Contents

Worth The Wait

Not By Sight

Worth The Wait

Chapter 1

Hello, beautiful."

Laney Wyatt glanced up from the landscaped, cobblestone path to see none other than Rand Mitchell watching her from within the shrubs decorating the side of his beautiful house.

His deep voice and bold gaze always unnerved her and today was no exception. Thankfully, the sight of the blood trickling onto his shirt from a cut on his forehead reminded her of why she was there and sent her into EMT mode.

His chin was scraped and raw, a white line of pain encircled his mouth, and there was no disguising the cuts and gashes on his arms, chest, and what she could see of his ribs. Still, he attempted to fix a smile to his insanely attractive lips, and her heart tripped when he aimed that shameless grin in her direction.

"I don't suppose you won't mention this to your father?"

"Patient confidentiality. My lips are sealed."

Dressed in cargo shorts, steel-toed work boots, and a faded shirt open across his broad, finger-tempting if now damaged chest, Rand was a guy's guy. He reminded her a bit of Tom Selleck, all big and muscled and tan and hairy but without the mustache. "Don't move, especially not your head. Just answer my questions verbally, okay? You fell off the roof?"

"Yeah. The ground really wanted to meet me. I would've driven myself to the hospital but..."

"But you fell off a roof," she repeated, ignoring the bushes pulling at her clothes to kneel beside him on the mulch. Hopefully they had softened his fall. "Jim, we need a collar and the backboard!"

Her partner dropped the supply kits within arm's reach and quickly retrieved the neck brace, muttering under his breath when a barberry bush took a hunk out of his inner forearm. Since Jim was now bleeding as well, she grabbed the collar and carefully placed it around Rand's neck.

"That's not necessary."

"Let the doctors decide," she ordered, unable to look at Rand directly because she'd always, always had a major crush on her father's friend. Worse still was that over the years, the crush had turned into a few fantasies that weren't sweet and innocent at all and had her silently apologizing in Sunday morning's service.

Laney forced herself to focus on getting Rand's stats, glad she could count on her training even though he made her feel like a schoolgirl talking to the football jock for the very first time.

Rand was speaking, so his airway was clear, and he was able to carry on a coherent conversation. She checked his pulse next. Strong and steady, if a little elevated, probably due to his pain.

"Do you always wear perfume when you're on duty?"

His electric-blue eyes held a curious gleam, and the question brought a flush to her face. "No sign of concussion," she said to Jim when he returned from the squad carting the backboard. "Any chest pain?"

"Are you asking because I'm old?"

If he was 'old,' she'd eat her shoe. Apparently owning a roofing business meant staying in shape and keeping a tan, at least when the owner worked as hands-on as Rand obviously did. She reevaluated her original description. He was Tom Selleck, the Marlboro Man, and every old-school Hollywood macho man combined. They just didn't make men like him anymore. She ought to know. She'd been looking. "I'm asking because I'm supposed to. Where do you hurt?"

"I'm fine."

She raised her eyebrows high. "You are, eh? Then why call us?"

He shrugged, grimaced at the move, and when his blue eyes locked on hers again she forgot to breathe.

Pull it together, Laney. He's just a man.

But he was *the* man. The one who made her heart go crazy every single time he came around.

He'd teased her as an awkward teenager, flirted with her at her father's diner as every guy had a tendency to do, but at some point in time, her feelings for Rand had changed in a major way. Only 12 years her senior, it wasn't *that* bit of an age difference, right?

"My right shoulder. I think it's dislocated. Every time I move I... get a little dizzy."

Which was obviously a big deal for him to admit. But easy enough to— Wow. Yeah, definitely dislocated.

Because he was propped awkwardly against the side of the house, she hadn't yet noticed. Good news was that appeared to be his most serious injury. His circulation was good, stomach soft beneath hard, toned abs that flexed when her trembling fingers touched him. "You're right about the shoulder. We'll get a wrap on you for transport to help hold it steady, but the doc will have to reset it."

It was a struggle to speak in a normal tone, especially when she had her hands all over him and his hot body. That really ought to be part of the training. How to not get distracted when the patient was *fiine*.

"I'm never gonna live this down. I've never fallen off, not in all the years I've been roofing."

She smiled at the depressed tone. "Just think of it as taking a mini vacation and getting a tour of the ambulance and hospital."

"And getting to spend time with you?"

Air froze in her lungs, and before she could think of a witty reply, Jim and the other two EMTs on duty appeared.

"Good to go?" Jim asked.

"Yeah," she said, more than a little breathless and kind of dizzy herself—all from Rand's comment and nearness.

"You're coming with me, right?" Rand asked. "To hold my hand?"

Her work buddies looked at her in amusement. It wasn't the first time she'd gotten hit on by a patient, but typically the men were either quite elderly or drunk.

Laney ignored her squad partners, knowing she'd catch some ribbing later for Rand's pained flirting, and huffed out a laugh. "They're my ride. I have to go with you."

Chapter 2

Sometime that evening Rand opened his eyes and stared at the white wall across from him, trying to remember what he'd done to hurt so much. It came to him seconds later, right before he realized he wasn't alone in the room.

"Hey," Laney said simply. "You're looking better."

She smelled like smoke. Not cigarette smoke but— "What happened to you?"

She shifted in the chair and shrugged. "Fire run."

"Anybody hurt?"

She shook her head and got up, moving close to his bed.

"No. I had to come back for some paperwork and wanted to stop by and check on you. You were sleeping so peacefully I didn't want to wake you."

"You should have. It's not every day I get to see you." Even in the dim light of his hospital room, he saw the blush that flooded her face with color. For a woman who had spent quite a few years working for her father in a diner frequented by the men in town, Rand found it amazing she could blush at all given what she had probably seen and heard. "You're missed at the Shake Shak."

7

"Dad just misses the cheap labor."

"I wasn't talking about him," Rand said, the words more revealing than he'd like.

Over the years, he'd watched Laney grow from a gangly young woman into a knockout beauty who turned every man's head between the ages of nine and ninety. But he was twelve years her senior and too old to be thinking about his friend's eldest daughter in such a way. It wasn't right. And there was the small fact that Frank would kill him, no doubt about that.

So why was it every time he saw her, he felt like someone slammed him in the gut with a wrecking ball? "Frank still giving you a hard time about quitting?"

"He wouldn't be Dad if he didn't," she said dryly. "Emma's been picking up my hours, but I've gotten several calls from Dad about how I left him in the lurch despite giving him six months' notice."

Buddy or not, Frank could be stubborn when he wanted to be, yet another reason Rand didn't want to tangle with Laney's father over something so personal. The man wouldn't forgive him —or her—if they crossed the line.

He'd thought about asking Laney out more than once—but he didn't want to cause a ruckus in her family, or ruin a long-time friendship. He was stuck between a rock and a hard place.

And twelve years' age difference was a big gap to span—full of baggage, one failed marriage, and more than a little awareness that he was no longer in his prime and should focus on women his own age. "Frank will come around in time. You make a great EMT."

"Thanks. Well, I should go and let you rest. Maybe I'll stop in again if you're still here."

"Doc said I'll be released first thing in the morning." None too soon, either. If not for the painkillers and the fact he lived alone, he could've been released, but his doc wasn't one for taking chances that he'd reinjure himself.

"Good for you. Just take it easy, okay? That was quite a fall. You could have broken your neck."

She stepped close enough to the bed for him to snag her hand and he took a long look into her eyes. "You sure you're okay?"

She made a sound in her throat.

"I'm fine. Just a long day."

Something about the way she said it made him think it was more, but she wasn't going to offer up any information. And he didn't have the right to ask no matter how much he wanted to.

He squeezed her hand and brought it up to his lips, brushing his mouth over her knuckles because it seemed so natural. Maybe it was the drugs but all of the reasons he'd told himself to steer clear were kind of foggy at the moment. "Thanks for coming to my rescue."

"Any time. Call the station if you, um, need anything. You know, with the insurance reports or… such."

She pulled her hand from his and was out the door before her words had time to really sink in.

Or such?

Minutes later, he still stared at the door where she'd disappeared, wondering if he had imagined Delaney Wyatt's visit to his room or the emphasis of her *or such*.

He settled himself more deeply into the uncomfortable hospital bed and sighed. Maybe the drugs were better than he'd thought.

LATER THAT SAME EVENING, Laney set her cellphone aside and leaned back in the desk chair at the fire station. That voice mail just proved how quickly things changed.

"Well?" Jim asked. "Everything okay with Emma's service dog?"

"Yeah. Roxy's stable."

"And your sister? How's she holding up?"

Laney picked up a pen and doodled on the edge of a notebook. "She was offered a job earlier today. She didn't think she would take it, but now she is. The guy's even offering room and board for Emma and the animals."

Jim whistled long and low. "Including the horse?"

His description of Goliath, Emma's Great Dane, earned a deeper frown from her. "Yeah, even Goli," she said. "Pretty amazing, isn't it?"

"Got that right. Not many people would take that on. What's the job?"

"Tutoring and babysitting. Take your pick. Uncle Bruce recommended Emma to a guy who wants her to help his brother cope with recently becoming blind."

And while Emma was staying with her new employer, who was obviously pitching in due to the fire that had destroyed their family home today, Laney couldn't help but feel a twinge of resentment.

Emma had said one of the reasons she'd accepted the job was so Laney and her father wouldn't have to worry about her and the animals. But with Frank sleeping in his small camper to watch over the contents of the sheds and property that hadn't burned, that left Laney on her own. Not that her family seemed to notice or ask where she was going to sleep.

You're how old? Grow up. You know it'll be easier for you to fend for yourself.

It would. But it was the principle of the thing.

You know good and well several people from church have offered to help. Even the guys at the station have offered. All you have to do is say yes.

But she hadn't. Her pride had gotten in the way of her

acceptance and she wasn't even sure why it was such an issue, but it was.

Since the car accident that had killed her mother and injured Emma, Laney had run herself ragged taking care of the family. Once upon a time, she'd dreamed of a big life, of becoming a doctor, living in Atlanta or some other large city. She'd given up her big dreams to live small, to do all the things expected of her. But having done that, where was their concern for her?

Emma called and left a message, and you talked to Frank at the site. You want them to hold your hand?

No. She didn't need that or want it. But hearing about Emma's good fortune and knowing her father would probably stay at his fiancée's home tomorrow or the day after didn't help Laney's mood at all. It still left her right where she was—homeless and alone.

By choice.

She rolled her eyes at her thinking and ran her hand through her already mussed hair. She'd no sooner left the hospital after transporting Rand to be checked out when the call had come in from dispatch.

Stone Gap Mountain, Georgia, was generous and supportive when it came to taking care of its own after disasters like the fire that had sent her afternoon into a spiral. But that support was definitely more focused on her blind sister and Frank, the owner of the Shake Shak. Where she fell into the mix she wasn't sure.

Oh, boo-hoo. Again, offers were made. You turned them down. You're the one with the issue. They tried! Why are you being so stubborn?

Maybe because the one she wanted help from hadn't offered?

Well he is in a hospital bed.

"Your shift ended a half hour ago. You decide what you're going to do tonight? You know you're welcome to come home and stay with me. Sleep on the couch or... whatever," Jim said with a too-casual shrug.

Jim had made no effort to hide his interest in her, but the spark just wasn't there. And the "whatever" he referred to was his bed, which she had no intention of hopping into, no matter how good of a match it might be.

Jim was good-looking and a heck of an EMT and firefighter, a reservist who had made three trips to Iraq and Afghanistan to serve his country. She should feel something other than friendship and admiration for his sense of duty but… it just wasn't there. Jim was fun to hang out with, train with, but he didn't make her pulse pound.

An image of Rand formed in her mind. His smile, his eyes. The way he made the blood surge through her veins whenever he was near. She shook off the shiver of response brought on by the thought. Not gonna happen. "I appreciate the offer, but I'm going to grab a bunk in the duty room and head back to the house first thing in the morning."

"You sure?"

"Yeah. Thanks though," she said, trying to sound casual about turning him down. Again.

"If you change your mind, the offer stands. I make a mean omelet. You don't know what you're missing."

Probably not. Jim was nice. Only a year or so older than her twenty-nine. He was perfectly suitable, so why couldn't she feel more than she did?

"Some girl's gonna be lucky when she snags you, Jim." But it wasn't going to be her.

"You like that old guy that flirted with you today?"

She jerked her head up in surprise and blinked, trying to cover her reaction. "Huh?"

"I saw you coming out of his room at the hospital when you said you had to use the restroom."

Oh. "I stopped in to check on him. He's a friend of my father's. I've known Rand since I was a… kid."

"Yeah, well, the guy was in serious pain today, but still couldn't keep his eyes off of you. If we hadn't strapped him down he probably would've made a pass."

She laughed off the comment and shook her head. *Too bad Rand had been strapped.* "Like I said, he's just an old friend."

"Old being the key word," Jim insisted.

"He's not *that* old." But she could see where the age difference might come up as an issue. After all, when they'd first met each other, she'd been twelve to his twenty-four.

"So you do like him?"

She opened her mouth to deny it but couldn't and knew Jim saw the truth on her face. She hated being obvious.

Jim stood. "Hey, no biggie," he said.

His expression had lost a lot of the welcome she'd seen on it earlier and belied his words.

"Let me know if you change your mind and need a place to stay. Even if it is the couch."

Chapter 3

The next morning, Laney squatted down in the charred remains of the razed house and fought back tears.

Remnants of metal littered the burned-out structure along with glass and smoldering rubble, with puffs of smoke still curling into the muggy August air. But it was the sight of soot-covered bits of her mother's china that left her unable to breathe.

It was gone. Everything was gone, and she couldn't even be angry with Emma for the loss. At least not verbally.

She stared down at the two-inch piece of broken china in her hand and rubbed her thumb back and forth over what was left of the image.

Old Country Roses. The gold-trimmed edge and painted roses of the pattern were mostly gone, another victim of the fire, but she saw them in her mind. Could picture her mother cradling the teacup so carefully in her hands as she sipped from the rim and stared out the kitchen window.

The pattern was special, used only on holidays and for Mama's morning tea. But sometimes when she and Emma had been young, Aunt Rose would come to the house, and because Mama declared the day special, they'd all have a tea party with little cookie cutter-shaped sandwiches and cakes. "Oh, Mama. I miss you. Why did we have to lose this too?"

Wiping away her tears, she forced herself to stand and continue her search through the mess for anything that might have survived the flames. There was little to be found.

She searched through a pile of rubble in the area she thought was her closet when the rumble of an engine and the crunch of tires alerted her to the fact she was no longer alone. She shielded her eyes from the sun and watched the big Dodge truck roll to a stop beside her Jeep.

Laney smoothed her hands over her jeans and waited expectantly for the driver's door to swing open.

"Hey," Rand said in greeting.

His arm hung in a sling, and his eyes were shaded by sunglasses, but neither of those things did anything to tone down his appeal. "Hey, yourself. You look a little more comfortable than the last time I saw you."

"I am. Thanks to you."

"Just doing my job. Um, if you're looking for Frank, he's not here."

"I'm not looking for him. Is there a reason you didn't mention that the fire you responded to yesterday was your own house?"

She wiped her hand over the sweat on her forehead. "Wouldn't have changed anything if I had. Is there something I can help you with?"

"I heard about what happened," he said with a nod toward the rubble, "and I thought I'd stop by. It's the least I could do after you checked on me last night."

"I was already at the hospital. You didn't need to make a special trip. You should be home resting."

His head swung right- to- left as he took in the damage. "You got a place to stay?"

"No, not yet. I mean, I've had a few offers but I don't want to impose. Do you know of something for rent?"

"Yeah. Come with me. Climb in and I'll show you."

"How about I drive?" she countered, indicating his arm. "Are you supposed to be out and about the day after closed reduction to set your arm?"

He tilted his head to one side, that oh-so-gorgeous smile on his lips. Why, oh why, did he have to get to her so easily? Why couldn't he just be like all the rest of her father's buddies? There, sometimes flirtatious just because it was their nature, but not the type to invade her dreams at night—since she'd hit puberty when she'd first found herself curious about the opposite sex.

"You going to lecture me or let me show you a nice little house that's available?"

Laney made her way over the debris and the cinder blocks that had formed the crawl space. "I'm coming," she said. "But if you wreck, you'll really top off my week."

If someone had said she'd wind up alone with Rand in a 1950s fixer-upper, she would have said that was crazy. But fifteen minutes later, she turned to survey the kitchen of the two-bedroom home on a quiet street not far from the station and clasped her soot-gritty hands to her chest to keep from ruining the pristine, light gray walls.

"What do you think? It's small, but you and Emma might be able to make it work."

"It's yours, isn't it?" She'd known via town gossip that Rand owned quite a bit of property in addition to his roofing business, but she hadn't given much thought to actually contacting him for a place to stay. And for him to bring her here… Did it mean something or was she just a romantic who wanted it to mean more than it did?

"Yeah."

"How much?"

"No charge. No—I insist. I'm a good landlord."

She sputtered at the statements. "You'd let me stay here rent-free?"

"Until you get back on your feet, yeah. I'd rather have someone I can trust living in it than rent it to someone who'll tear it up."

"That's… that's a very generous offer."

"So you accept?"

He wasn't really going to let her stay for free, was he? And if so, why? "I can pay rent. And it's just me. Emma took a job and is staying there."

"Good for her. But no rent. Not until you're back on your feet," he said. "It will take a while for you to buy furniture and things, settle in. Once you do, we'll talk."

He set the keys on the counter, and she shook her head, unable to believe he was just handing the house over to her. "Wait. Rand, why are you doing this?"

Just for a moment, for the briefest nanosecond, she thought she saw a flicker of something in his electric-blue gaze. But she had to be wrong.

Right?

Barely able to breathe due to the thoughts in her head, she moved toward the stove to occupy her hands. Four burners, an oven, a broiler. Yup, it was a kitchen appliance.

"It's no big deal. You need a place to stay, and I have one. I've known you how many years now?"

He said the words like a reminder. For himself?

"A long time," she said. "But I'm a grown woman now. I can take care of myself." She turned and watched as he digested her words. Had his good hand fisted in response?

Tired, achy. Feeling the strain of too much, the sight of his control—even if she'd imagined it—came as another blow, eliciting the sting of tears. She turned her head but not fast enough.

It was muggy in the house but she couldn't blame the stupid tears on that.

"Ah, sweetheart. Come here."

Rand's hand slid along the base of her back and then upward as he pulled her close for a one-armed hug.

"I'm sorry. It can't be easy losing everything in that fire."

Emma was safe— that was the most important thing. Emma, her dogs. things didn't matter. Things could be replaced. So why did it hurt so much?

Laney lifted her chin, much too aware of Rand standing so close and how wonderful it was to be held by him after waiting so long.

What would he do if she kissed him?

She didn't care that Rand was older, didn't care about anything but the way she'd felt about him for so long. About the comfort he offered her when she needed it most because she was finally free to do whatever she wanted.

With whomever she wanted?

She wasn't living in her father's home now. Did age really matter when she was almost thirty years old? Mature enough to make her own decisions?

Rand's nostrils flared as he took a breath, his thick, black lashes lowering over his eyes as he followed the nervous flick of her tongue on her lips.

He lowered his head, stopping when his mouth was a scant half-inch away. Suddenly his eyes widened, and he tensed, jerking away. Despite the humidity, she missed his warmth, his contact.

"Uh, yeah. We should go."

Rand left her standing there in the kitchen, dazed and breathless and more confused than ever.

Had that almost happened? For real?

Rand couldn't get out of the house fast enough, but Laney stood there, a slow smile breaking across her face because finally —finally!— she had proof that she wasn't the only one feeling the pull. That almost-kiss proved it.

Now— what did she dare do about it?

Chapter 4

The next afternoon, Rand set the bottle of painkillers back on the table unopened. He wasn't a masochist, but he hated the fuzzy, otherworldly dopiness he felt after a dose.

Last night, he'd needed a pill to sleep, but today the pain was bearable, and the bruises on his ribs only hurt when he pressed on them, his shoulder sore but holding its own.

The television commercial ended, and the news channel reappeared. A slick-looking dude with pasty-white teeth and fake hair smiled as he warned viewers about the heat index.

August was always hot, but the drought had yet to break, and the temperature had shot higher than ever today. The setting sun didn't alleviate the problem, and the temperature remained in the high eighties. And because Delaney Wyatt was never far from his mind, an image of her flashed in front of his eyes, and he didn't bother holding back the groan that followed.

Yesterday when he'd shown her the rental house, he'd come much too close to making a fool of himself. But when she'd lifted her face as though she was ready to be kissed, he'd almost given in to the temptation.

What was he thinking?

She was his friend's *daughter*.

The drive back to her Jeep was made in total silence, broken only by the radio blaring out the latest hits and the motor thrumming as he sped down the highway. But he'd been aware of her looking at him, her big, beautiful eyes staring at him. Like she was afraid he'd pounce on her? He'd almost crossed the line and instead of being her friend, a protector of someone smaller and younger and more innocent than himself, he'd…

Wanted to toss her over his shoulder like a caveman and claim her as his own. Forever.

He'd spent the evening staring at the wall, wishing he were younger. That Laney was older. That Frank Wyatt wasn't a friend who'd clobber him for lusting after the man's daughter.

But it wasn't only lust. He'd known Laney too many years for that. He'd watched as she'd held her family together in the aftermath of her mother's death and her sister's injury. Laney had dreamed of becoming a doctor, but after the accident, she had chosen a different path that would keep her close to home. What wasn't to admire about that? Respect?

She was smart, beautiful. Giving. Sexy but seemingly unaware of the real effect she had on the men around her. Before she'd hired on full-time at the firehouse, he'd found himself going to the diner too many evenings to count, just so he could sit and watch her while she waited on customers. Be close to her.

He'd even married the wrong woman for what he'd thought were the right reasons, all in an attempt to forget about Laney and her jail-bait status at the time.

"So, folks, crank up the AC, drink lots of fluids, and stay inside. It's going to be another scorcher tomorrow," the weatherman said.

Rand grabbed the remote and turned off the television, fighting with the devil on his shoulder urging him to go see

Laney, check on her, for the wrong reasons and the angel warning him about the jump from the pot into the flames.

A good man removed himself from temptation. He didn't go running after it.

But it was hot. Going to get hotter. Given all she had been through, wasn't making sure she was settling in okay the *decent* thing to do? Frank had his hands full post-fire. Emma was taken care of.

Who was taking care of Laney? Watching over her?

Muttering under his breath, he got to his feet and grabbed his keys.

A man never died from just looking…

LANEY, open up. It's me, Rand."

Laney held the damp towel to her chest and cringed. She had hoped a cool shower would give her some relief from the heat, but the coolness had ended the moment she'd turned off the spray. The last thing she wanted to do was put on clothes again, but she couldn't meet Rand at the door in her birthday suit. "Be right there!" she said as she rushed into the bigger of the two bedrooms and hurried to pull on some of the clothes from the church's disaster donation box.

Her Aunt Rose had dropped by this morning with a bag of T-shirts, shorts, jeans and other items, some of which fit, and some she tucked right back into the bag with a no-way-am-I-wearing-that laugh.

"What are you doing here?" Laney asked after she'd gotten decent and unlocked and opened the screen door to her unfurnished home. Rand stood on the other side, his arms full of a window-unit air conditioner. "And why are you carrying that with your shoulder? You'll pull it out of place!"

"It's fine. Doesn't help that you won't ask me in, though," he chided, a smile in his voice. "Want to move out of the way and give my shoulder a break?"

She backed up instantly and let him enter the stifling little house. Every window was open, and she'd borrowed a box fan from the firehouse, but all it blew was hot air.

"You're installing an air conditioner? Where did you get it? I called all over town looking for one."

"It's used but still in good shape. Took it from one of my properties when I had central air put in and I hang onto them just in case. Sorry I didn't already have this installed."

Rand looked around, side-stepping the blowup camping mattress she'd placed on the floor. The living room had two windows versus the single in the bedroom. Rand chose the one farthest from the door for the unit.

"This will only take a few minutes."

Since she couldn't exactly stand there and gawk— er, watch him work— she went to the refrigerator and pulled out a pitcher of sweet tea.

After obtaining the keys from Rand yesterday, she had gone on a mini shopping spree, finding pots and pans at the Goodwill along with some glasses and plates and other odds and ends, enough to get her started while she set up housekeeping and replaced things lost in the fire.

Laney heard the metal scrape of the window unit being put into place, only then remembering Rand could use some help with the lifting and positioning.

She set the pitcher aside and ran to help. "Got it. I'll hold it while you secure it."

He looked like he wanted to protest, but surprisingly he didn't. More of an indication his shoulder did in fact hurt.

Men. Why did they let their pride get in their way so many times?

That's not only a man-thing, you know.

She focused on holding the box unit still while Rand made the necessary adjustments and fastened it in. By the time he was finished, she needed another shower.

"All we have to do is plug it in and— air."

The blast of air coming out of the unit was lukewarm at best, but it was cooler than that inside the house. Second by second, it cooled even more, and before long, Laney was selfishly hogging the cold air coming out of the miniature vents.

"Better?"

She sighed deeply. "You have no idea."

Rand's husky chuckle sounded in response, very close to her ear.

"Glad I could help. Can't have you passing out from heat exhaustion."

Eyes closed in total abandonment, she murmured, "Tea."

"What was that?"

She turned to face him, the air blowing under her hair and cooling her neck. Oh, such bliss. "I have sweet tea. It's decaf, so it won't keep you up. I'll get you some."

"That'd be nice. Thanks."

Realizing she hadn't moved even though he'd agreed to the drink, she put her feet in motion and turned her spot in front of the AC over to him.

The pitcher had sweated a puddle of moisture on the counter, and she swiped it up and poured the tea, taking her time in order to steady her nerves.

Now that it was cool enough for her brain to stop frying, all she could think about was the almost-kiss that hadn't happened.

Halfway across the living room floor she met his gaze, and if she'd had any lingering doubts as to whether or not Rand struggled with the same thoughts, they disappeared. The air left her lungs in a rush because before he broke eye contact and cleared his throat, there was no mistaking the gleam in his gaze. "Um, here you go."

Like something from a novel, their fingers brushed in the exchange of the glass. Electricity zapped up her arm, and she watched as Rand took a drink, his blue eyes meeting hers again over the glass.

She licked her lower lip from nervousness and almost smiled in triumph when his eyes darkened even more. Yeah, she wasn't stupid. So what were they going to do about these feelings of theirs? Better still, how was she going to convince Rand to take a chance on them when they both knew there would be fallout?

"Uh, this tastes great."

Laney stepped directly in front of him on the pretense of seeking out the sweet spot of air, blocking his path before he could cross the room and put some distance between them.

She wasn't exactly sure of what she was doing only that something was propelling her on. Driving her. Making her think that the time had come.

Wasn't that always the message? To be patient and wait? Let things play out in the time and way they're meant to?

So who's to say this wasn't the time? The place? The way?

She had put everyone else first for as long as it was necessary. But now… "Are you hungry?"

Once again, his gaze lowered to her mouth and she wasn't seeing things when that little muscle in his jaw tightened and ticked.

"I should probably go."

"Why? There's no need to do that… Unless you just want to."

"No, but—"

"But?" Just once. If she didn't follow her heart just this once, she would regret it the rest of her life, always wonder what might have been. "I'm, uh, used to the station house and having my family for company, remember? Stay a while. I have some cold chicken salad in the fridge."

"Laney—"

"Or we could skip the food and... Talk about why you haven't kissed me after all of these years when I'm pretty sure you want to."

Rand's hands fisted at his sides, and his nostrils flared as he sucked in a breath.

"Laney, your father—"

"Isn't here and you can't use him as an excuse anyway. Not anymore. I'm a grown woman, well over jailbait age."

He closed his eyes and dragged in a ragged breath. "I'm still too old for you, darlin'."

"You might be a *little* older but age is just a number."

"My number is twelve years higher than yours."

Her heart raced in her chest, every thud coinciding with the voice in her head demanding to know what on earth she was doing, thinking. Saying.

But like a dam bursting, the words kept coming. She knew for sure that she wanted this. Him. Had to take the risk and say the words and know, one way or the other. "It means you're a man and not boy pretending to be one, that's all."

"Laney, what are you doing, sweetheart?"

"Am I wrong? You feel it, too, don't you? I know why I've waited. I think I know why you've never said anything— My father and life but— We're here now and I would very much like for you to kiss me."

"You're sure about this?"

"I've never been more sure of anything in my life."

He closed his eyes and inhaled, like he tried to muster up resistance or courage or—

Rand stepped forward and placed his drink beside hers. Without a word, he kept moving toward her and hooked his good arm around her waist, lifting her until his mouth covered hers in a hard, urgent, exploring kiss that took everything. Was everything.

"You're so beautiful."

"So are you," she whispered.

He groaned against her lips, kissed her again, and again. Like he couldn't bring himself to stop now that he'd started.

"We've got a rough road ahead of us, darlin'. Your father isn't going to be happy about this."

She nodded her head, wincing. "What he doesn't know won't hurt him. We don't have to tell him. Not just yet."

Chapter 5

A couple of weeks later, Laney watched as Emma and her friends, along with her blind student laughed, and talked in the Shak.

"Laney, you need a lift?" Jim asked.

"No, I'm good. Thanks." Like so many others in town, Jim had chosen tonight to grab dinner at her father's diner. She'd felt him staring at her several times in the past hour but ignored the sensation, too focused on trying to figure out her emotions where Rand was concerned.

"You sure? I don't mind."

She forced herself to make eye contact with Jim while giving him a firm shake of her head. "Thanks, but no."

He turned to go but hesitated, swinging back to face her again.

"Something going on with you?" he pressed. "You've been acting weird ever since the fire. Sure you're okay?"

Jim was sweet. He meant well. But right now the only thing his questions did was add to the stress already churning in her stomach.

In the time since she and Rand gotten together, Rand had said nothing about his feelings for her. When pressed, he'd certainly shown his desire to kiss her, but he hadn't actually *said* the words she found she needed to hear.

When he did speak—when they made plans to see each other away from the prying eyes of the small town and came up with the details of *how* they would accomplish it—there was always a mutter or two from him that made it clear he didn't like what they were doing.

But why? Because he felt they weren't right for each other? Because of her father and the age difference? Had his interest in her already lessened?

They talked, laughed. Held hands. Kissed. They made every minute of their time together count because their schedules and lives made every opportunity to see each other all the more precious.

She loved him. But did he feel the same?

What's the rush? her mind asked.

I've waited a lifetime for him— I don't want to lose any more time.

"Yo. Earth to Laney."

She blinked away her thoughts and shook her head at Jim. "I'm good. It's kind of you to ask though."

Jim didn't look convinced, not that she'd tried all that hard. It would be nice to talk to someone about her secret relationship with Rand, but she didn't consider Jim a wise choice under the circumstances.

At this stage, she didn't have anyone she could confide in, not when it would mean answering still more questions she didn't have a clue how to answer.

What was going on? Was it serious? Did she and Rand have a future? How could they when neither of them was ready or willing or prepared to acknowledge the relationship to their families? The world and its censure?

"Guess I'll see you tomorrow then. 'Night."

"'Night." Once Jim was gone, Laney's gaze shifted back to Emma. She practically glowed with the challenge of keeping the Shak running, and doing whatever it was she did with Ian, her student, who proved to be a big, sexy guy himself—not that Emma could see him. But after all she'd been through Emma deserved to be happy.

So why did it bring up all sorts of jealous thoughts because her little sister was enjoying her new life so much while she feared the backlash of going public about seeing Rand?

As though conjured up by her thoughts, Rand appeared out of nowhere. He hesitated and took a long look around the diner, then approached the table where she sat. He was about to join her when Laney panicked and grabbed her purse.

One whiff of them behaving as a couple or whatever they were, and her father would make both her and Rand's lives miserable. What if Frank guilted Rand into ending things? What if they came to blows? What if either of them said she had to choose? She wasn't willing to take the chance. "What are you doing?" Her voice came out as a bitter hiss.

"You said you'd be here," Rand said. "I got out of my meeting early and thought—"

"That you'd join me? Are you crazy?"

"It's crowded. Everyone is grabbing a seat where they can. It's not like we haven't shared a table before."

They had but— "That's different. My father was there too."

He frowned down at her, his gaze zeroing in on her purse. "So you're leaving because I was going to sit down?"

"I'm leaving because I'm ready to go home." She'd had enough of watching Emma and her friends. Their joy. Right out there in the open for God and everyone to see.

Rand's gaze narrowed on her, and she squirmed beneath the

intensity. Man, he really did have gorgeous eyes. And she loved staring into them. In private, when they were alone.

"I don't like sneaking around, Laney. You know what, I agreed to keeping us on the down low until we became comfortable with each other, but if we're going to do this, let's do it. But if you're not willing to be public about us, maybe we should… end things now and let it be."

Let it be? *Let it be* because she just wasn't ready to deal with other people yet? "Just follow me out in a few minutes. Go get a drink at the counter, and if anyone asks why you were talking to me, all you have to do is say you were asking if I'm liking the rental."

He wiped a hand over his face and grimaced.

"No. I'm too old to play games. If we're going to do this, we need to be real about it. Now."

Real? She *was* being real. She was almost thirty years old, and she deserved a life with whomever she wanted. Rand wasn't married. Wasn't involved with anyone else. They were both free to be together. But why did it have to be so complicated? "I'm leaving. I'll meet you at your place in a few minutes."

She didn't wait around for Rand's response. Mainly because she was almost afraid his answer would be no.

Laney made her way out of the diner, not bothering to say goodbye to Emma or her friends. None of them would even know or really care that she'd left until later, and even then they'd assume she left during the busy-ness of the night, which is exactly what she wanted.

The air was humid and sticky, tinged with scents of cigarette smoke and asphalt and honeysuckle. The noise from the diner shut off with the closing of the door, but the dull thud of the juke box and sporadic bursts of laughter could still be heard as she walked along the outside of the building and parking lot.

Frank would never understand. Never accept that she and

Rand could possibly have anything in common. He'd say it was lust or curiosity. Nothing real.

So was it true? Was *that* why she kept putting off confiding in anyone—because she didn't want to face the possibility herself? Because she wanted more and doubted Rand's feelings for her?

The radio was so annoying on the way to Rand's home that Laney turned it off. Almost immediately she wished she hadn't because it made her more aware of her jumbled thoughts.

The streets heading out of town were relatively empty, with only a handful of cars at the red lights and a few small groups of college kids walking to and from Zailer University.

As she drove out to Rand's house, images filled her head. She couldn't help but wonder what it would be like to live there. Like a girl playing pretend, she pictured herself as hostess to his parties, the lady of the beautiful house nestled along the lake.

She turned up his driveway, loving the age-old feel of the tree-lined drive, the way the four white columns rose into the air like soldiers standing guard.

The night sounds surrounded her as she got out and made her way up the porch steps. She sat in one of the big, black rockers lining the front when Rand pulled to a stop near her Jeep and got out, his expression still dark and broody from their earlier conversation.

Beneath the light of the moon, she was able to make out his masculine stride and broad shoulders. He looked tough and strong, and all she could think about was how much she wanted to be with him regardless of their age difference or the impact it would have on both their relationships with her father. So was this it? Time to face the music as it were and let the people who say they love her… prove it?

"What happened?" he asked, stopping in front of her long enough to tug her out of the seat and into the house behind him once he'd unlocked the door. "What sent you running out of the Shak tonight?"

She inhaled and sighed. How easily he could read her. Yet another connection they shared because no one else had ever seemed to know her so well. "Jealousy."

"I'm not following you."

He shut and locked the door behind them with a decisive click, one that sent electricity racing through her raw nerves. "I'm jealous, okay? What else could you call being upset that my little sister lucked into a job paying more than I make in two years?" she said, turning to drop her purse onto the entry table. "Everything has turned out better for her than it was before the fire."

"It's not better for you?"

Oh, that was the real question, wasn't it?

She could hear the tension in Rand's tone as he voiced the query, and when she turned, she saw that he waited for her answer, hands fisted.

In some ways, yes, better for her. She was finally free. Free to live her life the way she wanted. Love who she wanted. And she did.

But did he feel the same way? And if he did, why not say it? Why he was with her? Why couldn't he just say the words already? Say *something*. It would give her the courage to face everyone—especially her family—if she just knew she wasn't imagining feelings that may or may not be there.

His silence was very old-school alpha male, and she didn't like not knowing what he was thinking or his high-handedness in demanding she be the one to decide and speak first when it came to owning up to their secret relationship. It put all of the risk on her shoulders. "You know what, forget it. I shouldn't have come here. I'm leaving."

Rand grasped her arm as she moved by him, not hurting her but not letting go either. Her heart skidded out of control, and heat pooled low in her belly. All from his touch and that look in his eyes.

Okay, so maybe she liked the alpha-male thing a little.

"I'm not sure why you're upset, but you shouldn't be driving like this."

"Oh, so you actually *do* care if something happens to me?"

His eyes glittered in the dim light of the foyer. He let go of her arm but stepped toward her, matching her step by step as she backed up, all the way until her shoulder blades hit the door.

"You know I do. And if I didn't know better," he said, lowering his head until his breath hit her mouth, "I'd say you were trying to pick a fight with me. But you're smart enough to know to ask for whatever it is you want from me, right?"

Laney leaned her head against the door. She had to ask for what she wanted, demand it. But would he give it to her? "I want... *you.*"

"Honey, you have me."

The way he said it made it seem very real. If only it was true. "No, I mean... As crazy as it sounds, I'm in love with you. I have been for years and years but here we are and neither one of us is willing to tell Frank the truth because we both know what will happen and...." A huff left her, her eyes burning with stupid tears. She had to blink fast to get rid of them.

"Delaney... Honey, I love you too."

Her heart picked up speed once more. He'd said it. He'd actually said the words? "You do?"

His big, calloused hand cupped her cheek, held so she couldn't look away.

"You know good and well that I do. I think I've loved you since the first time I set eyes on you. When it wasn't legal," he added with more than a little disgruntlement. "I had to wait."

"I know but now..."

"I want you to be sure. Really sure. Honey, I don't want you to do or say anything to your family until you're all in, but tonight when I got there and couldn't even *sit* with you…"

"You love me."

Rand's thick eyebrows lowered even more as though he tried to will the knowledge into her.

"More than my own life. I love you," he repeated. "But people will gossip and be awful and you've got to be real sure you're ready for that."

Now that she knew for sure he felt the same way, she was ready for anything! "I am. Frank included. He loves us both. He'll get over it eventually. Especially when he sees that this is real a-and we're not just messing around."

"You'd better not be messing around." He dropped a kiss on her lips, lingering. "You're mine now. Don't you forget it."

The big clock in the foyer began to chime and she closed her eyes, the emotions inside of her too much to handle. "I've wanted to be yours for such a long time."

Rand lowered his head and kissed her, possessed her, mastered her.

Yeah, she'd tell her father. She'd tell everyone. Scream it to the world from the highest rooftop she could find.

And it was so worth the wait.

WANT MORE OF THE STONE RIVER SERIES? READ ON BELOW FOR A SNEAK PEEK AT EMMA'S STORY IN NOT BY SIGHT!

Kara? No, no, don't scream. I'm here to help you. Your father sent me." He raised his hand in a non-threatening gesture and smiled at the terrified nineteen-year-old girl backing away from him. Ian followed her slowly, matching every step with a longer one to close the distance between them. "Target located," he said into the transmitter, relaying the information to the others on the team.

The kidnapped debutante retreated another two steps, until her hips hit a table, and glass clinked together. Some unseen object fell over with a dull thump.

"D-don't touch me."

"My name's Ian. We're here to take you home, but you have to trust me. We don't have much time. Do as I say, and don't make a sound, okay? Hurry."

She didn't take his outstretched hand, so Ian grabbed her elbow, holding it tightly when she immediately tried to bolt. "Shhh. It's okay."

Gunfire erupted outside the mansion, and Kara's eyes widened at the sound, her mouth opening in horror.

"Kara!" a male voice shouted from somewhere in the house.

In Ian's ear, the transmitter picked up his brother's mid-battle curse.

"He got by me. Moving up the stairs!"

Adrenaline pumped through Ian's veins, but he remained focused on the task. "Let's go."

Kara tried to pull away again.

"Kara!"

The man shouting Kara's name was closing in fast. It was too late to get her out of the bedroom, so Ian shoved Kara into a corner and positioned himself in front of the whimpering girl. One of Kara's captors burst into the room, but the guy wasn't prepared to find Ian already there.

The man swung his gun up to fire, but two shots ended the forward charge. The man's grip on the semiautomatic held true, and bullets sprayed the wall, window, and Ian's shoulder before the gunman and his weapon fell silent.

The aftermath of the short firefight was deafening. Kara's screams ripped through the air as the kidnapper's blood began to pool on the hacienda's tile floor, Ian's boot the dam holding the fluid in place.

As he watched, blood dripped from his own gunshot wound into the mass, and the puddle grew larger. The flood quickly surrounded Ian's boots like a wellspring bubbling up from the ground, swept over his feet, thickening and darkening, dragging at his legs. He tried to get out of the coating veil, but it swallowed his calves and thighs, dragged at his chest, snaked around his neck.

He lifted his chin, twisted, and grappled for a handhold to escape as it swelled over his head and crashed together like the Red Sea. The tide sucked him down until the last bit of light diminished from view, and he was engulfed, suffocating, in inky, depths-of-hell black....

Ian MacGregor opened his eyes with a full-body jerk that rocked the bed beneath him. His heart pulsed in his ears but not loudly enough to drown out the sound of his breath chugging in and out of his lungs.

The air conditioning chilled the sweat on his skin as Kara Winston's rescue from a Mexican stronghold slithered back into the hole of his subconscious.

Awake, his claustrophobia was manageable thanks to the mind games he played with himself. But when he slept, his guard lowered, the nightmare took hold, and he woke up sensory-deprived and drowning, because even with his eyes open, the darkness didn't fade.

As a prisoner entombed in Iraq, he'd spent two full weeks underground without once letting his captors know how close he'd been to losing his mind. He'd known the guards would open the door eventually. They had to drag him above ground to beat and torture him, so he'd counted down the time until they returned, knowing he'd catch a glimpse of the sun through the canvas and bars above his head, something to ease the hours spent in darkness and hold him over until next time. But now?

What did I do to deserve this?

He wiped a hand over his face and scrubbed hard, hoping to rid himself of the fear that left him shaking like a puppy. He blinked a few times, desperate for a miracle.

Ian rolled himself off the bed and onto his feet. His head spun at the sudden shift of position, and it took him several seconds to orient himself and stay upright.

Hands out in front of him, he shuffled his way across the room until he bumped into a chair and felt his way around to the front. Halfway there, a prickle of awareness lifted the little hairs on his neck. "Who's there?"

"Me," Duncan said softly. "You okay?"

Nothing about this was okay. He hated being the entertainment for the household every time he dozed off.

How long had his brother been standing there? Watching him? Listening? "I'm good."

"You want to talk about it?"

"No." What did Duncan want him to say? Fear like his belonged to children who believed in monsters under the bed or ghosts in the attic. He was a soldier—at least he used to be. Thanks to his little side journey into Mexico, his medical discharge was complete and his CO five shades of ticked.

Ian leaned his head back against the cushion, but he didn't close his eyes. He couldn't, even though it wouldn't make a difference.

He couldn't escape the dark no matter how long he waited. Blindness was his own very personalized hell.

Why this?

"How about I stay? Keep you company for a while?"

Lost in the dark, Ian made a game of stringing obscenities together in his head, focusing on adding another and another, getting pretty creative in his anger. He couldn't *breathe*, and Duncan wanted to stay and *chat*? "Get out."

Every soldier knew there were prices to be paid and that sometimes the dice didn't roll in your favor. This was one of those times.

But no way could he have sat back and allowed Duncan to go into Mexican drug country on a kidnap-retrieval mission without some American-trained soldier tagging along for backup. Before the night was over, he was the one who had found and hauled the kidnapped nineteen-year-old away from the site of her four-week captivity.

The mission should have been over then, in and out of Mexico with no one the wiser. He had carried Kara through the jungle for two full miles with a bullet in his shoulder. To lose his sight during surgery? *After* they had made it back to safety?

Why?

"I can hang out for a while," Duncan insisted.

Ian stretched out a hand and fumbled to find one of the many empty liquor bottles on the table beside him. He hurtled it to the left of Duncan's voice, his rage growing hotter in response to Duncan's pitying tone.

The bottle splintered against the wall and scattered across the tile floor. "I said *get out.*"

"This doesn't have to be as bad as you're making it."

Duncan didn't know about the claustrophobia. No one knew. Smart soldiers showed no weakness. But at that statement, Ian started chuckling. Not as bad as he was making it?

Duncan muttered something and left, closing the door to the bedroom with a firm slam. Ian laughed harder, the dam inside him leaking like a sieve until tears wet the corners of his eyes, his stomach muscles ached, and he gasped for breath before wheezing out a few final chuckles.

Not as hard as he was making it... God help him, he was in hell, and there was no way out.

ONLY YOU WOULD INHERIT a pregnant Great Dane."

Emma Wyatt laughed as she filled a couple baskets of peanuts to have at the ready. It was hot out, and while The Shake Shak wasn't that busy at the moment, it would be soon. "Tell me about it," she said in response to Tasha's comment. "But what can I do? Goli is such a sweetheart, and Mr. Bowman knew not just anyone would take her."

"Got that right," Morgan said as she munched on one of the potato chips that came with her sandwich. "That dog is bigger than my kitchen."

Married right out of high school, Morgan was the only one of the *Besties* with a ring and a couple kids underfoot. She lived in an area called Rose Hill, the high-end section of Stone River, Georgia, boasting houses that were a minimum of thirty-five hundred square feet. Stone River was nestled in the Blue Ridge Mountains far enough north to make it a scenic drive for those wanting to view the foliage.

"Emma, I hate to tell you this, but that dog? She's *big*—and she's going to get even bigger when she gets ready to deliver those puppies." Morgan slurped the last of her soda, the noise obnoxious. "They'll be here before you know it."

"She's right, you know," Tasha said from her stool beside Morgan's. "You need to begin advertising those pups now. See if you can start a wait list and get people lined up before the big day. Maybe Jolie can design some ads for you. Her flyers for the opening of Cuppa Jo's were great."

"Do you know who the father is?" Morgan asked.

Emma shrugged and kept working, not letting the chatter keep her from her tasks. "I have no idea. It wasn't exactly a planned breeding."

"It rarely is, unfortunately," Tasha added in her serious vet's voice. "But it makes for a great mystery."

Morgan snickered. "It'll be even more of a mystery if they arrive looking exactly like their mama. The saddest part of this story is that even the dog's gettin' more love and attention than me," Morgan murmured sourly.

Tasha and Emma both sighed in empathy as expected, but neither of them pursued the comment. This wasn't the place to discuss Morgan's troubled marriage. That topic required an unlimited amount of chocolate, privacy, and usually more than a few tissues.

"Mr. Bowman didn't have any other dogs, so there's no way to tell," Tasha said. "Maybe you could advertise them with a Who's-Your-Daddy campaign. Have some fun with it."

Emma groaned. Leave it to her friends to come up with that one.

The *Besties*—Morgan, Tasha, Emma, and Jolie, who had yet to show today—had been friends since school. Emma had met Tasha in first grade when she'd taught Tasha how to tie her shoes. Morgan had come along in third grade when her father had moved the family to Stone River from Ohio for an industrial job, and Jolie was inducted the summer before ninth grade when her very strict parents had stopped homeschooling her and allowed Jolie to move in with her grandmother.

Ten years after graduation, they were still friends. The *Besties* were great at sarcasm, moral support, and laughter as needed, snarky comments guaranteed.

Emma grabbed a few mugs and aligned the handles the way she liked them for easy reach. She'd discovered when she'd first begun waitressing for her father at The Shake Shak that keeping her sanity meant staying a step ahead of the crowd. With afternoon sessions at Zailer University almost over, the late-lunch crowd would come streaming in shortly.

"Emma, can I get a root beer?"

She turned toward the man making the request and smiled. "Sure, Homer. You need peanuts, too?"

"You know me too well, darlin'."

Emma quickly grabbed a mug and moved to the machine. Once full, she set it aside to fill yet another basket.

A regular at The Shak and one of the town's best mechanics, Homer had a thing about skimping on peanuts, so she always gave him extra in exchange for the tips he left her. Every little bit helped when it came to saving up for her dream—a large kennel situated within walking distance of The Shak and her classroom at the university.

Emma delivered the soda and heaping basket of peanuts to the ever-patient Homer, then removed the dishes left two stools down by a different customer. That done, she grabbed the rag at her waist to wipe down the counter, the bell banging against the door barely discernible over the jukebox blaring by the two pool tables in back by the pinball machines.

The jukebox had to be turned down. The nonstop noise did nothing to help the headache she couldn't shake.

"So," Morgan said, lowering her voice so only they could hear, "where's Laney? I never see her in here anymore."

"She officially quit," Emma informed them. "Laney was hired on full-time as an EMT at the firehouse."

"Oh, wow. Bet your dad loved losing her." Morgan rattled the ice in her glass and slurped again.

Tasha made a sympathetic noise. "Sorry, Em. That's why you've been working so much, huh?"

"Yeah. But I'm not complaining," she added. "More hours means more money." Her sister's new job also meant their father was now leaning on Emma to take over all of Laney's responsibilities at The Shak, even though Emma also currently ran a small kennel out of her father's garage and had her hands full.

Every tip went into a fund for the future—namely independence and her own place.

She *had* to get her own place soon. No way could she continue living at the house, not when her father had announced his engagement to a local bank manager who planned to move in after the nuptials. Thank goodness they hadn't set a date yet.

What twenty-eight-year-old woman wanted to be the third wheel to her father's love life? Sharing meals? Downtime?

"Careful," Morgan warned, "you're starting to sound like me. Rory's pay cut has seriously dampened my spending. If not for the money I make on baking and decorating cakes, I'd be up the creek without my highlights. Speaking of which, I gotta go. Em, do you need me to drive you home? I've got a little time before my hair appointment. She's always running behind anyway."

"No, but thank you. Genie's taking me home."

"I wondered where your shadow was today," Tasha said.

"She's on her way, and stop calling her my shadow," Emma ordered. "Genie's had a hard time of it since her grandma died. She doesn't have any family and not many friends."

"Well, you make up for it, big softie that you are, taking in all the strays," Tasha said. "I love that about you."

"I love it, too. Hey, don't get me wrong. I feel sorry for Genie," Morgan said, lowering her voice. "I mean, she certainly doesn't have much going for her looks-wise, and I'm not even sure makeup would help."

Emma grabbed a container of glasses and set them into position. "People are more than their looks, you know."

"Of course they are," Morgan said. "But we live in a society where first impressions matter, even here in the backwoods of Georgia. All I'm saying is that maybe she would have more friends if she'd make an effort. Some days I wonder if she washes her hair. And those glasses of hers? Seriously, invest in some contacts."

"Wow," Tasha murmured. "You get harsh when you're grumpy, Mo."

"Oh, please, like you haven't thought the same thing? Being sweet and helpful isn't everything. She needs one of those heavy-duty, as-seen-on-TV makeovers," Morgan said.

Emma finished emptying the crate and set it aside with the other two from earlier. "I think people should be accepted for who they are." And it made her angry when people talked about how someone else should change and judged others when they didn't know the person.

Morgan would do absolutely anything for any of the *Besties*, but to hear her talk about Genie, you would think... well, the worst. Both about poor Genie and about Morgan, for being so mean.

Fact was, the few times Genie had been around the *Besties* had been brief, but the younger woman's awkwardness had been tangible, making them all uncomfortable. Genie was backward and painfully shy, socially challenged, characteristics that were apparent given her lack of personable graces.

"I agree. They should be accepted," Morgan said, "but we're not in Kansas anymore, Dorothy."

"All right, you two," Tasha said, her tone firm. "Morgan, aren't you going to be late?"

"Em, it's just an observation, right?" Morgan said.

"Right." Emma knew Morgan meant well despite her negativity. Morgan was having a hard time at home, and Emma had to give Morgan allowances for being cynical. Morgan wasn't a mean person. Which made Emma wonder what Rory was saying to Morgan about *her* appearance.

Rory was a supercritical guy, and after kids and baking for cash, Morgan had gained a few pounds. Emma couldn't help but think Rory was at the root of Morgan's critical comments.

The metal decorations on Morgan's purse scraped against the counter's surface and clinked together as she scooted off her stool. Her heels hit the hardwood floor with a clatter.

"Your uncle's here, Em," Morgan said. "Nice lunch, girls, but I've got to get my hair done and get home. If I don't have dinner on the table when Rory walks through the door, he gets persnickety."

"Mmmnfph—" Tasha said around a mouthful of sandwich.

"See you later." Emma gave her friend a good-bye smile and wave.

Several seconds passed before Tasha spoke. "They're fighting again. Bad."

"Yeah, I could tell. I wish there was something we could do to help." Morgan's marriage had been rocky the last few years, but recently things had gotten even more antagonistic.

"The first thing I'd do to help is kick Rory's rear for treating her like his own personal housekeeper, nanny, and cook combined. She supported him all through school, gave up her job because he wanted her to, does everything for the kids, takes care of the house, plus bakes for her spending money, and he doesn't lift a finger and treats her like dirt."

"Maybe Rory is having trouble at work or something. It doesn't excuse his behavior, but who knows?" Emma snagged a couple baskets and washed them down after emptying them of the remains and paper liners.

Tasha's sigh revealed her frustration, and she rattled the ice in her glass. "I hate to eat and run, but I need to go, too. I have to go out to Elmer Pruitt's and check on Barney."

Barney was the pet mule of one of the local farmers, and the thought of Tasha caring for the ornery beast kept the *Besties* in stitches.

"Yeah, ha ha. Laugh it up," Tasha said. "You're not the only one with bills."

"I know. Sorry for laughing. Drive safe," Emma said, swallowing her amusement.

"Will do. Your uncle is at sixteen," Tasha added, indicating the table Uncle Bruce had chosen. "Looks like he's having a good day today. Give him a hug from me, 'kay?"

"Absolutely." Emma grabbed an oversized coffee mug and filled it, adding cream and two sugars the way Uncle Bruce liked.

She stirred the coffee too hard, the liquid burning her fingers when it splashed over the rim.

There was nothing she could do about Morgan—or Tasha, for that matter. Tasha worried and fussed about Morgan's marriage, but Emma knew it only came as a result of Tasha not wanting to focus too heavily on *her* personal life and the death of her fiancé last year. Talking about Morgan's problems was easier than thinking of what Tasha had almost had but lost.

She said a quick prayer for her friends and for Uncle Bruce before turning and trailing her fingers along the edge of the long counter.

There was a reason she preferred kenneling to waitressing—dogs were a lot less complicated than people.

TWO HOURS after watching Ian emerge from a nightmare, Duncan MacGregor climbed off the back of his Ducati Desmosedici RR GP Replica and stared at the university town of his childhood.

The ride down the mountain and south along the interstate to The Shak had been fast and harrowing, meant to bring focus and clear his head. It hadn't worked.

All Duncan could think about was Ian in the hours of Kara Winston's rescue, how his brother had been the ultimate sailor, a true SEAL.

But when he compared that image to the current...

Gravel dust billowed up with every step Duncan took across the rear parking lot toward the diner, the particles floating briefly in the sultry August air.

Dark purple clouds teased the sky with the hint of rain even though it had been twelve hot, miserable weeks since a drop had fallen.

The blast of air conditioning cooled the sweat on his fore-head when Duncan entered the restaurant. He quickly spotted the man he'd come there to meet in the back and made his way toward the booth, wondering what Bruce Dibbs had been doing to put the dark bags under his pale blue eyes.

Duncan surveyed the environment on his way to the table. The diner was located only a few blocks from the university, but the clientele was diverse, thanks to the main highway running through town bringing bikers, truckers, tourists, and even the occasional farmer.

At present, there were four grizzled bikers parked in a booth talking about this year's Bike Week in Myrtle Beach, a handful of college-age guys huddled over books in the far corner, a lone woman at the counter talking to the waitress, and a few others who sat by themselves and commented on the race on the single big screen.

The waitress unloaded a tray of clean mugs but smiled in Duncan's direction as he passed by.

"Seat yourself. Menus are on the table, and Shirley will be out shortly if you have a food order. What would you like to drink?"

"A cold water and a Coke, thanks." Given the conversation about to take place, he needed a cool head.

"I'll bring them right over."

Duncan approached the booth with a smile. "Hey, Doc. Thanks for meeting me."

"It was nice to hear from you, Duncan. It's been a long time." Doc held out his palm. "How are you?"

Duncan chose to ignore the tremor he saw and hoped it was just a natural aging process and not the makings of more. His doubts grew when Doc's handshake resembled a cooked noodle. Dibbs had always had a strong grip and a steady stare, only one of which remained. "Fine. Have you been here long?"

"No, no. Rose dropped me off before going on to do the grocery shopping, but I come here as often as I can."

"The food's that good?"

A tired smile lifted one corner of his mouth. "I just like the company."

Duncan followed the older man's gaze and noted Dibbs stared at the waitress. The doc was happily married and had been for as long as Duncan could remember, making him wonder who the woman was.

"I heard about Ian. I'm sorry, son." The shrink tugged on his ear. "I take it he isn't doing any better?"

Duncan glanced around again, not wanting to admit the extent of his worries but knowing he had no choice. "No. That's why I'm here."

Dibbs' expression revealed his sadness at the news, his silver hair sparkling beneath the dim, old-fashioned lights above their heads. "I'm sorry to hear that. Your brother is a good man."

"Look, Doc, I know you're retired and probably enjoying yourself, but will you consider taking Ian on?"

"I'd love to, Duncan, but unfortunately I can't."

That wasn't the response Duncan wanted to hear. "I'll make it worth your while. You name it and it's yours. You and the missus ever think about a condo in Florida? A nice, long cruise? I'll make it happen. Ian needs you, Doc. He just needed to have a bullet dug out of his shoulder. He went into surgery able to see, but he woke up blind. Can't you give him a few hours a week?"

The old man stared at his hands, clasped loosely on the table in front of him. "I'm sorry, Duncan. I feel for Ian and for you. I want to say yes, but I can't."

Desperate, Duncan scrambled for ways to sway the old man. "Is it getting to the house? I'll arrange for a driver to bring you up the mountain or else we'll bring Ian to you. You won't have to worry about that. You can even take a room and consider it a working vacation if you like. Bring Rose. Neither of you would have to lift a finger. If you'll just talk with Ian and get him to—"

"I have cancer."

Duncan froze, mouth open to begin another round of promises and offers. A moment passed before he was able to speak. "I hadn't heard. I'm sorry."

Lifting the coffee cup to his lips, Doc took a fortifying swallow and nodded. "You've had your hands full since you brought Ian home to recuperate, but it's public knowledge now. Stage four, inoperable. They've given me three to six months. I intend to prove them wrong, but I am going to spend every bit of that time with my Rose."

The knot in Duncan's gut grew. He hated what Dibbs and his wife were about to face.

As to Ian... The retired shrink had been Duncan's one and only hope since Ian wasn't pulling out of his post-surgery spiral. Ian knew the doc, respected the man because Dibbs had unofficially counseled them after their parents' deaths by talking them through their grief over fishing and hiking trips. If anyone could get through to Ian, Dibbs was it. "I'm sorry for giving you a hard time. If there's anything I can do, just say it."

The older man's searching gaze held a shrewd glint. "Actually, there is."

Dibbs had never asked for anything in all the years Duncan had known him. "Anything."

"Good, because I'm going to hold you to your word."

Foregoing Ian's state of mind until another solution could be found, Duncan nodded. "What do you need?"

"Not me, Duncan, you. And Ian. I accepted your invitation today because I suspected the reason you wanted to meet. I've been giving it some thought, and I've come up with a solution. Someone I believe can help Ian much more than I could."

Duncan leaned forward over the table. "Who?"

Dibbs lifted his hand toward the counter at the front of the building. Duncan followed the gesture and spotted the waitress. She was at the fountain machine, her head tilted slightly as she waited for the glass to fill.

Duncan assessed her in a second. It didn't take long. One look at her face said she wasn't listed in a database somewhere. *Soft* was the word that came to mind.

About five six, she had jeans and a black and silver Shake Shak T-shirt that hugged her curvy frame. She looked sweet and gentle, her long, wavy hair and delicate profile the perfect combo for the old-fashioned diner.

"That is my niece, Emma. The Shake Shak is owned by my former brother-in-law, Frank Wyatt. Rose's sister, God rest her soul, married Frank and loved him with all her heart."

The psychiatrist stopped to clear his throat. Sadness rimmed the old man's eyes as he stared into the depths of his coffee cup.

The sight gave Duncan an idea of where the doc was going with the story, and he mentally scrambled to find an out, deciding he'd jumped the fence a little too soon with that promise of *anything*. "What happened?"

"A car accident. Lauren was killed instantly and Emma injured." Dr. Dibbs' blue gaze shifted back to Duncan and sharpened. "Duncan, I want you to hire Emma to help Ian."

Exactly what he hadn't wanted to hear. "Doc, you know I meant what I said, right? I'll do anything for you and Rose. I'll get you specialists, hire nurses, domestic help, send you on the trip of a lifetime—but I can't hire your niece."

"Why not?"

Duncan looked at the woman again and shook his head. *Ian would eat her alive.* "Doc, Ian's not himself. This isn't a job for someone as young as her."

"She's twenty-eight, your age or thereabouts, if I remember correctly."

She looked younger. A lot younger. "Fine. Someone as soft as she appears."

"You're being judgmental, Duncan. Shame on you."

Shame on him? Maybe it was the way her hair was pulled back from her face and how the length hung midway down her back, but he couldn't imagine pitting her against a former Navy SEAL as lethal as Ian. What was Dibbs thinking? "Doc, it's obvious you love your niece and think a lot of her abilities, but she wouldn't last a day."

"You're looking at the outside, but you're not seeing her strength. And you gave me your word, Duncan. I'm holding you to it."

"Doc… Ian's drinking, flying into rages. No," he said with a firm shake of his head. "For your sake and Rose's, I'm not hiring your niece."

Duncan straightened when he spotted Emma making her way over to them.

"Emma is exactly what Ian needs," Dibbs argued softly.

"Here's your Coke and a water," she said, setting the glasses on the table. "Uncle Bruce, my shift is over, but I'll be around for a few more minutes. Let me know if you need anything else, okay?"

"Emma, can you spare a moment? I'd like you to meet Duncan MacGregor. Duncan, my niece, Emma."

"Nice to meet you, Duncan," she said.

"Likewise."

The entry opened with a jingle of the bells attached to the push bar.

"Emma! How's my favorite girl, eh, sweetheart?" an older man called out. "We're celebrating George's paper getting published. Set us up with eight root beer floats, would you?"

"Sounds like a party, Professor Jackson. I'll be right with

you." Turning back to their table, Emma smiled. "Patty is just coming on the clock so I need to help her out."

"Come back and sit with us for a few minutes when you're done. Duncan and I have been talking about a job opportunity you might be interested in. It pays well," Dibbs added with a pointed smile at Duncan.

"Oh, really? That sounds intriguing. I'm sure I can spare a few minutes while my ride home finishes her dinner."

"Doc," Duncan warned as she walked away, not wanting to be put on the spot or made to feel bad the man wasn't getting the seriousness of Ian's behavior.

His gaze strayed to Emma as she headed back to the bar. Despite her words about needing to lend a hand, she trailed her fingertips along the tables and chairs, hesitating every so often to chat with customers.

"You're being stubborn, Duncan."

Duncan shrugged. "Like I said, it's a bad idea. If she needs a job, I'll ask around and see what I can do, but I'm pretty out of touch with things here. As far as Ian is concerned, what I really need is another you, Doc. Don't you know another shrink? My brother needs someone to—"

"To show him life goes on after being blinded," the man insisted. "Duncan, Emma is proof of that very thing."

"What do you mean?" For the first time since Duncan had sat down at the booth, he saw Doc's eyes take on their former sparkle.

"You didn't even notice, did you?"

"Notice what?" Duncan felt like he wasn't getting a joke when Dibbs out and out laughed.

"Duncan, there is a reason I'm recommending Emma for the job—she's blind, too."

Duncan swung his head to the right, searching until he spotted Emma as she repositioned herself behind the counter.

No way. How had he missed *that*?

Emma laughed at something one of the newcomers said to her as she retrieved a tray and began the process of filling the order for the floats. Once that was done, she replenished mugs for those sitting at the long bar and chatted up the customers. She even made a banana split, her fingertips sliding over the varying shapes until she found the right ones, like the way she'd trailed her fingers over the tables and chairs as she'd crossed the floor. To the unknowing observer, the gesture had looked innocent, casual. Even playful.

But despite the ready smile she wore for her customers, he now noticed other things. No matter how relaxed she seemed, there was an intensity about her, a quiet concentration as she focused on and performed her tasks.

Emma maintained contact with the counter or machines at all times, whether with her hands or her body, sliding her hip against the edge while she carried drinks to her customers or tracing her movements by the placement of the items behind the counter.

Blind?

"If you would prefer to consider it my dying request, so be it," Dibbs said, playing his sympathy card. "But with the perspective of death shadowing my every thought and action these days, I feel I'm seeing more clearly than you at the moment. I'm not only asking on Emma's behalf to spare her the indignity of continuing to perform a job she doesn't particularly enjoy, but also because I want Ian to get the help he needs. Two birds with one stone and all that," Dibbs said matter-of-factly. "And for the record, Emma knows all about handling herself around drunken men. Frank had his own issues back in the day."

"Her father?" Duncan asked, unable to pull his gaze from her.

"Yes. Emma was blinded in the accident that killed her

mother, and Frank didn't handle Lauren's death or Emma's disability well."

Who would?

Duncan continued to follow Emma's every movement, amazed at the ease with which she worked. He didn't mean to gawk at her but… she was amazing. "How long ago was this?"

An older woman appeared from the kitchen and took over as waitress. Emma emerged once more, only this time she called out to someone named Roxy.

"Fourteen years. Duncan, Emma can help Ian in ways I would never be able to because she understands. She's been there and experienced it for herself."

Watching Emma while listening to the doc's words, Duncan faltered. It was tempting. So tempting. But as good as she was, he couldn't offer her up to Ian like a sacrifice. "He threw a bottle at me today, Doc. Shattered it against the wall by my head. You really want her to be his next target?"

"Ian is scared and striking out, but I've never known him to be the type of man to release his frustration on those who can't handle it. You can take the things he does, and he knows that. Have you considered that maybe after all his years of fighting, what Ian needs to face this new development in his life is a woman's gentleness?"

No, he hadn't. But Emma Wyatt also wasn't just any woman. Like it or not, she couldn't *see,* and her disability added an element of risk to an already explosive situation.

His brother would never intentionally hurt a woman, but Ian was consumed in anger. A flare of temper, an accidental swing of his arm…

But what alternative did he have? With the doc unable to counsel Ian, choices were limited. And if Emma could teach Ian the confidence she displayed, maybe it was worth the risk?

How many people could run a busy diner blind? Maybe

Emma *was* what Ian needed. "I'll take her to meet him. But I won't promise to hire her."

I hope you have enjoyed WORTH THE WAIT and the teaser of NOT BY SIGHT. Listed below are links to the rest of the books so you can continue reading about Emma, Ian, and all of their friends.

Word of mouth and reviews are the two best ways an author has to gain attention for their books. While you're browsing the titles, please consider taking a moment to leave a short review.

Thank you,

Kay

The Stone River Novels

- WORTH THE WAIT
- NOT BY SIGHT
- MORE THAN LOVE (FORMERLY THROUGH THE VALLEY)
- TO PROTECT HER (FORMERLY LEAD ME NOT)
- CHRISTMAS AT HOLLY WOOD
- THEIR CHRISTMAS MIRACLE
- SECOND CHANCES

A slightly sexier version of this book was first published under the title THAT SOUTHERN SUMMER NIGHT by Ivy James.

For more information about Kay Lyons, please visit her website at www.kaylyonsauthor.com.

@KayLyonsAuthor (Twitter)

Kay Lyons Author (Facebook)

Author_Kay_Lyons (Instagram)

Kay Lyons, Author (Pinterest)

SIGN UP FOR KAY'S NEWSLETTER AND RECEIVE UPDATES ON NEW RELEASES, CONTESTS, PRE-RELEASE BOOK INFORMATION, EXCLUSIVES AND MORE!

Not By Sight

NOT BY SIGHT

A STONE RIVER NOVEL

KAY LYONS

Kindred Spirits Publishing

For more information about Kay Lyons, please visit her website at www.kaylyonsauthor.com.

You can also find her at one of the following:

www.kaylyonsauthor.com

@KayLyonsAuthor (Twitter)

Kay Lyons Author (Facebook)

Author_Kay_Lyons (Instagram)

Kay Lyons, Author (Pinterest)

Sign up for KAY'S NEWSLETTER and receive updates on new releases, contests, pre-release book information and more!

Chapter 1

Kara? No, no, don't scream. I'm here to help you. Your father sent me." He raised his hand in a non-threatening gesture and smiled at the terrified nineteen-year-old girl backing away from

him. Ian followed her slowly, matching every step with a longer one to close the distance between them. "Target located," he said into the transmitter, relaying the information to the others on the team.

The kidnapped debutante retreated another two steps, until her hips hit a table, and glass clinked together. Some unseen object fell over with a dull thump.

"D-don't touch me."

"My name's Ian. We're here to take you home, but you have to trust me. We don't have much time. Do as I say, and don't make a sound, okay? Hurry."

She didn't take his outstretched hand, so Ian grabbed her elbow, holding it tightly when she immediately tried to bolt. "Shhh. It's okay."

Gunfire erupted outside the mansion, and Kara's eyes widened at the sound, her mouth opening in horror.

"Kara!" a male voice shouted from somewhere in the house.

In Ian's ear, the transmitter picked up his brother's mid-battle curse.

"He got by me. Moving up the stairs!"

Adrenaline pumped through Ian's veins, but he remained focused on the task. "Let's go."

Kara tried to pull away again.

"Kara!"

The man shouting Kara's name was closing in fast. It was too late to get her out of the bedroom, so Ian shoved Kara into a corner and positioned himself in front of the whimpering girl. One of Kara's captors burst into the room, but the guy wasn't prepared to find Ian already there.

The man swung his gun up to fire, but two shots ended the forward charge. The man's grip on the semiautomatic held true, and bullets sprayed the wall, window, and Ian's shoulder before the gunman and his weapon fell silent.

The aftermath of the short firefight was deafening. Kara's screams ripped through the air as the kidnapper's blood began to pool on the hacienda's tile floor, Ian's boot the dam holding the fluid in place.

As he watched, blood dripped from his own gunshot wound into the mass, and the puddle grew larger. The flood quickly surrounded Ian's boots like a wellspring bubbling up from the ground, swept over his feet, thickening and darkening, dragging at his legs. He tried to get out of the coating veil, but it swallowed his calves and thighs, dragged at his chest, snaked around his neck.

He lifted his chin, twisted, and grappled for a handhold to escape as it swelled over his head and crashed together like the Red Sea. The tide sucked him down until the last bit of light diminished from view, and he was engulfed, suffocating, in inky, depths-of-hell black....

Ian MacGregor opened his eyes with a full-body jerk that rocked the bed beneath him. His heart pulsed in his ears but not loudly enough to drown out the sound of his breath chugging in and out of his lungs.

The air conditioning chilled the sweat on his skin as Kara Winston's rescue from a Mexican stronghold slithered back into the hole of his subconscious.

Awake, his claustrophobia was manageable thanks to the

mind games he played with himself. But when he slept, his guard lowered, the nightmare took hold, and he woke up sensory-deprived and drowning, because even with his eyes open, the darkness didn't fade.

As a prisoner entombed in Iraq, he'd spent two full weeks underground without once letting his captors know how close he'd been to losing his mind. He'd known the guards would open the door eventually. They had to drag him above ground to beat and torture him, so he'd counted down the time until they returned, knowing he'd catch a glimpse of the sun through the canvas and bars above his head, something to ease the hours spent in darkness and hold him over until next time. But now?

What did I do to deserve this?

He wiped a hand over his face and scrubbed hard, hoping to rid himself of the fear that left him shaking like a puppy. He blinked a few times, desperate for a miracle.

Ian rolled himself off the bed and onto his feet. His head spun at the sudden shift of position, and it took him several seconds to orient himself and stay upright.

Hands out in front of him, he shuffled his way across the room until he bumped into a chair and felt his way around to the front. Halfway there, a prickle of awareness lifted the little hairs on his neck. "Who's there?"

"Me," Duncan said softly. "You okay?"

Nothing about this was okay. He hated being the entertainment for the household every time he dozed off.

How long had his brother been standing there? Watching him? Listening? "I'm good."

"You want to talk about it?"

"No." What did Duncan want him to say? Fear like his belonged to children who believed in monsters under the bed or ghosts in the attic. He was a soldier—at least he used to be.

Thanks to his little side journey into Mexico, his medical discharge was complete and his CO five shades of ticked.

Ian leaned his head back against the cushion, but he didn't close his eyes. He couldn't, even though it wouldn't make a difference.

He couldn't escape the dark no matter how long he waited. Blindness was his own very personalized hell.

Why this?

"How about I stay? Keep you company for a while?"

Lost in the dark, Ian made a game of stringing obscenities together in his head, focusing on adding another and another, getting pretty creative in his anger. He couldn't *breathe*, and Duncan wanted to stay and *chat*? "Get out."

Every soldier knew there were prices to be paid and that sometimes the dice didn't roll in your favor. This was one of those times.

But no way could he have sat back and allowed Duncan to go into Mexican drug country on a kidnap-retrieval mission without some American-trained soldier tagging along for backup. Before the night was over, he was the one who had found and hauled the kidnapped nineteen-year-old away from the site of her four-week captivity.

The mission should have been over then, in and out of Mexico with no one the wiser. He had carried Kara through the jungle for two full miles with a bullet in his shoulder. To lose his sight during surgery? *After* they had made it back to safety?

Why?

"I can hang out for a while," Duncan insisted.

Ian stretched out a hand and fumbled to find one of the many empty liquor bottles on the table beside him. He hurtled it to the left of Duncan's voice, his rage growing hotter in response to Duncan's pitying tone.

The bottle splintered against the wall and scattered across the tile floor. "I said *get out*."

"This doesn't have to be as bad as you're making it."

Duncan didn't know about the claustrophobia. No one knew. Smart soldiers showed no weakness. But at that statement, Ian started chuckling. Not as bad as he was making it?

Duncan muttered something and left, closing the door to the bedroom with a firm slam. Ian laughed harder, the dam inside him leaking like a sieve until tears wet the corners of his eyes, his stomach muscles ached, and he gasped for breath before wheezing out a few final chuckles.

Not as hard as he was making it... God help him, he was in hell, and there was no way out.

ONLY YOU WOULD INHERIT a pregnant Great Dane."

Emma Wyatt laughed as she filled a couple baskets of peanuts to have at the ready. It was hot out, and while The Shake Shak wasn't that busy at the moment, it would be soon. "Tell me about it," she said in response to Tasha's comment. "But what can I do? Goli is such a sweetheart, and Mr. Bowman knew not just anyone would take her."

"Got that right," Morgan said as she munched on one of the potato chips that came with her sandwich. "That dog is bigger than my kitchen."

Married right out of high school, Morgan was the only one of the *Besties* with a ring and a couple kids underfoot. She lived in an area called Rose Hill, the high-end section of Stone River, Georgia, boasting houses that were a minimum of thirty-five hundred square feet. Stone River was nestled in the Blue Ridge Mountains far enough north to make it a scenic drive for those wanting to view the foliage.

"Emma, I hate to tell you this, but that dog? She's *big*—and she's going to get even bigger when she gets ready to deliver those puppies." Morgan slurped the last of her soda, the noise obnoxious. "They'll be here before you know it."

"She's right, you know," Tasha said from her stool beside Morgan's. "You need to begin advertising those pups now. See if you can start a wait list and get people lined up before the big day. Maybe Jolie can design some ads for you. Her flyers for the opening of Cuppa Jo's were great."

"Do you know who the father is?" Morgan asked.

Emma shrugged and kept working, not letting the chatter keep her from her tasks. "I have no idea. It wasn't exactly a planned breeding."

"It rarely is, unfortunately," Tasha added in her serious vet's voice. "But it makes for a great mystery."

Morgan snickered. "It'll be even more of a mystery if they arrive looking exactly like their mama. The saddest part of this story is that even the dog's gettin' more love and attention than me," Morgan murmured sourly.

Tasha and Emma both sighed in empathy as expected, but neither of them pursued the comment. This wasn't the place to discuss Morgan's troubled marriage. That topic required an unlimited amount of chocolate, privacy, and usually more than a few tissues.

"Mr. Bowman didn't have any other dogs, so there's no way to tell," Tasha said. "Maybe you could advertise them with a Who's-Your-Daddy campaign. Have some fun with it."

Emma groaned. Leave it to her friends to come up with that one.

The *Besties*—Morgan, Tasha, Emma, and Jolie, who had yet to show today—had been friends since school. Emma had met Tasha in first grade when she'd taught Tasha how to tie her shoes. Morgan had come along in third grade when her father had moved the family to Stone River from Ohio for an industrial job, and Jolie was inducted the summer before ninth grade when her very strict parents had stopped homeschooling her and allowed Jolie to move in with her grandmother.

Ten years after graduation, they were still friends. The *Besties* were great at sarcasm, moral support, and laughter as needed, snarky comments guaranteed.

Emma grabbed a few mugs and aligned the handles the way she liked them for easy reach. She'd discovered when she'd first begun waitressing for her father at The Shake Shak that keeping her sanity meant staying a step ahead of the crowd. With afternoon sessions at Zailer University almost over, the late-lunch crowd would come streaming in shortly.

"Emma, can I get a root beer?"

She turned toward the man making the request and smiled. "Sure, Homer. You need peanuts, too?"

"You know me too well, darlin'."

Emma quickly grabbed a mug and moved to the machine. Once full, she set it aside to fill yet another basket.

A regular at The Shak and one of the town's best mechanics, Homer had a thing about skimping on peanuts, so she always gave him extra in exchange for the tips he left her. Every little bit helped when it came to saving up for her dream—a large kennel situated within walking distance of The Shak and her classroom at the university.

Emma delivered the soda and heaping basket of peanuts to the ever-patient Homer, then removed the dishes left two stools down by a different customer. That done, she grabbed the rag at her waist to wipe down the counter, the bell banging against the door barely discernible over the jukebox blaring by the two pool tables in back by the pinball machines.

The jukebox had to be turned down. The nonstop noise did nothing to help the headache she couldn't shake.

"So," Morgan said, lowering her voice so only they could hear, "where's Laney? I never see her in here anymore."

"She officially quit," Emma informed them. "Laney was hired on full-time as an EMT at the firehouse."

"Oh, wow. Bet your dad loved losing her." Morgan rattled the ice in her glass and slurped again.

Tasha made a sympathetic noise. "Sorry, Em. That's why you've been working so much, huh?"

"Yeah. But I'm not complaining," she added. "More hours means more money." Her sister's new job also meant their father was now leaning on Emma to take over all of Laney's responsibilities at The Shak, even though Emma also currently ran a small kennel out of her father's garage and had her hands full.

Every tip went into a fund for the future—namely independence and her own place.

She *had* to get her own place soon. No way could she continue living at the house, not when her father had announced his engagement to a local bank manager who planned to move in after the nuptials. Thank goodness they hadn't set a date yet.

What twenty-eight-year-old woman wanted to be the third wheel to her father's love life? Sharing meals? Downtime?

"Careful," Morgan warned, "you're starting to sound like me. Rory's pay cut has seriously dampened my spending. If not for the money I make on baking and decorating cakes, I'd be up the creek without my highlights. Speaking of which, I gotta go. Em, do you need me to drive you home? I've got a little time before my hair appointment. She's always running behind anyway."

"No, but thank you. Genie's taking me home."

"I wondered where your shadow was today," Tasha said.

"She's on her way, and stop calling her my shadow," Emma ordered. "Genie's had a hard time of it since her grandma died. She doesn't have any family and not many friends."

"Well, you make up for it, big softie that you are, taking in all the strays," Tasha said. "I love that about you."

"I love it, too. Hey, don't get me wrong. I feel sorry for Genie," Morgan said, lowering her voice. "I mean, she certainly doesn't have much going for her looks-wise, and I'm not even sure makeup would help."

Emma grabbed a container of glasses and set them into position. "People are more than their looks, you know."

"Of course they are," Morgan said. "But we live in a society where first impressions matter, even here in the backwoods of Georgia. All I'm saying is that maybe she would have more friends if she'd make an effort. Some days I wonder if she washes her hair. And those glasses of hers? Seriously, invest in some contacts."

"Wow," Tasha murmured. "You get harsh when you're grumpy, Mo."

"Oh, please, like you haven't thought the same thing? Being sweet and helpful isn't everything. She needs one of those heavy-duty, as-seen-on-TV makeovers," Morgan said.

Emma finished emptying the crate and set it aside with the other two from earlier. "I think people should be accepted for who they are." And it made her angry when people talked about how someone else should change and judged others when they didn't know the person.

Morgan would do absolutely anything for any of the *Besties,* but to hear her talk about Genie, you would think... well, the worst. Both about poor Genie and about Morgan, for being so mean.

Fact was, the few times Genie had been around the *Besties* had been brief, but the younger woman's awkwardness had been tangible, making them all uncomfortable. Genie was backward and painfully shy, socially challenged, characteristics that were apparent given her lack of personable graces.

"I agree. They should be accepted," Morgan said, "but we're not in Kansas anymore, Dorothy."

"All right, you two," Tasha said, her tone firm. "Morgan, aren't you going to be late?"

"Em, it's just an observation, right?" Morgan said.

"Right." Emma knew Morgan meant well despite her negativity. Morgan was having a hard time at home, and Emma had to give Morgan allowances for being cynical. Morgan wasn't a mean person. Which made Emma wonder what Rory was saying to Morgan about *her* appearance.

Rory was a supercritical guy, and after kids and baking for cash, Morgan had gained a few pounds. Emma couldn't help but think Rory was at the root of Morgan's critical comments.

The metal decorations on Morgan's purse scraped against the counter's surface and clinked together as she scooted off her stool. Her heels hit the hardwood floor with a clatter.

"Your uncle's here, Em," Morgan said. "Nice lunch, girls, but I've got to get my hair done and get home. If I don't have dinner on the table when Rory walks through the door, he gets persnickety."

"Mmmnfph—" Tasha said around a mouthful of sandwich.

"See you later." Emma gave her friend a good-bye smile and wave.

Several seconds passed before Tasha spoke. "They're fighting again. Bad."

"Yeah, I could tell. I wish there was something we could do to help." Morgan's marriage had been rocky the last few years, but recently things had gotten even more antagonistic.

"The first thing I'd do to help is kick Rory's rear for treating her like his own personal housekeeper, nanny, and cook combined. She supported him all through school, gave up her job because he wanted her to, does everything for the kids, takes care of the house, plus bakes for her spending money, and he doesn't lift a finger and treats her like dirt."

"Maybe Rory is having trouble at work or something. It doesn't excuse his behavior, but who knows?" Emma snagged a couple baskets and washed them down after emptying them of the remains and paper liners.

Tasha's sigh revealed her frustration, and she rattled the ice in her glass. "I hate to eat and run, but I need to go, too. I have to go out to Elmer Pruitt's and check on Barney."

Barney was the pet mule of one of the local farmers, and the thought of Tasha caring for the ornery beast kept the *Besties* in stitches.

"Yeah, ha ha. Laugh it up," Tasha said. "You're not the only one with bills."

"I know. Sorry for laughing. Drive safe," Emma said, swallowing her amusement.

"Will do. Your uncle is at sixteen," Tasha added, indicating the table Uncle Bruce had chosen. "Looks like he's having a good day today. Give him a hug from me, 'kay?"

"Absolutely." Emma grabbed an oversized coffee mug and filled it, adding cream and two sugars the way Uncle Bruce liked. She stirred the coffee too hard, the liquid burning her fingers when it splashed over the rim.

There was nothing she could do about Morgan—or Tasha, for that matter. Tasha worried and fussed about Morgan's marriage, but Emma knew it only came as a result of Tasha not wanting to focus too heavily on *her* personal life and the death of her fiancé last year. Talking about Morgan's problems was easier than thinking of what Tasha had almost had but lost.

She said a quick prayer for her friends and for Uncle Bruce before turning and trailing her fingers along the edge of the long counter.

There was a reason she preferred kenneling to waitressing—dogs were a lot less complicated than people.

***

Two hours after watching Ian emerge from a nightmare, Duncan MacGregor climbed off the back of his Ducati Desmosedici RR GP Replica and stared at the university town of his childhood.

The ride down the mountain and south along the interstate to The Shak had been fast and harrowing, meant to bring focus and clear his head. It hadn't worked.

All Duncan could think about was Ian in the hours of Kara Winston's rescue, how his brother had been the ultimate sailor, a true SEAL.

But when he compared that image to the current...

Gravel dust billowed up with every step Duncan took across the rear parking lot toward the diner, the particles floating briefly in the sultry August air.

Dark purple clouds teased the sky with the hint of rain even though it had been twelve hot, miserable weeks since a drop had fallen.

The blast of air conditioning cooled the sweat on his forehead when Duncan entered the restaurant. He quickly spotted the man he'd come there to meet in the back and made his way toward the booth, wondering what Bruce Dibbs had been doing to put the dark bags under his pale blue eyes.

Duncan surveyed the environment on his way to the table. The diner was located only a few blocks from the university, but the clientele was diverse, thanks to the main highway running through town bringing bikers, truckers, tourists, and even the occasional farmer.

At present, there were four grizzled bikers parked in a booth talking about this year's Bike Week in Myrtle Beach, a handful of college-age guys huddled over books in the far corner, a lone woman at the counter talking to the waitress, and a few others who sat by themselves and commented on the race on the single big screen.

The waitress unloaded a tray of clean mugs but smiled in Duncan's direction as he passed by.

"Seat yourself. Menus are on the table, and Shirley will be out shortly if you have a food order. What would you like to drink?"

"A cold water and a Coke, thanks." Given the conversation about to take place, he needed a cool head.

"I'll bring them right over."

Duncan approached the booth with a smile. "Hey, Doc. Thanks for meeting me."

"It was nice to hear from you, Duncan. It's been a long time." Doc held out his palm. "How are you?"

Duncan chose to ignore the tremor he saw and hoped it was just a natural aging process and not the makings of more. His doubts grew when Doc's handshake resembled a cooked noodle. Dibbs had always had a strong grip and a steady stare, only one of which remained. "Fine. Have you been here long?"

"No, no. Rose dropped me off before going on to do the grocery shopping, but I come here as often as I can."

"The food's that good?"

A tired smile lifted one corner of his mouth. "I just like the company."

Duncan followed the older man's gaze and noted Dibbs stared at the waitress. The doc was happily married and had been for as long as Duncan could remember, making him wonder who the woman was.

"I heard about Ian. I'm sorry, son." The shrink tugged on his ear. "I take it he isn't doing any better?"

Duncan glanced around again, not wanting to admit the extent of his worries but knowing he had no choice. "No. That's why I'm here."

Dibbs' expression revealed his sadness at the news, his silver hair sparkling beneath the dim, old-fashioned lights above their heads. "I'm sorry to hear that. Your brother is a good man."

"Look, Doc, I know you're retired and probably enjoying yourself, but will you consider taking Ian on?"

"I'd love to, Duncan, but unfortunately I can't."

That wasn't the response Duncan wanted to hear. "I'll make it worth your while. You name it and it's yours. You and the missus ever think about a condo in Florida? A nice, long cruise? I'll make it happen. Ian needs you, Doc. He just needed to have a bullet dug out of his shoulder. He went into surgery able to see, but he woke up blind. Can't you give him a few hours a week?"

The old man stared at his hands, clasped loosely on the table in front of him. "I'm sorry, Duncan. I feel for Ian and for you. I want to say yes, but I can't."

Desperate, Duncan scrambled for ways to sway the old man. "Is it getting to the house? I'll arrange for a driver to bring you up the mountain or else we'll bring Ian to you. You won't have to worry about that. You can even take a room and consider it a working vacation if you like. Bring Rose. Neither of you would have to lift a finger. If you'll just talk with Ian and get him to—"

"I have cancer."

Duncan froze, mouth open to begin another round of promises and offers. A moment passed before he was able to speak. "I hadn't heard. I'm sorry."

Lifting the coffee cup to his lips, Doc took a fortifying swallow and nodded. "You've had your hands full since you brought Ian home to recuperate, but it's public knowledge now. Stage four, inoperable. They've given me three to six months. I intend to prove them wrong, but I am going to spend every bit of that time with my Rose.”

The knot in Duncan's gut grew. He hated what Dibbs and his wife were about to face.

As to Ian... The retired shrink had been Duncan's one and only hope since Ian wasn't pulling out of his post-surgery spiral. Ian knew the doc, respected the man because Dibbs had unofficially counseled them after their parents' deaths by talking them through their grief over fishing and hiking trips. If anyone could get through to Ian, Dibbs was it. “I'm sorry for giving you a hard time. If there's anything I can do, just say it.”

The older man's searching gaze held a shrewd glint. “Actually, there is.”

Dibbs had never asked for anything in all the years Duncan had known him. “Anything.”

“Good, because I'm going to hold you to your word.”

Foregoing Ian's state of mind until another solution could be found, Duncan nodded. “What do you need?”

“Not me, Duncan, you. And Ian. I accepted your invitation today because I suspected the reason you wanted to meet. I've been giving it some thought, and I've come up with a solution. Someone I believe can help Ian much more than I could.”

Duncan leaned forward over the table. “Who?”

Dibbs lifted his hand toward the counter at the front of the building. Duncan followed the gesture and spotted the waitress. She was at the fountain machine, her head tilted slightly as she waited for the glass to fill.

Duncan assessed her in a second. It didn't take long. One look at her face said she wasn't listed in a database somewhere. *Soft* was the word that came to mind.

About five six, she had jeans and a black and silver Shake Shak T-shirt that hugged her curvy frame. She looked sweet and gentle, her long, wavy hair and delicate profile the perfect combo for the old-fashioned diner.

"That is my niece, Emma. The Shake Shak is owned by my former brother-in-law, Frank Wyatt. Rose's sister, God rest her soul, married Frank and loved him with all her heart."

The psychiatrist stopped to clear his throat. Sadness rimmed the old man's eyes as he stared into the depths of his coffee cup.

The sight gave Duncan an idea of where the doc was going with the story, and he mentally scrambled to find an out, deciding he'd jumped the fence a little too soon with that promise of *anything*. "What happened?"

"A car accident. Lauren was killed instantly and Emma injured." Dr. Dibbs' blue gaze shifted back to Duncan and sharpened. "Duncan, I want you to hire Emma to help Ian."

Exactly what he hadn't wanted to hear. "Doc, you know I meant what I said, right? I'll do anything for you and Rose. I'll get you specialists, hire nurses, domestic help, send you on the trip of a lifetime—but I can't hire your niece."

"Why not?"

Duncan looked at the woman again and shook his head. *Ian would eat her alive.* "Doc, Ian's not himself. This isn't a job for someone as young as her."

"She's twenty-eight, your age or thereabouts, if I remember correctly."

She looked younger. A lot younger. "Fine. Someone as soft as she appears."

"You're being judgmental, Duncan. Shame on you."

Shame on him? Maybe it was the way her hair was pulled back from her face and how the length hung midway down her back, but he couldn't imagine pitting her against a former Navy SEAL as lethal as Ian. What was Dibbs thinking? "Doc, it's obvious you love your niece and think a lot of her abilities, but she wouldn't last a day."

"You're looking at the outside, but you're not seeing her strength. And you gave me your word, Duncan. I'm holding you to it."

"Doc… Ian's drinking, flying into rages. No," he said with a firm shake of his head. "For your sake and Rose's, I'm not hiring your niece."

Duncan straightened when he spotted Emma making her way over to them.

"Emma is exactly what Ian needs," Dibbs argued softly.

"Here's your Coke and a water," she said, setting the glasses on the table. "Uncle Bruce, my shift is over, but I'll be around for a few more minutes. Let me know if you need anything else, okay?"

"Emma, can you spare a moment? I'd like you to meet Duncan MacGregor. Duncan, my niece, Emma."

"Nice to meet you, Duncan," she said.

"Likewise."

The entry opened with a jingle of the bells attached to the push bar.

"Emma! How's my favorite girl, eh, sweetheart?" an older man called out. "We're celebrating George's paper getting published. Set us up with eight root beer floats, would you?"

"Sounds like a party, Professor Jackson. I'll be right with you." Turning back to their table, Emma smiled. "Patty is just coming on the clock so I need to help her out."

"Come back and sit with us for a few minutes when you're done. Duncan and I have been talking about a job opportunity you might be interested in. It pays well," Dibbs added with a pointed smile at Duncan.

"Oh, really? That sounds intriguing. I'm sure I can spare a few minutes while my ride home finishes her dinner."

"Doc," Duncan warned as she walked away, not wanting to

be put on the spot or made to feel bad the man wasn't getting the seriousness of Ian's behavior.

His gaze strayed to Emma as she headed back to the bar. Despite her words about needing to lend a hand, she trailed her fingertips along the tables and chairs, hesitating every so often to chat with customers.

"You're being stubborn, Duncan."

Duncan shrugged. "Like I said, it's a bad idea. If she needs a job, I'll ask around and see what I can do, but I'm pretty out of touch with things here. As far as Ian is concerned, what I really need is another you, Doc. Don't you know another shrink? My brother needs someone to—"

"To show him life goes on after being blinded," the man insisted. "Duncan, Emma is proof of that very thing."

"What do you mean?" For the first time since Duncan had sat down at the booth, he saw Doc's eyes take on their former sparkle.

"You didn't even notice, did you?"

"Notice what?" Duncan felt like he wasn't getting a joke when Dibbs out and out laughed.

"Duncan, there is a reason I'm recommending Emma for the job—she's blind, too."

Duncan swung his head to the right, searching until he spotted Emma as she repositioned herself behind the counter.

No way. How had he missed *that*?

Emma laughed at something one of the newcomers said to her as she retrieved a tray and began the process of filling the order for the floats. Once that was done, she replenished mugs for those sitting at the long bar and chatted up the customers. She even made a banana split, her fingertips sliding over the varying shapes until she found the right ones, like the way she'd trailed her fingers over the tables and chairs as she'd crossed the floor. To the unknowing observer, the gesture had looked inno-cent, casual. Even playful.

But despite the ready smile she wore for her customers, he now noticed other things. No matter how relaxed she seemed, there was an intensity about her, a quiet concentration as she focused on and performed her tasks.

Emma maintained contact with the counter or machines at all times, whether with her hands or her body, sliding her hip against the edge while she carried drinks to her customers or tracing her movements by the placement of the items behind the counter.

Blind?

"If you would prefer to consider it my dying request, so be it," Dibbs said, playing his sympathy card. "But with the perspec-tive of death shadowing my every thought and action these days, I feel I'm seeing more clearly than you at the moment. I'm not only asking on Emma's behalf to spare her the indignity of continuing to perform a job she doesn't particularly enjoy, but also because I want Ian to get the help he needs. Two birds with one stone and all that," Dibbs said matter-of-factly. "And for the record, Emma knows all about handling herself around drunken men. Frank had his own issues back in the day."

"Her father?" Duncan asked, unable to pull his gaze from her.

"Yes. Emma was blinded in the accident that killed her mother, and Frank didn't handle Lauren's death or Emma's disability well."

Who would?

Duncan continued to follow Emma's every movement, amazed at the ease with which she worked. He didn't mean to gawk at her but... she was amazing. "How long ago was this?"

An older woman appeared from the kitchen and took over as

waitress. Emma emerged once more, only this time she called out to someone named Roxy.

"Fourteen years. Duncan, Emma can help Ian in ways I would never be able to because she understands. She's been there and experienced it for herself."

Watching Emma while listening to the doc's words, Duncan faltered. It was tempting. So tempting. But as good as she was, he couldn't offer her up to Ian like a sacrifice. "He threw a bottle at me today, Doc. Shattered it against the wall by my head. You really want her to be his next target?"

"Ian is scared and striking out, but I've never known him to be the type of man to release his frustration on those who can't handle it. You can take the things he does, and he knows that. Have you considered that maybe after all his years of fighting, what Ian needs to face this new development in his life is a woman's gentleness?"

No, he hadn't. But Emma Wyatt also wasn't just any woman. Like it or not, she couldn't *see*, and her disability added an element of risk to an already explosive situation.

His brother would never intentionally hurt a woman, but Ian was consumed in anger. A flare of temper, an accidental swing of his arm...

But what alternative did he have? With the doc unable to counsel Ian, choices were limited. And if Emma could teach Ian the confidence she displayed, maybe it was worth the risk?

How many people could run a busy diner blind? Maybe Emma *was* what Ian needed. "I'll take her to meet him. But I won't promise to hire her."

Chapter 2

Ian sat in what had become his favorite chair later that afternoon when a sharp knock broke the silence. "Go away."

The door opened with a noisy rattle of the handle no doubt meant to alert him to the fact he was no longer alone.

"Hey," Duncan said in greeting. "I've brought a visitor."

"Get rid of them."

"Emma's already here. I thought you two could talk."

Duncan had barely finished the sentence when Ian heard the familiar sound of his brother's cell phone ringing. That phone was the first thing he'd heard when he'd come to in the hospital. Another indication of the busy life Duncan led as the owner of a major private security company—when he wasn't babysitting his blind big brother.

"It's Murdock," Duncan said. "You want to—"

"No." He had no interest in talking to his former CO.

Duncan deflated like a balloon, exhaling hard enough to pop a rib.

"Emma, this is my brother, Ian. Hang out for a second while I take care of this, okay?"

"Sure."

Duncan answered the call, his voice fading as he left the room. With every word his brother spoke, Ian's anger grew.

The sympathy calls from Murdock reminded Ian of what he'd lost and set his temper flaring again.

Silence filled the air, interrupted only by the distant sound of Duncan talking and the rasp of Ian's fingers against his beard as he rubbed a hand over his face and forced himself to focus on the here and now.

Emma... He didn't *know* an Emma. "You're a nurse?"

"No."

"A doctor?" That earned a laugh, and he heard the amusement in her voice as she responded.

"No. I'm a waitress most days."

Most days... What was she on the other days?

The question gave his curiosity a sharp poke. "What's your name again?" he asked, standing.

"Emma Wyatt. Duncan's thinking of hiring me to tutor you."

"Tutor me?" What did Duncan think this was, grade school?

"Yes. You know, to help you cope with your blindness," she explained. "Learn how to do everyday things without your sight. This meeting is to see if we're compatible."

His mood darkened even more at her explanation. Emma Wyatt was nothing but a glorified *nanny*.

"I'm sure Duncan will explain everything when he returns."

She sounded young. Happy. Way too happy. It was a struggle to keep his anger in check, but he reminded himself Duncan was the source. "I don't need a tutor. Duncan shouldn't have wasted your time."

Wasn't it enough that the house was already overrun with people? Duncan. His VP, Owen Redd. Quinn. Even his SEAL buddy Jagger planned to visit when he could.

Jagger had also gone into Mexico to rescue Kara Winston,

but it was amazing how uncomfortable soldiers became when one of their own was taken out of action. Like the bad mojo might rub off on them.

"Your brother disagrees," she said. "You can discuss it with him when he returns."

Having gauged the distance between them, Ian reached out, ignoring the rapidly fading buzz from his earlier drinking and the pounding in his head, the craving in his gut that made it clear he needed more. Soon.

He found her arm, a shoulder, and tugged her close, not leaving it to chance that she'd refuse the job offer. He wanted to make *sure* she said no. "You're here now. I'm sure we can settle the matter ourselves. You tell me if I need a tutor," he drawled, pulling her closer still.

"Let *go*."

"Maybe my little brother knows what I need after all," he said, lowering his voice as he murmured the insult.

"Don't be a jerk. I said let *go*."

Emma's shove set him off-balance. He automatically reached out to steady himself and used her to do it. That got him smacked, a hard wallop of a blow that whipped his head to the right and caused his ears to ring.

Great, now he'd be blind and deaf. A regular Helen Keller in combat boots.

"Get your hands *off* me. I came here for a tutoring job, not to get mauled by you!"

He winced at her tone, her words. Not so soft or sweet now, but he'd obviously succeeded in his goal. She would be leaving. ASAP.

Duncan's running footsteps echoed down the hallway. The cavalry to the rescue. Just in time to see her out.

"What's going on?" Duncan demanded.

Ian found the arm of the oversized chair and lowered himself to the surface. "Emma took offense to something I said."

"I couldn't leave you alone with her for five minutes? Ian, she's Bruce Dibbs' *niece*."

Ian stiffened at the news, the recent much-practiced string of curses reappearing in his head. Duncan couldn't have shared that bit of information right off the bat? "She said you were hiring her for me. What was I supposed to think?"

"To *tutor* you with your blindness. I was perfectly clear," Emma interjected.

"Yeah, well, like I said, I don't *need* a tutor..." He allowed the words to trail off so both Emma and Duncan would get the hint and leave him alone.

He wasn't normally crude to the opposite sex, quite the opposite in fact, but he wanted her gone. Now. And since he couldn't exactly show her to the door without potentially running into it, he had to do something to get rid of her. And make sure she wouldn't return.

"Oh, I disagree," Emma countered. "But blindness is the least of your problems. You need a lesson in manners more than anything."

"We each have our own ways of coping, sweetheart."

"Ian, what is wrong with you?" Duncan demanded.

More footsteps sounded in the hall, and Ian turned away from them. Was everyone coming to look at the circus freak?

An apology formed on his lips, but he wouldn't let it fly. She had to go. They *all* had to leave so he could figure out how to deal with the hand he'd been dealt.

"Owen," Duncan said, "would you show Emma to the living room and give my brother and me a few minutes alone?"

"No problem. This way," Owen urged.

Seconds passed before Duncan blew out a lung yet again, a sure indication a lecture brewed.

"What are you doing?"

Ian shrugged. "Wondering what you were thinking when you brought Dibbs' niece here."

"Oh, I dunno, Ian, maybe that you need someone to get you out of this room?"

Ian leaned his head against the cool leather. "You need to mind your own business and go back to Atlanta."

"What do you think I'm trying to do? The problem is I can't leave you, not like this. You won't leave the room except to raid the bar at night, you barely eat, and your liver is pickling at the speed of light. I'm just supposed to walk away?"

Ian's claustrophobia sank its claws ever deeper into his psyche, laughing its devil's laugh, because while he could have had a nice, pleasant conversation with Emma Wyatt, he'd ruined it and was now alone with nothing but a ticked-off brother, undeniable facts, and no route of escape that didn't involve ping-ponging off the walls and furniture like a blind mouse in a maze.

He swept his right hand out, found the bottle of Smirnoff on the table beside him. Still open from where he'd been drinking it before they'd interrupted him, the alcohol sloshed inside the bottle as he slammed the vodka back.

He was tired, frustrated. Mad at himself and sick to death of living in his head. He didn't need a tutor. What he *needed* was a knockdown, drag-out brawl. Something to get rid of his rage because he knew exactly what Duncan and the other men saw when they looked at him.

They saw nothing.

A man who used to be capable, a leader, a soldier. A man who used to *be*. Period.

Now? Ian lifted the bottle, touched the cool edge to his forehead, and pressed hard, until he dug the rim into his skin. Pain was better than nothing. He could deal with pain. Work through it. Block it out.

But no matter what he did, he couldn't block out the darkness.

Had he really sunk so low as to proposition Dibbs' niece? Come on to her like some heavy-handed jerk?

"I told myself I'd give you time."

Ian stilled, lifted his head at the sound of Duncan's voice. His brother had been quiet so long he'd wondered if Duncan had gone running after Emma to do damage control.

Ian swallowed the liquid, finishing the bottle off in noisy gulps because he knew it would egg on Duncan's anger.

"I've tried to put myself in your shoes. I've looked away, made excuses. I've ignored you drinking the house dry of booze so old—"

"Finely aged," he rasped.

"Enough, Ian. How long are you going to sit there wallowing in your own pity? How long? I promised Dibbs I'd look after Emma, and what did you do?"

He'd shoved Emma away just like he'd shoved Duncan away since the surgery. Better they stay away or risk getting dragged down with him.

"Go ahead. Enjoy yourself," Duncan ordered, his voice bitter. "But you'd better savor every drop because that's the last of the easy-access stuff."

Duncan's words were slow to sink in, but when they did, Ian stilled and wiped his mouth with his hand as the rush hit his bloodstream. He'd never been one to drink, preferring to keep his mind clear, but now… Coping. This was him coping. Couldn't Duncan see that? "This is my house."

Slowly, deliberately, he rolled his head on the smooth leather, toward the sound of Duncan's voice. "Bring me some wine from the cellar. We both know it's there."

Their parents had been wine snobs, hunting for the best

vintages to serve at the many political parties held here back in the day.

Duncan lost it and swore, highly unusual for him and a sure sign that Ian had stoked his little brother's anger to a fever pitch.

"No. That's it. You're done, Ian. You hear me? Done. I'm *sick* of this. Stop hiding!"

"*Hiding?*" he drawled, lifting his hand to indicate the room in all its glory. Not that he could see it. "I'm right here." He smiled at the way his words slurred. Either he *was* a little hammered or else Emma Wyatt had gotten in a better shot than he'd thought.

Yeah, his mouth was a little tender. *Score one for the wannabe tutor.* "I face reality every day. How am I hiding?" Ian pointed a finger in Duncan's direction. "If you don't like seeing me so much, get out and stay out. You brought me home. That's all I asked you to do."

"How long do you think you can keep this up?"

"As long as it takes." As long as it took to numb himself to the fear. As long as it took to figure out a way to survive in his own head.

However long it took to get the phobia under control so he could take a breath and not feel like a boa constrictor was wrapped around his neck and chest. The fewer people watching him do it, the better.

Ian moved to set the bottle on the table but missed. The bottle fell to the Egyptian tile floor their mother had fretted and fussed over choosing and landed with the unsatisfying sound of the bottle rolling away. No doubt he'd find it later the hard way.

"I know this hasn't been easy for you. I know——"

An embittered chuckle rumbled out of Ian's chest, effectively ending Duncan's inane comments. Was that the best his little brother could do? All this time since the diagnosis, and that was what Duncan was going with? "You put on a blindfold for a few minutes to see what it's like?"

"I'd feel the same way. I'd be angry and just as messed up, but you have to deal with this. The guys and I— we'll help you. Emma will *help* you."

"None of you can help me."

"So you think the alternative is to drink yourself to death?"

Death? No, he wasn't craving death. Oblivion? Yes. Light? By the grace of God, *yes*. Those things he craved. Anything to erase the total, all-consuming, clawing-him-to-shreds-from-the-inside darkness swallowing him whole.

Duncan moved closer, and the fact that he dragged his feet and made enough noise to *wake* the dead and alert the blind was just more proof of how much his brother pitied him.

Ian clenched his hands over the arms of the chair so hard his knuckles popped, and his fingertips went numb. His little brother could take his pity and shove it up his—

"You want me gone, Ian? Make me go. Prove to me you aren't some pansy who sits on his—"

Ian surged to his feet, arms out. He grasped the material of Duncan's shirt, and his vodka-hazed mind realized it was only because Duncan let him, but he didn't care. He hauled his brother close, his anger surging up another notch because baby brother let him do that, too.

"Bring me." Ian punctuated each word with a shake. "Another. Bottle."

It was a demand, a plea.

Why couldn't Duncan or the rest of them understand that, just for a little while, he needed to forget everything? *Had* to forget in order to create the mental muscle to cope?

"No. This stops now. If it were me, I'd want you to help me. I'd want you to get me help, which is exactly what I'm going to do for you."

It was a nice sentiment, but there were no magic pills or treatments, no transplants, no surgeries. Short of a miracle, there was no fixing what had been damaged when the post-op clot had obliterated his vision.

Ian gripped Duncan tighter, shook him harder. *"Give me what I want."*

"I know you, Ian. Knowing she's Dibbs' niece changes things, doesn't it?" Duncan breathed into Ian's face. "So now I'm going to do everything in my power to get her to come back and work with you, knowing you'll leave her alone because you *won't* disrespect Dibbs. He's dying. Did you know that?"

Shock rolled through him. And as much as he hated to admit it, yes, it changed everything.

"Ahh, obviously not," Duncan said slowly. "Well, it's true, and in case it hasn't sunk in, there are people out there like Dibbs who deserve to be acting like their life is over, but you aren't one of them. You're just acting like a coward."

Ian drew back and slugged Duncan at the insult. It was a bad shot, barely connected at all, but he put his weight behind it and caught Duncan by surprise.

The move sent both of them reeling, toppling onto the coffee table that shattered beneath their weight.

Ian's curses bounced off the walls as he floundered about. He scissored his legs and lucked into catching Duncan behind the knee. Duncan went down, but he slipped out of reach. Ian searched for his brother, ripping the air blue when he came up empty. From out of nowhere, Duncan yanked Ian to his feet and shook him like an unruly child.

"You can still be part of things," Duncan growled. "You can be an example to us all."

His little brother offered the lies like the proverbial carrot dangling from a stick, but they both knew in their line of work only the best survived. The sighted man, not the blind man who'd always be at a disadvantage, the one who'd always be the weak link. He was many things, but he wasn't a fool.

But even though he knew the truth of his future, he didn't want to learn to cope, to be stuck in the dark forever. He'd never shoot with accuracy, couldn't fly. Couldn't do what he did best because now...

Now he couldn't take a leak without wetting his feet.

"You can handle this." Duncan gripped Ian's neck and pressed their foreheads together with bruising force, no doubt so Ian couldn't head-butt him. "You *will* find a way to handle this because you're too good a man to act this way. I promise, Ian. I'll get you the help you need."

"You know what I need," he drawled, breathing hard from the brief tussle. More proof that he was out of shape, and the weeks since his release from the hospital had taken a toll.

Duncan shoved him away, and it was all Ian could do to stay on his feet. He staggered and tripped, his hands out like the blindfolded kid playing a game of Catch Me.

One hand hit soft leather still warm from his body, but it was enough to ground him and keep him upright.

"How is drinking yourself stupid going to help?"

"It's called coping!" He'd never see another thing as long as he lived. A sunset from the cockpit, the moon's reflection off the ocean's surface, the ripples in the desert sand. The way sunlight sparkled in a woman's hair.

He thought of Emma Wyatt and what she'd felt like the brief second he'd held her against him. Dibbs' niece or not, those few seconds of touch made him want more, a connection to something or someone that could *make* him forget. Take him out of his head, if only for a little while.

This wasn't living, wasn't life. He'd had a life. Guys who spent their days inside staring at a television or on the couch reading, maybe they could cope with blindness a little better, but him? "You won't bring me booze? Fine." He waited for Duncan to let down his guard and think he was giving in. When he heard Duncan's telltale exhale, Ian added, "Bring me a gun instead."

The silence following his statement was enough to reassure Ian that Duncan understood.

He didn't mean it—taking the coward's way out wasn't something he believed in—but he'd be lying if he said he hadn't thought more than once that it would've been better for him to have died on the operating table than to be the way he was now.

"You did not just say that."

Twisting the emotional knife, Ian shoved himself upright, desperate enough to push harder, the claustrophobic swamp in his mind closing in from all sides. "All this could be yours, little brother. The estate, the mountain. The money."

"Shut *up*."

Duncan had always worn his heart on his sleeve.

"Think about it. I know how to get the job done and not make it messy. One bullet and—"

Duncan cold-cocked him.

All Ian felt was the briefest hint of a breeze as his brother's fist flew toward his face, pain—then he opened his arms in welcome relief as his phobia lost its hold, and he began a spiraling slide into oblivion.

Finally...

So what happened?" Tasha demanded, her words echoing over the hands-free cell thingamabob she used while driving her Jeep back to Stone River.

Emma held the handle of the skillet atop the gas stove and adjusted the flame, listening for the sound that indicated a medium-low heat. Taco salad wasn't exactly new or exciting, but it was something simple and easy that didn't take long to prepare and one of her father's favorite meals.

What better way to broach the subject of her taking on the tutoring job than by feeding Frank first, then informing him she wouldn't be able to work Laney's shifts because of the opportunity Duncan offered?

Frank would probably try to talk her out of it, but she had to stand firm. Money like the kind Duncan MacGregor offered didn't come around every day.

"Hang on, I'm putting you on speaker while I cook," she said, setting the phone on the countertop beside the stove. "Okay, can you hear me?"

"Yes. Keep going," Tasha ordered. "I want to hear everything."

"Well, the meeting with Ian MacGregor was a disaster, but Duncan offered me the job anyway. And you won't believe how well it pays."

"Really? What'd you say? And what happened with Ian that made it so bad?"

"He came on to me——"

"*What?*"

A knock sounded on the back door.

"Emma? It's Genie."

"Hang on," she said. "Genie's here."

"Don't you dare hang up. I want to hear what happened."

Emma hurried to the door and let Genie in, automatically locking it behind her as her father required for peace of mind. As her father liked to put it, there were too many crazies in the world now to ever leave a door unlocked. "Hey, Genie. I'm on the phone with Tasha. Make yourself at home. Want some iced tea?"

"Yeah, but I can get it. Thanks."

Leaving Genie to serve herself as she had several times in the past, Emma moved back to the stove and the phone she'd left behind. "I'm back."

"So what happened?" Tasha asked, not even sparing a moment to greet Genie. "The suspense is killing me. He actually made a pass at you?"

Emma heard Genie gasp.

"Yeah. Now that I've had time to think about it, I think he only did it to get rid of me," she clarified. "But he grabbed me, so I slapped him."

"Good for you!" Tasha said. "But if that's the case, why would you want to tutor him? The pay can't be that good."

Genie pulled out a chair at the kitchen table and seated herself. Normally Emma wasn't quite as forthcoming with Genie and confided only in the *Besties*, but at least this way, Emma wouldn't have to repeat everything a second time. "It is that good. I'd be stupid to pass it up, and you know how hard I've been praying for something to happen so that I could do my own thing. The problem is... Duncan wants me to work with Ian at least three to four days a week for the next three months."

"That's not going to leave a lot of time for anything else."

"No, it doesn't," she agreed. But opportunities like this didn't come along every day, either.

She'd dealt with a few groping hands while waitressing, but if what Duncan said was true, Ian would mind his manners now that he knew she was Bruce Dibbs' niece. "It will mean not spending as much time in the diner and maybe cutting back on the PAWS classes, but it would take me *years* to earn what Duncan is offering. The next few months will be really hard, but it will be worth it because I'll finally have the money to get my own place. With Dad getting married—"

"This is your way out," Tasha said. "I get it. And I totally understand and support you. So you said yes?"

"No, not yet, but I'm going to. I ended the conversation with

Duncan by saying I'd think it over and get back to him, but Tasha, he said he'd take care of transportation and *everything*."

"Wow. Think your dad will handle your news okay?"

Emma laughed and stirred the meat a little harder, concentrating on squishing up the bits glommed together. "Probably not, but he has other things on his mind." Her father had told her multiple times she was welcome to continue living with him and his soon-to-be wife, that nothing would change, but who wanted to do that? She was a grown woman, one more than ready for her own home.

"Well, sounds to me like the timing couldn't be more perfect."

Tasha's voice crackled a bit due to the lousy cell service around the mountains.

"I know, right?" she agreed. "Now I just have to arrange schedules."

"I suppose it does make sense that the guy—Ian?"

"Yes, Ian."

"That he behaved that way," Tasha said. "I mean, think about it. What does an animal do when it's hurt?"

"It becomes viscous and strikes out at the people trying to help it." Emma grimaced. She had definitely been had. Too bad she hadn't kept a cooler head and confronted Ian on his behavior at the time. "I was totally ready to write him off as a jerk, but now I've got this hurt-animal image in my head. I have to try, right?"

Ian's anger had brought back a lot of old feelings from after the wreck. More than she'd thought it would.

"Only one way to find out. Follow your heart. But who better to help that guy than you? You've done so well."

"Hasn't been easy," she admitted. "And I couldn't have made it without you guys."

"Awww, shucks, you're making me blush," Tasha said with a sardonic snicker. "Don't be too thankful. Remember that time we took you to the mall wearing absolutely nothing that matched?"

"They did that to you?" Genie asked softly from the table, her tone horrified.

Emma nodded toward the younger woman. "It's not like you'd let me forget."

That set off another round of laughter from Tasha, and Emma smiled ruefully. At the time, she'd been furious and embarrassed by her friends' prank, mortified by all the snickers and comments from passersby that she didn't understand.

But a newspaper reporter had been trolling the mall and had seen her outfit as well as her friends leading her around. He'd asked about her clothes, interviewed each of the girls, and written a story about them. He'd also mentioned Emma's desire to kennel dogs and how her father had built her a couple pens in the family garage.

The response had been overwhelming, keeping her supplied in spending money all year long because she wasn't ready to tackle working at The Shak.

The hamburger simmered in the skillet, the sound sharper, indicating the meat was completely cooked. She drained the grease, soaked up the mess she'd made on the counter in her distraction, and laid the towel aside. A blind cook was a messy cook.

"I hear you puttering away. Making anything good?"

"Taco salad." Emma added water and the seasoning mix, holding her free hand over the skillet so she didn't knock the contents out of the pan as she stirred. She'd burned herself too many times to count over the years performing the same move, and her fingers, palm, and wrist bore several smooth scars. But she'd become a decent cook in the process. Stir-fries were her specialty. "Tash, I need to go. Drive safe, okay?"

Tasha had agreed with Emma's thoughts about Ian's injured-animal behavior. Ian had acted out. He didn't want her there, so what better way to push her away than to come on so strong? One slap and he'd backed down. That said something.

"Always do."

Emma said good-bye and pressed the End button. "Hey," she said toward Genie. "Sorry about that, but I knew she wouldn't let me hang up just yet."

"It's okay."

That was one of the things Emma loved about Genie—the woman was so easygoing. "What's up? I didn't expect to see you again today."

"You left your training whistle at class," Genie said. "I had it in my car to give to you, but when you went with that guy, I forgot about it."

"Oh, Genie, thanks. You didn't have to bring it all the way out here, though. I have others."

"It's not a problem. I thought— I wanted to help."

"And you did," she said, not wanting to hurt the woman's feelings after she had done such a nice thing. "Would you mind putting it on the ring with the others?"

"Sure."

Emma listened to the taco mix simmering in the pan. It had a ways to go. Enough time to get rid of Genie before Frank made it home. Emma needed to prepare her speech to break the news to her father.

"Taco night, huh?"

Wincing inwardly, Emma nodded, "Yeah. Not very elegant but I'm fixing my dad's favorite dinner because we have some heavy-duty things we have to discuss."

"The job offer?"

"Yes. He probably isn't going to take it well. You definitely don't want to be around to witness the eruption." There. No mistaking that, right?

"It smells great. I'm sure he will enjoy it."

"I hope so," she said somewhat awkwardly, not wanting to be rude but really wishing for time alone to work out a plan in her head.

Genie really was a sweetheart. In the past two years, she had pitched in at every opportunity without being asked. Or paid. Not that Emma could afford to pay the part-time college student, but very few people would ever consider working for free.

"So you're really going to take the job?" Genie asked. "Even though he acted like a jerk?"

"It's the opportunity of a lifetime. I'll be fine, Genie. I can handle myself."

The silence of the kitchen was broken by the bubbling of dinner and the low hiss of the gas stove.

"I know you can. I'm going to go so you can get ready. I just wanted to drop that off and make sure you made it home okay."

"I did. Thanks for watching out for me. I'm sorry you wound up driving to The Shak only to have to turn around and go home."

"No problem. See you in class tomorrow."

Emma led the way to the door, murmuring yet another thanks and good-bye.

Back at the stove, she stirred the soupy meat once more. Still not done.

The dogs continued to bark and jump at their gates, rattling them loudly enough to be heard through the wall separating the kitchen and garage.

She was quick at picking up the different pitches and knew the dogs the way most people knew someone's voice.

At present, she kept Goliath and three dogs for clients either on vacation, away on business, or recently home from the hospital and unable to care for their pet.

She also had two Lab pups about six months old that would

later go into training as service animals for the blind or disabled, and Roxy, her own service dog and graduate of the Seeing Eye program.

But one particular bark stood out from the others. That low-pitched *wuruff* belonged to Buttons, the Basset hound. A grumpy old fellow, the dog had a tendency to complain but not like this. At least not unless his dinner was late. He'd already been fed, walked and—was he *growling*?

He must have spotted Genie.

Roxy nudged Emma's calf, ready to go, and she petted the dog's soft head.

Some might think it silly, but Emma felt she and Roxy had an understanding. Roxy was her one and only, and so long as Emma didn't let the kennel animals into Roxy's domain on a permanent basis, Roxy didn't lead Emma face-first into anything.

"Emma?" Genie called from within the garage-kennel.

Frowning, Emma hurried to open the door, and the woman burst inside. "Genie, what's wrong?"

"The pups are loose. I tried to get them, but they won't come to me. They're heading into the woods."

Great. Just what she needed. "Roxy, stay," she said, rushing to the stove to flip the dial to low while removing the towel tucked into her pocket for ready use. She tossed it onto the counter with the others, lifting her white stick off the kitchen table as she passed. She grabbed the first whistle she found. "Pull the door shut so Roxy can't follow us, okay?"

"Yeah."

Genie followed Emma into the garage, and the door shut with a hurried slam.

Emma headed toward the yard. She'd long ago memorized the number of steps it took to get everywhere inside and outside the perimeter of her father's house, but the white stick came in handy when the dogs tumbled around her feet. She'd learned to shuffle instead of step after one too many falls from tripping over them. The trick was *not* shuffling in public out of habit when the dogs weren't around.

The barking became more frantic and frenzied when the animals spotted her. "Okay, okay, calm down!"

The garage held four individual cages that opened into run paths extending out into the driveway and yard. The setup gave the animals room to play off a leash but protection from the weather if needed.

The dogs made excited jumps at the kennel fence. Emma ran her hand over the metal mesh as she passed. Goliath. Penelope. Digger. Buttons. Buttons was agitated and panting hard. "Oh, you old hound, calm down before you make yourself sick."

Her statement was met by an excited bark off to her left—outside the kennel cages. "Having fun, are they?"

"Looks like it," Genie said.

"I wonder how they got out," Emma said, sighing.

"The gate is open. You should see Tucker's ears flopping. He might be ornery, but he's so cute."

Buttons licked her fingers in a sloppy kiss, as if he were apologizing for the pups' misbehavior. But she was the one to blame. She obviously hadn't fastened the gate correctly in her haste to get inside. "Tink? Tucker?"

Emma whistled, hoping they'd make things easy on her and return quickly.

There was a reason she'd nicknamed the pups TNT. Tink was usually well behaved, but Tucker was a firecracker who often riled Tink up in one way or another.

"Tucker?" This time she blew the training whistle. "Tinkerbell, *come!*" Emma could hear the pups in the yard, their tags clanking against their collars as they ran.

She gripped her cane tighter and left the shade of the garage.

Sweat immediately beaded her forehead as she followed the length of fence down the sloping yard, Genie beside her.

The sound of a splash drifted through the air, and Emma stumbled along the rutted path to the pond near the house. "Tucker, when I get my hands on you..."

All she received for her grumbling was an excited bark that relayed their fun. Baths were not Tucker's thing, but swimming in slimy, scum-coated pond water? Oh, yeah. He loved that.

Emma tried calling the dog repeatedly. Genie even found a small stick and waved it in the air hoping to entice him with a game of fetch. When none of those worked, Emma groaned. "Let's head back. I want to check on dinner and—"

Emma caught a hint of sound and paused, tilting her head to better hear it.

An alarm?

High and shrill, it didn't sound like their neighbor's security alarm but—*a fire alarm?*

The kenneled dogs began to bark and howl.

"Nooo." It couldn't be. She took off, running toward the house as fast as she could.

"Emma!" Genie called.

"We have to get back. Hurry!" Every step fueled the terror growing inside her.

The caged dogs barked nonstop in tune with the smoke alarm shrieking in the kitchen. *No. Oh, please.* "Just be smoke. Just be smoke!"

Emma stumbled up the three garage steps to the kitchen entry, but the moment she put her hands on the knob, she couldn't believe what she felt. Locked? It was *locked?*

She banged her palms on the door. "Roxy!" She kept twisting the knob, but it wouldn't budge.

Praying Roxy had gone to the front of the house away from danger, Emma hurried down the steps. "Genie, call 911!"

"Emma, we have to get out of here. What are you doing?"

"Call 911 and get the dogs out! I'll get Rox."

"Emma, no! You can't go in there!"

Genie grabbed Emma's arm and tried to stop her, but she yanked loose and kept going, around the kennel cages, out the open garage door, staggering over every dip and rut and rock to be found as she made her way to the front of the house. "Roxy, come!"

She pulled at the door, but the rarely used front entrance was locked as always.

Emma dropped to her knees and felt for something to throw at the window, but the steps were clear. No potted flowers for the dogs to dig in or knock over, no decorative gnomes to chew on. Nothing.

Not knowing what else to do, she pulled the shirt she wore over a camisole off her shoulders and wrapped it around her hand, barely sparing a second to take a deep breath before she plunged her fist through the window as hard as she could.

Choking smoke poured out of the opening, more smoke than would be created by taco mix getting cooked too crisp.

Emma coughed and jerked the shirt off her hand, holding it over her mouth and nose as she reached inside to unlock the door next to the window. *"Roxy!"*

What had she done? The question repeated itself over and over in Emma's head as the enormity of the moment set in. Sirens blared, every shriek tearing through her trembling body as help arrived.

The dogs continued to howl from within the older, rusting cage near the property line where Genie had led them all to safety, but Emma didn't waste her time trying to calm them. Nothing would help when they were so focused on the multitude of vehicles pulling into the driveway, on the engines and brakes and the crunch of gravel, the orders shouted as the Stone River Fire Department set out to battle the blaze.

"Emma? *Emma?*" Laney. Oh, of course her sister would be on duty today of all days.

"She's hurt," Genie said. "And she hasn't said anything since... since she got Roxy out."

The adrenaline and determination to save Roxy were gone, replaced with the overwhelming and numbing shock of catastrophe that left her entire body clenched into a hard knot.

What had she *done?* One little mistake, one moment of distraction—and she'd caused this?

"Were you burned?" Laney asked. *"Emma?"*

Emma heard the metal-on-metal scrape of latches being flipped a split second before her sister jumped into EMT mode, grabbing at her wrists, shoving a mask over her face.

"Stop pushing my hands away, and let me look at you," Laney ordered.

Emma stopped—but only because she wasn't aware she'd been pushing Laney away in the first place.

The hiss and crackle of the fire seared her mind, and she imagined the items in the house as they burned. Pictures, quilts. Precious memories.

What had she done? A nearly hysterical laugh bubbled out of her chest. "It's really on *fire?*"

Laney didn't answer. Not at first. And Emma realized she'd asked the stupidest question of all.

"Don't worry about that now, you hear me? Your arm is bleeding," Laney said. "Let me take a look. Hold still and let Jim put that oxygen mask back on you."

"No. No, I'm—" The elastic band of the mask pulled at her

hair and slid into position, cutting off her words. Laney and her partner obviously weren't listening to her.

She'd barely breathed any smoke after breaking the window to get Roxy, but her throat itched and burned, and her arm throbbed, like someone had repeatedly stabbed it. "Check Roxy." She pulled the mask off again. "*She* needs this. Roxy was inside the whole time."

"I'll check her but not until you put that back on," Laney ordered.

"We have another mask," Jim said. "I'm holding it in front of her now."

Jim's words brought a fresh sting to her eyes, one that had nothing to do with the smoke. "Laney...I'm *sorry*. I'm so sorry."

Laney ran her hand over Emma's head and fit the mask back into place.

"Just breathe. You're in shock. It's okay, Em. It'll all be okay."

How could it be okay? Only minutes ago, she was in the house and everything was fine and now...

How could she have made such a mistake? She was fine, alive, the kennel dogs safe, thanks to Genie. Rationally she knew that was all that mattered, but a part of her wanted to scream and howl like the animals because this *wasn't* a little mistake like stubbing her toe or burning cookies. She'd burned down their *house*!

It was gone. She didn't need her sight to know that. In the time she'd sat there surrounded by the dogs and Genie, waiting for help to arrive, she'd heard the fire roar through their small, old house, every hiss and pop and shatter of glass, the strange, rushing sound of the fire growing bigger, burning hotter.

What was left couldn't be more than the rubble being finished off by the flames. She only hoped, given the drought, the firemen were able to get it under control before the brush and forest caught, too. Their neighbors' homes? *Please, God, not that. Protect them.*

"Dad's here. Brace yourself," Laney said.

Emma barely had time to take a breath before her father swallowed her in a bear hug.

"Oh, baby girl. Thank God. You're okay?" Frank demanded.

She tried to nod but couldn't. She'd destroyed their home, their belongings. Everything. No, she wasn't okay. "Dad, I'm sorry. I don't know what happened."

"It's okay."

"It's *not* okay." Why did they keep saying that? How did you make up for something like this? All the years in the house, all the memories? Gone?

Emma felt the rubbery grip of Laney's fingers gently exploring the wound on her arm after Frank loosened his hold.

"The cut is long but shallow. More blood than anything. I don't think you'll need stitches, but the doc might not agree."

"Emma, you're alive. That's all that matters," her father said. "Any idea how it started?"

Emma wet her dry lips. "I was cooking and talking to Tasha, then Genie arrived to drop something off and when she left..."

"The pups were loose," Genie added. "I couldn't get them to come to me."

"So I left the stove to help her. I turned the heat down to low a-and—" She had to stop and take a breath, remembering how she'd tossed the towel onto the countertop. "The towel." Where had it landed? Too close to the flame? "I threw a towel onto the countertop and told Genie to shut the door. I didn't want Roxy nudging her way out behind us. I was just trying to get outside to the pups before they went too far. We were only gone a few minutes. The lock must have jammed. So I ran to the front and broke the window to unlock the door."

"You went back inside?" her father demanded.

"Dad," Laney warned.

"I had to get Roxy."

"For the love of— Emma, I know you love that dog—we all do—but you could've been *killed*."

"I had to try. Dad, she was waiting for me to get her. If I hadn't..."

"Ma'am?" a male voice said from her left. "I'm glad you're safe. My name's Deputy Parker. I understand you're visually impaired?"

So politically correct. "I'm blind, yes."

"What were you doing before the fire started?"

"Cooking. I-I think it may have started with a towel."

And with that statement, the questions began again.

Chapter 3

The sound of a groan woke Ian, but it wasn't until he heard the noise again that he recognized it as his own.

His head pounded like a Federation wrestler on his latest opponent, his mouth filled with copper-tinged cotton. He mustered up enough saliva to swallow and winced at the way his jaw ached as a result.

He needed a drink.

He moved his hand along the bed beside him for the ever-present bottle, only then remembering why his head hurt and swallowing was an issue. His baby brother had gotten better over the years.

Groaning again, he ignored the jackhammer in his head and rolled onto his side, shifting closer to the nightstand and the elixir that had gotten him through the last two months.

Nothing.

He swept his arm out again, scooting closer to the edge of the bed just in case his perception was off.

Alarm clock. Lamp—yeah, like he needed that—but nothing else.

Duncan's promise about ending access to alcohol bounced off the insides of Ian's aching brain and brought a surge of fear.

He swung his feet to the floor and stumbled toward the sitting area, hands out to feel the way to his chair and the table beside it. The bottles that had littered the top were gone from there as well. "Duncan!"

He winced at the pain shouting caused, his hands holding tight to his head to keep it on his shoulders. Maybe Duncan had missed his calling. With that kind of punch, he could've been a contender. "*Duncan!*"

"He left."

Quinn's quiet statement infuriated Ian. "What time is it?"

"Almost eight."

His buzz was gone, and with the clarity of sobriety came the soul-sucking awareness of what he faced. Stupid as it seemed, the claustrophobia was always worse at night, and while the sun might not have set yet, it wouldn't be long.

"You want some dinner?"

"Bring me a drink, straight up."

"Tea, water, cola, or coffee?" Quinn asked instead. "And don't think I'm not aware I sound like a freaking flight attendant."

Every breath rattled his brain. Only one thing would fix it. "Bring me a bottle, Q."

"I can't do that."

"Why? Because you're taking orders from my little brother now?"

Silence descended upon the room.

Ian growled out curses, all the while aware that Quinn waited, watched. "Did you know about her? That Duncan was thinking of hiring Emma Wyatt as a tutor?"

"Not until he showed up with her. Let me know if you change your mind about dinner. That I'll help you with."

"Don't walk away from me." Quinn couldn't walk away. He had to help, had to bring something that would take the edge off. Of all the men working to secure the house and grounds, Quinn should have been on his side. "I pulled you out of an Iraqi cell! I carried you across the *desert* when you barely remembered your own name! This is how you repay me?"

"Come with me," Quinn ordered. "I'm working on dinner. You can sit in the kitchen just like you sit in here. We can eat together."

And pretend all was right with the world? Normal? "Get out."

Ian didn't hear Quinn walk away.

The house was silent, but he knew—*knew*—Quinn and Owen Redd or whoever else remained, waited for whatever came next.

His head pounded harder, the blood pulsing through his body so fast he felt every squishing, too-fast pump.

He found the oversized chair in the sitting area, used it for a guide while he bounced from the chair to a side table. His hands landed on the base of a lamp he picked up and threw as hard as he could, because that table, too, was empty of the bottles he sought.

The crash echoed off the tile, insanely satisfying. So he wiped the table clean and moved on. The desk was next. The globe he couldn't see, the pins marking the locations he and his father had traveled scattering on the floor with little *pings*.

The phone, a photo frame, books. They slammed into the walls or bookshelves. Everything he could get his hands on, he hurtled into the black void.

Breathing hard from the exertion, Ian eventually stumbled his way through the chaos to the chair. He dropped down, his head lolling on the cool leather.

He gripped the cushioned arms in a sad attempt to anchor himself in the black sea, but it didn't work. He was still adrift. No light, no sensory awareness of direction. No hope. It was like being swallowed whole, then devoured bit by bit.

For the first time since the surgery, he faced his worst nightmare entirely stone-cold sober. No drugs. No booze.

A laugh erupted out of his chest when panic slithered up his spine.

This was what it was like to play chicken with the devil.

***

Needing some time alone after dropping Emma off at her house, Duncan found himself returning to The Shake Shak on his way back through town.

Emma was his best option for a difficult situation, but her hesitation to tutor Ian had been obvious.

Why bother attempting to help someone who wasn't willing to help himself?

Doc was right. Ian needed to be shaken up, and after watching Emma in action and hearing the slap she'd landed on Ian's cheek—seeing the red imprint of her hand on Ian's skin— who better than her to do the shaking?

Dibbs had mentioned Ian needing Emma's softness, but in Duncan's estimation, Ian needed her spunk.

Emma might look like the girl next door, but she had backbone. A quiet, steel-honed class in the confident way she carried herself and behaved that gave him hope.

Fifteen minutes after his arrival, Duncan finished off his cola and set it aside. He studied the billiard table for a decent shot, his thoughts on ways of convincing Emma to take the offer.

"Hey."

Duncan swung around to find Owen Redd pulling a cue stick from the display.

"You okay?"

Duncan narrowed his gaze on the other man. "Why wouldn't I be?"

"I was, uh, outside Ian's room today. Before you knocked him out."

That meant Redd knew what Ian had said. "He's having a rough time, but I've got a plan."

"Good. Then I won't feel guilty when I beat you… Boss."

Duncan smirked and watched as Owen racked the balls and tossed the triangle aside.

"Oh, my— Shirley! Shirley, come here, it's Emma."

Duncan swung around and watched as an older waitress hurried toward the younger one who'd stepped out of the kitchen.

"A fire?" the woman said, her hand fluttering to her throat as she paled. "Are you sure?"

The younger woman nodded. "Emma's okay. She refused to go to the hospital and insisted Laney take her to the vet clinic so the dogs can be checked over. They're there now. Brad just got back to the station. He says there's nothing left. The house went up like kindling."

Duncan exchanged a quick glance with Owen before they simultaneously tossed the sticks onto the table and headed out the door.

"I'm over here."

Owen led the way to his Denali, and they squealed out of the parking lot toward the east side of town. The vet clinic wasn't far.

Painted animal murals decorated the side of the cinder-block building, the colors beginning to chip and peel near the foundation.

Duncan was out of the vehicle before it rolled to a stop. It was after business hours, nearing nine.

The waiting room was empty. He kept going until he found

Emma and four other women in the back, one of them wearing a lab coat. Emma stood beside an exam table, soot-and-tear-streaked, her shoulders and arms, nearly every inch of her, covered in grime. A large bandage was wrapped around one arm from elbow to shoulder, but even though it looked new, it was dirty as well.

Emma's large Lab was on her side on the table with an IV inserted and oxygen in place. The dog tracked his arrival with her big brown eyes but didn't lift her head or attempt a tail wag of greeting.

"We're closed," said the woman with a stethoscope pressed to the dog's ribs.

She was tall and thin, pale, her dark brown hair tucked behind her ears and a serious look to her heart-shaped face.

"I'm here to see Emma," Duncan said.

"Who are you?" the blond of the group asked. She was shorter and plump, with pretty blue eyes. Two other women stood beside Emma, but they remained quiet.

Duncan ignored the question and moved deeper into the room. "Emma, are you all right?"

A brief smile curled the corners of Emma's full lips. "I'm fine. Thanks for checking on me, Duncan."

Duncan stared at her, wondering how anyone could undergo what she'd been through and look the way she did yet still remember her manners. More proof Emma Wyatt was an amazing woman.

"Duncan, you don't have to feel guilty. I understand."

He frowned at the statement. "What do you understand?"

"That you're trying to think of a nice way to retract the job offer. I wouldn't hire me right now, either. Not when the fire was my fault."

"Your fault? What happened?"

Emma had anticipated Duncan's question, but she hadn't counted on the hard lump that appeared in her throat when he asked it.

Three hours after she'd stood in the kitchen stirring the pan of seasoned meat, she still tried to come to grips with the reality of what she'd done, however accidentally.

Laney, Genie, and the *Besties* had offered condolences and repeatedly told her it could've happened to anyone. They had shared stories of how they'd left pans on the stove to run to the bathroom or answer a call or the door. How they'd locked themselves out of their cars. And maybe, occasionally, they had done those things, but the fact that it had happened to the local blind girl just...

Bit the big one. "I screwed up. I left a-a towel too close to the stove in my rush to check on the pups."

She'd worked so hard to prove herself in the years since the accident. To prove her abilities. And with a single, stupid mistake, she'd wiped the slate clean so that the only thing people would remember was how the blind girl had burned down her family's house.

As much as she would like to blame Genie for the locked door, Emma knew she couldn't. Genie wasn't the one cooking, and even though the lock on the door had been sticking for the last few months, Emma had forgotten that fact when she had ordered the girl to pull the door closed. The entire incident, from fire to lock to the house being razed, was her fault and her fault only.

Now every bone in her body ached as if she'd run a marathon, and Roxy had breathed too much smoke because she wasn't bouncing back as she should.

Oh, and she and her father were homeless. But the icing on the burnt cake? Having Duncan MacGregor see her like this. Was anything else going to go wrong today?

"We all make mistakes, Emma. And that's not why I'm here. How's Roxy?" Duncan asked kindly.

Given the careful tone of his voice, Emma stiffened. What did he see, what did they all see, that she couldn't?

Emma ran her hand down Roxy's side and felt the way the dog's ribs swelled and sank with every breath. "Tasha?"

"Her vitals are a little better, stronger than they were when you brought her in, but given her age, I'd like to keep her overnight and run some tests, just in case."

"Of course."

"I need to check the other dogs," Tasha said. "They looked fine, but I'll give them a once-over."

"I'll help," Jolie said, her exit marked by the way she shuffled her shoes along the floor.

"I'll give them a hand," a man said.

Emma recognized Owen Redd's voice from earlier today. "Morgan, go home," Emma ordered. "There's nothing you can do, and it's past the baby's bedtime."

"It is but—"

"But nothing," Emma said. "Go on and give Rory a break. You know he's probably pulling his hair out by now."

Rory had little patience with his children, a fact they'd all caught on to early in Morgan's marriage to him.

"I'll stay with Emma," Genie said.

Morgan inhaled, her bracelets jingling as she moved or gestured with her hands. Morgan had always talked with her hands, even as a kid.

"Okay. I'll go, but only if you promise to call me if something changes or if there is anything I can do. *Anything*."

"I will."

Morgan wrapped Emma in her arms. "I'm so glad you're safe. Please don't ever scare me like that again."

Emma forced a laugh, trying to lighten the mood. "Come on, it's good to get your blood pumping every now and again."

Still hugging her, Morgan's chuckle filled her ear. Emma squeezed her friend a little more tightly before letting go, unable to remember a time in the last few years when Morgan didn't smell like buttercream icing. Now was no exception. The scent of birthday cake frosting brought comfort and memories of happier days. "Thank you for coming to check on me."

"You know I'll stay if you need me," Morgan said.

"I know."

"Where are you sleeping tonight?" Morgan asked. "I have to know you're okay before I leave."

"She can stay with me," Genie offered. "I have a big house to myself."

"That's really nice of you, Genie," Emma said, "but I'm not sure what I'm going to do just yet. I won't know until I know more about Roxy's condition."

"Well, call me and tell me what's going on, okay?" Morgan asked.

"Deal." Emma waited for Morgan to exit the exam room, careful to stay by Roxy's side in case she tried to get up. Roxy didn't move, even though Morgan was one of the dog's favorite people because she baked doggie treats as well as human cakes.

"How are you holding up?" Duncan asked.

She briefly closed her gritty eyes and struggled to keep the semi-smile pinned to her lips. "The truth? I'm embarrassed. My taco salad has never been that hot before," she said dryly. "How did you find me?"

"I was at the diner when they got the news. Your arm needs attention."

"It's just a scratch. Laney already took care of it. Look,

Duncan, as you can no doubt see, now's not a good time. You're off the hook. I totally understand your not wanting to hire me after tonight, and it's okay. No hard feelings."

"And if I don't want to be off the hook?"

She couldn't fathom him *not* wanting to be. "Pardon me?"

"Emma, I've seen grown men go into full panic mode at less than what you handled tonight. My job offer stands. In fact, I'm going to increase it."

Increase it? She struggled to focus. Did he just say he was *increasing* it?

"You must have guessed I tried to hire your uncle before learning of his diagnosis."

She hadn't given it much thought, but it made sense. Uncle Bruce's counseling expertise would serve Ian's needs much better at the moment.

"Given the distance to the house, I offered to let Bruce and Rose stay there full-time. I'm extending the same offer to you."

Blood rushed past her ears, clouding her hearing. "Wait...what? You want me to live there?"

"Why not? You'll have your own room and bath. And it will mean easier access and more time with Ian. I assure you you'll be perfectly safe," he added. "You can kennel the dogs there, too."

That wasn't extending the offer; that was going above and beyond. "I don't understand. Why are you doing this?"

"Emma, you've been blind how long?"

She blinked at the question. "Fourteen years."

"I'm sure today wasn't the first time you've cooked something."

"No, of course not." But burning her house down was nothing to sneeze at.

"I thought as much. I'm extending the offer because Ian's recovery means everything to me. I realize we've only known each other a matter of hours, but anyone seeing you work the diner knows you're a competent, capable woman. One accident isn't an indication of your abilities. There is a lot you can teach Ian."

"Other people could teach him the same things," she countered, wondering if she was dreaming. Maybe she'd inhaled more smoke than she thought?

"Ian doesn't need an occupational therapist; he needs to know someone like you. Someone who understands what he's going through. So the tutoring job now comes with room and board, plus a raise in pay. It's only fair considering you'd be spending more time dealing with Ian on a daily basis. Your uncle mentioned you'd like to have your own kennel one day. Maybe with an apartment attached?"

It was like a shot to the heart, dangling that temptation in front of her. Was this really happening? "Yes."

"Looks to me like you could really use that now, and I can make it possible."

She slipped her fingers into Roxy's thick fur and stroked. "Genie, would you excuse us a moment?"

"Emma, you can stay with me," the girl insisted. "The animals, too. You don't have to do this."

She managed a smile and nod of thanks. "Thank you. I'll keep that in mind."

Several seconds passed before Emma heard Genie crossing the exam room to the door.

Her own kennel. She hadn't thought any further than getting the dogs to the clinic for Tasha to examine.

Now Duncan offered her a dream come true?

She thought the job offer had gone up in flames with the house. How could she possibly turn this down?

But the money wasn't the only reason she couldn't say no.

After meeting with Ian today, she hadn't been able to stop thinking about her own stay in a hospital rehab, how sterile and cold it had been. Everyone there had been a stranger, and while they'd been kind and generous and helpful, she would've much rather been working one-on-one with someone in her home.

"Emma, you need a place to go, one that accepts animals, and you need it tonight. Am I right?"

She had to make herself focus on Duncan's question. "Yes. Some of the dogs go back to their owners in a couple days, but the pups and Roxy are mine. You're serious? You would let me keep them? Board them and continue the pups' training?"

"Yes. You can even continue to kennel other dogs if you like. If it's not too much for you with your other responsibilities. The stable is clean and has a concrete floor. You can use the stalls for pens."

Which, not to be greedy, would allow her to earn even more money to put toward her dream. Hope surged so fast and was so overwhelming her head spun. She wanted to say yes. Scream it. But she had to be sure Duncan knew what he was in for. "Dogs have accidents. Make messes."

"So do blind men who haven't figured out how to care for themselves."

That they did. Emma ignored the overwhelming task of attempting to tutor Ian and concentrated solely on her animals and the future. Her future. "What if Ian refuses to work with me? What then?"

"You stick to your guns while we all work on him to bring him around. Emma, I assure you Ian's behavior this afternoon won't happen again."

"What happened this afternoon?" Jolie asked from the doorway.

Emma inhaled and sighed. This was a conversation that needed to be held in private, but with her friends in the building, that seemed to be impossible. "Nothing. Just...a misunderstanding." Emma hugged her arms around her front, her mind slow to take it all in. "Is something wrong, Jo?"

"No. I came to grab something for Tasha… Got it. Yell if you need me. Okay?"

"Yeah."

"Your friends are protective of you. That's good," Duncan murmured when Jolie left the room.

"Yes, it is." But more often than not, they were too protective, and being treated like a child grated on her last frayed nerve.

"Emma, Ian didn't know you were Dibbs' niece. He wouldn't have behaved that way had he known. That was my mistake. And trust me when I say that from now on, he'll be sober," Duncan said. "Give Ian three months of tutoring, and I'll make it the best decision you've ever made."

"A room and pay?"

"The fifty grand I promised."

"Fifty thousand dollars *on top of* room and board? That's... What's the catch?" There had to be a catch.

"Only one. You can't quit. Dealing with Ian's foul moods and temper won't be easy, and I can guarantee you'll want to walk out on a daily basis. The catch is that you can't. Take a break and let him brood, sure, but you can't quit. The offer is generous enough to get you what you want while making sure Ian gets the training and knowledge he needs. And if he needs more, we'll make it six months for a hundred thousand."

Emma braced her trembling body against the table in front of her. She could do *so much* with that kind of money. She could help her sister replace the things lost in the fire, help her father rebuild what she had destroyed. And Roxy...

Vet bills were expensive, and while Tasha wouldn't charge for her expertise, the medication and supplies had to be paid for.

"Ian will do and say whatever he can to push you away

because he's not going to like this or want your help. I don't doubt you'll earn every penny."

Ian MacGregor might not come on to her anymore due to her ties to Uncle Bruce, but that didn't mean Ian wouldn't try to make her life horrible just to be left alone. Was she up for that? "You sound desperate."

Almost as desperate as she was for independence.

"I am."

She thought of Ian's behavior and recognized his actions for what they were. Fear. Loss. No one understood better than she did what it was like to wake up in the dark. It got to her that Ian's emotions were so *raw*. "I feel for him. I remember lying there in the hospital, the seconds turning into hours when I realized I couldn't see," she said, petting Roxy, every stroke bringing a new memory. "I can't describe the absolute terror... I felt like my life was over."

"I know Ian's thinking the same thing. But from where I'm standing," Duncan murmured, "it looks like your accident was the start of a new chapter for you. Ian needs help to realize that it can be the same for him."

Her mother had always said things happened for a reason. That no matter the plans or events, God would use them. She wouldn't go so far as to say that the house had to burn down as part of an overall plan but... what if fire was the catalyst to shove her out the door? Only in God's hands could something so horrible be turned into something good.

Stroking Roxy, she inhaled. When she'd lost her sight, she'd quickly grown tired of being told she couldn't or shouldn't do something because she was blind. It had forced her to grow up, to get out of her shell and fight for what she wanted. How was taking this job any different?

"What do you say?" Duncan asked.

"Say to what?" Tasha queried as she reentered the room.

Jolie shuffled in behind Tasha, and while Emma didn't hear Owen Redd's return, she felt the man's presence. Genie wasn't far behind, the smell of smoke following her.

Emma quickly explained the change in Duncan's offer, that it now included room, board, and a place to kennel the dogs.

"Seriously?" Tasha's tone revealed her surprise and disbelief. And more than a little suspicion.

"Yes, seriously," Emma repeated, hoping Duncan knew better than to be insulted or alarmed by her friends' responses.

"*Emma...*" Jolie breathed. "After everything that's happened today, shouldn't you think about this?"

"I have." One wasn't supposed to love material things, but hearing the hiss and burn of the house had hurt in so many ways. Her mother's collection of Old Country Roses china and the lace tablecloths, favorite books. All gone.

The photos and albums had become unimportant to her. They were simply pieces of paper she couldn't draw anything from. But the things she could touch and hold, cherish... She mourned their demise. And while she knew her father and Laney wouldn't hold a grudge, she didn't want them worrying about her or the dogs on top of having to deal with that loss and their own well-being.

Tasha moved close, her perfume reaching Emma's nose and mingling with the smoke smell wafting from Emma's clothes. "Emma, you can stay with me," Tasha said. "Take a few days to consider all your options."

Her friends wanted to protect her. But the time had come for her to stand on her own, and while technically she wasn't *on her own* just yet, accepting the position was the first step that would get her there. "You have five cats and I'm allergic. Plus the dogs are an issue. Duncan says there is a stable I can use to kennel them."

"Morgan then," Tasha countered, keeping her voice low

despite the fact Duncan was right there listening to every word. "You know how she loves to play hostess. She wouldn't mind at all."

"The last thing she needs is someone else underfoot. She and Rory have enough problems as it is. And I know you'd let me stay," she said to Jolie before her friend could add her thoughts, "but Goli has *morning* sickness."

"Goli?" Duncan asked.

She was still so used to only having Roxy and the pups, she'd forgotten Goli's new permanent position with her. "Yes, uh, I forgot to mention I have a Great Dane, too. I inherited her from one of my clients when he passed away, and she's pregnant. Does that make you want to reconsider?"

She heard Owen struggling to smother a laugh, and the sound helped her place him in the room, by the door.

"No. My offer stands," Duncan said. "Like you said, I'm desperate."

"Emma," Jolie said, caution lacing every letter of her name.

"How can you consider just *moving in* with strangers?" Genie asked, clearly appalled at the thought.

While their worry was valid, her decision came surprisingly easy. "Uncle Bruce wouldn't have recommended I take the job if he didn't trust Duncan. You all know that."

"But you could stay with me," Genie said, her tone matching Jolie's with a mix of urgency and worry. "The animals, too. Really, it's no problem. I'll help you."

"Genie, I appreciate your offer, but I'm afraid the university would frown on having one of its instructors, even a part-time one, staying with a student. Besides, if I did accept, that would still leave the issue of transportation to the MacGregors'. Duncan's offer is the best solution," she said gently, trying not to hurt the girl's feelings.

Laney and her father would have to be told, but surely it would be an easy sell?

"Does that mean we have a deal?" Duncan asked.

"Yes. It's a deal. I accept." Emma held out her hand, the strength of Duncan's grip and the grit of soot and dirt between them forging a bond unlike any she'd made in her life.

Chapter 4

I called ahead after you agreed," Duncan said as he rolled to a stop outside the MacGregor house an hour and a half later. Duncan had dropped Owen off at The Shak to ride the Ducati back home, while Duncan drove Owen's SUV up the mountain with Emma and her animals in tow.

She could only imagine what they looked like with Goli's massive head sticking out one window, Button's tongue flapping in the breeze of the other, and the pups pacing the third-row seat. Little Penelope sat on Emma's lap, and the Yorkie trembled uncontrollably with nerves.

Digger's owners had heard about the fire and called the diner, which had given them Tasha's number. The owner's son-in-law had come to the clinic and retrieved Digger, saying he'd care for the dog until his in-laws' return from vacation.

Thankfully Tasha had volunteered to make the remaining calls to the dogs' owners, informing them that the animals were safe, had been checked over, and that Emma would be in touch tomorrow.

"The stable should be ready," Duncan added.

"I'm sorry for all the trouble."

"Not at all. The stable has been empty for years, but it's in good shape. The dogs will be safe tonight, and whatever else needs to be done can be taken care of tomorrow after you've gotten some rest."

Yeah, right. Like sleep was possible after the events of the day?

She had calls she needed to make. And then there was the guilt she felt because she would spend the night in a nice house, whereas her father would probably sleep in his tiny camper by the pond.

Or maybe at his fiancée's home.

She reminded herself that her father had mourned her mother for fourteen years. He deserved happiness. She couldn't begrudge him wanting to remarry. Even if it wasn't easy to accept.

Frank had been surprisingly supportive of her decision to accept Duncan's offer, a fact she blamed on her father being so overwhelmed by the fire and the aftermath he was relieved to have one less worry. Laney had been in the locker room at the fire station when Emma called, so she'd left a message with the details and Duncan's phone number. "Duncan? I can't thank you enough. I am well aware most people wouldn't have hired me under the circumstances."

"Like I said, Ian needs someone real. Someone who's been where he is. One mistake doesn't change that fact."

A whine sounded behind her, and Emma turned in the seat and held a hand out for Buttons to sniff. "Shhh. It's okay, boy. We're here."

Duncan shoved the vehicle into Park and unbuckled his seat belt before his earlier statement had a chance to sink in. When it did, she asked, "Wait, who did you call? There are other people here besides you and Ian?"

The ignition chimed when Duncan opened the door, and despite the multiple snouts panting in the back, she heard the scrape of the key leaving the ignition.

"One, plus Owen when I need him to stay. The rest are workmen, and they're only here during the day."

Good. That was good. Wasn't it? "I don't want to put anyone out."

"You won't. Quinn is the only one you'll regularly have to deal with. The workmen are gone now, but a few were here when I called earlier. They helped Quinn ready the stable for a little overtime."

"What are the workmen doing?" She couldn't imagine trying to figure out the layout of a house under repair. Couldn't he have mentioned that fact earlier?

"They're installing walkways, gates, alarms, and state-of-the-art security equipment."

Oh, wow. How wonderful it would be once it was finished, especially if Ian would be living so far up the mountain alone. "This Quinn person. He works for you, too?"

"No. Quinn is a loner, but he's a buddy of Ian's. Quinn oversees the ground crew and watches over Ian when I'm not around."

Now that was a friend. When push came to shove, not many people were willing to turn their life upside down to be so accommodating.

"Emma, there will be times when I have to travel to Atlanta, and you'll be here alone with Quinn and Ian. Is that a problem?"

She was nervous enough at the thought of living here with Ian and Duncan. Now to discover there was a third man—a stranger—all under the same roof?

She thought of her friends'—her church's—reactions to that and cringed. Nurses or aides were used to going into houses to care for someone, but they were typically sighted and they didn't stay. But unable to drive herself or take off on her own should something happen, she was stuck here at their mercy. It was enough to daunt the boldest of women. Especially when one particular man didn't want her around.

"I know we're asking you to place a lot of trust in us, but I promise you will be safe."

"It's not a problem. I'm just trying to take it all in." After all, what was the difference from being the only woman on a male-dominant business trip? She had to woman-up and not allow herself to give in to the what-ifs or to the impact gossips might have when they shouldn't be gossiping in the first place. This was a job, a live-in job.

"Come on, the sooner we get the dogs settled, the sooner you can shower and go to bed yourself."

"Yes. Thank you," she said, feeling for the door latch with one hand while gathering little Penelope in the other.

"Quinn sticks close if I'm busy," Duncan told her. "But he'll keep his distance unless you need something and seek him out."

Duncan's voice grew closer as he rounded the front of the large vehicle.

"To be honest, Quinn puts up with Ian's moods better than I do," Duncan continued, "so if Ian does give you a hard time and I'm not around, Quinn will step in."

"Hopefully I won't need either of you to step in. I like to fight my own battles."

"I can see that," Duncan murmured. "I tend to lose patience with Ian these days, but you've already proven you're up for whatever attitude he tosses out."

She hoped so. Pity got a person nowhere fast, and even though she felt it now because of her stupid mistake, she knew there was no use in crying over what was done.

The fire had happened. Grieving over things lost wouldn't help her, only hold her back. Ian needed to learn the same. It was time to pick up the pieces and move on, and by taking this job, earning the money, she could help him in the process of helping herself.

"You ready to do this?" Duncan asked.

She was too tired to move. All she wanted was to get the dogs cared for so she could take the longest shower she'd ever had in her life, rid herself of the smell of smoke, and try to come up with a plan for how to pull off the miracle Duncan expected of her.

She needed this job, not only for her sake but also for her family's. If the insurance company protested the claim or denied her father compensation because of some technicality, she had to be ready to hand over her pay so her father could rebuild. It was only right. "Ready as I'll ever be."

"The stable is this way."

With Owen's help, they retrieved the dogs from the large SUV. Duncan's grip on her arm was light but sure as he led the way into the stable-turned-kennel. The air was tainted with the smell of bleach.

"Quinn, it looks great. Thanks for getting it prepared," Duncan stated after performing the introductions.

Emma managed a smile, not sure where to face because she didn't hear anything to indicate where the man was standing. "Nice to meet you, Mr. Quinn."

"Just Quinn."

She turned her head to the right, but he didn't say anything more. Nor did he move, or if he did, she couldn't hear it with the dogs barking and panting and sniffing out their new home. Nathan Quinn was obviously a man of few words.

Duncan led her deeper into the stable, where Owen waited with a leashed Goli. The moment Emma was within licking distance, Goli's large tongue swiped over her knuckles before the big baby of a dog nudged her massive head into Emma's stomach for a more thorough scratch.

"As far as stables go, this one was four-star back when my grandfather was alive," Duncan told her. "The floor is concrete and easy to clean, the walls solid. There's even a window unit upstairs to keep things from getting too uncomfortable. Quinn's found some blankets and pans for food and water."

"I'll close the stable doors at night so there's no chance of an animal getting in to stir them up," Owen added. "I sleep in the apartment upstairs when I'm here, so I'll be around if anything happens tonight. Why don't you introduce me to everyone?"

Emma was touched that Owen Redd was making such an effort to learn the dogs' names and personalities. Penelope was the one she worried about the most, but with the pups already going inside with her, Emma was hesitant to take in yet another dog.

She listened as Owen talked to the animals and petted them, paying special attention to Penelope. Given the way the man made over the smallest dog, she wondered if Owen would take Penelope upstairs to the apartment with him.

"You should leave the pups with me tonight so you can rest," Duncan said. "If they need to go out, I'll handle it."

"That's very generous of you, but I don't want to trouble you any more than I already have."

"Emma, you've had a difficult day. I'm sure I can handle it for one night."

"I'm going back to the house."

Emma would recognize Quinn's sandpaper-and-ground-glass tone anywhere. It wasn't quite...normal? "Was your voice damaged?" she asked without thinking.

The very air stilled. Even the dogs were quiet in the seconds following her question. "I don't mean to offend you," she added. "My sister says I can be blunt, but without my vision, why waste time wondering when a simple question will do?"

Owen chuckled. "She's got a point."

"Let's finish settling the dogs so you can take a shower and turn in," Duncan urged.

"Yes," Quinn said. "It was damaged."

"Mind if I ask how?"

"Yes."

She smiled in spite of the fatigue she felt. "Okay then. I won't ask."

Both Duncan and Owen chuckled, and with the sound, her nervousness calmed. Nathan Quinn's foreboding quiet was unnerving but nothing she couldn't handle so long as he answered as honestly as he just had. Working at The Shake Shak had introduced her to a variety of people. Some were talkers, some weren't. Obviously Quinn was the latter.

"Don't take it personally," Duncan said after the man apparently left the kennel. "Quinn likes his privacy."

Duncan's gentle grip settled on her arm, and as much as she wanted to protest and insist on caring for the animals herself, Emma knew where to draw the line. She didn't know the layout of the house, or the location of the stable or yard in reference to the house, and until she did, letting the men pitch in made sense. Control wasn't easy to give up, but it was only one night, and she couldn't let her pride override her common sense. Besides, the sooner she went to bed, the sooner she could wake up and check on Roxy. "Thank you. All of you. I appreciate it."

"This way," Duncan said. He led her back into the sultry mountain air heavily laced with the earthy smell of the woods and sweet honeysuckle. But no matter which way she turned her head to try and get a better whiff, the acrid smoke permeating her clothing and hair overpowered her attempts.

"Is the house within walking distance?"

"Yes, why?"

"I'd like to get my bearings. I'll be spending a lot of time going back and forth between the house and kennel. Is there a path between the two?"

"Not yet, but I'll have something rigged up for you first thing in the morning."

So accommodating. Duncan was going out of his way to make sure her needs were met. All so she could help his brother.

But no matter how pleasant and welcoming Duncan and his men were, Ian would be the true test of her mettle. Thank goodness she wouldn't have to deal with him tonight.

Ian's nerve endings itched with the awareness of the late hour, the sensation interrupted by the sound of something going on outside in the direction of the stable.

Owen's SUV had arrived twenty minutes ago with its low, thrumming engine, Duncan's bike following close behind. Doors opened and closed, then...barking?

The itching got worse, pushing him out of the chair. Duncan no doubt had emptied the kitchen and dining room of what little alcohol had been kept on hand for social occasions, but their parents' wine collection remained downstairs. All he had to do was get it.

From the cellar.

Self-disgust filled his head. He knew the signs of alcoholism and he walked a very narrow line these days. But if it took the edge off...

He shoved the guilt away to focus on remembering the twists and turns of the layout. The house was big and old, with many additions to the main section forming an angled U around the pool and what used to be the gardens in back.

Maybe coming here wasn't such a good idea, but he couldn't hack another moment in Duncan's Atlanta townhouse, listening to the world go by him as if nothing had ever happened.

He wanted to be left alone, and even if it meant putting up with Duncan and all the workmen readying the house for a blind occupant, once the updates were completed, Duncan and the others would leave. And when they did... what then? Crawl around the house waiting on the years to pass? How would he survive? Eat? What would he do?

Slowly, inching his way along his room because of the broken glass and the shambles he'd created earlier, he finally made it to the door, out into the hallway.

"Hey," Duncan said from the left. "Where are you going?"

The slight breeze blowing through the house thanks to the newly updated AC system carried a not-so-pleasant scent. "What's that smell?"

Wildfires weren't only a danger in the west. The house sat atop a mountain surrounded by woods.

Still want to live here alone?

"The smell is me."

His grip on the door trim tightened as he recognized Emma Wyatt's voice. It was late, too late for her to be traveling the mountain roads alone. "What are you doing here?"

"Emma's moving in," Duncan stated matter-of-factly. "She'll be staying in the room beside yours."

"No. I don't want or need a tutor." Ian held out a hand and inched forward, toward the sound of their voices.

Ian didn't stop until Duncan's hand pressed into his shoulder, warning him he was in danger of bumping into something. Most likely *her*. Up close, the burnt smell made his nose twitch with the threat of a sneeze. "That's not wood smoke."

"Very good," Emma said dryly. "You're right, it's not."

"What happened?" he demanded.

"Ian," Duncan warned. "I'll fill you in later."

"Fill me in now," he ordered.

"My house burned to the ground this evening."

Duncan squeezed Ian's shoulder to the point of pain, but Ian didn't know if it was a subconscious move or a warning. Either way, it was a reminder of the blow Duncan had landed earlier and the fact that if Ian smarted off, Duncan would likely hit him again. Tempted, he asked, "How did it start?"

"In the kitchen," Duncan said, his tone sharp.

The vague response added to the intrigue teasing Ian's brain. He almost smiled. Finally there was something to focus on instead of the phobia. "How?"

"Oh, for pity's sake, it was *my* fault, okay? That's what he's not saying and what you want to hear, isn't it? I accidentally started the fire while I was cooking. There, story over."

She was angry and upset, tired, from the sound of it. Probably in shock. But it was the hint of vulnerability Ian heard in her voice that cut through his irritation that she had returned. "Somehow I get the impression there is more to the story."

"What do you want me to say?" she asked softly. "I'm human. I make mistakes, and this time—" her voice cracked with emotion but she quickly cleared her throat— "my father lost his home as a result. Happy?"

Duncan was right. This wasn't the time. And since she was there because she no longer had a home to go to, well, kicking her out wasn't an option.

Annoyed as he was at his brother's insistence about the tutoring thing, he wasn't heartless. "You're welcome to stay as long as you need to."

"Thank you."

"No problem. Just be sure that while you're here, you stay

away from me," Ian ordered, carefully backing into his room so he could shut the door before Duncan saw the damage to the bedroom and commented on it in front of their guest.

Emma already thought the worst of him, and while he didn't care, he had his pride. He wasn't some stoner trashing a hotel room for the thrill of it, and now that his rage had been spent, he would admit to being ashamed of what he'd done.

The bedroom had once belonged to his parents, many of the antiques and items he'd broken and thrown handpicked by his mother. Considering Emma's words about accidentally setting fire to her father's house, his behavior felt petty and small.

She'd lost her valuables by an accident she obviously regretted, whereas he had deliberately destroyed the room in a temperamental rage. Claustrophobia or not, that was childish and unacceptable.

He held his hands out in front of him as he shuffled his way back across the floor toward the chair he had so recently vacated. Desperate as he was for a drink, he would wait, bide his time.

Dance with the devil a little longer and see how close to the edge he could get before jumping.

I can practically hear the steam coming out of your ears," Emma said to Duncan as he showed her to her room. "Don't worry about Ian. It's okay."

Duncan frowned, wishing he could be as casual as Emma and shrug off Ian's behavior. Given his anti-tutor stance of earlier, Ian had gone soft on her, no doubt due to the seriousness of the fire. But ordering Emma to stay away from him wasn't okay.

Which brought up the question—how would they get Ian to

cooperate? He'd been so focused on getting his brother help that he hadn't given much thought to the next step.

Shaking his head at the entire mess, Duncan led her to her bedroom, staying quiet because he could tell she counted off the steps. "Here's the bed. The nightstand is on the right, phone's on top. The TV is directly across from the bed on the dresser."

"Okay. Got it."

"The bathroom is here," he told her, walking her to the doorway. "Sink's first, toilet, and then shower-tub. Towels are in the cabinet across from the sink. I've hired a cleaning company from Atlanta to come in once a week and take care of things, so any laundry you need done can be taken care of then."

"I can do my own laundry but thanks."

Duncan turned at her wry announcement and wound up bumping into her. He steadied her by her elbows. "Sorry."

She laughed, the smile lighting up her soot-smudged face. "No problem. But for future reference, quick stops or sudden turns need to come with a warning."

He stared down into her beautiful, unseeing eyes. Not quite blue, they had enough gray in them to make him think of metal. Strong, maybe a little bent, but unbreakable.

Covered in soot and sweat and more than a little dog hair, Emma exuded a natural beauty few women could claim sans makeup and a small fortune in hair products and a fancy wardrobe.

"Duncan, I hate to put you out, but I don't suppose you have some old clothes I could borrow? Anything's fine. Just until I get these washed?"

She plucked at the stained and bloodied flannel shirt she'd put on over her grungy tank.

"Of course. I'm sure I can round up some T-shirts and shorts or something that will fit you. If you'll leave your clothes outside the bathroom door, I'll come back in and grab them to wash tonight. Are you hungry? Thirsty?"

"I don't want to be more trouble than I've already been."

"Emma, you've had a long day. Clean clothes and a bottle of water or snack are nothing."

"Once I know my way around, I'll be able to handle the care and feeding of Emma," she stated firmly. "I just don't want you or the others to think you have to wait on me while I'm here."

Of course she didn't. Ian sat in his room demanding booze and food, but Emma wanted no special treatment. Yet another thing to admire about her even though he was saddened by the reality she lived.

"I insist. Tomorrow you can take over again, but for tonight you stay put, relax, and try to rest. I'll go grab those clothes."

That said, he placed his hands on her shoulders to hold her still while he moved by her in the narrow space.

Emma had spunk and an intriguing feminine strength. He wondered what she'd been like before her accident, if they would've been friends, had he known her back then.

"I appreciate it. Thank you."

Duncan released her. "You're welcome."

He moved toward the door but stopped again.

"Something wrong?" Emma asked.

He hadn't made any noise he was aware of to indicate he was still there, but of course she would be able to tell. Apparently it was true that a person's other senses were heightened when one failed. "Nothing. I just wanted to remind you that Ian will do his best to bully you into quitting, but...I'm begging you not to give up on him. He needs you, Emma. We all need you. Until Ian's capable of taking care of himself and handling things here, we're in limbo."

"I understand. I'll do my best to not let you down."

Duncan groaned softly, the look of exhaustion on her face

registering at last. Leave it to him to add more pressure instead of making her feel at home. "No, I apologize for putting you on the spot when you need time to regroup and settle things with the fire. Forget I said anything."

"Duncan, it's fine. I can hear how worried you are about your brother. There's not a whole lot I can do to help my dad other than work the diner as much as possible and stay out of the way, but I'm sure whatever needs to be done can be managed around my time with Ian. Since he's so resistant, we'll need to take things slowly. At least at first."

Agreeing, Duncan excused himself and went to find her a change of clothes. He liked that she was planning her strategy. Ian wouldn't know what hit him.

Chapter 5

A noise woke Emma. She checked her watch, the press of a button and the digitized voice telling her it was 2:02 in the morning.

She'd been so exhausted after the day's events that the moment she'd stepped out of the shower and dressed in the shirt and gym shorts Duncan had provided, she'd handed over her clothes and turned down the offer of food in favor of sleep.

Now she was awake, hungry, and embarrassed that Duncan MacGregor had gotten a firsthand glimpse of her underwear. Being unable to see the colors of clothes meant she didn't focus on them as much as some women, and her closet had mostly consisted of jeans and Shake Shak tees, some hand-me-down flannels from her father she used for work shirts with the dogs, and little else. As for her underwear, suffice it to say she had never been to Victoria's Secret.

A thump sounded outside her door, the sound followed by a growled curse. No mistaking that. Definitely Ian. But what was he doing?

Her stomach rumbled long and loud, accompanied by a

gnawing ache the likes of which wouldn't go away by sipping water.

Maybe Ian had left his room to find something to eat? If so, she could use it as a chance to talk to him, show him a few tricks of the trade when it came to midnight pantry raids. Without being obvious about it, of course.

Emma pushed the sheet away and rolled to the edge of the bed, her toes digging into the plush carpet.

She knew the way to the kitchen. During her first visit— had it really only been yesterday?— Owen had taken her to the kitchen for a drink while they waited for Duncan to reappear after his talk with Ian.

Standing, she automatically tapped her leg to signal Roxy only to stop with a sick twist in her stomach because Roxy wasn't there.

It felt strange not having the dog immediately come to her side, as if a part of her was missing. *Please, God, take care of her.*

Rubbing the tension from around her eyes, she inhaled and forced herself to focus on creating a mental map of the house, at least what she knew of it so far. She grabbed her white stick that one of the EMTs had found and returned to her and quietly left her room, not wanting to wake anyone else. If she and Ian were going to work together, she needed to counter his bad moods on her own, without Duncan's presence or influence demanding good behavior.

But once she stood in the hallway, she realized the kitchen wasn't the direction Ian had gone.

On her left, toward what she assumed was the end of the hall, she heard the rough, ragged sound of breathing.

"Ian?" She moved closer, slowly, not wanting to startle him if he was sleepwalking.

"Are you okay?" she pressed, inching closer.

"Go back to bed."

"Tell me what's wrong." She reached out, her fingertips finding the sweat-dampened material of his shirt, the muscles of his shoulder bunched and rock hard beneath it. "Maybe I can help you."

"No."

"How about we go to the kitchen? Get something to eat? Drink?"

A low laugh rumbled out of his chest. "What I want is down there."

"Down there?"

"The wine cellar."

She closed her eyes and focused, feeling the ever-so-slight breeze of musty air on her face. So that was what it was. He stood at the threshold of the cellar door. At two o'clock in the morning. "Ian—"

"Go back to bed, Emma. You can't help me. Unless you're willing to go down there and get what I want, the best thing for you to do is leave me alone."

She dropped her hand from his shoulder but didn't move otherwise. He wasn't going to scare her away. "I won't enable you. That's taking the easy way out, and you don't need to drink to get through the night."

"Easy?" he repeated, a rough huff of a laugh following the bitterly uttered word.

"Yes. You have to learn new things, and it's hard, but I can help you. Teach you what you need to know," she said. "If you cooperate, you can go down there and get that bottle yourself. *If* you still feel you need it."

IF ONLY IT *were that simple.*

Ian stood with his hands braced high against the frame of the cellar door, Emma Wyatt's calm words promising more than she could deliver but tempting him all the same.

Over the soothing tone of her voice, however, the devil laughed, the raucous noise echoing throughout the dark recesses of his mind.

Black was black. Dark was dark. What did it matter, going down there, when he couldn't see anyway? When it was no different than the dark hallway, his dark bedroom? His freakishly dark mind?

There was no difference.

But his brain knew. Because of his awareness that it was underground, he couldn't force his feet to take that first step.

Sweat trickled down his temple onto his cheek. As if someone were raking a knife over his skin, the stream burned. Physical proof of his weakness.

Every time he tried to move forward, he froze, and the throat-closing, chest-squeezing sensation overtook him, barring the way better than any door ever could.

As a child, irritated with his younger brother's antics during a party his parents had hosted, Ian had followed the catering staff down to the cellar and hidden from Duncan. He'd fallen asleep after a while, but when he'd woken, the cellar door had been locked from the outside. He'd been trapped in the dark for *hours* until his parents came looking for him in the wee hours of the morning when he wasn't in his bed.

"Ian?"

"You can't help me." When were they going to get that? He was the only one who could get himself through this. The only one who could fight the battle in his head.

Her hand flattened against his back once more.

"You're trembling." She sounded confused. "Do you have a fever?"

Ian turned, holding on to the door when his head spun with a wave of vertigo the docs said would eventually wane. He found her hand, removed it from his body because her touch made him think of other ways to survive the night. How sad and pathetic was that? She sounded young, but she could be as old as Eve, as ugly as a hag, and he wouldn't know it.

Emma's breath hitched in her throat at the contact, and after what he'd done to her in his room, he supposed she had reason to be leery. He gently squeezed her fingers. "Go back to bed."

"Learning to deal with your blindness and accepting it doesn't mean you're giving up."

"That's exactly what it means."

"No, Ian. It simply means you're ready for the challenge of viewing life another way. Being creative. So how about it? Instead of roaming the house at night looking for something you're not going to find in a bottle, what if you think about all the things you want to learn how to do," she suggested softly. "We'll focus on figuring out ways for you to do them."

"It won't work."

"Why do you say that?"

"Because I want my life back," he growled. "I want to do the things I did before, things that can't be done by a blind man."

"The blind can do most anything a sighted person can do. It just takes a little more thinking to pull it off. And if it hasn't yet been done? Be the first. Ian, there is *always* a way. Wouldn't figuring out *how* to do those things be better than this? Getting drunk isn't a solution. It's nothing more than temporary."

She turned her hand in his grip, making him aware that he'd been holding on to her the whole time.

"Interesting..."

He didn't want to ask. He wanted her to shut up and go

away. To hold on and stop the darkness from closing in on him. "What?"

She slipped her hand from his, and he missed the warmth of her touch.

"You're not shaking anymore."

His breath huffed out of his lungs when he realized she was right. The craving inside him had dimmed a bit while talking to her. Being distracted by her.

"What's going on?" Duncan asked from the end of the hall. "Ian, what are you doing?"

Not what Duncan obviously thought. But if he could find a way to descend into the cellar, a way to go down there and breathe, maybe he could get to a place within himself where he could live with what he'd become. Rise to the challenge, like Emma had said.

The only way to conquer fear was to face it, and the cellar was his test, his demon in physical form. If he could go down there...

"Emma, go back to bed. I'll take Ian to his room."

Emma didn't move. He could feel the heat of her body next to him.

"Would you like me to stay?" she asked. "Talk with you about those things you'd like to do?"

It would get him through the night, at least another hour or so. He wanted to say yes, but he was too on edge. Afraid of what the darkness might drive him to do in a bid to escape it.

Listening to her prattle on about how he could do anything would sever the last of his threadbare nerves because no matter how much he wanted it to be true, it wasn't. "How could someone who burned down her house teach me anything?" he said. "I already told you, Emma. Stay away from me."

Emma was in her bedroom putting on her shoes the next morning when a knock sounded on the door.

"Emma? Rose Dibbs is on the phone for you," Duncan said. "Come to the kitchen when you're through. Breakfast is ready."

"Thank you," she called, walking around the bed to the table where the phone was located. "Aunt Rose?"

"Oh, Emma. How are you, dear? I was going to call you last night, but I thought you'd have your hands full. Once I heard you were okay, I made myself wait until this morning."

"I'm fine. And I did have my hands full. Thanks for understanding." The caring and warmth in her aunt's voice brought the sting of tears to Emma's eyes. Her aunt was dealing with so much with Uncle Bruce's cancer and terminal diagnosis. "How's Uncle Bruce feeling?"

"Today is another good day. We've seen some hard times, and we'll weather this one, don't you worry. Tell me about you. You must be heartbroken. And so scared!"

"I am, and I was. More than anything, I was terrified because Roxy was still inside."

"So I heard. Oh, Emma, I know you love that dog, but why did you go back in? You could've been killed!"

Maybe some people would have let their pet perish, but Roxy wasn't just a pet to her. "I didn't really think about anything other than getting her out. And I didn't go back inside, not really. Roxy was waiting for me by the door. Tasha said—" Emma had to stop and take a breath. "I talked to Tasha a few minutes ago, and she said Roxy has been sleeping a lot."

"Poor old thing. She's worn out from the excitement."

Emma tapped her fingers on the table by the bed. "I hope

that's it, and it's nothing more serious. Wait— How did you know to find me here?"

"Bruce called the firehouse first and talked to Laney. She said you'd left a message. I have to say we're happy to hear that you accepted the job. Duncan and Ian are both very nice men. It's perfect. I'm happy things have turned around so quickly for you."

Emma twisted the old-fashioned phone cord around her finger, vaguely wondering if the phone system would be updated like everything else in and around the house. She needed to ask, so she could learn how to use it and teach Ian. "Well, I don't know about perfect, but I'm here, and I'm determined to do what I can."

"I know you will. Now tell me, what are you doing for clothes? I'm in charge of the church's emergency ministry supplies, and I'd be happy to go through and pick out clothing for you from the donations. There were some nice things the last time I looked."

"That would be wonderful. I was hoping one of my friends would come by and take me to the thrift store, but if you wouldn't mind, that would be great. I'd rather not spend a lot, and I wasn't looking forward to having to shop. You know I don't like it."

Her aunt laughed, the sound warm and reminiscent of Emma's mother's.

"I know, dear. I'll take care of everything. Perhaps Laney or Duncan can come pick up the clothes later? I'm not sure Bruce is up for the drive, and good day or not, I hate leaving him alone. He wouldn't want me telling you this, but meeting with Duncan wore him totally out."

"No, I understand. I'll ask someone to do it." Duncan was a busy man, and she hated requesting that kind of favor, but maybe a call to one of the *Besties*—or perhaps Genie, since the girl wanted so badly to help?

"Good. So, anything special I should look for? Something feminine?"

Emma opened her mouth to speak, but a laugh emerged instead. "Aunt Rose, why would you say that?"

"Oh, Emma. You can't blame me for trying. The MacGregor brothers turn a woman's head, both of them tall, dark, and handsome."

"You're *matchmaking*? I think you're forgetting I'm here to work, not socialize. Duncan is my boss, and Ian will technically be my student. It's not good to mix personal feelings with professional ones."

"Yes, well, sometimes it can't be helped," Aunt Rose murmured, a smile in her voice. "Just remember to slow down every now and again, Emma. Life is too short to spend it working all the time."

Emma shoved her hair off her face and fingered the ends, her thoughts focusing on the sadness that would permeate their family when Uncle Bruce was no longer with them. "I know. Aunt Rose? Promise you'll call if you need anything. I can help you clean or stay with Uncle Bruce while you run errands. I don't mind."

"You are too sweet, and I will call if I need help," she promised. "Actually... Emma, I hate to ask, but I wanted to make sure you are still going to court next week? To talk to the judge about Zack Dupré?"

Oh, no. Last week Aunt Rose had asked Emma for the favor regarding a former student who had gotten himself into trouble. Emma had agreed because Aunt Rose never asked for anything, but now... "Aunt Rose, I'm not sure how I can help or if it's a good idea with all that's happened."

"Emma, I know the timing is horrible, but please don't back out. In fact, maybe now is the best time for you to ask that Zack work for you, considering all the changes in the last twenty-four hours. He could help you with the dogs as you settle in there. I know it's iffy, but I think if someone shows up, takes an interest in his case, Zack might be given community service instead of jail time. He's a *good* boy."

"Aunt Rose…" What would Duncan think if she asked to bring a stranger—a criminal no less—to his house?

"Emma, I know it's a lot to ask, but please—he's worth the trouble."

It *was* a lot to ask. But Emma was always the one needing this or that, especially after her mother had died in the car crash. That Aunt Rose asked now, with Uncle Bruce so bad…

Time and again, Uncle Bruce and Aunt Rose helped those in the community, for the sheer pleasure of lending a helping hand. Wasn't it time Emma paid it forward? After all, where would she be had Uncle Bruce not recommended her for the job? Zack Dupré was obviously one of Aunt Rose's favorite students, otherwise she wouldn't be taking such an interest in his case. "Of course I'll do it. I'll go to court."

"You will?"

Emma winced but nodded. "Yes. I'll see what I can do."

"Oh, Emma, thank you. He's a sweet boy. Really. His life hasn't been the promising one it should have been. He's just gotten turned around."

Emma hoped that was the case. Aunt Rose had won numerous awards during her years teaching at Stone River High School. She had been given honors as a mentor, and voted Georgia Teacher of the Year. And had circumstances been different with Uncle Bruce, Emma knew her aunt would be the one appearing in court on Zack Dupré's behalf.

Their conversation shifted to other things, and right before Emma prepared to say good-bye, she asked, "Before I forget, have you checked with Dad about getting clothes for him?"

"No, dear. I thought your father would prefer to handle that himself."

"Probably so," Emma agreed, fingering the soft blanket beneath her on the bed. Her dad had a penchant for bowling and Hawaii-themed shirts unmatched by anyone in town. A closet full —gone. But she had hoped, however mistakenly, that the act would be a bridge for her father and aunt to cross. Ever since the accident that had killed her mother, the distance between her father and Rose and Bruce had grown.

Memories from that horrible day surfaced in her mind, hazy thanks to the head injury she had received. She and her mother had been talking, and the next thing she knew, her mother was crying and—

"Emma, dear, Bruce is calling for me. I have to go."

Emma snapped out of her daze. "No problem. Give him a hug from me."

"I will. And I'll get those clothes ready for you. Oh, and if you flirt with any of those men, don't feel guilty. Just have fun."

Emma couldn't help but laugh. "Good-*bye*, Aunt Rose."

"Bye, hon."

Setting the phone back on the base, Emma squared her shoulders and stood. "Here we go," she murmured, smoothing her palms down her freshly washed jeans.

The moment she entered the kitchen, all conversation between the men gathered at the table stopped. "Good morning. I hope I'm not too late?"

A chorus of deep male voices called the greeting back to her in welcome. All, she noted, but Ian's.

"Ian prefers to eat in his room," Duncan said, apparently tuning into her thoughts.

It was easy enough to guess why.

Sighted people took eating for granted, but the reality was the angle of the fork, being able to stab something and raise it to your mouth, wasn't easy when you couldn't see what you were doing. It was like eating spaghetti with a spoon—blindfolded.

"Emma, have a seat," Duncan said.

The words were accompanied by the scrape of a chair and Duncan's hand grasping her elbow to show her the way. "Thanks."

"How do you like your eggs? Quinn's proven himself to be a decent cook, and he's at your beck and call."

She bet the man loved hearing that. "Poor Quinn. I won't hold you to that statement," she said to the room as a whole.

"Scrambled or fried, take your pick."

Quinn's voice came from her left and a little behind her, his injured voice raspy and very Clint Eastwood-ish. "Scrambled."

"Toast?"

"Yes, please. But I can make my own breakfast. Don't feel like you have to cook for—" She broke off, only then remembering what had happened the last time she'd cooked. "I hope you all know I'll never make that mistake again."

"I'm sure you'd do fine," Duncan said, "but Quinn isn't fond of people mucking up what's become his kitchen."

Someone nudged her arm. Owen, she deduced, since the other two men had made their whereabouts readily apparent.

"I made one mistake, and they've never forgiven me," Owen said from her right. "Another cook so soon might send Quinn over the edge."

"With good reason," Duncan added.

"In my defense, it's not my fault it splattered," Owen countered.

"It was on the ceiling," Duncan informed her.

She smiled at the bickering, quite comfortable since the quibbling reminded her of the *Besties*. It was obvious that the men were friends.

"Emma, you're going to take it easy today, right?" The scrape of a chair being pulled into the table placed Duncan somewhere on the far end.

"Toast. One o'clock."

She heard Quinn settle a plate in front of her. Emma raised her hands onto the table and moved them forward until she touched the edge of the plate. "Do you have butter? Or jam?"

"Here."

Owen placed the container in her hand.

"Or I could—"

"No, but thank you." Having already found her utensils, she scraped a portion out of the carton with the tip of the knife, careful to hold the mass against the lip of the bowl while she picked up a piece of toast.

Aware that all the men watched her and that they were curious like most people, Emma buttered her toast and took a bite, glad to finally have food since she'd gone back to bed hungry after her meet-up with Ian in the hall.

"Would you like orange juice?" Duncan asked.

She heard Quinn at the stove scrambling her eggs. They were almost done, from the sound of things. "Please. Owen, would you like some more?" she asked when she heard the man set his glass on the table, the hollow sound indicating its emptiness.

"Uh, yeah. Sure."

"Allow me," she said. "The juice?"

They had to see she was perfectly capable of buttering her toast and pouring her own juice, just like they had to stop catering to Ian's demands that he eat in his room or whatever task they were doing that Ian should be doing for himself. Yes, helping hands were needed but not for every little thing.

"Seven o'clock," Quinn said from the stove.

She found the handle of the plastic gallon jug and lifted it by its handle. Almost empty. Even better. "Owen?"

Hand out, she accepted the glass Owen gave her and poured

him a perfect portion, listening closely as the glass filled, before handing it back to him. Still, she frowned at their collective sigh of relief. They were on pins and needles waiting for her to screw up.

That had to stop. Yes, she'd spill, and she'd make messes, and she'd do all sorts of embarrassing things—and some cool things, too?

Wondering if she dared... Oh, why not?

She tilted the jug up and her head back, holding the plastic several inches above her mouth as she poured, finishing off the remainder without spilling a drop.

Owen sucked in a ragged breath.

Quinn muttered a soft grunt.

And Duncan simply released a surprised chuckle.

Emma set the empty jug on the table, glad her point had been proven. "Okay, so now that you know I'm capable of feeding myself, we need to talk about Ian."

"What do you want to know?" Duncan asked, amusement giving his voice a nice, appealing tone.

She shoved away Aunt Rose's advice to flirt with Duncan and Ian and focused on the task at hand. "We'll get to that later. Who Ian was isn't who he is now. What I want to discuss are the ground rules about how you treat him. Things are going to change. Starting today."

Chapter 6

The moment Ian opened the bathroom door, he knew he wasn't alone. His senses went on immediate alert, the little wet hairs on the back of his neck standing on end. "Duncan?"

The bounce of a ball preceded a soft laugh. "Guess again."

Emma. "What do you want?"

"To talk to you."

"We have nothing to say to each other."

"I disagree. So do Duncan and his men."

Duncan and *his* men? His little brother might control those in his security company, but Ian didn't think Quinn would appreciate being lumped into the mix. "Get out. Unless you're wanting an eyeful when this towel comes off."

"You know you're only hurting yourself, right? The longer you drag this out, the longer it'll be before you're independent. Or is that it?" she asked softly. "Do you like them having to wait on you? I suppose it is a power trip of sorts because it keeps them close. I don't know a lot about what you did before you were blinded, but according to Duncan, you were a man who liked to take charge. It makes sense that you'd try to manipulate them now, I suppose."

Manipulate them? Anger barreled through him. He wanted to be left alone, and she thought he was manipulating them? "Emma, you're Bruce's niece, and for that reason alone, I'm trying to mind my manners."

"Thank you."

"But get out of my room."

"Ahhhh. I hit too close to home, didn't I?"

Ian ran a hand over his head and set off across the floor to the bed for the jeans and T-shirt Quinn set out for him every day.

He hated that Emma saw him walking hunched over like an old man, arms outstretched to find his way.

Hitting the edge of the mattress, Ian swept his hand over the covers. Not only had the bed not been made but his clothes were missing as well. "I don't want them waiting on me hand and foot."

"But you're making no effort to learn, so where's the breakdown? Are you looking for something?"

Ian tried to ignore the taunt but wasn't quite able to do so. Quinn stepped forward more often than not, but Ian knew it had more to do with him saving Quinn and getting the man across the desert than the desire to turn into a butler. "My clothes."

"What color was the shirt?"

"I don't care. Where are they?"

"I talked with Duncan and the others this morning. I considered waiting until I had some things of my own squared away, but then I realized you've brooded long enough. It's time to dive in. From now on, no one will wait on you. You'll fend for yourself. We'll start our lessons with that, and I'll also show you how to match your clothes, how to fix your own meals. It isn't rocket science."

"Get out." His hands fisted so tightly his nails bit into his palms and several of his knuckles popped. Who did she think she was?

"You need to know *how* to do certain things, regardless of whether or not you *need* to do them."

"Why should I care what color my shirt is if I can't see it? *Get out.* The towel is coming off."

"Go ahead."

She threw the ball again. A dog went scrambling, bouncing off his calf as it passed. "Emma, where are my clothes?"

The dog skidded to an abrupt stop somewhere near the nightstand and began to bark and whine.

"Uh-oh, Tink. Did it roll under something?"

The leather chair where she sat squeaked as Emma got to her feet.

"I can't find it, Tink. Where'd it go?"

The dog continued to bark, the incessant noise threatening to drive Ian over the edge. He waited impatiently, surmising that Emma dropped to her knees and was apparently searching for the ball. "Emma..."

He wanted to see her, know what she looked like, but without asking her or Duncan or one of the others, he'd never know. Yet another thing robbed from him, his ability to assess the people he came into contact with.

Ian rubbed the heels of his hands over his eyes and counted to twenty when he felt something—her *hair?*—brush against his knee. "Get. *Out.* You can get the dog another ball," he said, turning away.

"Actually, I thought I would stick around, and we could talk about what happened last night in front of the cellar door."

The very thing he didn't want to discuss. With anyone. "I can only think of one reason why you're still here when I'm ready to get naked." He smoothed his hand over his chest, down to the knot, and ignored the warning voice in his head that he shouldn't.

"Oh, please. You think I don't know what you're trying to do?"

The challenge in her voice grated on his nerves. "How much is Duncan paying you?"

"A lot."

"I'll match it if you walk out and leave me alone."

Silence. Ahh, a weakness. She considered it.

"He said you'd try that," she murmured, "and it's tempting. But I gave Duncan my word."

"Break it."

"No."

"Suit yourself, but this is your last warning." He was done with this conversation. A man should have peace in his home, in his bedroom. "You've got five seconds to exit."

"Why are you so determined to not get help?"

"Four."

"I'm not leaving just because you're too afraid of having to deal with what's happened to you."

"Three."

"Why didn't you go down those stairs last night?"

"*Two.*"

"Do you always go wandering around the house at two o'clock in the morning?"

"One," he growled.

"I get it, okay? I know what it's like to want to break something because it feels as though you're broken inside and you don't want to be alone in the dark, but that doesn't mean—"

He grabbed the towel from around his waist and tossed it in her direction, hoping he wasn't far off the mark. Then he waited for her reaction. A gasp, a slap. Something. Anything to shut her up because she *was* hitting too close to home with her comments.

But the towel dropped to the floor with a disappointing, water-heavy sound, and Emma made a noise, as if she struggled to restrain her... laughter?

She laughed at him?

"Oooh, we really do have a temper, don't we? Or an ego."

"You were warned."

"So I was. Too bad your big, dramatic display is for nothing. None of them told you, did they?"

"Told me *what?*"

"Ian, I lost my sight when I was fourteen. I can't *see* you, so parade around naked all you want. The joke's on you."

It took a second for her words to sink in.

Less than that for him to feel like the biggest idiot on earth. She was blind, too?

"But if you think you can't deal with what happened as a grown man? Try being an emotional teenage girl. One with an attitude, who'd had her world ripped apart in a single second. I didn't just lose my eyesight that day, I lost my mom, too. The person who could have helped me and guided me the most. She died, and there I was, stuck in the dark."

The breath in his lungs emerged in a rough exhale. No, this was a ploy, a story to gain his cooperation. When he interrogated someone, he said whatever it took to make a connection, get the person on his side, think he was sympathetic.

But something about her words rang true, and he knew it wasn't just a story. Shock pulsed through his veins.

Duncan had hired a *blind* tutor—a woman, no less, who'd lost her vision so young there was a chance she'd never *seen* a naked man—to show him how to *cope?*

No, he hired Dibbs' niece, knowing you'd keep your hands and your attitude to yourself.

But he hadn't.

And he didn't want to.

Her revelation had just put a whole other spin on things because if it was true— she actually *did* understand how he felt. And after last night and the way her touch had brought him back from the edge, he found her lack of sight and understanding of his mindset more appealing than anything he could remember.

"Ian, I know what it's like to wake up expecting something different, to believe I was dreaming. That all I had to do was open my eyes and I would be able to see again. But day after day would pass, and I would open them and… *nothing*. I know what it's like to have everything taken away and how hard it is to even think about starting over again. But I also know it's *possible*.

"You have to start at the bottom and work your way up. Figure out new ways and make new plans. From what I've heard, you were a man who thrived on challenges. Where is that man now? Why is he hiding in this room?"

There was that word again—hiding. Emma's voice challenged him. Direct but soft-spoken, lined with steel. Her words made him forget the darkness, forget the claustrophobia. Made him feel ashamed of his behavior and determined to do better. But how?

"What if your life isn't over? What if it's just beginning, but you're so stubborn you refuse to adapt as a blind man? What then? What's in your future? Because you're never going to find out sitting here."

He laughed at that, unable to stop the sound.

"What? You don't think you have a future?"

"No," he stated, brutally honest.

"Oh, well, okay. I guess you won't have one then. Not unless you believe it. Until you believe it, you'll be stuck here with nothing left," she said, the pitch of her voice changing in challenge. "Which—coincidentally—is what you have right now."

It was. And he hated her for pointing it out. "Ask Quinn to bring my food when you leave."

"No." She released a resigned sigh. "When you're hungry enough, you'll come to the kitchen after it. I meant what I said. From now on, no one in this house is going to wait on you. It's time for you to get a grip."

Something hit him square in the chest, and he caught it instinctively. The towel. She'd nailed him with it, unlike his disappointing near-miss with her.

His hands fisted on the material, and he felt ridiculous standing there as he was, holding it in front of him like some Victorian bride. "You have a lot of nerve thinking you can teach me anything, considering the reason you're now staying under my roof."

"Maybe I do. But at least I was brave enough to face the world and *try*. What have you done?"

***

It took everything inside Emma to calmly walk out of Ian's bedroom as though she hadn't been standing there talking to a naked man the entire time.

She leaned against the wall at the end of the hallway and tried to catch her breath. Her heart thudded so hard in her chest she pressed her hand over the spot as though that would help slow it. Ian had thrown his towel at her. His towel!

It had been warm from his body, smelled like soap and something that was undeniably male. Undeniably him?

She'd tried to play it cool. If she was going to succeed, she couldn't allow him to unnerve her. No matter what he threw at her. But when she'd misjudged the distance while looking for Tinkerbell's ball and brushed against Ian's leg? She wouldn't have noticed except a few strands of her hair had caught in his, and she had felt the slight tug as she had pulled away. How utterly mortifying.

Laughing wryly, she shook her head. "What do you think, Tinkerbell? It's going to be an interesting job, isn't it?"

A low bark was her answer. That and a whine that indicated it was time to take a trip outside. "Yeah, I could totally use some fresh air, too. Let's go."

Using the rope running from the house to the kennel that Duncan had established and shown her after breakfast, Emma made her way to check on the dogs.

She spent the next hour or so on the phone to the dogs' owners, reassuring them of their safety and care. Finally she was down to one task—that of asking someone to haul the clothes from Aunt Rose's house up the mountain to the MacGregors'. Any of the *Besties* would be happy to help her, but Morgan would be home with the kids, Tasha at the clinic, and Jolie gearing up for the grand opening of her coffee house.

Sighing, she dialed Genie's number and hoped the girl was available. "Genie?" she said when the younger woman answered. "Hey, it's Emma. How are you feeling today after the excitement of the fire?"

There was a slight pause.

"I'm fine. Have you changed your mind about staying there?"

Wincing because of the hope she heard in Genie's voice, Emma said, "No. I'm, uh, calling to ask a favor, though. Please feel free to say no—"

"What do you need?"

Emma explained the situation with Aunt Rose and waited, breathing a sigh of relief when Genie agreed.

The call completed, Emma headed back out to her new kennel.

She lavished the dogs with extra treats, supplied by Tasha, in an attempt to settle her thoughts and work out her upset over everything that had gone wrong the last twenty-four hours. For a person whose days normally moved at a snail's pace as she filled orders and played with her animals, she hadn't yet adjusted to warp speed. "Oh, ugh. You guys smell, you know that?"

The dogs reeked of smoke, and baths were definitely in order. Someone was pounding away on something not far from the stable. The pounding stopped when she emerged, leading her to believe they'd spotted her. Catching a whiff of Owen's cologne, she smiled. "Hey, Owen. I hate to ask, but I could use some help. It'll only take a few minutes. If you have time."

"What do you need?" Quinn asked.

Whoa, where had he come from? She hadn't heard or sensed Quinn, but then the banging had made hearing a little difficult. "Um, a water hose, old towels. Dog shampoo or Dawn dish detergent if you have it. Something gentle to get the smoke smell off the dogs."

Something landed on the ground with a thud, presumably a hammer.

"I'll get it for you," Owen said.

The man turned toward the house, and after a few steps, she heard him break into a slow jog.

"Did you talk to Ian?" Quinn asked.

Small talk from a man who rarely spoke was unnerving. "Yes. He's angry because we're not all jumping to do his bidding but fine otherwise."

"He needs to eat. He's lost weight."

"He'll eat when his stomach is hungry enough to overtake his fear," she said softly.

"Owen's coming. I'm going back to work."

She nodded her understanding and listened closely.

Nothing. She heard *nothing*. Who moved that silently?

"Here you go," Owen said. "I have towels and soap. Come this way, and I'll show you where the hose is."

"Thanks. Um, Owen?"

"Yeah?"

"Where is Quinn?"

"Do you need him?"

"No, I just— I'm trying to place him and... Where is he?"

"He's standing about ten feet to your right getting ready to stretch wire for one of the gates. Why?"

"No reason," she murmured, pinning a smile to her lips. She wasn't sure how Quinn could have traveled such a distance without her hearing something— his shoes dragging through the grass, his clothing rubbing together as he walked, the change in his pocket rattling—but obviously she was going to have to find some other way to identify Quinn's presence or else always be surprised when he appeared out of nowhere.

Owen located a hose and a bucket for her, but she shooed him back to what he'd been doing when he'd offered to help her get started.

The first thing she did was gather up the old blankets the dogs had been given last night and put them in the wash. No use giving the dogs a bath if they wound up smelling like smoke again.

Bathing the dogs was actually a chore she enjoyed. Today it enabled her to focus on them rather than the fire and the damage done by her actions, and for a little while, she was free to enjoy the sun and warmth and fun of the animals, the little things that were important, rather than Ian's sour mood and their very awkward conversation this morning.

The sun rose higher in the sky, and the day grew hotter by the time she finished washing, brushing, and caring for the dogs. She saved Penelope for last and paid special attention to the little lapdog, brushing her gently until Penelope's long fur was soft and silky.

After a walk around the yard, she'd head back to the house to call her father and Laney, check in with them and make sure all was as well as could be expected. She had apologized numerous times yesterday, but she felt the need to say it a million more.

"There you are. I've been looking for you," Duncan said, his long strides closing the distance between them. "I heard you've had a busy day."

She smiled as she gave Buttons an extra scratch beneath his chin. "A very relaxing day compared to yesterday." She stood and tightened her grip on the thick leash in her hand, knowing from experience the dogs would immediately scramble in their excitement to get started.

They did, the leash going taut, but she didn't budge just yet.

"What are you doing?"

"It's time for a walk," she said, wondering at the question when the answer was obvious. "Did you need to see me? Something to do with Ian?"

Silence ticked off via the multiple pants of the animals at their feet.

"Don't take this the wrong way but—who's leading who?"

She laughed at the joke, because now that she wasn't so sensitive about her blindness, she could. One day, Ian would be able to laugh about it, too. On the good days, anyway. "They're walking me, of course. I don't know my way around yet."

Duncan chuckled as she'd intended.

"Mind if I join you?"

"Not at all. Would you like them to lead?"

Another husky laugh rumbled out of his chest. "How about I lead?"

She lifted her hand, and Duncan grasped it, looping her arm through his. That was something she liked about Duncan. He might run an office in Atlanta, but the callouses on his fingers said he was a hands-on kind of guy. That appealed to her. She'd always found everyday working guys more attractive than those with hands softer than hers.

With the pups on one side and Duncan on the other, they set off down the driveway, the gravel crunching beneath their feet.

"I'll have another rope set up between the stable and the side yard fence. The dogs can do their business there."

"Thanks. That would work well. And thanks again for tacking up the rope this morning."

"No problem. Before long, the rope will be replaced by a walkway with rails and a gate system sectioning off the pool and the garden as well as the stable and front and side yard perimeter. Like a grid. Ian will always know exactly where he is."

"That sounds wonderful. Your brother is very lucky to have you putting such thought into the upgrades. Your mother's garden is toward the right?"

"Was, but yeah. She had every flower imaginable planted there. Now it's an overgrown mess."

"Can't be too bad. I can still smell the blooms of what's left." A few steps farther down the road, she asked, "Do you mind if I ask what happened to her?"

"Not at all. As much as she loved her garden, she was allergic to bees. She was getting a rake from the shed when she stumbled upon a small nest."

"Oh, Duncan."

"She was only stung twice, but it was enough. And it was a long time ago."

Maybe it was, but that didn't mean it wasn't tragic, especially since James MacGregor was taken from him and Ian so soon afterward. "I remember when the senator was killed. It was all over the news. I'm so sorry. You and Ian must have been terrified being so far from home when it happened."

"We were, although I think Ian felt guilty more than anything."

"Oh?" She heard Duncan inhale. "You don't have to tell me, of course, but... any insight into Ian's thinking might give me an edge in helping him."

They took several more steps in silence.

"Basically, Ian had stayed out all night despite his curfew. Dad was understandably angry because Ian had snuck out to go to a party. When Ian finally came home, they fought, and Dad went out for a run to cool down—but he left his bodyguard in the hotel to make sure Ian didn't leave again. Next thing we knew, there was a knock at the door, and the London police were on the other side. Me being younger, Ian stepped up and took care of me. Since he was sixteen, almost seventeen, he was allowed to be my guardian so long as we stayed enrolled at the military school we attended as Dad wanted."

Emma heard both the sadness and the love in Duncan's voice. "That sounds very intense. For you and Ian both."

"It was."

"And now you're taking care of Ian."

Duncan stopped walking. She firmed her grip on the leash in her hand and dug in her heels so the dogs wouldn't tug her along behind them.

"When you asked us to tell you about Ian this morning over breakfast... Emma, we didn't expect to go on vacation and come home orphaned but Ian... He blames himself."

"Most people would."

"I know. But he never once complained about getting stuck with his little brother. Not once," he repeated.

"Maybe not," she replied, "but that doesn't give Ian a free pass to behave as he is now. In the beginning, sure, but it's time to face facts."

"Ian didn't expect to wake up blind."

"Trust me, no one ever expects to wake up blind." A warm

tongue licked her fingers, and she automatically began to pet the four-legged owner.

"I know we have to get Ian to turn a corner with what happened, but I feel like he's due some complaining. I've probably let him get by with too much. I definitely let him drink too much for too long."

"Duncan, you didn't force him to drink."

"I'm simply saying Ian deserves some slack because the guy he used to be, the guy who stepped up to take care of me back then and the one who gave up his R and R to help rescue a young woman from a bad situation, *is* still there, somewhere."

She sensed Duncan's need to defend his brother and nodded, her heart softening. Duncan was doing his best to help Ian. Now it was up to her to see that Ian understood how important it was that he took control of his life. "I understand."

"Looks like Buttons wants us to keep walking. Come on," he said, taking her arm and tugging her gently to the left. "Some rough terrain ahead," he told her, tightening his grip and steadying her. "How are you doing at learning the inside of the house?"

"That's going to take me a while," she said honestly. "You and Ian have a lot of rooms and a lot of furniture. It will take time to help Ian learn to navigate it all."

"So if it's difficult for you, it's even more so for Ian?"

"Not necessarily. Ian knew the layout and where everything was before he was blinded, so he has some mental references. I don't."

They rounded a slope in the driveway.

"Buttons found his spot," Duncan said.

"I can tell."

"How?"

"The slack on the leash and the way he's not tugging on it."

Emma felt Duncan's stare on her face and found herself fighting the urge to fidget.

Her hair was brushed and contained in a hair band, her clothes damp and covered in dog hair. Aunt Rose had proclaimed Ian and Duncan both handsome, but this was the norm for her. Still, the feminine side of her wondered what Duncan thought even though she told herself she didn't care. Beauty came from within, and she wasn't looking for anything from Duncan except a paycheck.

"I don't know how to talk to him," Duncan murmured.

Her smile was forced, and she hoped Duncan didn't notice. "He'll let you know when he's ready to talk."

The dogs pulled on their leashes, ready for more exploring.

"So that's it?" Duncan asked. "We wait? Surely there's a next step."

"There is, but waiting him out is definitely part of it. First we let him do things for himself. It's hard to watch someone struggle, but it's necessary."

"That advice sounds like it comes from experience."

She couldn't help but laugh. "Most definitely. I learned all the tricks. Every time someone asked me to do something, I'd be all pathetic and say, "But I can't, I'm blind." Finally the *Besties* had had enough and told me to get over it."

He chuckled. "Friends are good like that, aren't they?"

"Totally. But siblings are good, too, and you've reached that stage with Ian. Tiptoeing around him only makes it more obvious that you're uncomfortable with him and what happened. That compounds the problem and makes him feel more self-conscious."

"He has nothing to feel self-conscious about. It just kills me that one stupid mistake changed him from a highly honored soldier to the guy in the house no one can stand for long."

"Ian isn't a soldier anymore," she said. "That's the problem. He has to figure out who he is now."

Emma allowed Duncan to lead her back toward the kennel via the sloping front yard.

Grass pulled at her shoes, and she smelled the earthy scent of old mulch and wild onions in the sultry humid air.

"I hate that the only reason Ian is blind is because he helped me with a case."

Something about Duncan's words struck a chord inside her. "You and I have that in common then. I've always felt guilty about the accident that killed my mom. I'm not even sure why, only that I feel that way."

"Survivor's guilt."

Maybe. Probably. But sometimes she couldn't help but believe it was more.

"Doc told me a little bit about what happened. What do you remember?" Duncan asked.

Emma took several steps, focusing her thoughts on that horrible day. It wasn't something she liked talking about, but seeing as how Duncan had shared his parents' deaths with her, she couldn't refuse. "I remember the sunshine. It was a beautiful day, not as hot as today, though. I remember wanting to go somewhere but not being allowed and...saying something to Mom. Not the actual words but... my tone, I guess. We were in the car, and she turned and looked at me like I had slapped her."

Her skin prickled with unease because the awareness of whatever she'd said hovered in the shadows of her mind. There, but inaccessible. "I was a typical fourteen-year-old smart-mouth. I can only imagine the stupid thing we were fighting over or what I said to her before the crash."

"Accidents happen, Emma. And teenagers are like that. I'm sure your mother wouldn't expect you to carry the guilt."

"No, she wouldn't. But that's when the crash happened. She

was looking at me with that expression and then... there was a truck. We hit it head on."

The crunch of gravel beneath their feet sounded loud in her ears, echoing off the canopy of trees shading the drive. It helped her place where they were on the road between the house and the kennel. When they stepped into the sun's path, Emma felt like she was baking, even though it had to be mid-nineties in the shade.

"I'm sorry for your loss."

"Me, too. It just goes to show how quickly things can happen."

They crossed the width of the gravel drive and moved back into the grass.

"Will Ian ever be the same?" Duncan said after a few steps. "I guess that's a stupid question. I know the answer."

Her heart ached at his words, but she had to answer honestly. "Ian will never be the same, no matter how much he wants to be. He knows it, and deep down you know it. Everything has changed. It's a process, but after a while, you'll be able to accept him as he is without wanting to coddle him."

"You know, if kenneling doesn't work out, you should try being a shrink like your uncle."

She smiled at Duncan's words but shook her head. "No, dogs are definitely easier than people. I'll stick with them."

Duncan was a good man, looking out for Ian the way a brother should. She wasn't used to talking to a man so openly, but her walk with Duncan was nice. Unexpected.

Which is why she hated bringing up Aunt Rose's request regarding Zack Dupré.

The sound of a vehicle motor climbing the long drive stilled Emma's words, and as the vehicle came closer, Emma heard a familiar rattle. "It's Genie," she said, pleased. "She's bringing clothing for me from Aunt Rose." She plucked at her post-dog-bath jeans Duncan had so kindly washed last night. "One pair doesn't go far, and I need clothes for my shift tomorrow."

"You're working at The Shak? You don't think it's too soon?"

"I'm scheduled to work, and seeing as how my father has his hands full dealing with the aftermath of the fire, the last thing he needs is to have to find a fill-in waitress. Plus, my PAWS Class takes place immediately before. I can't miss them. It'll be fine." She hesitated, then said, "You realize I will be working at The Shak and managing my responsibilities on top of helping Ian, right? You didn't think I would give them up even though the living arrangement changed?"

His hand settled over hers, warm and rough against her skin. "Yes, I knew you'd continue to work, but I don't want you to rush back after all you've been through."

The tension in her shoulders eased at his statement. "I'm fine."

The dogs went wild, barking and scrambling in the gravel to run toward Genie's vehicle as she topped the rise.

"I still owe you an apology," Duncan murmured.

"For what?"

"Your lack of clothing. I should have driven you to town."

"I'm certain you have better things to do than take me shopping." She refused to mention how frugal she could be in preferring clothes from Rose's church's emergency donation box than spending her own hard-earned and much-hoarded cash. "I could tell Aunt Rose really wanted to help, but she doesn't like leaving Uncle Bruce alone for long when every minute counts. Picking out clothes for me gave her something to do in the house besides sit and worry about him."

She waved in the direction of the car.

Genie rolled to a stop near them and cut the engine.

"Hey, Genie. Thank you so much for bringing the clothes to me," Emma said.

Genie got out and made a sound of frustration.

"Is something wrong?"

"I didn't expect it to be so isolated," Genie said, her voice hushed. "Emma, please say you'll come home with me? Now."

"I'm *fine*." Emma patted Genie on the arm. "Do I smell Aunt Rose's oatmeal cookies?"

"Yes. But it's not too late to change your mind," Genie added. "My offer stands. I have plenty of room."

"And I thank you, but it isn't necessary. Duncan has been nothing but nice and welcoming."

"What about the other one?" Genie asked, her voice growing cool. "Has he been nice?"

"Ian is... Ian," Emma said, aware Duncan listened to every word.

"What does that mean? What did he do?" the girl demanded.

"Nothing, Genie. Calm down," Emma said, refusing to go into details when she could well imagine Genie's shock and horror at the towel incident. "Please don't worry. Ian needs time to get used to me, but he will."

"And if he doesn't? I'm afraid for you. What if he hurts you? I stared at the ceiling all night last night thinking about it."

Emma wasn't sure what to say to that. Truth be told, she was nervous enough about the whole situation without adding Genie's fears to the mix. But she wasn't a woman who lived in fear. If she did, she would find a hidey-hole and...act just like Ian?

"You have nothing to worry about. Ian would never intentionally hurt Emma," Duncan interjected.

Emma wished she could say something to ease the girl's mind. "Would you like to come in? I could use some help learning my way around. That is, if you don't have plans?"

"That sounds like a wonderful idea," Duncan said. "Would you mind?"

"No," Genie said simply. "I don't mind."

"Then I'll leave you ladies to it," Duncan said. "Genie, thank you. Given all Emma's been through and the chaos of the remodel, I appreciate it, too."

The girl took hold of Emma's arm, gripping it a bit too tightly. "Emma's my best friend and number one in my life. I'd do anything for her."

Emma smiled at Genie's comment despite her discomfort. "Great. Now Duncan's free to get his work done. Unless you need the dogs to show you the way back?" she asked, teasing him.

"I think I can manage on my own."

Duncan's chuckles drifted back to Emma as he walked away, and Emma turned to Genie. "See? He's nice, right?"

"I suppose."

Obviously, Emma wasn't going to get Genie to budge in her thinking. "Come on, I'll show you the kennel before we go inside. I can't wait to hear your description. And tell me—is the outside of the house as big as the inside seems?"

Chapter 7

Ian stubbornly ignored Emma's statement that he wouldn't be able to eat in his room and waited in vain for Quinn to bring breakfast, then lunch. With every minute that passed and every growl of his stomach, Ian's anger grew.

He heard Emma in the house talking to another woman, but Emma didn't knock on his door, no doubt fearing his reaction and mood.

Ian closed his eyes and leaned his head against the leather back, imagining a sunset, the way the light rippled off the surface of the ocean, the steady hum and whirl of a chopper's blades as it swept over the surface.

The calming technique was one he'd learned in his cell in Iraq, one of the few things that worked to allow him to retain control over the panic, but just when he started to feel a small measure of relief, his stomach growled again.

Where was Quinn?

No sooner had the question formed than he heard someone opening his door. "It's about time. I'm hungry." He waited impatiently. "Quinn?"

"Quinn is outside, working hard in the heat like the other men," Emma informed him. "I would have told you sooner, but I was waiting for you to wind down from your tantrum."

The sweetness of her tone belied the sting of her words. Tantrum? "Where's my food?"

"In the kitchen, exactly where I said it would be. I thought we could pitch in and help the men by fixing sandwiches for them."

"You thought wrong." He sighed when he heard multiple pants. Bad enough she'd brought one dog with her this morning, but now there were several in his room, one of which was brave enough to nudge his hand with its nose. He jerked away and wiped his fingers on his shirt. "If you're frustrated with my lack of cooperation, get out of my house so I don't bother you anymore."

"You'd like that, wouldn't you? Then you could use my leaving as your excuse for being too afraid to try."

His fingers twitched with the desire to wring her neck. He wasn't afraid to try. He was...

Afraid to fail? Afraid the claustrophobia would win?

He opened his mouth to deny the accusation but couldn't. "Are you going to stand there and tell me you have no problem with this? You don't care that you have to walk around in the dark all the time?"

The admission cost him more in pride than he cared to admit.

"No," she said softly. "No, of course not. I was terrified." A soft, bitter sound emerged from her. "I was *fourteen*. How do you think I felt?"

He heard the emotional connection in her voice. He was being a jerk. He knew he was being a jerk. But for a guy who'd been trained to be a soldier, having to start over and learn the rudimentary basics of living was just wrong.

"Ian, I was angry and bitter, scared. I hated everyone because it had happened to *me*. I totally rocked the whole *why me* thing for a while."

A rough sound left her chest. A laugh, a huff. He wasn't sure which.

"Do you know I was asked to the prom by seven different guys? Wanna guess *why*?"

"Because they felt sorry for you." Pity was the worst. He hated pity.

Another laugh, this one more caustic than the last.

"No. They asked me because one of the morons came up with the brilliant conclusion that the blind girl would be so desperate for a date she'd do *any* despicable thing they wanted for a chance to go. They weren't shy about setting up the rules ahead of time, either."

His hands tightened over the arms of his chair, his mind well able to imagine hormonal teenage boys saying those things and laughing as they did so, her lack of sight giving them an anonymity of sorts.

"But you know what's worse, Ian? This time I *am* the desperate blind girl. My family has been devastated because of my stupid mistake, and I refuse to be something else they have to handle on top of the fire. You've made it very clear I'm not welcome. But do you have any idea why I'm willing to come back to your room again and again?"

"Please, tell me," he drawled, not bothering to hide his sarcasm because it took him away from feeling a connection with her and the way her words affected him.

"I'm here, I'm putting up with your *bull*, because I want my own life. I want my own business and my own home, and I want them enough to listen to your foul mouth and nasty attitude when the truth is you've got two good arms and two good legs, training and skills and education most men don't have and couldn't afford. But you're sitting here bellowing out orders and demanding food like a spoiled *brat*. It would be a lot easier, a lot simpler, if I were to accept your offer and leave you to wallow in your self-pity, but I refuse. I will not quit just because you won't get your head out of your butt."

There was passion in her voice, anger, determination. The strength and courage and bluntness he couldn't seem to find. "You can't help me, Emma. When are you going to get that?"

He raised his head, aware that she'd moved across the floor and now stood next to his chair.

Emma's hand slid onto the leather back near his head, found his shoulder and arm, moved down until she took his hand in hers.

"I can if you let me. I *was* you. I've said the same things you're saying. I've behaved the same way and pushed people away because I thought it would be easier. That it wouldn't hurt as much. Ian, I *do* understand. You and I are both stuck in this big, black void, and it sucks and it isn't fair, but don't you want to be free? To be able to count on yourself? Be independent?"

"The money Duncan's paying you is your independence?"

"In a way, yes."

His hand tightened on hers. "Then take the deal I'm offering you."

"*No.*"

"Why not?"

"Because independence comes with responsibility. It's about being an adult, one who keeps my word when I give it, and gives back to someone who needs my help more than he realizes."

"I don't—"

"Yes, you do! Get it through that thick, hard head of yours. I'm sticking this out. Maybe you can't have your eyesight back, but you can have other things. Make other plans. *What* do you want? Is this really it? To sit in this room and let the world go on without you?"

He tightened his grip over her hand, the softness of her skin offset by work-roughened spots. *A waitress most days.* A kennel owner on the others.

How could she run a diner blind? Care for the dogs? How many times had she been hit on by customers? Bitten by dogs?

It didn't matter because she did it anyway.

He teetered on the edge of a cliff. Believe her, or go about it his own way, in his own time, floundering about like he'd been for the last couple months but not making progress. Obviously she'd devised a way and felt she could help him.

No, he wasn't satisfied listening to the world go on without him. He wanted more. Wanted everything she said. But how? "I can't *have* what I want."

"Oh, Ian."

Her other hand slid over the top of his knuckles. He was surrounded by her softness, the smell of her. A lifeline in the dark. One he wanted to grab and hold so tightly she became part of him so he wasn't alone.

"I swear there will come a time when it won't be so bad. You're in survival mode right now. Putting one foot in front of the other to get through the days. But if you trust me, just a little bit, you'll wake up one morning, open your eyes, and start your day without that moment of panic when you remember you're blind. It'll just be another day you're alive."

"That's a mighty big promise to make." One he'd give anything to have come true.

"I know. But if you're willing to work and think and be creative, you can do just about anything you want to do. You are the only one holding you back."

Emma offered a future, dangling it like a carrot. But how was it possible?

"Let's go get something to eat. Come with me?"

Going to the kitchen appealed. He was beginning to hate this room. It was twenty paces by seventeen, large and luxuriously appointed despite the age of the house. But it had become another prison. "I don't want to eat in front of the others."

"Fine. But you can eat in front of me. After all," she said, a smile in her voice, "I can't see you if you spill."

Another carrot. Another indication that she wanted to help him, that she understood. Holding on to her, Ian got to his feet and took the first step.

That was the thing about rock bottom. Once you hit it, you couldn't sink any lower.

Fifteen minutes later, Ian listened while Emma fought an impromptu game of tug-of-war with Tucker over her white stick.

"Tucker, *no*. Let go!"

"Guess I'm not the only one not cooperating," he said.

Emma released a huff. "Nothing I can't—" She inhaled sharply, a squeak sounding on the floor like her shoe slid against the tile. "Handle. Tucker, let—ah! Got it! Bad, Tucker. Bad dog!" she scolded.

Tucker whined.

"Keep it up, Tuck, and you will be kicked out of school before you ever make it in."

"What do you mean?" Ian asked.

"I raise pups and prepare them for various assistance programs. But I'm afraid Tuck's not going to make it. He's distracted too easily and not growing out of his puppy-tude."

Puppy-tude? Ian laughed to himself and shoved another potato chip into his mouth.

Upon entering the kitchen, Emma had set to work on making lunch. When asked to help, he had declined, but in the end, he had made his own sandwich. Other than squirting on too much mustard and giving up on the tomato slice that kept falling out, it tasted okay.

The kitchen door opened, and he heard the voices of the men as they entered. Just that quickly, his appetite fled, and Ian pushed his plate away.

"Finished already?" Emma asked.

"Yeah." If he had to guess, he'd only eaten half of the meal, but it was enough to take the edge off his hunger. In the midst of a mission, he'd gone without. Doing so now wasn't a chore. It wasn't like he expended energy doing nothing but sitting or pacing.

He couldn't help but wonder what Quinn and Duncan would think, seeing that Emma had managed to get him to the kitchen in the light of day.

Then he knew. All conversation came to an abrupt stop, presumably when they spotted him.

"Hey, Ian, Emma," Owen finally said.

"Did your friend leave?" Duncan asked.

"Yeah. Genie had some errands to run, but we explored a bit and got the clothes Aunt Rose sent sorted and put away."

"Good. Maybe that will help take the edge off her worry. Ian," Duncan said, "Winston called again."

His brother's voice held more than a little challenge.

Maxwell Winston had called quite a few times since Ian had left the hospital, all the calls having one purpose. "The answer's still no."

"I said yes. We either meet with him and Kara in Atlanta or here. I agreed to let them come here, since I knew you'd prefer it."

He refused to be backed into a corner. "You meet with them then. Leave me out of it."

"They don't want to talk to me," Duncan said.

Ian stood and carefully moved around the corner of the table to where Emma now sat. Almost immediately, he heard the pups get to their feet, their claws clicking on the floor.

It would be just his luck to trip over one of them, but he refused to put his hands out in front of him to feel his way to the door. Instead he found Emma's shoulder, slid his hand down her arm, and wrapped his fingers around her thin wrist. "I'll walk you to your room," he said, urging her to her feet.

Emma hesitated a split second before she caught on, and he thanked God she understood what he wanted—and complied without protest or pointing out his inability to do such a thing. One wrong turn and he might lead them right into a wall. Or the pool.

"Of course."

Head high, he shifted his hand to Emma's shoulder and let her set the course, the pups following. As they left the room, he was aware that the men who'd followed him into the Mexican jungle were quiet.

They made it out of the kitchen and down the long, adjoining hallways without incident, but he didn't release the breath he held until they neared his room.

"They miss you, Ian."

They entered his bedroom, the tinge of air freshener not disguising the smell of spilled booze leftover from the last six weeks. "I'm useless to them."

"You are definitely not useless. What can I do to convince you?"

"I was discharged from the military for a reason," he said in response. "What good am I to them? Duncan's business is security. I can't be a bodyguard or investigator. I can't patrol an area."

"So? You can do other things."

"I don't know how to *do* anything else. I was trained to be a soldier. I don't know how to be blind."

"Then let me—"

"Emma, please, for the love of God, stop. You're not independent. You're never going to *be* completely independent and neither will I."

"That's not true!"

"It is. Why do you think it is so hard for me to stomach this? I hate what I've become, and you can lie to yourself all you want, but it won't change the truth. Now get out of my room and take those sorry mutts with you."

By the next morning, the stress of the fire, Roxy's health, and Ian's latest response to her presence in his life left Emma feeling the need for normalcy. Working the diner would require all her concentration, so hopefully she could set aside the other problems, at least for a while.

Even though she'd made progress in getting Ian out of his room, she felt as though he'd taken a step back once Duncan announced the upcoming visit from Maxwell Winston. Ian had stayed in his room the rest of the day, refusing them all entry, and went without dinner instead of returning to the table.

Baby steps, she reminded herself.

But maybe on the drive to The Shak, she could ask a few questions, and Duncan could explain why meeting with the Winstons had sent Ian back into hiding.

She used the time she had before leaving to organize the last of the clothing Genie had delivered. Aunt Rose had sent two large bags filled to the top, smelling freshly washed. There were pajamas, jeans, a couple flannels, tank tops, and even two dresses Emma knew she'd never wear, but obviously Aunt Rose hoped she would.

Thankfully her church's dress code was casual, which meant so long as she was modestly dressed, pretty much anything was okay. Her pastor believed coming to church and worshiping the Lord was more important than how she dressed.

After touring the house and the kennel, Genie had helped mark a few of the clothes so they were recognizable via touch and promised to return soon to finish the job—and no doubt check on Emma again.

Now standing beneath the shower, Emma lifted her face until the water rained down hot and hard.

All the happiness she could have felt for her progress in life with her blindness was tainted by the bluntness of Ian's words regarding never being independent. His comment had pierced her heart with truth and, nearly twenty-four hours later, still wouldn't let go.

No, she would never be wholly independent. But wasn't independence what she made it to be? She held a job, ran a business.

Shame on Ian for trying to belittle her achievements. He was the one bound up in bitterness and fear, not her, and she prayed for Ian to find the strength to realize it.

What she had to remember was that Ian was doing exactly as Duncan had warned, pushing her away, trying to be rid of her. Saying the things he thought would hurt her most. She'd given him the perfect ammunition by revealing her dreams for him to stomp on.

But she couldn't let Ian take her accomplishments away from her. She had to stay strong enough to help Ian find his footing again. Because in doing so—she'd take the next step in *her* future. And that was a goal she wasn't willing to give up.

Unable to stay in the heat any longer, she felt for the knob and flipped it to cold, gasping at the temperature difference.

Sometimes the cold brought clarity. Not today. So she got out and dried off, looking forward to some time out of the house.

The dogs had been cared for, and she had stacked the lunch-meat, condiments, and cheese all in one spot in the refrigerator so as to be easy to find and told Ian he could make his own lunch if he chose.

Leaving Ian unfed and hungry nagged at her, but she couldn't give in to his stubborn behavior. One sign of weakness and he would press the advantage. Give an inch and he'd take a mile.

Remembering she still needed to call her father, Emma got dressed and entered the bedroom, sitting on the edge of the mattress to make the call but standing nervously before the first ring sounded in her ear.

"'Ello?"

"Hey, Dad. It's Em. How are you?" The towel around her hair got in the way until she pulled it off to better hear his response.

"I'm fine, sweetheart. I think the question is how are you?"

"Settling the dogs and such."

"I figured as much. Been busy myself."

Yeah, she could imagine. "So, have you talked to the insurance company?"

"Stop worrying, Emmalee. Yes, I've talked to them. The fire marshal ruled it accidental, and everything is proceeding as expected. Payment will happen as the house is rebuilt, but my local guy said he'll give me a partial in advance for the contents to get me through until then."

"Thank goodness. Dad, I'm so——"

"Don't say you're sorry again. I know, baby girl. I'm not upset with you. You're upset with yourself enough for all of us. I'm just happy you're safe."

She curled a wet tendril around her finger. "But I feel so guilty, and I don't know what to say. Where did you and Laney sleep last night?"

"You don't need to say anything. I stayed in the camper last night, and your sister slept on one of the cots at the firehouse."

"The firehouse? Why not stay with Aunt Rose?"

"I don't think she wants to be that far from the station. Don't you worry about her. Your sister will find a place soon."

"Okay, so what about you? You can't stay in the camper the whole time. It's too hot."

"I know, I know. I spent the morning getting everything inside the sheds locked up tight or put into storage. Just stopped by the diner to check on things. Emma, Helen and I decided to move up the wedding. We're getting married as soon as we get the license."

Emma stopped twirling her hair. Married? Now? *"What?"*

"The fire changed things. I lost your mother, and I have nearly lost you twice. I want to be with Helen. I love her. She's a nice woman."

"No one says she isn't, but, Dad, I'm fine. There's no need to—"

"There is a need. I've lost too much to wait on the right time or the right day, and I won't move in without being married. I don't want people thinking badly of her."

She didn't know what to say. Her father required a special approach. To tell him he was rushing into something, that he was wrong, would only make him dig his heels in deeper.

But what would happen if things didn't work out here? With Ian? Where would she go? She couldn't move back in with her father and...Helen.

You're thinking of yourself, not them.

"I can almost hear your mind whirling." A deep sigh echoed over the phone. "You don't worry about a thing, sweetheart. If it doesn't work out with your job, you know you're always welcome to live with me and Helen. We're planning a spare bedroom and bath just for you."

Ian's words of dependence came back to her in a flash. No. She wouldn't move in with them. She couldn't. "Dad, are you sure you're not angry with me? For causing the fire?"

"Our decision to move up the wedding has nothing to do with you, Emma."

"But it does. If I hadn't accidentally burned down the house, we wouldn't be having this conversation. You wouldn't be moving anything up."

"But now I am. For the record, I think Helen likes the thought of you staying with us sometimes. She never had children."

"I'm not a child." And she wouldn't be treated like one.

"Oh, she knows that. How about we get together for dinner or something soon, so you two can get to know each other better?"

Not exactly on her list of Must Do's. "What about Laney?"

"Your sister is usually working, but, yeah, she's welcome to come to dinner. Of course."

"I meant... Laney lived with us until the fire. Does she get a room?"

Silence followed her question, and Emma bit back an Ian-like response.

"Emma, Laney's wanted to move out for years. I'm sure she'd rather do pretty much anything than move in with Helen and me."

But they expected *her* to move in because they thought she couldn't look after herself?

"I'm not rushing into anything, Emma. I thought I'd be alone the rest of my life. It's what I deserved. Helen caught me by surprise."

Her father wasn't one for making statements like that. Ever. "What do you mean, 'it's what you deserved'?"

"Oh, just an old man talking. Every marriage has its problems, and your mother and I had ours as well," he said mysteriously. "I just never thought I'd be happy again. Now enough of that. Are you heading in to work?"

That was it? That was all he was going to say? "Yes, I'll be there, but I'm going to have a short PAWS class and stop and check on Roxy before I get there."

"How's the old gal doing?"

"Tasha's running more tests today."

"She'll bounce back. You'll see."

With so many changes taking place, Emma couldn't imagine not having Roxy by her side.

After she said good-bye to her father, Emma finished getting ready. The new-to-her clothes felt strange on her body, the material not as soft as she liked. Since she couldn't see fabrics or colors or the things sighted people looked for, she'd become a material snob, choosing textures that felt good against her skin.

Ian's words about how they'd never be truly independent slid through her mind once again, taunting her so much her hands fisted over the edge of the bathroom sink.

Once upon a time, she'd been in love. Right after high school, she'd met a guy attending college at Zailer. They'd hit it off and started dating, but just when things were getting serious, Mark had backed off, citing school, pressures from family, and so forth for the decision. She'd confronted him and discovered the thought of spending his life with a blind woman was at the core of his retreat.

It wasn't long afterward that Mark transferred to another university. And only six months after that, she'd discovered he'd gotten engaged.

Mark's behavior was a smack in the face to her I-can-do-anything mantra. It had shaken her, hurt her. But she couldn't let Mark or Ian or anyone else decide her fate. "Time to show him how it's done."

Chapter 8

Ian nearly took a dive off his chair when something dropped into his lap. Music blared from the speakers, but he tilted his head and heard the *pant, pant, pant* of whatever dog had snuck into his room.

Ian plucked the ball from his lap and threw it toward the bedroom door, hoping the dog would go with it.

Instead, the ball hit a wall and bounced several times, and the only thing audible was the unmistakable scramble and happy grunts of one of Emma's four-legged pals. "Get out," he ordered the dog. "Go on, go!"

A low whine allowed Ian to place the animal near the hearth.

Man, was his aim ever off. "Don't you dare hike your leg, you mangy mutt."

Emma might have made a deal with Duncan, but it was still Ian's house. He had to establish a rule about the dogs staying out of his room. The last thing he wanted to do was step into a pile of dog doo.

Warmth touched his leg once again. The dog nudged Ian's

thigh with his head, and the ball dropped onto his lap once more. Ian grimaced at the slimy feel.

Tucker. It had to be Tucker. Tinkerbell minded too well, and he knew for a fact both dogs were supposed to be outside in the kennel while Emma was at work. "Stupid dog. You escaped, eh?"

The dog stopped panting long enough to lick its chops and yawn. Loudly.

"Bored? Maybe you're not such a stupid dog," he said, scratching Tucker's head and ears. "Keep holding back and pretending to be dumb, and Emma might send you packing."

If only that would work for him. He'd refused to cooperate and tried to rid himself of his well-meaning and too-stubborn-for-her-own-good tutor, all for no good.

Emma was nothing if not persistent.

Tucker nudged the ball in Ian's lap, a definite order to throw it again.

Apparently Emma's dog was just as stubborn.

Ian picked it up and tossed it across the room once more. "Fetch." Tucker took off, his tail hitting Ian's leg as he turned to give chase.

The dog retrieved the ball and brought it back to Ian.

Tucker was obviously capable of learning basic commands. But what if Tucker was the smarter of the two of them? "Am I the old dog, Tucker? Is that it?"

The old dog set in his ways, one who didn't want to change because it meant accepting this new reality.

What if he couldn't do it? Who was to say he possessed the ability to start over again? Reading, writing—did blind people still use *Braille*?

The thought of having to begin again—literally from scratch —and be a thirty-three-year-old kindergartner scared him.

Maybe he *was* a coward.

Ian gripped the dog's large head in both his hands and

rubbed hard. Tucker began to growl playfully, the ball forgotten. "Which is it?" he asked the dog. "Are you a stupid dog, or are you pulling one over on us because you don't want to spend your days playing fetch and follow the leader with some loser who trips over his shoes?"

Tucker grunted and licked Ian's wrist.

Ian smothered a laugh. "Yeah. That's what I thought."

⁂

Duncan offered to drop Emma off at Tasha's vet clinic on his way to Atlanta. It was strange, riding down the mountain with him. As much time as she spent around guys in the diner, she was rarely alone with men.

Duncan was polite, definitely a flirt. But all of the years at the diner had given her enough insight to know a lot of men saw her as safe. Safe to flirt with, safe to talk to. She didn't take Duncan's tone or teasing to mean more than simple conversation.

"Call Quinn or Owen if you need a ride home," Duncan said as he pulled the SUV to a stop.

She gathered her purse and white cane before opening the door. "I'll be fine. Thanks for the ride."

The chime on the entry door sounded as Emma let herself inside Tasha's clinic. The receptionist greeted her, the welcome followed by several other pet owners in the waiting area.

"Hey, Em," Tasha said, her shoes squeaking a bit on the tile floor. "Good timing. We need to talk."

Taken aback by Tasha's professional voice, Emma swallowed. "What's going on?"

"Come on. Let's go back and see Roxy."

Emma's stomach curled into a hard knot. Whatever Tasha had to say, it didn't sound good. "Tash? Roxy's okay, right?"

"Em," Tasha's voice lowered as she led the way down the hall. "Something showed up in the scans. This way," Tasha ordered, grasping Emma's arm. "Roxy's over here."

Tasha led the way. In seconds, Emma knelt by Roxy, who was lying on a cushion on the floor.

Her mind raced with a jumble of prayers and pleas and panic. "What's wrong with her?"

"The test results are back and..."

"Just say it," Emma begged, desperate to get the waiting over with.

"Sometime between her last check up and now, Roxy's developed tumors. They're big and they're multiplying fast."

Her hand tightened in Roxy's soft fur as she struggled to take it all in. "Tumors?"

"I can do surgery and remove what I see."

Emma shook her head. "But?"

"I'll know more when I get in there. You'd said she hasn't been feeling well lately? Before the fire? This is why."

"I should have brought her in sooner. I thought it was just her age."

"You are not to blame. I wish all my pet owners were as diligent as you. Em, it hasn't been that long since her last visit. No matter how much we hate it, sometimes these things just happen."

Maybe. But not to Roxy. Emma pressed a kiss to Roxy's bulky head. "Okay, so, surgery, right? That will help?"

"Yes. That will help and give us more information."

"So let's do it." She couldn't imagine her life without Roxy at her side. At least for several more years. "What about chemotherapy? Radiation? Do they do that on dogs?" She sounded desperate, but she *was* desperate. Roxy was... *Roxy*.

"The course of treatment is up to you, but given her age, I would caution you to think hard before taking that route."

She ran her hand down Roxy's head, over her ribs. Despite the oxygen Roxy still wore over her nose, every breath was a tired pant. "What do you mean?"

"She was four years old when you got her. The life expectancy of a Lab is eight to twelve years and..."

"She's twelve." But she couldn't just give up. Roxy deserved more than that. She was such a good dog, such a part of their lives. "Tash, please, you have to do everything you can. I know she's just a dog to some people, but she's so much *more* than that to me."

"I know. And I will."

It took everything in Emma not to climb into the oversized dog bed and curl up around Roxy. She wanted to. Needed to. "When can you do surgery?"

"Today. I'll take a look and find out what we're dealing with. Stay positive."

She closed her eyes and nodded. Positive. She had to stay positive. Roxy would not die this way. It was too cruel. "Thank you."

The words were next to impossible to get out over the lump in her throat.

"Come on. Let's let Roxy rest. You can sign off on the surgery, and we can get things going in the right direction before your class."

"If she's having surgery, I should stay. What can I do?" she asked, her voice husky. "There has to be something I can do."

"Em, you're only a few minutes away. The best thing you can do is stay busy and pray, not pace my waiting room. Go, do your thing, and come back tonight when you're done with your shift. I'll keep you posted. I promise."

Tasha pulled Emma into a hug, surrounding her in a cloud of warmth and friendship and perfume. But more telling than what Tasha did was the words she didn't say.

Because Tasha never said Roxy would be fine.

The weekend passed in a constant battle of wills with Emma fighting to get Ian out of his room for meals and being forced to endure his petulant attitude, visiting a recovering Roxy, caring for the kennel dogs, and working her shifts at The Shake Shak.

Tasha was right, though. So long as Emma stayed in motion and focused on a task, she wasn't consumed with worry about Roxy or her father or the general state of life as she presently knew it. She put one foot in front of the other and moved until she fell into bed so exhausted she almost didn't wake when she heard Ian outside in the hall, back at the cellar door.

Given the circumstances and Ian's determination to wallow in self-pity, Emma didn't force her tired body out of bed to talk to him. She lay there unable to sleep, until Ian shuffled and stumbled his way back to his room.

She knew better than to let Ian's bad attitude rub off on her, but right now, she also knew her limits, and her patience was stretched thin and filled with holes.

Roxy was recovering from surgery, and while the tumors were cancerous, Tasha thought she'd gotten them all. They were waiting for word on more tests, but Emma hoped to bring Roxy home soon.

Home to where? How are you going to take care of her? On top of every-thing else?

She'd find a way.

Emma rolled onto her side in the queen-size bed and pressed her face into the pillow. So many changes in so little time.

Surely from here things would get better?

On Monday morning, Duncan took in Emma's appearance as he approached her in the yard, noting she wore lip gloss, blush, mascara, and powder that did nothing to lighten the dark shadows beneath her eyes. "Morning."

"Good morning to you, too."

The sunlight was strong and highlighted the freckles on her skin, the gleam of auburn-gold in her brown hair, the way her blue-gray eyes picked up the color of her blouse. "Can I ask you something?"

"Sure."

"How do you do the makeup?"

A smile pulled at her full lips. "That's what brought you out here? You need makeup tips?" she teased.

"No, but answer that question first."

"Lots and *lots* of practice. After I was blinded, Laney helped me figure out a system. So long as I always use the same products, it's fine. Once I mixed up the blush and eye shadow and wound up with red eyes and gray cheeks. According to Laney I looked like a zombie."

He laughed at the visual. "Well, you don't today. You look beautiful."

"Thanks. So what's up?"

He fell into step beside her as the dogs meandered around the yard on their leashes. "I'm surprised to see you up already. No one would blame you for sleeping in."

"I have responsibilities, Duncan. The world doesn't stop just because something bad happens."

A truer statement had never been said.

"I could rely on you and the others to guide me around the grounds, but considering I can tell where the yard ends thanks to the driveway, I'll learn the area much faster on my own if it's from necessity."

He stared at her in awe, struck by her sheer determination. "You're amazing, you know that?"

"No, I'm not," she said. "What I am is too lazy to expend the energy hunting one of you down every time I need something."

The giant Goli took a leak while Penelope strained at her harness to go exploring in a nearby bush. Buttons sat on his fat haunches and looked ready for a nap. "All I'm saying is that one of us would've taken care of the animals for you."

Emma had worked the evening shift last night, closing the diner at eleven. One of the waitresses had dropped her off around midnight, but here she was, bright and early.

"I don't expect you to help me. I am sorry about waking you up last night, though. I didn't think about getting a key before I left."

"No problem, but I am having one made for you today."

Goli finished her business and began leading the other dogs and Emma toward the driveway. Buttons protested the move for a couple seconds before giving a blustery grunt and complying.

Duncan fell into step beside her, pulling her hand through the crook of his arm. "They seem to get along well."

"Yeah, they do, thank goodness. I've had some in the past that couldn't be near each other without fighting, and it made walking them difficult."

Duncan could tell something was bothering her. "Are you okay?"

"Yeah."

"That doesn't sound very convincing."

A weak smile curled her lips. "No, probably not. I was holding out hope that the masses Tasha found were benign but...they aren't. Roxy has cancer."

"I'm sorry to hear that."

"Yeah, me, too."

"Is there anything I can do?"

"There you go again," she said, giving him a brief smile. "No. But I appreciate you asking."

"Let me know if that ever changes. I mean it." She'd had a hard few days, and things seemed to be getting worse, not better. The fire, Ian. Her dog was dying? It was a heavy load to carry.

"Can I give you a ride into town? I'm heading that way."

"I'd like that. I have to be at the courthouse by— Oh no."

"What? What's going on?"

Emma groaned softly. "I forgot to tell you. Things have been so busy... Aunt Rose asked for a favor before the fire, and even with all that happened, I didn't have the heart to say no."

"Say no to what?"

"One of her former students has a court date today. Aunt Rose wants me to ask the judge to assign the guy to work in the kennel and help me with my PAWS class as community service. I figured given the circumstances and how it'll take me a while to find my footing here, an extra hand wouldn't be a bad idea. I don't want you or your men to have to stop what you're doing whenever I need help. I should've run it by you, but it slipped my mind with the news about Roxy."

Goli came over and nudged Duncan's leg, almost knocking him sideways. He petted the huge dog and admired the ease with which Emma handled herself with the Great Dane. But working with animals wasn't the same as working with criminals. "Do you know why he's appearing in court?"

"No. But I can't imagine it's too bad if Aunt Rose is sticking up for him."

True. Rose Dibbs had a soft heart and wouldn't risk putting Emma in danger. But it was little comfort given today's society. Not being physically dangerous didn't mean the guy wouldn't rob them bli— He broke off the mental expression, glad he hadn't said the words aloud and stuck his foot in his mouth.

"It's your house. You can disagree and totally shut the idea down," she said. "No hard feelings."

Duncan was tempted to do just that, but he thought about Rose and Bruce and shook his head. "No, it's fine. I don't mind you helping the guy so long as he's trustworthy. Only time will tell. I would appreciate it if he keeps his distance from the house until we can get a gauge on him, though. The kennel has a bathroom and small fridge in it, so anything he'd need is there."

"I understand. Thank you."

"My pleasure. Rose has always looked out for those she called 'her kids.' I'm sure this is another example of that. Now for my favor," he added, wondering if Emma could work some magic on Ian.

They resumed their walk, their shoulders brushing against each other periodically. "I need Ian to sit in on that dinner with Maxwell Winston and his daughter."

"Where have I heard that name?"

"Most likely in the news. He's a businessman based in Atlanta and an associate of mine, not to mention a friend."

"That must be it. Should I guess why Ian is so opposed to the meeting?"

He shouldn't tell her, but maybe if Emma understood, she could convince Ian to change his mind. "I need your word you won't discuss it with anyone. Not even your friends."

"Of course."

"I mean it, Emma."

"I won't breathe a word," she vowed. "What happened?"

"Max's daughter got herself into some trouble on a recent vacation in Mexico. She was taken and held for ransom, and Max hired my company to rescue her. Ian was on leave, so he came along, too."

"That's when he was shot."

"Right. Ian went against military rules to help us. Long story short, Kara's now in therapy, and she and Max are asking for a face-to-face with Ian so she can put the incident behind her."

Duncan inhaled and sighed, wishing he could get the knot between his shoulder blades to release. "Ian is the main person Kara wants to see, and I can't help but think it might do him some good as well."

"It might. I know I've gone to visit the scene of the accident several times over the years."

"Do you think you could convince Ian to sit down with Kara?"

"I can try—I just can't make any promises."

Chapter 9

Emma tried not to be nervous in court. She had met with Zack Dupré's attorney on the courthouse steps before entering the historic building, aware of the scents of pine and polish and old paper. There was a distinct mustiness to the courtroom, as if the windows hadn't been opened in quite a while.

"I've reviewed the case, but I understand you have someone willing to speak on Mr. Dupré's behalf?" the judge said, his voice ringing with authority.

"Yes, Your Honor. Miss Emmalee Wyatt."

"Go ahead."

Emma inhaled and tried to look both suitable as a potential boss and yet helpless due to the circumstances that brought her there as she explained her plight to the judge. "So you see, Your Honor, I could use the help right now, and if the court chooses to honor my aunt's request to help her former student, you'd be doing us both a favor."

Silence followed her words. Other than the shuffle of papers and the jingle of some kind of metal clinking together behind her where the spectators sat, Emma waited for a response.

Tension gathered in her shoulders, her muscles beginning to ache from the strain.

It was hard to sound sincere when, honestly, she felt for Zack Dupré, but if he'd stayed out of trouble, neither of them would be there right now. Maybe she was a bit jaded, but she couldn't help but think Aunt Rose was being played.

And you'll keep that from happening to you, how?

She was doing a good deed. God would watch over her, even if it came in the form of Duncan and the others creating not only a foolproof system of gates and walkways for Ian but also a state-of-the-art security system. They'd make sure Zack didn't go anywhere near the house.

"Considering the nature of your work, Ms. Wyatt, and recent events, I'm going to grant your request—with several conditions."

"Thank you, Your Honor."

"Mr. Dupré, you are hereby on probation. Barring death or hospitalization, you are to work with Ms. Wyatt as needed according to her schedule. Failure to do so will be a violation of your probation, and you will serve three months in the county jail as a result of your noncompliance. Do you understand?"

"Yes, sir," Zack said from the other side of the attorney standing to Emma's right.

"Mr. Dupré, I hope you understand how lucky you are to have not one but two people willing to step forward to help you in this matter. I know Ms. Wyatt's aunt and all she's going through. In the same situation, I guarantee you that most people wouldn't give you a second thought. I'm going to trust that she sees something in you I'm not capable of seeing at the moment and that you won't disappoint either of us. Or Ms. Wyatt, for that matter. Do you understand me?"

"Yes, sir."

"Ms. Wyatt?"

"Yes, Your Honor?"

"If you have any problems with this young hoodlum, you come directly to me. Do you understand?"

"Yes, I will." Emma jumped when the gavel banged against the desk, then smiled sheepishly in embarrassment.

"Court dismissed."

Emma lowered herself into the chair behind her under the guise of retrieving her purse and white cane. The reality was it gave her quaking knees a break, and she was thankful the nerve-wracking process was over.

"Ma'am? Thank you for doing what you did."

She turned her head toward the sound of Zack Dupré's voice and hoped she hadn't let her love for her aunt get in the way of common sense. "Don't thank me yet. You have a lot of work ahead of you. I'm still settling in and won't need you until Monday. Think you can stay out of trouble until then?"

"Yeah. I don't want to go to jail."

"Good." After a deep breath and a brief mental tussle to steady herself, she held out her hand. Duncan had given her the ultimate of second chances. The least she could do was offer the same to Zack, right? "Here's to new beginnings, Mr. Dupré."

For both of us.

I can't believe you just went to the courthouse and did that," Genie said to Emma later that same day.

Emma's head pounded with a headache she hadn't been able to shake all afternoon, but she managed a grimace of a smile in Genie's direction, reminding herself that Genie meant well. "Aunt Rose wouldn't have asked me to do anything that put me in danger. It'll be fine."

"You don't know anything about him, Emma. Just like you don't know anything about those men in that house."

All true. And if she were honest, she would admit to being nervous about having someone working with her—for her—who was there because of a court order. But it was done. And until Zack Dupré gave her reason to reconsider, she had to move forward as planned. "It'll be fine," she repeated, both for her own benefit and Genie's.

Emma went about her duties, filling baskets and checking orders, while Genie kept talking about all the bad things that could happen. Like she hadn't already thought of them herself? What if Zack wasn't an animal person? What if something happened to one of the dogs in her care? There were so many things that could go wrong that she didn't need to add Genie's pessimism to the list.

"I'm going to go get gas, but I'll be back to pick you up later."

"I'm going to the clinic to see Roxy again. I can get another ride home."

"Don't be silly. I'll meet you there."

"Emma, I need a couple more sodas over here!"

"Coming right up!" Emma answered. Lowering her voice, she grabbed two glasses. "Um, sure. If you don't mind. Thanks a lot, Genie."

Emma turned and carried the drinks down the length of the counter to the other end. Not long after, she heard the bell on the door jingle.

She felt a niggle of regret that she'd been about to blow Genie off, but she had enough on her plate without adding Genie to it. Right now, the last thing she wanted was to have to deal with someone else's emotional issues. She had too many balls in the air to juggle blind, and Genie's neediness was draining.

Two hours later, her back ached almost as badly as her head, and she realized both were early warning signs her period was about to strike.

Her shift was over at nine o'clock, and she made her way to Tasha's clinic, every step marked by the tap of her white cane against the concrete sidewalks. She was so lost in a daze she almost missed the buzz of the crosswalk signal and stopped just as the rush of a car, music throbbing and rattling store windows as it passed, scared her enough to stumble back onto the curb.

Pay attention, Emma. You know this isn't the place to daydream.

By the time she'd walked the four blocks to the clinic in the stifling evening heat, her shirt stuck to her back and sweat beaded her forehead. She hated to sound like a spoiled southern belle, but she hated being *sticky.*

The scent of dog poo assailed her nose as she approached the clinic's entry. How rude. Tasha had planted a yard off to the side of the building where customers could walk their dogs. A sign was even posted, but it had obviously been ignored and the mess left behind. Some people just didn't think about others or take responsibility for their pets.

The clinic door's metal handle was hot to the touch.

"Hey, Emma," Tasha's receptionist said.

"Hi, Rita. You're here late." Emma smiled at the woman from her church as she readjusted the cane in her hand.

"Just catching up on some paperwork when the phone isn't ringing off the hook. I'm on my way home now. Tasha's in her office."

"Thanks. Have a good night."

"Emma? I'm so sorry about the fire and all that's happened. If there's anything I can do, you let me know, okay? We're here for you. All you have to do is ask."

The show of compassion caught Emma off guard, and she blinked the sting of tears away. "Thanks. I appreciate it."

Emma entered the hallway leading to Tasha's office, confused when she picked up the faint hint of Morgan's favorite perfume. "Knock, knock. You busy?"

"Come in. We've been waiting for you," Tasha said.

Unease settled deep and made her stomach burn. We? "What's going on?"

"Em, I'm so sorry," Jolie said.

A surge of fear squeezed her stomach until she wanted to hurl. "Roxy's *dead?*"

"No."

The squeak of the desk chair's wheels alerted Emma that Tasha had stood. Two seconds later, Tasha's arm wrapped around Emma's shoulders.

"Come sit down."

Tasha all but shoved her into the chair, but Emma didn't protest because her legs shook so badly. "If she's not dead, what's wrong? Is she worse?"

"Yeah, I'm afraid she is. I'd hoped she was making a turn-around after the surgery, but her blood count is through the roof, and several tumors have reappeared."

"So soon?" Emma whispered, barely able to get the words out. How could this be happening? All at once. She couldn't do this. Handle this, too. *God, please, not this, too.*

"Yes. They're multiplying fast. I'm sorry, Em. At this point... we've had to give her increasing doses of painkiller just to keep her comfortable. She's in pain."

Emma struggled to hold herself together. She wanted to yell. Scream. Cry like a baby because she was so tired of always having to put on a brave face and be strong. "I don't want her to hurt."

"I know."

Silence followed her words, like Tasha and the others waited for her to come to the conclusion that had gathered them there by her side. "This is it? Nothing can be done?"

"No. Sweetie, I am so sorry. To be honest, I don't think she'll make it more than a few more days, and if she does, they will not be easy ones. But ultimately the decision is yours."

"Can I see her?"

"Of course."

Knowing Roxy was going to die "one day" was something every pet owner feared, but for that day to be today... "I need a few minutes."

"Take as long as you like. I'll show you where she is and give you time alone," Tasha said.

Morgan sniffled as Emma walked by. "We're here for you, Em."

"Always," Jolie added.

The back room smelled like disinfectant, the air conditioning and cinder walls giving the room a chill.

"She's over here."

A metal gate was opened and swung wide. Em dropped to her knees, hands out to feel for the cage.

Roxy whined, the sound barely audible.

"She's happy to see you. She's wagging her tail."

Tasha patted Emma's shoulder.

"Let me know if you need anything. I'll come back in a while."

Emma nodded, unable to speak. When the door closed behind Tasha, Emma reached out and found Roxy's thick, soft head. Rox panted hard, every breath an obvious struggle. "Hey, Rox. You aren't feeling very well, huh? Yeah, I know. It hurts, doesn't it? I'm so sorry."

She pressed a kiss to Roxy's head, memories flashing through her mind. "We've had some fun, haven't we?" she whispered. "There won't *ever* be another dog like you."

Roxy licked Emma's hand, her tongue dry, whimpers low and barely audible.

"Oh, Roxy, I don't want you to hurt." Emma lowered her forehead and pressed it against the dog's. "I need you so much. Ian— He doesn't get it, you know? I need you to help me show him how it can be."

She shifted to lie down beside Roxy, snuggled Roxy's head against her chest, and buried her nose in Roxy's soft neck. "But you're tired. You've been such a good girl. You've had a nice life, yeah? Mrs. Parker loved you before she died, and when I got you... You shouldn't suffer. Not at all, because it's not *right*. I've always told you there's a special place in heaven for dogs like you. I have to believe that because now... you'll get to see it."

Roxy whined again, the sound forlorn. "I'm going to miss you so, *so* much. But you're ready, aren't you? You just don't want to hurt anymore?"

As though understanding her question, Roxy licked Emma's cheek and snuffled out a sigh.

"Just know *I love you*. Always remember that, okay? But don't forget me, because I won't ever forget you."

Emma stayed curled on the floor by Roxy's head a long time, until a soft knock on the door alerted Emma to the *Besties'* presence.

"Em?"

She couldn't speak for the tears choking her, so she simply nodded.

"I thought I'd say something. Is that okay?" Jolie asked.

Another nod was all she could manage, too choked up, too on edge. While Tasha got the medicine from a nearby cabinet, Emma felt her friends surrounding her. Jolie to her right, squeezed in between Roxy and the wall of the kennel, and Morgan across from them, probably dressed up as she always was in a bid to boost her confidence but willing to brave Tasha's vet clinic floor anyway.

"Tasha's ready," Jolie said.

Emma dug her fingers a little deeper into Roxy's fur.

A hand slid over Emma's, the lack of rings making it easy to identify Jolie's.

"Ashes to ashes, dust to dust. Dear Heavenly Father, you brought Roxy into Emma's life and filled it with joy and happiness. Not a sparrow falls from the sky if it's not Your will, and we understand that You gave Roxy to Emma for a reason. It's hard for us to let go, but we ask that Roxy's passing be a gentle one and that she finds a home in Heaven to await Emma's arrival. Roxy has been a good pet and a wonderful and loyal friend who has served Emma well. Please comfort Emma as she says goodbye and bring Emma solace from this loss. We ask these things in Jesus' name. Amen."

Soft amens followed the prayer, and Emma clutched Roxy closer. Tighter.

"I'm giving her the medicine now," Tasha whispered.

Nooo. Emma buried her nose in Roxy's neck and cradled her old friend in her arms. "I love you. I love you, I love you, I love you."

Roxy's breathing slowed, every inhalation softer and shallower.

One.

Then another.

Until she breathed no more.

An hour later, Emma stood outside the vet clinic in the middle of one last group hug when she heard a familiar rattle. The car slid to a stop, and a door slammed shut.

"It's your shadow," Morgan murmured.

Emma immediately shook her head and moaned. She couldn't handle more right now. She didn't have the strength. In wanting to help, Genie would only bring more stress. "I can't— Guys, please."

"Go. I'll run interference," Tasha said.

"Emma! Emma, what's happening? Why are you all here? Oh, Emma, you're crying."

Jolie wrapped an arm around Emma's shoulders and nudged her toward the right.

"Emma will talk to you later, Genie." Jolie opened the car door and urged Emma inside.

"Wait! What are you doing?" Genie asked.

"I'm taking Emma home," Jolie said.

"But that's why I'm here," Genie said. "I can drive her."

"I'm sorry, Genie. I didn't know—" Emma broke off, unable to go on.

She just wanted to go home. Wanted to burrow beneath her covers and hide.

"Jolie is taking Em home," Tasha said firmly. "Genie, we're sorry for the mix-up, but it's been a rather rough evening. We'll take care of Emma, though. You can go on home."

"Emma, what's going on?" Genie's voice rose. "What happened?"

Someone must have answered Genie's questions.

"Oh, no— Why didn't any of you call me? I would've stayed with her. I should've been here."

Just before the car door closed, Emma was able to make out Tasha telling Genie that things had progressed quickly. Genie's upset was muffled by the glass but still audible.

Oh, sweet girl. She really was sweet, but right now it was all Emma could do to hold herself together.

Jolie climbed behind the wheel and started the engine, the blast of air conditioning blowing Emma's hair into her face.

"Em? You okay?"

Emma closed her eyes and leaned her head against the rest behind her. "No. Please, just take me ho—" She broke off, remembering that home was now burnt rubble thanks to her. "Take me to the MacGregors'."

So much change in such a short time. Had she really wondered how things could get worse? How she'd ever be able to function without Roxy by her side?

Ian listened as Emma tolerated the men fussing over her like a bunch of mother hens. He sat at one end of the long kitchen table, Duncan at the other. But where their comments were accompanied by the periodic scrape of utensils against their breakfast plates, he simply sat there, his stomach growling.

Later, when they were gone, the room empty, he'd eat.

"We'll take care of everything," Duncan told her. "Since you aren't sure where you'll be living, I'll pay to have Roxy's remains cremated, and you can bury her when you're settled."

"That's very generous of you, but I can't accept. I can handle things myself. Tasha said it's not that expensive."

"Consider it a gift. I insist."

Duncan refused to take no for an answer, but Ian was glad to hear it. Emma had been through enough. And though he might consider her a hired pest, he could tell from her behavior what the dog had meant to her.

"I had better head out," Owen said. "I think I just saw the first truck pull up."

"I'll meet you," Quinn said.

Duncan excused himself from the table as well after his cell phone bleeped out an instant message.

"Emma, take it easy today," Duncan ordered.

Emma didn't respond verbally, and Ian grew frustrated at his inability to see her expression.

His belly growled again, long and loud.

"Would you eat, already?" she said the moment they were alone. "Your stomach has been making noises for the last half hour. It's driving me insane."

Not needing to be told twice, Ian found his fork and dug in, wondering how he would counter her grouchiness and then deciding to let it pass.

Throughout breakfast, he'd heard the others' comments about the omelet, but the *smell...*

He didn't bother trying to cut the egg concoction, didn't care that it was cold. He simply stabbed it, bent over his plate and bit a chunk out of it. He finished his food in no time flat, and despite his efforts not to, he spilled bits of mushrooms and onions. Muttering silently, he tried to find them and toss them on the plate so Quinn wouldn't see the mess.

"I'm going back to my room for a little while. I'll come by yours later and show you how to keep track of your clothes, sorting them, washing, and that type of thing."

"Emma—"

"Ian, you need to learn it, and today you will," she said firmly.

Ian heard the scrape of her chair and scooted his back as well. She had to pass him on the way to the door, and the moment she did—

He held both hands out, grabbed her, and pulled her close, between his knees. A sharp gasp followed his move, but he was careful not to hurt her or let his hands settle anywhere inappropriate. "I'm sorry about your dog," he said before she could escape.

Ian gentled his hold and noted the way she held herself tense, as if one hint of weakness would make her crumble.

It took her a moment, several deep breaths, before she said, "Thank you."

He got to his feet, still holding on to her. "I know what it's like to lose a pet," he said. "When I was six, I had a dog. He slept with me, ate with me, played with me."

She swallowed audibly.

"What happened to him?"

"My father was getting deliveries here at the house. He heard another truck pulling up and asked that I go to the door. The dog shot by me before I could stop him, and he ran right under the wheel. The driver couldn't stop in time."

"Oh, Ian. And you saw this? At six?"

"Yeah."

"That's horrible."

"No more than you having to put down Roxy," he said, tugging her closer.

Emma smelled sweet, like oranges and honey. Felt soft and womanly. Her back was narrow, tense, so he rubbed the heel of his palms in the tender flesh between her shoulder blades. Emma breathed a soft sound in response, and the tension eased by minute degrees.

He set his jaw, determined he wouldn't act like a jerk this time.

She surprised him when she pressed her face into his shoulder.

"Did you get another dog?"

"No. He—Blue—was one of a kind. I didn't want another one."

A rough sound left her. "And here I've brought a slew of them into your home. No wonder you don't like them. Or me."

He wasn't about to tell her he was adjusting to the canine company—and hers—better than he'd ever thought possible.

"If you tell anyone I let you hold me, I'll deny it."

Her fighting spirit was coming back, and it made him smile. He squeezed her gently. "And why is that?"

"Teachers are supposed to be strong and tough, but today...I don't feel like either."

He pressed a kiss to the top of her head, every protective instinct he had clamoring to the surface faster than the next.

He liked holding her. Liked how she felt in his arms. He imagined Emma as beautiful but realized her looks didn't matter. It was how she made him feel. Amazing how perspectives changed. "Today you don't have to be strong. But I do think you're tough."

Her moist breath seeped into his shirt when she sighed.

"So are you, Ian. That's why everyone gets so frustrated with you. You can do this."

Maybe in some ways but not in others. Not yet anyway. He didn't want to talk about his blindness. He was sick of talking about it. Sick of thinking about it. It was nice to focus on something else. On her. Nice to think of her needing the hug he gave her.

"You know it's true," she said, her words muffled by his shirt. "You just have to find something to inspire you. Isn't there something you used to do that you think you can't do now? Something you miss? Something you'd like to do for fun? And don't you dare make a snarky comment, or I'll smack you again."

He smiled at the threat and retracted the words that had appeared automatically, giving her questions some more thought. Given the need, he could still point a gun and pull the trigger. He might not hit the target, but sometimes multiple shots worked as well as a deadly one. But that wasn't what she meant. And because he could tell she needed a distraction from all that had happened, a purposeful way she could help him, he said, "Darts."

She wanted a challenge? He'd give her one.

"Darts?"

"Duncan and I used to play a lot, even won some tournaments during our days in the military. If you want to prove that I can still do the things I used to do, teach me to play darts and win, fair and square. You think of a way for me to do that, and maybe I'll go along with some of your tutoring lessons."

"No maybe about it. You'd have to agree."

"Fine," he said, releasing her. "I agree. But that's for later. I heard you pacing your room last night. You need to get some rest."

"I'm sorry I kept you up."

"I wasn't sleeping."

"Seems to be a lot of that going around." She inhaled and released a gusty sigh. "I'm going to take advantage of you feeling sorry for me and hold you to your word, you know."

"You have to find a way first."

"Oh, I will. You wait and see. Come, Tink. Tucker."

Ian listened to them head toward the door before he sat back down, determined not to let this meal go to waste. Quinn had also made bacon, and there was fresh fruit. Ten minutes ago, he'd been ready to spend another day battling the darkness with no hope of true escape. Now he realized he looked forward to seeing what Emma could come up with to force his cooperation. If nothing else, it could be amusing.

"Ian?" she murmured.

"Yeah."

"Thank you. For the hug that didn't happen."

"Any time."

"Do you need me to help you back to your room?"

"No."

"Good for you," she said softly.

There was a measure of pride in her tone. Pride he felt himself at not running back to his rabbit hole. It wasn't much...but it was a start.

Chapter 10

It was early evening before Emma awoke from her much-needed nap.

Talking with Ian had helped. It had also given her some insight to his way of thinking. The loss of his dog had scarred him, so much so he hadn't wanted another. That sort of distancing was a coping mechanism, and it made sense that Ian retreated to work through his grief over the loss of his vision. The trick now was to help him out of his comfort zone.

She showered away the cobwebs and worked on her appearance, not wanting to give the men any more reason to pity her. With her hair divided into fairly equal sections, she stood in the bathroom and braided the length in two loose ropes that hung over her shoulders while she contemplated Ian's request.

Ian wanted to play darts—accurately. And having played since childhood while working at The Shak, she knew exactly how competitive things could get in the leagues. Ian wouldn't accept anything less than mastering the challenge. And why should he?

Hair done, she moved into the bedroom and straightened the

sheet and blanket on her bed even though she'd be climbing back into it soon. When she was sure her room was in order, she walked down the hallway in search of what she needed to grant Ian's wish.

One hallway led to the foyer, and she eventually ventured upstairs, running her hands over every table she found.

A door on her right opened abruptly, and she jumped. She'd thought everyone but Ian was out of the house.

"What are you doing up here?" Quinn asked in his unusual voice.

Emma found herself wanting to take a step back, realizing she had intruded. "I'm looking for something. A clock."

"You're wearing a watch."

"It's not for me, it's for Ian."

"He can't see it."

"No, but he can hear it. Do you know where I can find one?"

"Down the hall, top of the stairs."

"No, that one won't work. Ideally, I need a table clock, a loud one, and a table to set it on."

"Why?"

If Quinn ever spoke in full paragraphs, she just might keel over from the shock. Still, she found it sweet that he'd stayed and kept Jolie company last night in the kennel. Emma had sought comfort from Goli and had spent several hours snuggled up to Goli's massive body. Jolie wouldn't leave, not even when Quinn chose to stay in the kennel as well. Given his many responsibilities with Ian and with the remodel and security being installed, he should have been in bed last night, not watching over them. "Can you keep a secret?"

"You'd be surprised."

Of that she had no doubt. Quinn seemed to be the most mysterious of all the men, the one who let the others speak while he listened and observed. Jolie admitted that Quinn unnerved her, but given her backward and shy personality, it wasn't hard to understand why. "Ian wants to play darts. If I can show him a way to play, he's agreed to cooperate with lessons and let me help him."

"And the clock?"

A new intensity filled Quinn's tone. What he didn't say with words, he expressed other ways. He was worried about his friend. "The clock will act as a focal point he can hear. It simply has to be loud enough to be heard if others are in the room talking."

"Come with me."

Quinn took hold of her arm and guided her down the hall to yet another hallway, into the wing she and Genie hadn't explored because it wasn't part of the house currently being used.

She heard the clock before they drew near. "Is it small? Unobtrusive?"

"You decide."

He placed one of her hands atop the wooden base.

Emma felt it, measuring, and smiled. "Perfect. Can I take the table, too?"

"You take the clock. I'll bring the table."

Emma's scent reached Ian seconds before the sound system shut off. "I was listening to that."

"And now you're not. Come with me."

"I'm not hungry," he growled, in a foul mood because he wanted a drink to take the edge off the encroaching evening. His decent mood of the morning was gone. She needed to leave.

"This isn't about food. It's about darts."

"Darts?" That surprised him. He'd figured it would take

longer for her to scheme up something. "Emma, you know I can't—"

"Since when does a soldier say *can't*? And I assure you, you can. Unless you aren't going to honor our deal, and this is your way of crying uncle?"

If she'd figured out a way for him to play, he was sure going to make it work to his advantage. "Where?"

"The den."

"Why not here?"

"You want to spend more time in your room?"

"Let's go." Ian was on his feet and waiting for her when she crossed the floor to him.

Taking his hand, she placed it on her shoulder and led them out of his bedroom and down the hall to the study.

"I don't know what you've come up with, but it's doubtful it will work."

"He of little faith. It'll take some practice, but if you can aim, it will work. Trust me."

Beneath his hand, he felt the warmth of her skin, the slender bones and angles, the scent of her hair in his nose as he walked a step behind.

If she could teach a blind man to play darts, he'd keep his word, no matter how difficult or inept he felt relearning the chores meant for children.

"Here we are," she said, pausing to shut the door.

The scent of his father's favorite cigars still lingered in the air after all these years, bringing with it the memories of guilt and anger he'd felt after his father's death. But it also brought back memories of good times, too. Like studying while James MacGregor worked at his big desk, listening to his mother play the piano down the hall.

"I asked Quinn to move the dartboard and a couple other things into this room so you'd have privacy to practice."

He appreciated the thoughtfulness. "Thanks."

"You're welcome. Now—what do you hear? Concentrate and tell me."

He frowned at the request but focused his attention on the room. He heard a fly in the window, the buzzing stopping intermittently as the insect hit the glass. Outside, someone mowed the yard, but the sound of the mower didn't drown out the sound of hammering.

"Good," she said when he recited that back to her. "What else? Ignore the fly, but concentrate on sounds only in this room."

It took some effort. Between the fading intensity of the setting sun outside the window and the knowledge the claustrophobia was right there on the edge of his subconscious, the only other thing he was aware of was Emma's hand covering his where it rested on her shoulder and... "A clock."

"Exactly. Where is the clock?"

"Straight ahead."

"Yes. Now don't take offense, but we're going to start off easy, okay?"

"What do you mean?"

She led him forward, her white cane tapping lightly against the rug-covered wood floor. Left, right, left. Step by step.

"The clock is centered on a table exactly three feet beneath the dart board. I had Quinn measure it because he said you were good with distances."

He got the concept. But being good with eyeing distances visually and doing it blind were two different things. More of a challenge.

He smiled, glad she couldn't see it. Because the idea was ingenious. "Focus on the clock, aim above it?"

"Quinn marked the tournament distance with a piece of tape on the floor by the desk. You can start there right off the bat or closer and work back. You ready to give it a try? You said if I found a way, you'd cooperate. Time to soldier up."

He wished he would've met Emma before. Known her before. Given what she'd been through in the last few days, he wanted more than ever to see her. Did she lift her chin while issuing that challenge? What did she look like? He'd held her, but it wasn't the same as being able to picture her face in his mind.

"Ian, you can do this. I know you can. Learning how means you are rising to the challenge. All the stuff you need to know? It's about strategy and tricks, planning. Isn't that big in the military?"

He closed his eyes and wiped his hand over them, pressing to relieve the tension. "Yeah."

"So learn the strategies," she said. "Turn it into a mind game if you have to. All the other stuff will fall into place if you do, and you will be amazed at how easy it is once you have a system. How to cook, use a white cane. How to go where you want to go and do the things you want to do *without needing help*. Isn't that worth spending some time with me?"

As much as he didn't want to be blind, he didn't want to be blind and useless even more. Helpless. Or the reason Duncan potentially lost his focus on a job and came home in a body bag.

His pride wouldn't let him accept help from Duncan or Quinn, but Emma showing him these things was different. Maybe she was rubbing off on him, but spending time with her was no longer such a bad thing to consider. "Fine."

"You agree? You'll do it? Even when you're mad at me and frustrated and want to quit? You'll trust me enough to stick with it?"

"I just said as much, sweetheart. Don't beat a dead horse." He moved the hand still resting on her shoulder, slid it up her neck, brushing her chin and running his thumb lightly over the fullness of her mouth. Feeling her tense, he said, "Sorry," and began to pull his hand away only to have her hold it in place.

"It's, um, okay," she said softly. "Go ahead if you're curious. I don't mind."

He didn't understand at first. All he'd wanted to do was touch her, but then it sank in that she was giving him permission to "see" her. He wasn't about to turn that down, but how did he go about it? He'd never done that before. Never had to.

"Like this," she said.

She slid her hand atop his and flattened his palm to her cheek and jaw.

"Feel the shape of my face, then use your fingertips to trace my eyes and nose. It will help you visualize."

Careful to keep his touch gentle, he followed instructions and took a moment to note the design of her features, frowning in frustration when he came up with a list of descriptions he couldn't piece together.

Small ears held long, dangly hoop earrings that were smooth and simple. Narrow face, prominent cheekbones. Soft, silky skin. Her eyebrows were arched, her lashes long enough to make an impression as they feathered over his thumbs. A straight nose, rounded at the tip. Wide, full lips that made him think of kissing her.

Shaking his head, he closed his eyes and arranged the features in his head, adding a squared chin and jawline. Those weren't at all surprising considering the stubborn nature she'd exhibited so far. And there, right in the middle of her chin, the tiniest of indentations.

He followed the shape of her jaw to the braids that stopped just below her shoulders. Her hair was loose by her face but the braids were thick. He liked the way she smelled and dipped his head lower, closer, to take a breath. "Your hair is long."

"Yes. And brown. It used to be dark brown but the *Besties* say it's gotten lighter over the years. Um... Ian, we should get started."

He'd gotten to her. He had been focused on his task, on the sounds of the room like she'd told him, which was why he heard the hitch in her breath, the slight tremble in her voice, the nervous flutter of her hands against his chest as she tried to put some space between them.

Dibbs' niece, he reminded himself.

Lifting his hands from her, he took a step back. "Where are the darts?"

Emma rolled over in her bed in the wee hours of Wednesday morning, wondering what it was that had disturbed her. She listened closely, hoping Ian wasn't out in the hallway again, so desperate for a drink he found himself at the cellar door.

A dull thud sounded, followed seconds later by another. Then another. Silence followed along with the awareness of the sound's origin. She imagined Ian feeling his way along the floor and the wall of the den, finding the darts to retrieve them.

Floating on the edges of sleep, she remembered how Ian had touched her face, stroked his fingers down her hair, over her mouth. For a moment, she'd found herself leaning into him, wondering if he was going to kiss her.

Her mind wandered, strayed into the dangerous what-if territory. Ian was technically her student and still reeling from his blindness and trying to adjust. She couldn't let herself get drawn in. And what about her? Too much had happened recently for her to think straight. She had no business thinking about any man that way at the moment.

Just a fleeting thought. Nothing to worry about.

Her mind drifted on to other things. Her father's upcoming wedding. What she was going to do now that Roxy was gone.

Soon, the thuds began again, and she smiled, closing her sleep-gritty eyes before burying her face in the softness of the pillow.

Better darts than the cellar door.

The next morning, Ian was in his room when a knock sounded.

Before he could tell whoever it was to go away, the door opened, and in an instant, the soft tread identified his visitor. "Get out."

"How rude," Emma chided. "What's got you so crabby? If you're that hungry, you didn't have to wait on me to come get you."

Like he would go to breakfast without her?

He didn't like the way he was starting to depend on Emma, distraction or not.

"Did you play darts all night?"

He'd returned to his room an hour ago, when he'd heard the others stirring. "I'm sorry if I disturbed you."

"You didn't. I'm just wondering why you're in such a mood today. Something happen?"

She'd happened. Playing darts with Emma had been a lesson in humility.

She'd laughed a lot. She'd teased. She'd kept him from drowning in anger when he couldn't hit the dartboard on the first try the way he'd wanted to. Or the second. Or the third. Not even the twentieth.

Every time one of the darts had bounced off the wall and

fallen to the ground, he'd felt like a failure, although by the early hours of the morning, he'd been hitting the board and sticking more often than not.

But touching Emma yesterday, using his hands to "see" her, had been a huge mistake. It made him aware of how attracted he was to Emma even though he didn't have a clue what she looked like.

Emma kept the darkness at bay—until she left the room or the house, and he was alone with it again.

"I've brought visitors. Hope you don't mind. Say hello to Ian, guys."

The sound of panting and multiple paws reached his ears, and because he was in a bear of a mood he said, "I don't want dogs in my room."

"Too late. They're here."

"Emma, please. Get out. We'll...work later."

"I can't. I have a shift to work at The Shak. Come to breakfast."

"I'm not hungry," he lied just before he heard a high-pitched bark.

Emma released a deep sigh.

"Wow. Back to that, are we?"

He shut his mouth. He had agreed to cooperate, and he knew it.

"How about some fresh air?"

Fresh air wouldn't help what ailed him. "No. I'd prefer uninterrupted peace and quiet."

"Tinkerbell, *fetch*."

She really was going to sit there and play with her dogs?

"You made progress yesterday, Ian. And last night, from the sound of it."

"It's just darts."

"It's not just darts. Look, I know it's hard to accept. I know everything in you rebels and wants things to return to the way they were before, but it's not going to happen, and the sooner you accept it, the better it will be."

"Better?" he repeated, the word bitter.

"Yes! Ian, we're the lucky ones. You were shot, and you *lived*. You had a blood clot travel to your *brain*, but you *lived*. If that's not lucky—if that's not *blessed*—I don't know what is. How old are you?"

"Thirty-three."

"So you had thirty-three years of sight. And being your father's son and in the military, I'll bet you've seen most of the world, haven't you?"

Nearly every continent, as well as major cities, rice paddies, and beaches that made a man thankful to be alive.

"I've always dreamed of traveling. I've heard the water in the Bahamas is sooo blue it looks like a sapphire."

"It does in spots. In others it's bright turquoise."

"It sounds beautiful. You should be thankful you got to see it."

Her words brought about reluctant agreement. Waking from a troubled doze with the massive headache had left him having a pity party for himself. Yes, in a way, he was lucky. Hard as it was to swallow. "How can I be content, Emma? Having had my sight, how can I be content now? Are you happy being blind?"

"No."

"But you can stand there and tell me you wouldn't change a thing?"

"Of course I would. We would *all* change something, blind or not. But I've learned to count my blessings rather than whine about what I don't have or can't get."

He sucked in a deep breath at the insult. Grown men didn't whine. And soldiers...

"Why spend your life grumpy and miserable and locked in

this room? Why not focus on the positive? That is the difference between how Duncan and the men treat you now and how they'll treat you when you get off your butt and prove to them you're still the man they knew."

"I'm not the man they knew, and I'm sick of being treated like a child. They pity me. All of them."

"Then let them! Pity is a good emotion to feel so long as you're not feeling it for yourself. Let people feel pity for you; let them help you if you need help. It's not a be-all end-all kind of thing."

"I can feel them staring at me," he grumbled, giving in to the anger inside him. Anger was better than pity. She was right about that.

"So wear sunglasses. I have a lot of blind friends online who wouldn't dream of going out without sunglasses. They feel it helps give them a buffer. If you like, I can have the *Besties* look for some for you. Morgan loves doing stuff like that."

He hadn't thought of sunglasses, but it did appeal. "That... Thank you. Have Duncan give you some cash."

"Glasses aside, Ian, you have to learn to be a man people don't pity, to not be someone who draws attention to himself by not knowing how to help himself. You change the attitude, and you'll see the difference."

Tucker licked his knuckles, and suddenly Ian found himself petting the dog. If it took a dump on his floor...

"So, one more thing before I stop lecturing."

"Can't wait to hear it," he said dryly.

"Duncan told me about Mr. Winston and his daughter coming to see you."

"Duncan can handle it. He shouldn't have said anything."

"I'm glad he did. Duncan asked if I would talk to you about them."

Of course he had. Duncan knew strategy. And the fact Ian

hadn't tossed Emma out the door meant she was his weak link. Sometimes. "It's not going to happen."

"You can't sit there and listen to what they have to say? Let them thank you so the girl can have closure?"

Ian ran a hand over his hair. He heard the ball bounce and roll, heard the frantic scramble of the dog's paws as it chased its target. "The Winstons are none of your concern."

"They are when they impact your progress. What's holding you back? You have shut yourself off from everything and everyone, and I feel like there's something... something more than embarrassment or even pity involved here. Talk to me. Maybe I can help."

"You can't." She wouldn't understand. How many people were claustrophobic *and* blind? She obviously wasn't or she wouldn't be ready to take on the world.

"You won't give me a chance? You can trust me, Ian. What's it going to take to prove that to you?"

He held his silence, hoping she'd give up. Hoping the desire to share his secret would go away.

"Fine. Maybe one day soon you will confide in me. But hear me when I say this, okay? Sitting here? You're never going to be a man again, just some shell of a person people continue to pity because you're too wound up in the past to see what you can do with your future. Tucker, no. *No.*" An exasperated sigh left her lips.

Ian listened closely and heard the sound of puppy growls. Tucker and his sister were fighting over the ball.

One of the dogs suddenly began to whimper and whine, then bark.

"Potty time, eh, Tink? Ian, would you like to come with us for a walk? It's a beautiful day outside."

For the first time, he was able to distinguish between the dogs' pitches. So that was how she did it. "Why bother if I can't see it?"

"Oh, Ian. Because you can smell it in the air, feel it on your skin. Even taste it."

Now that was intriguing. "How do you taste a beautiful day?" Surely she didn't mean... No, that was his mind thinking of her. Of kissing and tasting *her*.

"Come with me and I'll show you."

"Show me?"

"Yes."

Surprising himself, Ian got to his feet, unable to resist the lure of Emma Wyatt.

Chapter 11

She didn't let him kiss her. Emma's reference to tasting the day came in the form of honeysuckle vines growing on the old garden trellis. Using a rope Duncan had apparently tied from the kitchen porch post that intersected with the gazebo in the garden and then stretched on to the stable-turned-kennel, Emma led Ian out into the hot sun and muggy air.

The scent of honeysuckle surrounded them, and he let Emma talk him into sipping the nectar buried in the base of the petals. It was good, sweet. A reminder of his childhood when his parents were both alive and well.

The sun felt good on his skin. Bees buzzed, birds sang, the sounds overshadowed by the whack of hammers, drills, and saws being used by the workers. Duncan had kept Ian informed of the upgrades, though he'd listened with half an ear, too focused on his next drink to pay attention to the details of alarms, grids, and safety measures.

Duncan had also mentioned something about turning the cellar into a fireproof panic room. Ian couldn't help but laugh at the irony there. Were he ever to be locked in it, there would definitely be some panicking going on.

He would have to tell his brother the truth at some point, but Ian hoped to conquer his phobia before the work on the panic room began. No use creating something he'd never use.

He wasn't sure where the men were at the moment, but throughout his walk with Emma, he felt the neck-prickling sensation of being watched. But when he turned his head in that direction, the feeling would go away.

It made him self-conscious and hyperaware of every bumbling step he took by Emma's side. The ground was uneven in spots and made him feel like a clumsy boy who hadn't grown into his feet.

And no doubt the men were surprised to see him outside at all.

"You're tense. Just relax. Take a deep breath. Oh, do you smell that?"

He inhaled, tripped over a patch of overgrown grass, and swore.

"Watch your step."

"Hard to watch it when I can't see where I'm going."

Emma's laughter filled the air. "Aren't you Mr. Sunshine today. Anytime I trip in public, I like to pretend I'm dancing. Makes people laugh."

"What am I supposed to be smelling?" he demanded, refusing to do something so ridiculous. But when he imagined her doing it, it made him smile. Almost.

"Life. That's the smell of life, Ian. You are alive. The day is whatever you choose to make it, warmed by the sun and sweet with honeysuckle. You don't get this smell in your room. In there, life just passes you by."

After a late lunch, Emma walked Ian back to his room so she could go get ready for work. He didn't like the idea of her working at a diner, couldn't imagine how she managed to not get taken by the patrons. And what about the losers hitting on her? How was she treated when she wasn't able to defend herself?

A part of him was curious about the logistics of waitressing blind, but a bigger part of him was ashamed that she did so much while he did so little. And her laughter today during their walk...

That's the smell of life, Ian. You are alive. The day is whatever you choose to make it, warmed by the sun and sweet with honeysuckle. You don't get this smell in your room. In there, life just passes you by.

He understood what she was saying. He'd known a few couch potatoes in his life. The only excuse he had was that she didn't have to deal with claustrophobia the way he did. If he didn't always feel like he was being swallowed up, maybe he could focus on the future. But he had to get a grip on his phobia first. Shouldn't he be used to it by now?

A cold nose pressed against his hand. He frowned at the dog's determined intrusion, but given the time of day and approach of evening, Ian didn't mind. "You sneak away again, Tucker?"

Tucker had come to Ian's room the same night Emma had put Roxy down. And while the dog was a pain in the rear and determined when it came to forcing Ian to play tug-of-war and fetch, the animal proved to be good company as well.

Ian could hear the men in the other end of the house. Mostly bangs, and every now and again, a burst of ornery laughter. The sound brought back memories of missions, the ribbing and conversation that came after a job done well.

Quinn and the others were probably cooking dinner. Hanging out. "If you want any scraps thrown your way, you'd better get going," he told Tucker, rubbing the dog's ears. "I won't take you."

He'd grown used to Emma forcing him down the hall for his meals, even though he waited and ate after the guys were finished and the room emptied. Hearing them, he couldn't bring himself to go on his own, not without her there to lighten the mood when he walked in and everyone got quiet.

A low whimper emerged from Tucker.

"What's the matter? You in trouble again?"

"Yeah, he is," Quinn said from the doorway. "He ate two of your father's personalized golf balls."

Ate them? "Does he need a vet?"

"Doesn't look sick to me. Just guilty. It was a three-pack, and the balls have since reappeared in the hallway."

Ian rubbed Tucker behind his ears and received a thorough swipe of the tongue for the effort. He ought to be angry, but a deep belly laugh caught him by surprise. "Got bored, did you? Eh?"

"Dinner's almost ready. You coming?" Quinn asked.

Ian hesitated. He didn't want to spend the evening with the black cloud in his head, but he didn't feel comfortable with the others, either. "I'll eat in the den. You mind bringing it there?"

"How's the dart throwing?"

"Improving."

Ian didn't hear his friend leave, but after a moment, he stood and patted the leg closest to Tucker. "Tucker, *nu'la.*"

Surprisingly, Tucker moved beside him and pressed his side against Ian's leg. Unbelievable. "Good boy," Ian said with a pat on Tucker's head.

He sidestepped to put some distance between them and repeated the command. "Tucker, *nu'la.*"

Once more, the dog moved to Ian's side, and Ian praised the animal with a few vigorous rubs of the dog's head.

"What did you say?" Quinn asked softly.

Ian had thought he was alone, but he felt a measure of pride in Tucker's response. "It means 'come' in Cherokee."

"You're teaching the dog Cherokee?"

"I've experimented a few times, but he seems to understand it better than English. I learned it in school when I did a paper on Native American Code Talkers in World War II."

His too-serious friend chuckled, but Ian's thoughts remained on Tucker's quick responses. Would it hurt to train Tucker in Cherokee so long as it didn't interfere with Emma teaching the dog English commands?

"I'll bring the food to the den."

Ian nodded his thanks. After the walk outside and "tasting the day," he did feel better, not that he'd tell Emma that. But she was right. He needed to lighten up and laugh at something, and the thought of Tucker responding to him rather than Emma brought out his competitive side.

If keeping his sanity was all about strategy, maybe for now, until he came up with a better plan, throwing darts and occupying himself training Tucker would be enough to keep the claustrophobia at bay.

Duncan walked into The Shake Shak an hour before closing. He sat on a stool opposite the counter and talked with Emma while she closed up for the night.

Her father hadn't shown up as planned due to an excavation snafu at the house site, and she'd worked Frank's shift to keep her mind off of Roxy and the other life-based balls she juggled.

"Something wrong?" Duncan asked, taking her hand and placing it over his forearm as they prepared to leave.

"No. Thanks for the ride home. I hated to ask Genie because it would put her on the roads so late. You calling on the way from Atlanta saved me."

"Any time. I spent quite a bit of time watching you."

"Oh. Wow. Okay." Nothing about that statement unnerved her at all.

"Don't be self-conscious."

"It's a little hard not to be. Did I do anything embarrassing?"

He laughed, probably thinking it was a joke. But really. Had she?

"No. You're teaching me quite a lot about the abilities of the blind, Emma. Things I never knew or even considered until meeting you. Now if only some of that knowledge will rub off on Ian."

"He's coming around. Slowly," she said, thinking of Ian's joke earlier today. It was more a frustrated statement of fact about not being able to see where he was walking, but said in the tone Ian had used, there was no doubt he had poked fun at himself. It was a good sign and one she was glad to hear.

Thank you, Lord.

"That's good to know. I think his teacher has a lot to do with it."

She smiled at the compliment. "It takes time, Duncan. No one wants to accept that this is it. Day after day of darkness? It's depressing. I mean, it's one thing if you were born blind and never knew what it was like. From day one, you learn to make do, and you dream of what could've been, but you don't actually know what you're missing. I have friends who've always been blind, and some of them say while it's not any easier, since they've never seen a sunset or whatever, they don't miss it as much as someone like Ian."

"Or you?"

She tilted her head to one side, nodding. "Or me," she agreed. "I miss color. I *love* color. Flowers, rainbows. One year for my birthday, my parents let me paint the walls in my room anything I wanted."

"Sounds like a scary concept for a parent."

"I'm sure it was. And when I picked out the brightest, wildest colors... I have no doubt they regretted their decision. But they didn't say anything, not even my father, who is a white-wall kind of guy."

"What did you paint? Some kind of colorful peace sign?"

"Nope. I made a mural of all my favorite things. I painted a cross and a huge rainbow, a clown fish, lots of bright green grass, and giant flowers. One flower took up the entire wall."

"Sounds like a great room for a kid."

"It was. What was your room like growing up?"

"I went to military school. I had a roommate and gray walls."

"Oh."

"Don't look so sad. It was fine. Ian was right down the hall, and with that many boys in one spot, there were a lot of antics going on in any given day. It was like rooming with a lot of brothers."

The image made her smile, and despite the sadness of his childhood due to his parents' deaths, she was glad he'd been able to see the positive. "I can imagine. So from there, I'm guessing you and Ian went into the military and then...?"

"Private security for me and what was supposed to be career military for Ian."

She wasn't sure what to make of that. How did one decide to do that sort of thing? "Why did you choose private security?"

Duncan nudged her toward whatever vehicle he'd brought to drive her home.

"My father wasn't mugged like the news reports said," Duncan admitted. "He was out on a run, but he was taken and held for three days before his captors killed him and dumped his body on the street like a piece of trash."

"Duncan." She didn't know what to say to that.

"The U.S. does not negotiate with kidnappers," he murmured, as if by rote. "Ian stayed in the military because some of the missions he was sent on were secret rescue missions, but as soon as I felt I had the training I needed, I got out."

"For private security."

"Why not? It pays well, and I protect people with families and homes they want to make it back to when they travel."

"People like your father. That's very admirable."

"It's a living, like any other."

No, it was more than that. Duncan put his life on the line to protect others. So had Ian. The brothers were both to be admired for the sacrifices they had made. "Was Ian a good leader?" she asked softly. "He was his team leader, correct?"

The smell of the hot pavement was thick and sharp in her nose, tinged with cigarettes and mulch. For the first time, she realized she couldn't smell Duncan, not a hint of soap or shampoo or cologne.

Come to think of it, she didn't remember ever picking up a scent from Ian, either, other than when she was close enough to smell his breath or skin. Just the scent of... man. Was that on purpose? To not be detected if the wind happened to blow the wrong way? She had to think so.

Duncan unlocked the vehicle and opened the door for her.

"Step up. I brought the SUV. As to the question... Ian was the best," Duncan said as he steadied her with a hand on her arm. "That's why all of this has been so hard."

She could only imagine. Having been pulled from that life and thrust into one of darkness... Some men would have wished for death or even taken it a step further and ended their lives, unable to cope with the aftermath of having their sight taken away.

The fact that Ian was still here and bellowing orders said something to her—he wanted to cope. If only she could figure out what held him back.

How's Jolie?" Ian asked the next morning as they walked toward the den with the pups in tow.

"She's fine. The broken window has been replaced, and everything is back to normal."

During her shift at the Shake Shak, Emma had learned a brick had broken the front window of Cuppa Jo's. The police considered it a college prank or the act of a drunk—or both—but thankfully Jolie's security alarm had gone off, preventing further damage or theft.

Emma stopped and felt for the edge of the doorframe to guide Ian inside without incident. She liked coming to the den. It smelled of rich, sweetly pungent cigars and old leather.

The fabrics in the room varied in texture from smooth to grained to velvety soft. There was a window seat, too, and she had developed the habit of curling up on it while Ian practiced.

She liked the feel of the sun on her face, and in between dart throws and her verbal instructions on how to go about doing this or that, Ian told her anecdotes about his childhood.

According to Ian, the bench Emma favored had also been his mother's chosen spot because it overlooked the terrace that led to the pool and the courtyard garden.

Little by little, Emma was adding to the mental map in her head, learning the twists and turns of the large house and how the rooms were arranged on the grounds.

Those weren't the only things that had to be memorized. Everything sighted people took for granted, she had to learn by feel and memorization. The placement of all the furniture was an issue, remembering what rooms were what. Even learning where the utensils were in the kitchen. Confining her efforts to a handful of rooms in the twenty-room house didn't help as much as one might think because it still took time.

While she led Tink and Tucker to the window seat to keep them out of Ian's path, Ian found the darts and began tossing them. The first throws always went wide and hit the walls, the sound shallow.

Ian threw the last dart and walked toward the board to fetch them with shuffling steps. "Lift your feet," she ordered.

Ian immediately stopped where he stood.

From across the room, she sensed his tension and embarrassment that she'd pointed out a flaw. "I'm trying to help you, Ian. Don't shuffle when you walk. If you're afraid of running into something, let me show you how to use a white cane."

"No."

"Okay, fine. A service animal—"

"No."

"Why on earth not? Because they're for *blind* people? Guess what? You're blind. Stop standing in your own way."

"Maybe I wouldn't feel the need to shuffle if your dogs weren't always underfoot."

"That's an excuse and you know it. The dogs aren't over there. Do you think I'd take a chance on you hitting them with a dart?"

Ian muttered under his breath.

"Tinkerbell, down. Good girl," Emma crooned when she detected Tinkerbell's immediate response. Tink's hot doggy breath bathed Emma's ankle. "Tucker, down."

Not in the mood for Tucker's disobedience or Ian's attitude, she gathered patience from her reserve stores and tried again. "Tucker, *down.*"

The leash attached to her wrist indicated Tucker was on his feet, tugging against the restraint to cross the room to Ian. "No."

Tucker whined and the leash pulled taut again.

"Tucker, *down*." Emma bent and tried to nudge the fifty-pound pup in the correct pose, but Tucker eluded her and rose to his hind legs, placed both front paws on her shoulders, and swiped his tongue across her chin. "Tucker, no! No!"

Tired from a sleepless night spent listening to Ian throwing darts with increasing force, Emma pushed the dog back on all four paws and grabbed Tucker by his collar, burying her hands deep into his silky fur. *"Down."*

Tucker stood firm, pulling against her hold, and Emma's last frazzled nerve snapped. The fire, Roxy's death, Laney's apparent abandonment because her sister hadn't called or stopped by the diner since leaving them at Tasha's vet clinic that horrible day, her father getting *married*. It was too much. Too, too much. Now Tucker's disobedience topped off the list, and she couldn't handle more.

"Emma?"

Oh so thankful Ian couldn't see her less-than-stellar moment, Emma hid her face in Tucker's thick neck and hugged the mischievous dog, inhaling long, slow breaths she tried to keep quiet, all in an attempt to stem the hot prickle of tears. She would not cry when she had so much to be thankful for. She would not stoop to Ian's self-pitying level. She would *not*.

But just when she'd almost calmed the barrage of emotions she felt, a choked breath escaped her.

"Emma?" Ian demanded. "What's wrong?"

Determined, she lifted her head and swallowed. "Nothing."

"Don't lie to me."

"Everything's fine."

"Yeah, right. You're lying. I can tell."

"How?" she demanded in an attempt to bring them back to a teacher-student level. Not everything was about not running into furniture. A wise blind person learned to tell when someone was being deceptive.

"Stop. Now's not the time to try and teach me."

"I think it is," she said softly, thickly. "How do you know I'm lying?"

"The sound. Your voice. When you said nothing was wrong, the pitch changed."

"Very good. Sighted people tend to watch for visual clues to what the other person is saying. Some say over ninety percent of communication is visual."

"Answer the question."

She rubbed Tucker's ears. "I had a moment of weakness."

Emma released her grip on Tucker's neck and stood. Tucker immediately took off, the leash on Emma's wrist jerking her hand away from her body.

"I have him. Let go."

Emma pulled the leather off her wrist and allowed Ian to take control of her errant canine. "He likes you."

A sharp rap sounded on the den's door.

"We're blind, not deaf," Ian said to whomever was on the other side.

Emma smiled. She liked it that Ian was becoming more comfortable talking about blindness, even in the general sense, rather than avoiding all references to it.

"Time for lunch," Duncan said through the door. "Emma needs to eat even if you don't."

Ian sighed his frustration at being interrupted. "Let's go."

"You're not going to complain about having to go to the kitchen today?" Ian didn't respond and Emma startled when she suddenly sensed Ian directly in front of her. "Oh!"

Ian had moved closer. Without shuffling. Without making a sound, actually. She wouldn't have known he was there at all except for her sensory awareness of him, of his warmth and the energy she felt when he was near.

Ian's hand found her arm and slid up to her shoulder, not

stopping until he cupped her face in his hand. Her breath stalled in her chest.

"I'm sorry for your losses," he murmured. "All of them. And the fact you're having to put up with me on top of everything else you've been through."

"It's... You're not so bad."

"But I'm not making it any easier on you, am I?"

"You wouldn't be nearly as interesting if you did," she said lightly.

"Emma, you can still take the out I offered. Duncan would understand. So would I."

She placed her hand over his and closed her eyes, ignoring his words yet relishing the simple, gentle gesture for the show of warmth and caring that it was. *And the fact he's trying to get rid of you?* "Would you understand?"

"If it's what you wanted, yes."

Wait, what? What *she* wanted? Wasn't it what *he* wanted? "I'm not going anywhere. You're stuck with me," she said, her voice firm. "Nice try, though."

Ian released a sound, possibly a laugh, and pulled her against his side, hugging her close.

"I'm trying, you know."

He whispered the words into her hair, but she heard them loud and clear. "I know you are."

Chapter 12

After lunch, Emma insisted they go back to Ian's room, much to his displeasure. "I'll hire it done."

"Why, when you can do it yourself? Here, like this."

Emma's hands guided his as he tried to attach the square-shaped button onto the bottom of his shirt. Sewing. She wanted to teach him sewing. So far all he'd managed so far was to bleed on the thing. "I don't have the— Sh-whh-ow!"

Her throaty chuckle blew the little hairs at the base of his neck. With her leaning over him as she was, he smelled the scent of her hair, the heat of her body burning into his because she was so close.

Like it or not, he was beginning to react to her. First because she was a woman, second because she was Emma. Strong, frustrating, irritating *Emma*.

"Poor baby," she crooned, her tone teasing. "Ian, you don't have to be good at it, but you need to know how to do it and what the different shapes mean. The best way of remembering the system and being able to pick something out to wear at a second's feel is to do it yourself, at least once. What shape means blue?"

"Round flat." Ian poked himself in the finger with the needle yet again. "Ah."

"Are you bleeding?" she asked, a smile in her voice.

"How should I know?" he grumbled, wondering how something so simple could be such a pain. He'd sewn up soldiers in the field. He'd sewn up his own wounds a time or two. Now he couldn't sew on a button?

"Let me see. Which one?"

He didn't need a nursemaid because of a needle stick, but her concern was sweet. "My thumb."

Emma took his hand in hers and ran one of her fingers over the area. "I don't feel any moisture. I think you'll live."

She let go of his hand. He felt her retreat—until he snagged her arm and drew her close again. "You think I didn't hear you gasp a few minutes ago?"

Her bubble of laughter brought a smile. For someone he'd hated when he'd first met her, she'd grown on him in a very short amount of time. And then some.

"Fine, you caught me. But I'm used to it. I expect I'll stick myself and have learned to handle the pain, unlike *someone* I know."

She thought him a wuss? "Those are fightin' words, Ms. Wyatt. Odds are you bled on my shirt," he told her, tugging on her hand until she had to adjust her position and lean forward, over him, even more.

"Ian?"

Her breath tickled his ear. "Time to pay up. I'm thinking recompense is in order."

He shifted in the oversized chair, held on to her arm with one hand while he used his free hand to find her shoulder.

From there, Ian slid his fingers into her hair and used his

recently pierced thumb to tilt her chin until he felt her breath on his lips.

"Ian, wh-what are you—"

Hoping that his aim this close was true, he slowly closed the distance between them, his lips hitting a little high and to the right. He quickly adjusted and fastened his lips over hers.

She tasted good, like honey and sweetness.

"Ian... Ian, s-stop." She drew away, her breath raspy and unsteady, like his. "We can't do this. I have to be able to teach you a-and that means keeping a professional distance. Besides, how do I know any woman wouldn't do?"

"I wasn't thinking about any woman just now. I wasn't kissing any woman. Only you. Besides, no other woman would want—" He broke off, realizing how he'd made that sound, but too late to stop the words.

"Ahhh, I see. No *sighted* woman would want you, but I'm blind and desperate enough to want an egotistical, self-pitying guy like you?"

He kept hold of her arm when she tried to pull away, careful not to hurt her but intent on maintaining contact because he didn't want to argue with a voice in the dark. "I didn't mean for it to sound that way."

"But it's what you're thinking, isn't it? Well, here's a clue since you obviously don't have one. I'm smart enough to realize you kissed me because I'm here, I'm convenient, and you want a distraction. Oh, and I'm blind, which means I'm acceptable because you're what? Intimidated at the thought of dating a sighted woman now?"

Hot embarrassment flooded every muscle in his body. "You're putting words in my mouth." But she'd certainly nailed his thoughts. He'd just meant... He didn't know what he meant, but it wasn't what she thought. "You can't blame me for wanting to kiss you."

"Oh, and why is that?"

"Fishing for compliments?"

"Of course not!"

He chuckled and held tight when she tried to push him away again. "You can't blame me for kissing you when there is so much about you I admire," he clarified. "You're a strong, fascinating woman. And, yeah, I'm intrigued. Wasn't that the point of this little experiment of yours and Duncan's?"

"If you hint that Duncan is paying me to sleep with you one more time, I'm going to smack you again," she said, giving him another shove.

Ian grabbed her by the waist, pulled her into his lap. She flailed a bit, but he was bigger, stronger, and in the space of a heartbeat, he'd lowered his head until his nose brushed hers. "I'm sorry. I did not mean that the way it sounded."

"Let go."

"Not until you hear me out. Emma, any woman wouldn't do. Just you," he murmured.

"Why should I believe you?"

He stroked her cheek with his thumb, fascinated by the softness of her skin. "Before you came, all I could think about was being blind, or getting booze. Now... You make me want to do more. Be more." He squeezed her. "Be someone you respect and like and want to be around, too."

"You're saying sweet things, Ian, but you're also trying to dig yourself out of the hole you've just dug."

Maybe he was trying to remove his foot from his mouth, but he meant every word. "Fine. I like how you know what it's like to be stuck in the dark, how you don't let it stop you. I like how brave you are because it gives me hope. I think," he drawled, his voice lowering even more, "I like you because I admire you more than you irritate me."

"Now there's a compliment."

"You know," he drawled, snuggling her closer, "sometimes when a woman goes on and on, there's only one way a guy can think of to shut her up."

Emma couldn't stop her head from whirling after Ian lowered his mouth to hers and kissed her again. Maybe she was crazy for being sucked in by his words, but with Ian's arm beneath her back, the way he cradled her shoulder in his palm and shifted her closer for better access, she couldn't deny him. Or herself.

His hair was long and cool beneath her fingers. As one kiss fed into another, she explored him, running her hands down his neck, over the top of his shoulders.

"Emma, you are amazing."

His lips found the spot just beneath her ear in the sensitive curve of her neck.

His touch made her skin tingle. "I-I refuse to be your play toy."

"I'll happily be yours."

Such a male response. One that brought a blush to her cheeks. "Fine. As my play toy, I want you to go to the Winston dinner. We have until the end of the week to get you ready for it."

Ian stilled and sighed, the expansion and contraction of his chest reminding her of where she sat.

She lowered her forehead to his, rubbing noses with him. "I know it can't be easy meeting with them, but this girl obviously needs closure. And you... You have to stop running from what happened and accept it."

"It's not that simple."

She opened her mouth but just as quickly closed it. What to say? "Why isn't it? Tell me, Ian."

Ian was silent a long moment. She knew she ought to feel self-conscious sitting on his lap the way she was, but with his arms now loosely linked at her hips, she waited, giving him time.

"I know it sounds childish considering the circumstances, but I don't want them here because I know what's going to happen."

"Go on," she urged.

"Meeting them...makes it real. I saved the girl, and I don't regret it but... I wish I wouldn't have gotten shot. I wish I wouldn't have had surgery—"

"You had a bullet in you. Surgery wasn't optional."

"I wish I wouldn't have been blinded. I can't... How do you do this?"

His voice was rough, hoarse. His emotions surrounding them in a bubble of heat. His arms hardened around her before Ian pulled her closer, resting his forehead against her upper arm. This time she didn't fight him at all.

"What if instead of thinking of this meeting as the end of who you were, you think of it as a beginning? The first step to the next part of your life? Part of a bigger plan for you?"

His lips brushed against her arm, and she allowed herself to enjoy the comfort of being held by him.

She was wrong about him not having a scent. It was subtle but there. Clean soap, warm skin, salt. Just...Ian. Her bitter, broken Ian.

Lightly, she ran her fingertips over his face. How strange to have kissed him but not "seen" him. She had only Aunt Rose's description of handsomeness to go by.

Blunt nose, crooked at the base as if it had been broken. Hard, slanting cheekbones, firm mouth. A stubble-roughened chin.

"How can it be the first step when I'm useless?"

"You are not useless, Ian. You're blind. It's only *one* aspect of you, but you're letting it define you. You need to find a new purpose, a new mission. Am I useless?" she asked, anger erupting from deep within her. Was that what he thought of her? "Because every time you say that, you're not only referencing you but also me and every other blind or challenged person out there. I resent it."

His lips brushed her arm again, and just that easy, her anger turned to emotions like caring and pain and empathy.

Ian couldn't return to work as a SEAL. He wasn't just mourning the loss of his vision but having a complete identity crisis. It was a blow to his masculinity, to who he was inside.

So what would convince Ian to change his attitude? He truly didn't strike her as a person who sat back and felt sorry for himself, but something kept him chained.

And she was smart enough to know she couldn't free him. He had to do that himself.

"Duncan asked me to join the group for dinner," she said casually. "Let me help you, and Mr. Winston and his daughter will leave never knowing how hard this is for you. Ian..."

She sought to offer comfort and support, and it seemed only natural to shift against him and slide her hands around his neck, to hold him. "No one wants to be blind, Ian. But we are, and we have choices to make in regard to how we deal with it. Make a choice. Right now. Put the past behind you and make peace with what's happened. If you do that, I can help you move on."

She felt every rise and fall of his chest, every breath he took a slow release of air against her cheek.

"Trust doesn't come easy for me."

"It doesn't come easy for any of us, but you can trust me. You know my agenda," she told him. "You know I need the money Duncan's paying me, but I get paid no matter what. But helping you? That's something I *want* to do. It hurts me to know you're like this. That you feel this way. I can help you find your footing. I can help you learn to cope, but you have to stop retreating every time you make progress."

"You'll be here?"

"Yes."

"Not just for the dinner. Until I know everything I need to know? No matter how long it takes?"

No matter how long? First he tried to get rid of her, now he was asking for a commitment?

Out of fear. Out of anxiety. But where will it leave you?

Saying yes risked her heart. She liked Ian. Cared for him far more than she should. The longer she stayed, the greater the risk.

But whatever the future brought, she wanted this time with him. No matter where it led or how much it hurt in the end. "Yes. I'll be here."

Chapter 13

Emma was a nervous wreck sitting at the dinner table beside Ian. It would have helped if he weren't so nervous. His grip on her knee stopped just short of painful, and she knew he was completely unaware of his hold.

Maxwell Winston was charming and older, from the sound of his voice. He'd immediately tried to play the gentleman and escort Emma to the table when dinner—catered by a restaurant in town—was announced. She'd run her hand over Ian's forearm in a reassuring gesture before declining and stating she already had an escort.

Dressed in the blue dress Aunt Rose had given her and pumps a half size too small, she had guided Ian to the table without incident. But despite a menu she and Quinn had worked hard to perfect because it allowed Ian more leeway in not making a mess, Ian refused to eat and sipped from the wineglass he held in his right hand since her knee was in his left.

A single glass with dinner was nothing to worry about, but on an empty stomach...

Kara Winston had barely said a word. Other than a brief

hello when introduced, the girl sat directly across from Emma, her fork pinging off the plate as she picked at her food. From the sound of it, Ian wasn't the only one who wasn't eating.

"So, Emma, you are a teacher?"

Maxwell—Max—was trying to make conversation. Emma managed a smile and discreetly tried to ease Ian's hand off her knee. "Of sorts. I teach a class at the university called PAWS for a Cause. It serves as a public service credit. We take in puppies that will later be used as service animals and raise them to the age that they can enter the appropriate programs. The dogs' food and vet care is paid for, so the students benefit from the experience and volunteer their time."

"Sounds like a wonderful endeavor," Max said.

"It is. Some of my adopted owners have raised pups every year they've attended Zailer University and gone on to stay in the program after they've graduated. It's very rewarding."

"I imagine so," Max said.

Silence descended once more, broken only by the scrape of knives and forks. Duncan came to the rescue, questioning Max about a political figure recently in Atlanta news.

Finally dinner was over, dessert served and eaten. Max, Duncan, Owen, and Quinn excused themselves from the table to smoke cigars out on the terrace.

"I'll give you a few minutes alone," she said, firmly removing Ian's hand from her knee.

Juggling her white cane in the unfamiliar heels took some doing, and she worried about falling on her face.

"Emma?" Ian said from the table.

She heard the tension in his voice, the anger that she was abandoning him. "Yes?"

"Never mind. We'll discuss it later," he said, the words sounding ominous but in a decidedly personal way.

A shiver raced over her spine. Later promised to be...interesting.

Realizing he was now alone with Kara Winston, Ian downed the last of his wine and wished he knew where Duncan had left the bottle. As much as he'd been drinking recently, the single glass had taken zero effect.

"You must think it strange that I wanted to see you."

Ian raised his head and tilted it slightly, more in Kara's direction. This afternoon, Emma's friend had stopped by with no less than ten pairs of sunglasses for him to try. It was embarrassing to have a total stranger fussing over him, but before the woman—Morgan—had entered the den, Emma had squeezed his shoulder and said, "She's going through a hard time right now, too. Say one word to make her cry, and I'll run you into a wall."

Duly warned, he'd kept his mouth shut and let Morgan try pair after pair of glasses on him until she'd eventually chosen two for his use and deemed the rest unsuitable, adding in a soft aside to Emma that the chosen ones gave him a sexy, bad-boy quality.

Right now he was simply glad there was a barrier between himself and Kara. He wasn't sure why it mattered, but it did, and he was extremely grateful to Emma for making it happen.

"To be honest," Kara continued, "I didn't want to. The meeting was arranged by my father and my shrink. But now I realize my shrink was right. I needed to do this. See you."

"I hope it helps you."

"Oh, it has," she said, a huff of a laugh following her words. "Sitting here watching you with your friends and girlfriend has made me realize you need to know exactly what you did that day."

A prickle of unease crawled up his neck at her tone. "Which is?"

"How you couldn't see what was right in front of you."

Come again?

"The irony is amazing if you think about it. Personally, I think it's hysterical how Karma's gotten her revenge."

Ian shifted, his gut tight as a drum. "What are you talking about? What couldn't I see?"

"How you, the supposed hero, murdered an innocent man. The man who came to rescue me—"

"I came to rescue you, Kara. Duncan and the others came to rescue you."

"No. No, you came to *retrieve* me like some pet who'd gone astray, and in doing so, you *killed* my boyfriend, not my kidnapper."

Ian froze in his chair, shook his head. No. That wasn't right. Intel said the "friend" was in on the kidnapping plot. Kara was wrong.

But her bitterness made him doubt his actions. Had he and Duncan missed something when they'd gone to get Kara out? All the men involved were members of a confirmed drug ring.

"You're thinking about it, aren't you? *Good*. Because it's true. Raj was a good guy. He was nice and sweet and real, and you didn't even hesitate before you murdered him."

"He was going to shoot me and probably you in the process," Ian said, barely recognizing his hoarse voice. Was Kara right?

"He was coming to protect me. Every day for the rest of your life, I want you to think about how being blind is what you deserve for killing him."

He flinched at her words, his mind reeling. He'd done a lot of praying since waking up in the hospital. Prayers that had gone unanswered. Was this why? "Kara—"

"I don't want to hear excuses. You murdered him. Coming

here tonight wasn't about closure or whatever crap my shrink spews to my father. It was about me wanting to see your face and know you got exactly what you deserved."

Her chair scraped against the wood floor as she stood, and the rapid tap of her heels indicated her upset as she stalked to the French doors leading from the dining room to the terrace.

The door slammed behind her, leaving Ian alone.

"Ian?" Emma called softly a few seconds later. "What happened?"

"Take me to my room," he ordered huskily, shooting to his feet.

"But they're still here. Maybe we should—"

"Take me to my room. Emma... *please*." He heard the tap of Emma's white stick on the floor and tried to disguise his sigh of relief. But the moment her hand found his, he clutched it tight. "Help me."

***

A noise woke Emma early Monday morning. She rolled over and tried to go back to sleep, but just as quickly, her lashes lifted because she knew where the sound had come from. The hallway.

Ian.

She shoved the sheet back and sat up. She'd taken Ian to his room earlier hoping to discover whatever it was that had put him in such a spiral, but he'd kicked her out. At a loss as to what to do, she had returned to the main part of the house and found Duncan bidding the Winstons good night.

Not having any answers for Duncan or herself, she had gone to bed, exhausted by the tension surrounding the event.

What had taken place between Ian and Kara? Ian had come so far in the last week, and she hated the thought of a setback.

She opened the door, careful to keep the pups inside her bedroom. At the end of the hall, she heard Ian muttering a string of obscenities, his voice bitter and broken and chock full of hatred. Fear?

"Ian?" Emma smoothed her hands over his back. His shirt was damp with the heat of his skin. "Ian, what's wrong?"

"Go back to bed."

She ran her hands over his taut back, slow and easy, soothing him as best she could. "Talk to me. What's wrong?"

When he didn't speak, she stepped closer and wrapped her arms around him, hugged him. She remembered in the time immediately following her accident, when she felt so out of control and desperate, her senses overwhelmed, how Laney would grab and hold her and not let go, no matter what. A compression hug to calm the nerves and lower blood pressure. To keep the person from panicking.

She squeezed him tighter and pressed a kiss to his back. "I'm not leaving you."

Silence met her words, but she didn't alter her hold on him, and eventually she felt his breathing ease.

"What if it's true?" Ian said gruffly.

"What if what's true?"

"Kara. She said..."

He repeated what the Winston girl had said to him, and Emma was shocked. How could anyone be so cruel knowing all Ian had lost? Kara had done an unspeakable amount of damage in the time she had been here. "She's angry and striking out, Ian."

"But is this my punishment for killing him?"

"Stop it," she ordered. "Stop right now. You were in danger. He had a gun, right? You believed he was holding her for ransom?"

"Yeah. The intel was all there."

The trembling she felt beneath her cheek was subsiding ever so slowly. Emma still didn't let go. "Then focus on that. Ian, Kara is a confused teenage girl. She hasn't had time to adjust. Think about it. The boy she cared for was accused of doing something horrible, and she's trying to rationalize it. She's not seeing the bigger picture, only the one in which she and her boyfriend were the victims, and he was a good guy. She's hurting and she struck out at you. That doesn't make what she said true. Your injury isn't a punishment from God."

"How can you be sure?"

"I just am," she said, loosening her hold when he turned and yanked her against his chest. He was a little rough, but she understood his need for contact, for something to center and ground him. "Ian, things happen. People get hurt. But *I* believe God can make things better. And," she added quickly, "you don't need alcohol to get through this."

He pressed his face into her hair. "I just want to forget."

Her heart broke for the pain she heard in his voice, felt in the way he held her. "Ian, what keeps bringing you here?"

"It doesn't matter," he said against her temple. "When you're around, it doesn't matter."

Words ended when he pressed his mouth against hers. This wasn't a sweet kiss like before but one born of desperation and need. One minute she was standing there and the next Ian had her pinned against the wall with his body, his hands angling her head just so to deepen the kiss.

She let her head fall back against the wall with a soft thud and a whimper smothered by Ian's lips.

They had to stop. She had to stop this. But her hands fisted in his hair, holding him close.

"Come to my room," he breathed.

She gripped his head, her fingers buried in his hair. Held on while he called to life every fleshly desire banked within her for so long.

"Please. Say yes," he whispered into her ear, nibbling the sensitive skin beneath.

Goosebumps covered her in response. "Ian, we can't."

"We can."

Stated so convincingly, she struggled to remember why they couldn't. Especially since she'd fallen for him so quickly. Ian was Ian. Strong, silent, and brooding. Sweet, gentle, and as lost in the dark as she was. "*I* can't," she whispered. "I promised myself— Marriage… I promised myself I would wait. No matter how long it took."

Ian flattened her against the wall with his body even more, as if he wanted to absorb her.

She struggled to stay strong, but she had to say no because she wouldn't let herself be used as a distraction. Wouldn't let her heart rule when it came to something so personal and meaningful to her.

She planted her trembling hands on his shoulders and firmly pushed. "Ian, please. Talk to me."

His hands slid to her face, one thumb stroking over her lips. He kissed her again, but this time his hunger was restrained though no less apparent. He wanted her, wanted more, but he was heeding her refusal.

"Go to bed."

"Ian—"

"Go."

She shifted sideways against the wall, removing herself from Ian's embrace even though her body mourned the loss of warmth.

Ian was her student. New to blindness. Confused. Angry. Searching for comfort. The list of reasons to say no was endless and heartbreaking. Until he came to terms with things, she had to be the strong one so neither of them gave in to temptation and did something regretful.

Emma hurried back to her room and let herself inside. She leaned against the door, feeling the pups' snouts sniffing her legs, their noses cold against her super-sensitive skin.

She folded her legs beneath her, back against the door as she slid down and seated herself on the floor. The pups immediately took advantage and sought attention.

She petted them, but they didn't change her focus as her body slowly became her own again, rather than one craving the man she wasn't supposed to want.

Chapter 14

So, you ready for this?" Emma asked later when Zack Dupré showed up for work. They'd already stowed Zack's lunch in the miniature fridge in the kennel, and she'd showed him where the bathroom facilities were for Zack and the men working on the security system, making it clear this was the only area in which Zack was permitted access.

Emma had to stop and cover her mouth when an extended yawn caught her by surprise.

Sleep had eluded her after Ian had kissed her in the hall, her mind too focused on him and his need for the wine at the bottom of the cellar steps. She had prayed for a long while after returning to her room, both for Ian to overcome his need for alcohol and for herself and her unusual response to Ian's kisses.

She'd dated over the years and been kissed before, but never had she responded like that.

"I guess," Zack said. "I'm not sure what I'm supposed to do, though."

"I'll show you," she told him, managing a smile. "You ever have a dog?"

"No."

Not what she had hoped to hear. "Well, now you have several, and they have to be fed, walked, and groomed." She introduced Zack to the pups, then went on to the others barking excitedly from their pens. "Today is bath day. Goli is first. She's expecting puppies and is a little sick, but she's pretty easy to handle. I'll hold her because she isn't used to you, but in the future, make sure you have her leash tied to something, or she'll take off. She likes to be chased. It's a big game to her.

"Buttons is contrary, so I usually wash him next or save him for last, depending on my mood. You're lucky. Usually I have more dogs, but Penelope's owners picked her up this morning. Before we start the baths, though, you have another chore. You need to clean out the pens and shovel the side yard where the dogs do their business."

"I have to shovel dog crap?"

"Yes, you do." She nodded firmly. She wasn't going to take it easy on Zack. The jobs she gave him were the things she had to do. Granted, Laney or Genie usually shoveled the dog piles once a week because Emma couldn't see them, but that responsibility was now Zack's for two reasons: First, she needed to know that Zack would do whatever he was told in order to stay out of jail. Second, how well he worked with the animals would tell Emma what she needed to know about Zack but couldn't see. "Unless you'd rather go back before the judge with your complaint?"

"Where's the shovel?"

She laughed at his quick turnaround. "The shovel should be along the wall there somewhere. Toss everything into the woods, away from the house. While you do that, I'll wash the bedding and hose down the pens."

"Then what?" Zack asked.

"Then comes the actual bathing. Don't worry, I'll help you, and I'll even do you a favor."

"What's that?"

"While you shovel, I'll take the dogs for a walk so they don't decide halfway through the bath they have to go—on you."

"Niiice. But thanks," he quickly added.

"What's going on?" Genie asked from the kennel entry.

Emma turned her head toward the woman and smiled. "Genie, hi. Just showing Zack the ropes. And I could ask you the same thing. What are you doing here?"

"It's—I always come to help you on bath day."

Yes, but she and Genie had already had this conversation. "You're welcome to stay if you like, but Zack will be handling things for the next six months. Remember?"

"Yeah. Yeah, of course I remember. I just thought... I'd come by and check on you."

"That's sweet. Thank you. So far so good, as you can see," Emma said, feeling a bit awkward even though she wasn't sure why. "You should go enjoy your day. We'll be fine."

"Oh, yeah, sure. So I guess I'll see you at class?"

"Wouldn't miss it."

"And you'll be there, too, Zack?" Genie asked.

"Yeah."

"So...tomorrow then," Genie said.

Emma smiled and nodded. "Yep—unless you'd like to stay?"

"No, that's okay. I'll run to the store. Need anything?"

Emma almost made up a list just to give Genie something to do, but on one of her trips up and down the mountain, she had picked up her necessities. "No, but thanks."

"Did I replace her or something?" Zack asked after Genie left.

"Not officially. Genie was a volunteer, but I felt bad about taking up all of her free time. It's fine. Let's get to work. Go grab that shovel, and we'll get started."

Half an hour later, Emma stood holding Goli's collar with the leash wrapped tightly around her hand while Zack bathed the massive dog. "She likes you, you know."

"Yeah?" he asked. "How can you tell?"

"She's standing still. Usually by this time she's—"

As though understanding her words, Goli dipped her head and began that doggy-shake that starts at their head and ends at their tail. And given the size and length of Goliath's body...

Emma couldn't hold in her laughter. Or on to Goli's head. The giant Great Dane swung around, and from the sounds of things, she was giving Zack her own brand of paws-on-the-shoulders doggy kisses.

"Stop, dog, stop!"

Zack's reaction was the key to everything. Instead of being upset, Zack protested the sloppy kisses with laughter, the rhythmic *clink* of Goli's tags indicating Zack petted the animal rather than shoving her away. Animals sensed what people sometimes overlooked, and in Emma's estimation, now was one of those times.

Zack wasn't the bad boy he pretended to be. No one who could so immediately relate to animals could be truly bad.

"Are they all like this?"

She smiled. "Most. Think you can handle it?"

"Yeah. I always thought big dogs were mean."

Emma shook her head and found Goli's leash once more. "I've always found smaller dogs to be more aggressive. They have Napoleonic attitudes and think they're bigger than they are."

Goli settled down, and Zack went back to washing her.

"So tell me about yourself," Emma said, hoping to prod the kid into revealing as much as possible. "Aunt Rose said you have a younger sister?"

"Yeah. She's fourteen."

"Ah, so you're the big brother, eh? Is she pretty?"

"Too pretty."

"Oh?"

"The girls at school give her a hard time. She's pretty, but we don't have a lot of money, you know? I try to give her nice things when I can, but jobs are hard to find these days."

"I suppose it is hard when they find out you've been in trouble," she said, having decided long ago that honesty was always the best route.

"Yeah. But I haven't been in trouble for anything major. I mean, the last time— I was defending my sister. The guy deserved the punch."

Emma thought over his words and noted the protective way Zack had when talking about his sister. "I know of a job at the diner, and I'd be willing to offer it to you on a trial basis—so long as you stay out of trouble. You interested?"

"Yeah, sure. I guess. It pays, though, right? It's not like this?"

"Yes, it pays," she said, smiling. "It won't pay much at first, but it's steady and it's legal, and if you do well... you never know what might happen."

"Cool. But I don't have a diploma or anything. I quit school to work when my dad got hurt."

"You don't need a diploma to be a busboy. My father owns The Shake Shak. The more you help out the waitresses, the more willing everyone is to share their tips."

Zack whistled. "The Shak is a busy place."

"Yes, it is. You can earn good money."

"What about your father? Doesn't he have to say okay before I'm hired?"

"Actually, I do most of the hiring."

"You?"

She laughed at his surprise. "Yeah, me. Don't underestimate me, Zack. I may be blind, but I have superpower senses when it comes to reading people."

The guy was quiet for a while, and Emma could practically hear his mind whirling.

"What do your superpowers tell you about me?" he finally asked.

She ran her hands over Goli's nose and chin. "That you want a chance to prove yourself. So don't disappoint me."

***

Three hours later, Emma sent Zack on his way down the mountain and was headed toward her room for a much-needed shower when Ian called out her name. She bit her lower lip, her body going on immediate alert because Ian had refused breakfast this morning, and this was her first contact with him after last night's kiss. "Hey. Hungry?"

"Come here."

A zing shot through her at his husky command. "Ian, I smell like wet dog. Give me twenty, and we'll go find some lunch."

"Emma—"

"Twenty minutes," she said, hurrying away so fast she almost tripped.

She couldn't help it, though. All the time she'd had last night and this morning to come to terms with her reaction to Ian? None of it had helped. His *come here* had put her right back into the moment.

But then what? Getting involved with Ian was a bad idea. If she and Mark or the other guys she had dated so briefly couldn't make it, what were the odds she and Ian could have anything serious? If that's what Ian was interested in at all?

He wants a distraction. Period.

But what was her excuse? Why was she so caught up in him? Her emotions were a tangled mess where Ian was concerned.

She showered and dressed, taking her time despite the twenty-minute limit she'd set. Unable to put Ian off any longer, she made her way to his room only to find it empty.

Tucker pulled on his leash so hard it slipped from her loose grip. "Tucker, no. Come!"

She hurried Tink out the door and listened as Tucker scrambled down the hall, the leash snagging on table legs and whipping around, making things clatter as it trailed behind. "Come on, Tink."

They followed Tucker all the way to the den, where Emma heard Ian greeting the dog.

"Thought you were going to hide away in your room all afternoon."

"I'm not that late," she said, feeling a twinge defensive. And guilty because if she'd thought for a second she could get by with postponing this after-kiss moment, she probably would have. "Do I smell food?"

"Quinn brought lunch to us here. Close the door so the dogs don't escape."

She did as ordered, the soft click of the latch sending an unmistakable shiver down her spine.

"I suppose I should apologize for what happened in the hallway last night."

"Are you sorry?" The words slipped out before she could stop them, and she grimaced.

Really? Why are you asking him that?

"Sorry I kissed you? No. I'm not sorry at all."

Okay. So. Now she knew. Question was—what was she supposed to think about that?

"Come and eat, Emma. You've been going nonstop all morning."

She made her way toward Ian, following the sound of his voice. "You should have come outside. Joined us."

"And get sprayed every time the dogs shook? No thanks."

She laughed at the wry amusement in his voice. This was an Ian she could work with. Talk to. But the one last night? He was someone so intense she wasn't sure she could handle him.

She stopped walking when she got close enough to feel his body heat, close enough that he reached out and grasped her elbow while pulling out her chair with his free hand. "Thanks."

Once she was seated, he leaned over, his mouth and nose disturbingly close to her hair.

"I can be a gentleman when I choose."

"Good to know."

His hands smoothed over her shoulders, his fingers lingering on the sensitive skin of her neck in nearly the exact spot he'd kissed last night. Her body hummed, and she found herself trembling in response.

"Emma?"

"Y-yes?"

"I'm definitely not sorry."

She closed her eyes at the feel of his breath on her skin and sighed. *Neither am I.*

On Tuesday, Ian dug in his heels just inside the doorway of The Shake Shak. How Emma had managed to talk him into this, he would never know.

After lunch yesterday, she had grilled him on button shapes and meanings, clothes colors, and even talked him into using a white stick. They had spent hours walking around the den, then the hallway, then the lower floor of the house. In the process, he'd heard her laugh more than she ever had, and something about it made him want to please her.

When she had asked him to come with her to her PAWS Class, he hadn't been able to refuse—and was curious enough about what she did, bored enough to want to get out of the house to agree. But coming to the diner? "I don't want to be here."

"Stop whining," Emma ordered. "And don't tell me you're not tired of sitting at home."

"You didn't tell me you had all these stops to make when you dragged me out of the house with you."

"If by 'all these' you mean one extra stop, of course I didn't. You wouldn't have come. It won't take long, so stop being a baby. I just need to meet with Tasha and Morgan about a birthday party for Jolie. Can you believe she's never had one? Ever. Are you really going to deny us a few minutes of planning time?"

Emma pushed him deeper into the interior. At least it was cool inside. At ninety-eight degrees and eighty percent humidity, his sweat was sweating.

"Good grief, relax, would you? Your back is harder than a rock."

He smiled briefly at her words and let his feet drag a little more because it meant she'd keep her hands on him. "I'll have a double hot fudge milkshake. And you take me to the deepest corner of the restaurant and let me enjoy it in peace."

"Fine."

Ian allowed her to lead him deeper into the building, hating the way conversation stopped when the occupants saw them. "Do they have a problem?" he asked, uncaring if the diners heard him or not.

"They're probably just curious. You're an unfamiliar face, remember?" Emma said. "Come on. Over here. It's a round booth in the corner."

"Emma, hey," an unfamiliar female voice said.

"Hey, Tash. You're early."

"I was starving. Need any help?"

"No, she doesn't," Ian replied, afraid the woman would take over and Emma would disappear.

"I'm all set up at the counter," Tasha said. "Morgan's here, too. She's on the phone."

"Status report?" Emma asked.

"I'm amazed she hasn't neutered him."

Ian grimaced at the statement on behalf of all men.

"What now?" Emma asked.

"Okay, first, don't get mad at me for not telling you this sooner," the woman said, "but Morgan made me promise not to say anything because you had enough on your plate."

"Oh, no. What happened?"

"The day Roxy...passed, Morgan had to take Rory's car since her van was in the shop. She made a few stops, and when she came out, there was a note under the windshield wiper—from a woman. It said something about how she couldn't wait to see him again at their usual spot."

"Tasha, tell me you're kidding," Emma begged.

"'Fraid not. Anyway, Morgan did some digging inside his car and found some receipts for a motel outside town."

"What?" Emma gasped.

"Yeah. Apparently Rory wrote off the room as a tax expense."

"No!"

"But it gets worse," Tasha said. "Morgan managed to keep her mouth shut—an act I really would've liked to have witnessed for myself—and went to the motel that night after Rory called and said he was working late."

"And he was there," Emma said.

"Oh, yeah. And if that wasn't insulting enough, he'd picked Morgan's van up from the shop and driven it—with the happy little family stickers smiling in the back window."

"Oh, I can't imagine," Emma said, her tone heavy with worry for her friend. "Is Rory still living at home?"

"Nope. With his mother. Which is better than where he'd be if I'd caught my husband cheating. I don't understand why men get married if they're just going to break their vows."

Emma sighed. "I don't, either. Why can't they appreciate what they have?" She asked. "Ian? Any suggestions for why we don't appreciate our blessings better than we do?"

He wasn't an idiot, and it didn't take much to figure out the gist of Emma's reference. "You promised me a milkshake," he said, sliding into the booth she indicated by removing his hand from her shoulder and placing it on the table.

"Yeah, yeah. What about food?" she asked. "Maybe some nachos? Pretzels? How about a turkey sandwich, hold the extras?"

Those he could handle in public. Emma looked out for him despite his grumbling about being there. "Surprise me."

Emma squeezed his hand as though in approval, and he felt a sad sense of satisfaction because he knew he'd made her happy by agreeing.

"I'll be right back. Tash, go easy on him. He's not Rory."

"She can go with you," Ian suggested, even though he'd felt the breeze created by Emma moving rapidly away. He envied that, her ability to turn and walk, move, so freely. Emma claimed it came with time and practice. He couldn't imagine ever being able to take a step and not wonder if he was about to hit a wall or the ground.

"Oh, that's okay. I'll keep you company," Tasha said.

He heard the aged bench seat squeak as Emma's friend lowered herself into the booth. "And now that she's gone, answer me this—how is she holding up? Please tell me you're not so self-absorbed you haven't noticed how she's doing after losing Roxy and her house burning down."

He thought of how Emma had let him hold her, of the intensity of the kisses they'd exchanged since. "She's coping." Better than he was. Yet another thing to envy. "She's focusing on Goliath and the pups. And me."

"So I see. And how's that going?"

"Emma is a good tutor."

"Wow."

"What?" he asked.

"You like her."

Ian wiped a hand over his face, mindful of the sunglasses he now regularly wore whenever others were around, and settled back in the seat.

It was true. What wasn't to like? Emma was smart, capable, funny, kind. Sexy. Every time she touched him, she made him want more. Which brought him to the question of—what could he offer her? Were mutual attraction and a common disability enough? "Shouldn't you be planning a party?"

"Nice deflection. That's what someone does when a question hits too close to home. Interesting. Oh, stop worrying. Here she comes. Emma to the rescue," she said cheerfully. "One piece of advice, though. Don't hurt her. You hurt her and you'll answer to all the busybodies Emma calls her best friends."

The following evening at Jolie's birthday party, Duncan saw the way Ian went on instant alert the moment Emma stepped near their table. He wasn't sure how Ian knew it was Emma, but it was amazing to witness.

Ian stiffened in his seat, straightened, and sat up tall, as though Emma could see him. Once, Ian even ran a hand over his head as though to smooth his hair.

Duncan took it all in and smiled, glad to note Ian's focus had changed to something more than booze and hiding away in his room. "Do you remember that girl we saw at the train station in Prague? The brunette with the big, beautiful blue eyes?"

"What about her?" Ian asked.

"That's who Emma reminds me of."

Ian squirmed on the cracked leather seat of the corner booth. Duncan knew Ian wanted to get up and stalk away, but he didn't know his way around the restaurant, and that fact was the only thing keeping Ian grounded.

"What are you doing?"

"Just trying to give you a reference. Emma is curvier but—"

"Shut up," Ian ordered. "I don't want or need you to describe Emma to me."

"Ian, I'm saying this because you like her. It's obvious every time she comes near you."

"Yeah, well, she's made it clear I'm her student and nothing else."

"So change her mind," Duncan said, lifting his glass to his lips.

"You don't think I've tried? She says I'm not ready for a relationship."

"Are you?"

Ian ran his hands over his head and squeezed his neck.

"I don't know. Nothing is going to make me the man Emma needs. I'll always be at a disadvantage, unable to do things, unable to protect her."

Was his brother going to make him spell it out? "Protect her from what? Ian, you're out of that life now, and realistically she's only in danger of getting a dog bite. Civilian life is different."

His brother scowled, obviously not happy with the response.

"Isn't it about time for you to return to Atlanta?"

Duncan fought his frustration, knowing Ian tried to pick a

fight with that question. "So that's it? You're just going to sit there and do nothing?"

Ian fisted his water glass and drained the contents.

Apparently that was his answer.

Emma, I need to talk to you."

Something in her father's voice warned Emma of his mood, but his grip on her arm confirmed it. "Uh, sure. Excuse me, Genie."

"Is everything all right?" Genie asked, concern lacing her voice.

"I'm sure it's fine," Emma said to reassure the girl, hoping it was true.

"But you'll be back?"

Emma's heart twisted at the sadness in Genie's voice. She had made a point of inviting Genie to Jolie's party out of politeness, but now Genie was glued to Emma's side, making it hard to play hostess and work the counter as backup waitress. "Of course. I'll find you again in a bit, okay?"

"Okay."

Frank tugged Emma across the crowded room to a quieter area near the kitchen. Given the crowd and food orders, the swing door flipped back and forth multiple times in less than a minute. "Dad, what's up? We're slammed tonight. Can't this wait?"

"Emma, what are you doing?"

"Excuse me?" Her father rarely used that tone with her. He and Laney often got into fights, but—

"What are you thinking, hiring him?"

Wait, what? "Him? You mean Zack?"

"Who else would I mean? Yeah, *Zack*."

Her father practically spat the name. Emma was taken aback by the vehemence. "What's wrong? Zack's doing great. The waitresses love him."

"We should have discussed hiring him."

"Why? You gave me the responsibility of hiring and firing two years ago, and you've never had a problem with my decisions until now. Aren't you the one who told me the best workers are those who not only want a job but need it?"

"I've seen him around town, and I know he has a record. He's not a good candidate for anything but an orange-vested road crew."

Her father had always spoken his mind, but that was harsh even from him. "Dad, Zack's made some mistakes. He readily admits that. But he's trying to turn his life around. That's why Aunt Rose asked me to work with him, because so many people think the same way you are right now. If you refused to serve customers who had a record, how many people would you have left? But they're still good customers, still good people deep down."

"Rose *asked* you to take him on?" he asked, sounding incredulous.

"Yes." She explained that Zack now worked with her at the kennel thanks to the judge's ruling. "See? Even Aunt Rose knows he deserves a second chance, otherwise she wouldn't have recommended him."

Her father muttered something she wasn't able to make out.

"The question is why would you agree to do such a thing? Emmalee, where's your head? Wasn't it enough that he's your helper? Why bring him here?"

"The kennel job doesn't pay, and Zack has a family he's trying to help support. And," she stressed, "we were short a busboy. Look, Zack's worked the last couple of nights, and we haven't had a problem."

"He'd be stupid to rob us on the first day."

"He's really good with the dogs."

"They're *dogs*, Emmalee. Pets like anyone, even masters who abuse them."

"You're not being fair."

"I don't want him here."

"Fine. I'll coordinate his schedule so he always works with me or the other manager. You'll never see him," she said, hoping against hope she didn't regret being so rash. Why was her father so upset? "Dad, give Zack a chance. I'll keep my eye on him," she said, smiling up at her father.

"Not the time, funny-face," he said, using the nickname he'd given her as a child because of her ability to find the humor in most any situation.

But this one? "You can't fire him. We need a busboy. Ask Shirley how well Zack's done. You know she'll tell it to you straight."

Despite the jukebox blaring and the chatter from the patrons, her father's sigh was loud and clear and full of reluctance.

"Fine. He can stay, but you keep him away from the cash registers. I don't want him ringing out. Not even once."

"Deal." It wasn't a harsh demand since busboys didn't handle checks anyway.

"You stay away from him, too."

"Going to be hard to do when he works for me," she countered, shaking her head at the unreasonable request. "Instead, I'll promise you I'll be careful. How's that? But you have to be nice. At least until Zack gives you reason not to be."

"One screw-up and he's out of here."

"I know. He knows, too. I made that clear."

"Good. So you're coming to the wedding?"

"Wouldn't miss it," she said, secretly wishing she could do just that. "I'm bringing a guest, too."

"Not Zack."

Frank's complaint made her grin. "No, not Zack. I'm going to ask Ian," she decided abruptly. "He needs to get out more."

Ian had done well yesterday during her PAWS Class. He'd sat in the back of the room and listened while the dogs went through their training. Zack had helped clean up, then drove them back up the mountain in the vehicle Duncan had allowed Zack to borrow for the occasion. All in all, it had been a good day. Maybe Ian would be willing to try for another day out and attend the wedding.

She was distracted from her thoughts when her father tugged her close and kissed her forehead.

"Bring whomever you want. Just not the busboy."

Chapter 15

Emma heard the signal beep at the street corner indicating the light had changed. She stopped at the crosswalk, feeling the knobby ridges on the slant leading into the street against the tip of her white stick, and gently yanked on Tink's leash to stop and heel.

She had decided to start taking the pups out with her one at a time, seeing as how together they proved too distracted. And since she didn't want any kind of a tug-of-war scene in Jolie's coffee shop, Emma had brought the calmer Tink along for the excursion.

Traffic in front of her slowed, and seconds later, the signal at the corner beeped again. She was proud as punch when Tink followed the cue and immediately stepped forward.

Not knowing what type of service Tink would later perform meant keeping the verbal commands to a minimum. The focus of the PAWS class was obedience, getting the dog into the groove of what its future might hold.

On the opposite street corner, her thoughts returned to Ian as they always seemed to of late, until the moment Emma crossed the threshold to Cuppa Jo's, and the smell of coffee and choco-late and all sorts of baked yumminess hit her and made her mouth water.

Distracted easily or what?

It was the bane of all chocoholics, she mused. "Here we are, Tink. Behave, okay?" she said as she juggled the leash, her purse, and the white stick.

"Hey, Em," Jolie called from behind the counter, her pen-filled apron hitting the edge with several *clinks*. "I've got it right here. I saw you coming."

Emma smiled. Instant gratification wasn't always a bad thing. "I'm predictable, huh? Thanks," she said, accepting the cup and setting it down to dig her wallet out of her purse.

"Not at all," Jolie said with a laugh. "Thanks again for the party last night. It was fun, but you shouldn't have gone to the trouble. Hey, no charge. Today is on me."

"It was no trouble at all," Emma said, frowning when her fingers came up empty.

"Is something wrong?"

Emma concentrated on the wallet playing hide and seek. Gum, tissues, lip gloss, breath mints, dog treats.

One by one she sifted through the items in her bag, moving them from side to side as she identified them. She twisted her hand, fingers splayed, but still couldn't feel it. "I can't find my wallet."

"Elaine, will you watch the counter for me?" Jolie asked. Apparently she received an answer, because Jolie ducked beneath the moveable countertop and grasped Emma's arm. "Come on. I'll help you look."

Seconds later, they were at the corner table, and Emma resumed searching her purse. "I still can't find it. Would you mind?"

A knot had formed in her stomach. She wasn't the forgetful

type—or unorganized. The blind had to be organized or else always look like a fool. So where was it?

"I don't see it. Red, right?"

"Yeah. The one you bought me for my birthday two years ago."

"Oh, Em. I hate to tell you this, but it's not here. Any idea when you had it last?"

"At The Shak. I left my purse behind the counter because I didn't have time to run it into Dad's office, and I got cash out of it to pay my part of your cake."

"Oh, geez, Em. I'm so sorry. Do you think maybe it didn't go into your purse? Could it have fallen behind on the shelf?"

"No, I put it inside. You know how I am about stuff like that."

"Yeah, so... that means someone must have taken it."

Jolie didn't accuse anyone outright, but Emma knew what her friend was thinking. Em wanted to give Zack the benefit of the doubt, but Aunt Rose had filled her in on Zack's situation, and his past was full of petty theft charges. "It might not be Zack."

"But what if it was?"

Emma sipped her coffee to buy herself some time before she had to respond and shrugged. "Then I'll deal with it."

"How?"

"I'm not sure. I mean, I never carry my credit card. I barely had any cash in it. The only thing I even have to replace is my campus ID, and no one ever checks those."

"That doesn't make a wrong a right. Are you going to ask Zack about it?"

"No. What if it wasn't him?"

"*Emma.*"

"How would you like being accused of stealing just because you had in the past? What if he really didn't do it and I dump that accusation on him? Maybe I did screw up and not zip my purse. I was rushed."

"But like you just said—you don't make mistakes like that."

"I don't burn houses down, Jolie, but it happened, didn't it?" Her eyes burned and her nose prickled with the threat of frustrated tears she refused to shed. People made mistakes. She wasn't immune, much as she'd like to be. "It could have dropped out of my bag as I crossed the parking lot last night. I could've dropped it somewhere along the way in this morning. Who knows? I'll check the shelf where I stashed my purse, but I'm not going to accuse Zack. He's innocent until proven guilty, not the other way around."

In a blatant attempt to change the subject, she slurped her drink. "So, about last night... What is up with you turning down Quinn's request for a dance?"

"What? Nothing. You know I'm not a dancer."

"Jolie." Emma drawled out her friend's name, knowing "nothing" wasn't an answer. "I get that he's intense. Is he not handsome?"

"No, he's— Em, I'm just not interested."

"Why?" Emma fingered the cupholder keeping her fingers from being burned by the too-hot coffee.

"I'm a busy woman."

"Not that busy. There are some nice guys in this town, and sometimes you seem so lonely."

"You're one to talk. You haven't exactly been pounding the pavement on dates, you know."

"I know. But you and I both know it takes a special person to handle the whole blind thing. Look, no pressure, okay? I just want you to be happy."

"I am. Some people actually believe you don't need a man to be happy."

Emma forced a smile she didn't feel, her mind immediately

shooting to Ian and how quickly she had grown close to him. How happy he made her at times, despite his temper and silence about the cellar.

She pressed the button on her watch and gasped at the time. "Oh! I have to go or I'll be late for class."

"Ian's not tagging along with you today?" Jolie asked.

"No, he said he had something he wanted to do. I wanted so badly to ask what it was, but I didn't because it's progress and better than brooding in his room, whatever it is."

"Keep me posted. It sounds intriguing."

Emma stood and immediately felt Tinkerbell's response as the dog stood and prepared to work. "Good job, Tink." To Jolie, she said, "We're okay?"

Jolie got up and gave Emma a tight hug. "*Besties* till the very end."

Half an hour later, Emma frowned when she couldn't find her binder. She stored her crate of class materials in the classroom at the university for simplicity's sake. The instructor she shared a room with never bothered it, but the crate wasn't in its place.

She groaned her frustration and turned toward the front of the classroom. She'd have to wait for Zack or one of her students to get there to help her find it.

Three steps into the ten-step distance, she ran knee-first into a student desk. "Ow! *Ow!*"

Seriously? There was a sign up on the wall. Nothing was to be moved!

Ten minutes later, her knee still throbbed when her students began to arrive. Amid laughter, chatter, and the click of the dogs' nails on the tile floor, Emma felt ill-prepared and embarrassed at having to ask for help. She had hoped Zack would arrive a few minutes early to restore order to her morning, but apparently that wasn't going to happen. "Good morning, everyone."

A chorus of replies shot back at her, with a few low barks thrown in. "If anyone is free, I could use a hand getting ready. I'm a bit scattered today."

"I can help you," Genie said, approaching. "What do you need?"

Emma led the way to where the crate of materials was usually stored and lowered her voice. "Do you see my training manual? I've misplaced it."

"Sure, it's right here."

Emma fought off the rush of heat that threatened to flood her face. "Thanks. Where was it?"

"In the crate. I'm sorry, Emma. If I'd known Zack wasn't going to be here, I would've come in earlier to help," Genie said.

"Thanks. I'm sure he's probably just running late." *With your wallet?* "Um...I need the orange cones. Would you mind?"

"Oh, sure. They're over by the wall."

Genie retrieved them, and Emma fought for composure. Okay, so it was an accident. The crate of supplies was there, just a little out of place. No big deal.

Probably a new cleaning person. Someone too focused on his job to read the signs posted around the room. "Thanks, Genie. I appreciate it."

"Sure. Do you need me to pitch in until Zack gets here?"

"That would be great."

"Want to get something to eat after class?" the girl asked, her tone hopeful.

Remembering her wallet-less state, Emma shook her head in regret. "I can't today. Sorry. But some other time, okay? My treat."

Later that afternoon, Emma knocked softly on Ian's door. "You in there?"

She listened closely, but when he didn't respond, she turned and went into her room, figuring Ian was in the den with his darts.

Emma walked to the dresser, where she placed her purse every night, smoothing her hands over the surface to search for the missing wallet.

Nothing on top, nothing on the floor beside the dresser. Maybe it had fallen into an open drawer? She checked there, too.

Nothing.

She'd gone back to the bar after class and checked the shelf and the lost-and-found box in the office, but there was no sign of her wallet there, either. It was gone. But that didn't mean Zack had stolen it, even if he hadn't shown up for class today. Or called with an excuse.

Giving up the search, Emma left her room and ventured down the hall to the den. Outside the door, she heard the low thump of the darts hitting the board, not the wall. She knocked before entering. "Hey, you're sounding good."

"He's definitely winning," Duncan said, the words followed by a laugh. "Ian's notched his darts to tell them apart, and I'm not allowed near the board until he counts up the points."

A sharp measure of pride filled her. Ian was figuring things out and learning fast. Just like she'd known he would once he got out of his own way.

"Thanks for rescuing me. Ian, we'll finish this later," Duncan said, moving by her to the door.

Emma dipped her head in a nod, smiling.

"Where are you going?" Ian asked.

"Work. See you both—uh, later," Duncan said, sounding awkward.

Emma didn't take offense at Duncan's words, but she wondered if Ian would.

She used her cane to find her way to the couch and collapsed onto the cushions with a sigh.

"You sound tired. Bad day?"

Wow. So Ian was letting his brother's comment pass? Another step in the right direction.

Tink rested her head atop Emma's foot. "You could say that." She heard Ian shuffling his feet as he walked toward her. "Stop."

"Why?"

"Where's your cane?"

He said something under his breath. Not a curse, but something that wasn't nice.

Still, she also heard him change directions and the sound of what appeared to be his cane sliding against the edge of the desk as Ian found it.

His next few steps were slow, but he didn't shuffle. "Much better."

He found his way to the couch and sat down beside her.

"What's wrong?" he demanded.

"Just one of those days."

"Tell me about it. You can't have a bad day and not let me enjoy it a little."

His teasing brought out a reluctant smile. Why not? Maybe venting a little would help. "Well, it began with me losing my wallet."

"Any idea where?"

"No."

"Could it have been stolen?"

Not him, too, she thought. But wasn't she coming to the same conclusion? "I don't think so, but anything is possible. But from there, things went downhill. I guess I was rattled. I kept misplacing things and running into things. My knee still hurts from where I banged it on a chair."

"Which one?"

She was startled when Ian's hand landed on her leg. "Uh..."

"Slide down," he ordered, pulling her legs across his knees before she even had time to take a breath.

Her protest died when he began to massage her calves and moved up to her knees. Who knew *knees* could be so sensitive? He didn't venture higher, and she was grateful he kept things appropriate so she wouldn't have to stop him since it felt so good.

"Did your PAWS class go well otherwise?"

"It was okay. What about you? How, um, did Tucker behave while I was gone?"

Ian tensed, his grip squeezing a bit tighter.

"Fine. We just...hung out. Quinn is taking him for a walk now."

"I guess I should go check on Goli and the others."

"Want some company?" Ian asked. "I've been in here all day."

Surprise shot through her, followed by a thrill. "That would be great."

One of Ian's hands shifted again, slid from her knee up to her arm, following the path until he lightly skimmed her face. Emma held perfectly still.

The rough pads of his fingers and thumbs slid over her forehead, her nose, around her eyes and cheekbones. Down to her mouth.

Her heart beat so hard and fast blood gushed past her ears, but nothing could drown out the soft whisper of Ian saying her name before he used his hold on her to lean forward and brush his lips over hers with unerring accuracy.

Tingles flooded her veins. She didn't have a ton of experience with men, but she had enough, though it didn't prepare her for the way her head spun from a single kiss.

She tore her mouth from his. "*Ian.* I'm your tutor. Business and pleasure… You're getting better, growing more confident. It's wonderful, but I don't want to do anything to jeopardize your progress o-or hurt you."

"You won't hurt me."

"Fine," she whispered. "Then I don't want to do anything that might hurt *me*."

He brushed a chaste kiss over her cheek, his sigh blowing moist against her skin.

Seconds passed but Ian didn't respond to her words. And that was answer enough. She swung her feet to the floor and scrambled to safety even though the last thing she wanted at the moment was to play it safe. Was this where she was meant to be? She needed time, distance, and a lot of prayer to figure things out. "Let's go check on the dogs."

Okay, so are you ready for this?" Emma asked Ian later as she stepped close. The way he smelled… The scent needed to be bottled and sold. Love Potion Number Whatever.

Love?

Her mind immediately backpedaled from that four-letter word and settled on…like. Like was better. Like was a perfectly good word. Because she really liked Ian. And the liking was growing into…

Too much like.

"I know which button to press on the microwave," Ian said.

His grumble drew her out of her inner debate. "You can't microwave everything. Besides, one minor ice or snowstorm, a windstorm for that matter, and the electricity is off until you get the generator up and running. You need to know how to use the gas stove in case of emergencies. Unless...you don't want me using it because of what happened?"

"Emma, please ignore the comment I made the night you arrived, and accept my apology. You won't catch anything on fire. What happened with your house was an accident you won't ever repeat."

She certainly hoped not. Never again would she ever step away from the stove while cooking. "Okay, so let's get started. We have all the ingredients ready to go; the pan is on the back burner. Time to light things up. You remember the order of the knobs?"

"Front burner is first, back burner, the oven knob, then the front and back burner knobs for the right side."

"Good. Another thing to always remember is your clothing when lighting the burner. Make sure your shirt tail is tucked and nothing is touching the stove."

"Now what?"

"Um..." She had to clear her throat to speak. "Light it up like I showed you." She had to step away from him to momentarily focus on their task.

Ever since he'd kissed her, she'd been able to think of little else but him and her and the possibility of a *them*.

But there were too many other factors involved. Like her employment. Wasn't it poor taste to date a student, no matter the age?

Besides, Ian wasn't ready to be with anyone, not when he was just finding his way. And even though she was attracted to him, she couldn't ignore her dreams of independence. The money she earned tutoring Ian would go a long way toward funding her kennel and living independently, but how independent could she be if she got involved with him? Could she be with someone and still be independent?

"Is that right?" Ian asked.

Once more, Emma force-focused on their task, on the hissing sound of the flame emitting from the burner. "What do you think it is?"

"Medium high."

"Very good. Watch your hand and arm as you place the skillet on the burner."

"How do I know if I knock the hamburger out of the pan?"

Maybe she was a masochist, but she thought it fitting that Ian's first lesson was taco salads. "You'll hear a pop as it burns, but to keep it from happening, you put your hand over the skillet until you can feel the heat but don't touch the metal."

"Ow." Ian cursed. "Sorry," he said, sounding sincere.

"I understand. As to the meat, it takes a few tries to get it right. Here, I'll show you." She found his hands and placed them just so.

He was a big guy, tall and lean. Her nose fell somewhere at mid-bicep, and she couldn't help but notice he had the perfect shoulder to lean on—which may have been why she'd leaned on it a few times already. "Um, about there. Feel the heat?"

"Yeah."

"Don't burn yourself. Another way of keeping track is to use the lid to the skillet. Hold it against the edge as you stir, and it'll catch whatever you knock out. But it gets hot, too, and you'll burn yourself on it if you aren't careful. When you're done stirring, tip the cover as you reposition it, and the hamburger will fall back into the skillet."

"Okay, say I've done all that. How do I know when it's done?"

"You listen to the sizzle. Hear how it's low? Bubbling in moisture? When it's done, the pitch is higher and you'll hear the change because it's drier. You'll also smell the difference because if you leave it too long it starts to...burn." Emma was suddenly conscious of his hands over hers, of the way she leaned into him. "Um, this needs to cook for a few minutes," she said, pulling away.

Ian didn't let her go far.

"Wait."

His arms locked around her, blocking her retreat. Emma swallowed. "What?"

With one arm around her waist holding tight, Ian's fingers found her chin, gently tugged.

"I did well. Don't I get a reward?"

A nervous laugh erupted from her. "Ian..."

His lips closed over hers, ending her words. Ian gathered her closer, up on her toes, and he kissed her until her head spun and breathing didn't seem quite so important.

Nor did the obstacles standing in the way of their being together. A fact that acted like a splash of cold water.

"Ian."

His name was a gasp. A warning. A plea. Every emotion she felt all rolled into one. Emma pulled away. "You h-have to stop doing that."

"Why?"

"Because you've been through a lot. It's understandable that you'd consider me a friend. Turn to me."

"Emma, friendship isn't what I want."

"What are you saying? That you want more?" More, as in dating? Oh, now that was tempting... But would it ruin everything?

"I'd at least like the opportunity to figure things out."

"Does that mean you're ready to tell me what's going on with the cellar door?"

Silence filled the air between them.

"Not yet. That's not to say I won't ever confide in you but... it's not easy for me."

That she could understand. Ian had been taught to be a private person. First as his political father's son, then as a SEAL entrusted with secrets of national security. "But in time?"

"Yeah. I just have to get a handle on it first. Look, Emma, I'll be honest. I'm not convinced I have a lot to offer any woman, but thanks to you, I'm learning to deal with being blind. Rest assured my kissing you has nothing to do with you being blind or my tutor but because... you're tough and motivated and I admire that. Can't those reasons be enough for now?"

It was more than enough under the circumstances. She nodded but then had to find her voice. "Yes. For now."

He slid his hands over her face and lifted it for his kiss. This one was slow and sweet and full of promise.

"Emma?"

"Hmm?"

"The hamburger is burning."

Chapter 16

Ian shuffled his way to the kitchen Friday evening, counting off the steps like Emma had taught him, and wondering if there would ever come a time in his life when he wouldn't be counting but able to enjoy the world around him again.

He'd never given it much thought before, but now he knew the intense concentration and skill of the blind. To be able to get from place to place, to count money and know he wasn't getting ripped off, to do things for himself rather than relying on others.

"Good timing," Quinn said from across the room. "Want a snack?"

"No. Where's Emma? I thought I heard a car earlier."

"You did. Now she's swimming."

"With?"

"No one. Her friend dropped her off and left. Emma's alone."

The words sent a shiver of fear down Ian's spine. She could be hurt. How did she know where she was going? When to stop? She could hit her head, get a cramp, and go under because she didn't know which way to go. She was *blind,* for pity's sake.

"She's been doing laps for about ten minutes. If you're worried, go out there."

"And do what? If she gets in trouble…"

"You'd let her drown?"

Quinn's statement was a challenge.

But swimming now? The thought of being in water with no sense of direction tightened his gut into knots.

"You could always sit by the pool."

Sit, not swim. Yeah, maybe he could do that. And yell if she did get into trouble. He certainly wasn't about to suggest Quinn go in his place. He felt enough for Emma to be jealous of another man looking at her in a bathing suit soaked to her skin. Skin he couldn't see. But how to get there without making a fool of himself?

"I'll walk you out before I turn in."

Quinn led the way out the door, down the terrace steps to the pool. As they approached, Ian heard the sound of Emma's rhythmic splashes as she sliced her way through the water, heard her inhale and the silence that followed as she flipped for another lap.

She was a strong swimmer.

"She goes under for about five to six seconds before breaking surface."

Ian nodded once. He'd been doing the same, counting the seconds of silence before the splashing began again. "Thanks."

Quinn squeezed his shoulder.

"It's muggy. Want to sit on the steps?"

It didn't take a genius to figure out what Quinn was doing. His friend was trying to get him as close to the water as possible.

Maybe it was a good first move that would help get him over the barrier of actually getting in. "Yes."

By the time Emma made it back to the shallow end of the

pool, Ian sat with his feet and lower calves in the too-warm water.

"You're a good swimmer," Quinn said when the splashing stopped. "Right, Ian?"

"Yeah." He listened as Emma struggled to catch her breath.

"I used to be," she said, laughing softly. "Now I barely crawl, and I'm out of breath when I get there."

Ian heard her move through the water, toward him.

"I'll be in my room," Quinn said, his footsteps carrying him toward the house.

"You coming in?"

Instant unease swept through Ian. "No. I'm good on the steps."

"Ian, I know you can swim." Her tone lowered, softened. "Picture an oval in your mind."

"I'm fine here."

"Because you can't see?"

Her husky murmur drew closer.

"I thought SEALS were practically born in the water."

He'd graduated top in his class. Learned to swim with his hands and feet bound. With a blindfold on. The Navy's Hell Week had been just that, but he'd gotten through it, knowing once the exercise was over, he'd be able to see again. That it would last only as long as it took him to get to the surface.

"I think it's kind of liberating, personally. Sure you won't change your mind?"

His curiosity got the better of him. "What are you wearing?" If anything could distract him from his phobia and the convoluted mix of fear and the desire to touch her, her response was it.

A low, throaty laugh filled the air and eased some of the tension he felt.

"Does it matter?"

"I guess not."

"Needless to say, I'm covered," she told him, amusement thick in her voice.

"You are the most amazing woman I've ever met," he whispered.

"You're not so bad yourself, you know. When you aren't barking out orders," she teased.

"I just wish... I wish I could see you."

She found his arm, his hand, and carried it to her face.

He jerked and pulled his hand away.

"That's not what I want."

"But it's what we have, Ian. I thought you had finally started to accept that?"

"How can I?"

"How can you not? The sooner you do, the sooner we—you," she corrected softly, "can move on and have whatever comes next."

His hand stroked her back, fingers on the bones of her shoulder. "How do you do it? How do you swim like that?"

He wanted to talk about that now?

She thought about the days after the car accident, the weeks and months where she'd been so angry she'd considered jumping into a pool and not swimming at all. People who said they'd never once, not in their entire life, contemplated suicide were liars. Everyone did at least once, especially after something so brutal happened. "It was either swim or drown," she whispered. "I felt like I'd lost everything. But I'd been on the swim team for four years, and when Tasha said they were going to replace me if I didn't show them I could still do it, it became a mission."

"How do you find your way in the dark, in the water?"

"I picture the other side, and I don't stop until I get there." She squeezed his forearm, the gesture leaving a cool trail. "It sounds stupid but... that's how. Trust me, riding a bike wasn't nearly as easy."

He stilled and sucked in a breath. "You ride bikes?"

"Yeah. And I have a lot of scars on my elbows and knees to prove it."

"Why?"

The way he asked made it sound as though he was working through something in his mind. She wanted to ask what but knew he'd tell her when he was ready. *Baby steps.* "All my friends were going on a bike ride at the state park. I wanted to go, too."

"So you just did it?"

"No. It took time. Practice. A lot of wrecking. But I didn't want to be left behind. Sometimes, that's incentive enough."

This time when she took his hands in hers, he didn't fight the move. She brought it to her cheek. "This?" She pressed a chaste kiss into his palm. "Maybe it's not perfect, but it's real. It's who we are."

"I don't want to be blind. I want to see you, Emma. I want to see you when you smile, when you're giving me a hard time. I just...want to see."

"You can't. We *can't*. It's something you have to accept."

Ian fisted his hands in her hair, pulling some of the strands. The stubble on his chin was rough against her cheek as he tugged her to him once more, kissed her with a desperation she remembered all too well.

She let the kiss go on for a long moment until she ended it and pulled away. "Ian, only you can decide. What are you going to do? Sink or swim?"

Ian opened his eyes a couple hours later, unable to sleep. After ending their kiss, Emma had insisted on returning to the house and then to their separate rooms.

But now all he could do was think of that kiss and how it had felt. Being with her soothed the demons of the dark, another Emma-only factor no one else possessed.

But he knew his feelings for her were growing...

And if he wanted to keep her, to share more kisses, he had to accept his blindness like she said. Accept the loss of certain abilities and freedoms. Become someone else entirely.

The someone he now was.

"I didn't want to be left behind...."

For her, a future with her, he'd find a way to face the phobia. She was right. He didn't want to be left behind. And as his eyes grew heavy, he knew the truth—sometimes not wanting to get left behind really was incentive enough.

***

The weekend flew by, every waking moment and most of Ian's sleeping ones filled with Emma. When she asked him to attend church with her on Sunday morning he agreed—but only if he could sit in the back.

While she taught him how to maneuver the landscape around the house, he and Emma played with the pups, and he asked the questions on his mind about training them to become service animals. Emma was obviously well suited for the job, patient with them, especially Tucker, who never ceased to cause trouble of some sort.

"What's got you so deep in thought today?" Emma asked on Monday.

"Yesterday," he murmured honestly. "Thanks for making me go to church with you. The sermon was... inspiring."

"I'm glad."

She looped her arms around his neck and pressed a quick kiss to his lips, the first time she'd ever made the first move. He considered it progress. Maybe a reward for going to church?

"Quinn put a lot of research into this computer program, and I can't wait to learn it with you."

"You're using me to further your own educational pursuits?" he complained. His thumb skimmed over her lip. "It's going to cost you."

Emma's throaty laugh filled his ears. "Oh, really?"

"It's only fair."

"Hmmm. I think I know just the thing..."

Emma proceeded to raise herself on tiptoe and pressed her lips to his once more, this kiss slower and more tantalizing. Before it was over, he decided to attend church more often in the future.

After spending so much time with her, living with her, he didn't want to be without her. Emma kept him grounded, kept him from losing himself in the dark. Made him focus on other things besides the chaos in his head.

Nights were easier to bear. Whenever he drifted off and the darkness closed in, he lost himself in what-ifs and what the future could hold. But they couldn't be together for real until he conquered his phobia. For his sake and hers. For the life he imagined them having together.

The only question was...how?

Chapter 17

Okay, everybody stop. Emma, what is up with you?"

Emma froze at Tasha's question and forced herself to swallow the bite of cake she'd just taken inside of Cuppa Jo's.

"Mmm...hmmm?" She hadn't wanted to leave Ian, but she was supposed to meet Genie for a movie before going to work her shift at The Shake Shak. Then Morgan had called an emergency meeting of the *Besties* to vent over the latest episode with Rory, and Emma had canceled her plans, hoping a *Bestie* chat would help her untangle her emotions.

The entire time she'd sat there, she had searched her brain for a way to discreetly bring up her change of relationship with Ian, but obviously something had given her away.

"Emma Wyatt," Tasha said, tsking.

"What?" Jolie asked.

"She's blushing!" Morgan all but hooted.

"Shhh," Emma ordered, unable to stop the flood of searing heat gushing into her face. "Keep your voices down, please?"

"What did she do?" Jolie demanded in a secretive whisper.

"Well, Emma? What *did* you do?" Tasha wrapped her arm around Emma's shoulder.

"Stop," she said, laughing in embarrassment.

"Question isn't really what but with whom?" Tasha queried. "The gorgeous but workaholic brother, Duncan, or the gorgeous but brooding brother, Ian? Hmmm?"

Emma wanted the floor to open up and swallow her. The *Besties* discussed everything with very little off-limits, but that didn't mean she was used to talking about *her* personal life, only theirs.

"Well?" Jolie asked.

She took a sip of her ice water and tried to pretend it would cool the heat scorching her cheeks. "Um, Ian and I...have become closer."

"Whoa, wait a minute," Morgan interjected. "It was consensual, right?"

"Of course! Ian would never hurt me."

"But you said the first time you met that he implied you were a prostitute…" Jolie said.

"I know but that— He was trying to scare me away. " She shook her head and smiled, unable to stop it. "Since then we've grown close and… we've kissed and talked."

"But?" Tasha prodded. "Because we can all hear it in there, Em."

She shook her head firmly. "Not for the reasons you think. I don't regret getting to know him but…" She'd be lying if she said she hadn't woken up with a bit of confusion—on multiple occasions. "He's wonderful. He's learned so much, and he's nothing like the man I met that first day."

"That's good, not 'but' worthy," Morgan said. "What's the problem?"

Morgan really knew how to press an issue, maybe because she was stalling about talking about her own wealth of issues.

Emma inhaled and sighed. Sometimes it helped to talk to her girls. They were all women of faith, women who tried to live a godly life despite their own stumbles and trials. "It's not a problem per se. It's just that since working for Duncan, I'm closer than I've ever been to my dream of being independent. You know how much I've wanted to live on my own. But now I've met him and I just wonder how I can be with Ian and...be free. If it's even possible?"

Silence followed her words, and an even bigger bolt of fear slid down her spine.

Emma turned to Tasha. "Say something."

"Oh, hon. I'm not the one to ask. I'm as confused as you right now. I've, um, been getting to know Owen," she whispered.

"What?"

"Shhh," Tasha demanded of Morgan.

"Tash?" Emma waited for her friend to continue. "When? *How?"*

"The night of Jolie's party. I...kind of received some bad news that day."

"So that's where you disappeared to," Jolie said in disapproval. "You didn't say anything," Em whispered. "And what bad news?"

"What's to say? I'm confused and... I feel guilty. I loved Adam, and I planned to spend my life with him."

"Adam wouldn't expect you to be alone forever," Morgan said.

"Are you two seeing each other now?" Jolie asked.

"It's complicated. Owen...wants to see where things lead, but I said I have to think about it."

"And the bad news?" Emma pressed.

"Apparently I ticked off a customer because someone turned me in to the authorities claiming I'm dealing drugs out of the clinic."

"*What?*"

"Are you serious?"

"Who would do such a thing?"

"I have no idea who did it, but it floored me," Tasha said, releasing a gusty sigh. "I mean, I'd never do something like that."

"You don't have to defend yourself to us, Tash. We know better," Emma said. "Is that how you turned to Owen?"

"I'd like to say yes but...I don't know. Maybe? He's a good listener. Has great advice. But shouldn't we be talking about *your* new development?"

"We are, in a way," Emma said, her heart breaking for her friend because Tasha was a strong, capable, independent woman, but after losing her cop fiancé, she was afraid to fall for someone again. And the hassle of fending off such a horrible claim? "I can't allow myself to fall for someone who can't handle his blindness, much less mine."

Tasha's laugh didn't hold any true humor.

"It's weird, isn't it? Both our situations are the same as before but different. I feel like I've betrayed Adam and for what? How can I think about falling for another man who is married to his job? Adam and I had so many fights over the danger he faced, and after he died, I swore I wouldn't ever date another man who put his life on the line."

"So what are you going to do?" Jolie asked.

"What is there to do? Owen is here now, but he doesn't know where he'll be in the future. I can't do it. I'm not going to see him again," Tasha said.

"But... can't you work something out?" Emma asked, her heart tugging with sympathy because of the hurt in Tasha's tone and the newfound friendship she'd made with Owen Redd. She didn't know him well, but he was a good friend to Duncan, and she respected that bond and loyalty.

"I can't. And now," Tasha said, her voice firming, "we're

talking about you. And Morgan is definitely next since she's the one who called us all together. So, Em. Can you be with a man and still be free? Your answer represents an age-old question."

"What do you feel when you're with him?" Morgan asked.

Bombarded by questions, Emma rubbed her temple and the headache that plagued her. "I feel…torn."

"Yeah?" Tasha urged.

"He is wonderful. Nice and kind. I don't want to miss being with him, because he really is a good man, but I feel like I can't let myself get too involved, because he's so stuck on focusing on each and every limitation life has to offer now that he's blind."

"Whereas you blast through them. Maybe he just needs encouragement?" Morgan asked.

"Maybe. I don't know."

"Emma, are you saying you don't care for him?" Jolie murmured.

"I never said I didn't care for him." She cared. Sometimes she thought she cared too much. "I do. A lot." But right now Ian had enough to deal with without feeling more pressure from her. "It's just Ian is struggling to cope with his blindness, and he leans on me for help, which is perfectly fine but…then I think of Mark and how he couldn't handle the realities of it… I wonder."

"What?" Jolie placed her hand over Emma's and squeezed.

"If Mark couldn't handle it, how on earth can Ian when it's blindness times two?"

"First, Ian isn't Mark. You shouldn't compare them," Jolie said.

"That's true. And by being blind, Ian has a perspective Mark didn't possess," Tasha added.

Morgan made a noise. "But it *is* true. Ian's learning from her now, but a time will come when they will be equal, and the novelty of being together will have worn off. That's when reality really sets in. If they stay together and build a relationship, he'll have to deal with what comes next. The good, bad, and the ugly," Morgan said, her tone indicating she talked from the experience that had brought them together today.

Emma released the lip she held between her teeth and shrugged. "I can't change what's done. And I don't regret kissing him. I guess, for now, I'm going to take things slow, enjoy my time with Ian, and... see what happens."

"And eat cake," Tasha murmured, her mouth obviously full.

"And eat cake," Emma repeated, digging her fork into her chocolate treat. "Morgan? You're up. What's the latest with Rory?"

"I've asked for a divorce," Morgan announced. "As it turns out, Rory didn't get a pay cut and he hasn't been working late. The last three years of our marriage have been a lie because everything he did was to b-be with her. I feel like such an idiot."

"You're not."

"Don't say that!"

"He's the adulterer, not you."

"I know. I've done everything I could to save our marriage, but it's the strangest thing. Now that I've told him we're through, all I feel is relief. I *know* this is the right thing for me and the kids, even though it's horrible, too. Is that weird?"

Two hours later, Emma let herself out of Morgan's van while Morgan hit the button to open the sliding rear door for Tucker to tumble out.

"Have a great shift. Thanks for talking me off the ledge," Morgan said.

"Right back at you. And thanks for the ride," Emma said as she gathered the leash in her hand and juggled the white stick, her purse, the dog, and a backpack of freshly baked dog treats. "I would be sooo late if not for you."

"That's what *Besties* are for. See you later."

Emma hurried toward the entrance of The Shake Shak, but when she approached, she realized someone stood holding the door, the cool air from within the building rushing out and lifting the hair stuck to her neck. "Thanks."

"You're welcome," Genie said softly, hurt clouding her voice.

Emma bit back a groan. Of all people to see her get out of Morgan's van. "Genie, hey, I'm sorry about canceling today. Morgan had something she really needed to talk about, and she's been so busy with...things...that we haven't seen much of each other lately."

"It's fine."

Inside, Emma hesitated. "Would you like to come to dinner this evening? At the MacGregors'?"

"You don't have to invite me."

"I want to invite you, Genie. To make up for being so rude and canceling at the last minute. I've done that several times lately, and it's poor manners. Quinn is grilling out tonight. He's quite the cook. Say you'll join us?"

They walked toward the counter in sync, the dog at Emma's side.

"Sure. That sounds like fun. I can drive you home."

"Oh, um—thanks," Emma said. "That would be great. If you don't mind."

"Why would I mind? How many times have I told you, Emma, you can always count on me."

Ian was in the kitchen with Quinn later that evening when he heard someone else enter the room.

"Hi," Genie said, her tone awkward. "I, um, was wondering if I could get a bottle of water? Emma went to change clothes."

"We only have tap," Quinn said.

"That's fine."

Ian heard the clink of glasses, the sound of the faucet being turned on and off. "How's it going?" he asked, feeling the need to be sociable since Quinn wasn't the type.

"Fine."

"I need to check the steaks."

Ian didn't hear a sound as Quinn exited, but seconds later, Genie cleared her throat.

"Can I talk to you about something? It's about Emma."

"Sure. Something wrong?" he asked, frowning as he waited for the woman's response.

"I don't think so. It's just that guy she hired because of her aunt... Zack?"

"What about him?"

"Did Emma tell you her wallet was stolen?"

Ian froze with his glass of iced tea halfway to his lips. "She said she had misplaced it."

"Yeah, well, that's just it. Emma doesn't misplace things. Ever. She's fanatical about everything being where it's supposed to be, so she keeps track of things. But since she hired him, her wallet's disappeared and..."

"And?" he prodded, wanting to hear whatever it was the girl had to say.

"And I don't want to get him in trouble, but I'm worried. Emma says it's all a coincidence but—"

"What's going on, Genie?"

"Well, her wallet went missing, and Zack hasn't shown up for class."

"That's against his court-order placement."

"I know. I tried to talk to Emma about it on the way here tonight, but she doesn't want Zack to get into trouble. She says he'll show up, but I just don't know. Please don't tell her I told you this, okay? She'll be mad at me."

Ian set the glass in front of him, his fingers sliding over the condensation. Emma had a tender heart. She wanted to see the good in everyone, even when bad was present. "I won't tell her, but I will check into it."

"Good. Emma's a wonderful teacher, isn't she?" the girl said.

"Yes." A good teacher, a good woman. He hadn't wanted her to leave this morning, but she'd insisted on meeting her friends. Was he the topic of their discussions?

"So... you like her?"

Emma calmed him, dragged him out of the darkness so that his entire focus was on her or a task she felt he needed to learn. She got to him. Like? No, what he felt for her was more. "Things are complicated."

"Yeah, I can imagine. I mean, how would you do it if you and Emma got married or something? Getting around, holding down jobs, kids? Two blind people chasing after a sighted child? No offense," Genie quickly interjected. "I'm not trying to be rude. It's just if I was Emma, I couldn't... I mean, I'd want to be with someone who could... Um, I'm really sticking my foot in my mouth, aren't I?"

That she was. But it was an honest statement of concern, and his thoughts raced as he finished the woman's sentences in his head. If she were blind, Genie would want to be with someone who could see, someone who could be a helpmate. That's what she was about to say. "Like I said, it's complicated."

"Yeah. Well, I just wanted to mention Zack's behavior to you. I know you can't do anything to help, but I thought your brother might be able to check on Zack or something, you know? He's in security, right?"

"Yeah." He was very aware of the fact he could do little to help Emma. Looking beyond kids and a future together with all its complications, here was yet another one—safety. He refused to have a family he couldn't protect. Duncan could keep Emma safe. Any other man in the house could help Emma with this situation. Except him.

Reality set in, stripping away confidence. Taking away every positive, forward-thinking thought he'd had since being with her.

Ian sat on the stool in the kitchen a long time after Genie's footsteps faded away, his thoughts on Emma and the future. Genie had made a valid point that emphasized his thoughts from the beginning.

He couldn't offer Emma anything but a future of darkness and a lifetime of having to run to someone else for help when she needed it. Who was he kidding?

"Hey," Duncan said as he came into the kitchen. "Those steaks are calling my name. I could smell them the whole time I was in the office trying to finish up. You coming?"

"Yeah," Ian said, unmoving. "Duncan, wait. Has Emma said anything to you about that guy she has working for her?"

"Not much. I had the guys keeping an eye on him when he was here, though. Why?"

Swallowing his pride because Emma's safety was more important, Ian filled Duncan in.

"So she hasn't said anything to the judge?"

"No."

"Could be a coincidence, but it's doubtful," Duncan continued. "Don't worry. I'll check on Zack and find out what's going on."

"Thanks."

"Ian... About you and Emma. You doing okay?"

Ian opened his mouth to comment but just as quickly closed it, unsure of how to respond.

"A day at a time?"

Ian took a long sip from his iced tea before nodding. "Yeah."

The door off the patio opened.

"Steaks are done. Get'em while they're hot," Owen Redd said before the door closed again.

"Come on. If we don't get out there and claim our share, Owen and Quinn will eat them all."

Ian walked toward Duncan. His brother grasped his hand and lifted it onto his shoulder to grip, and in that moment, Ian wanted nothing more than to whirl Duncan around and lay into him like that day weeks ago, just to blow off some steam.

He hated being led around like a mentally challenged child. Hated having to rely on Duncan or whomever was around to help him. Hated—

"Ease up, brother. Any tighter and I'm going to need a sling later."

Ian loosened his grip with a muttered apology.

"Don't worry, okay? Emma will be fine. I'll see to it," Duncan said as they crossed the threshold onto the terrace.

Yeah. Duncan would see to it, make sure Emma was protected.

All because he couldn't do it himself.

Emma pressed a finger to her ear to block out the various sounds of barking and the student trainers' voices present for the next PAWS class. "Dad, I can't hear you very well. Class is about to start. Can I call you later?"

"No! I need to talk to you now. I found your wallet stashed in a bag in one of the employee lockers. *His* locker. Emma, I *told you* that kid was no good. Why didn't you tell me he'd stolen it?"

She closed her eyes and bit back a groan. Zack hadn't shown up for class again today. "Dad, are you sure? How do you know it was Zack? Did you see him put it there?"

"How can you think he's *not* the one who put it there?" her father countered.

"Just because you found it there doesn't mean Zack took it. Anyone could've stuck my wallet there."

"You're working awfully hard to defend that boy."

"And you're working awfully hard to convict him with no proof. Why do you hate Zack so much?"

"I know a bad seed when I see it," Frank muttered.

"He is wonderful with the dogs."

"That doesn't make him honest. Emma, I—"

"Dad, I have to go. I'll be by sometime to pick it up. Just leave it in the office, okay?"

"All your money's gone. So is your university ID."

Great. That was the one thing she'd hoped to recover. "I'll stop by the office today and get a new one. I should have done it already." But she'd hoped to discover her wallet had dropped out of her purse inside someone's car and have it not be an issue.

The barking grew in intensity as the dogs greeted each other, and Emma felt her nerves beginning to stretch and wear thin. "I *really* have to go. I'll call you later, okay? Love you. Bye."

"Problem?" Ian asked from where she'd left him waiting on her to escort him to the back of the room.

"No, not a problem. My dad found my wallet," she said, filling him in on the details.

"But you don't believe it's Zack?" Ian questioned.

Emma wet her lips and wished for a little quiet to process things. "I don't want to believe Zack stole it, no."

"So where is he?" Ian asked.

Emma rubbed her throbbing temple. How was she going to tell Aunt Rose that things with Zack weren't working out? "I don't know."

"You can't ignore blatant parole violations, Emma."

She nodded, knowing Ian was right. She wanted to give Zack the benefit of the doubt, but her confidence in him faltered in the face of his absence. "I know."

Two hours later, Ian stood in the back of Emma's PAWS classroom. They had just returned from an exercise on the campus to take the animals for crosswalk training. It was only the first of many exercises, but one the animals in this particular class had yet to officially experience until today.

Since Ian was in attendance, Quinn was playing chauffeur. He'd dropped Ian and Emma off this morning but had just called Ian to say an accident on the mountain road had delayed him.

Ian found himself impatient—and suddenly aware of what was bothering him.

The dogs had learned how to cross the street with the signal —which was more than Emma had taught him to do at this point. He was a Navy SEAL. How hard would it be for him to go back outside, cross the street, and return? It was a challenge he felt compelled to take on, one he had to master on his own. Do— or get left behind.

Ian let himself out of the classroom, counting off the paces to the stairs. The exit door. The corner.

He found the button on the crosswalk light with ease. Listened to the tone that indicated the light had changed and heard the approach of a car slowing to a complete stop. All the things Emma had told them to listen for because the dogs would learn to pick up on such things as well.

His heart beat like a drum, but he set off across the street, tapping his way to the opposite corner.

Once he was standing safely on the curb, he paused, feeling ridiculous because he couldn't wipe the smile off his face.

He'd done it. Piece of cake. So why not see what else he could do?

Making a quick decision, he set off down the sidewalk. He'd walk around the block, return to the corner where he'd crossed, and be back inside the building by the time Quinn arrived to take them home.

It was as simple as making a mental square, pathetic in its simplicity but a start just the same.

Frowning, he realized it took all his concentration to filter through the background noise around him. Cars, a bus. People talking. Kids screaming as they ran by chasing one another. He made it to another crosswalk, his cane tapping against the pole. With military precision, he made a quarter turn to tackle the next street, taking his time as he tapped his way along.

He passed a restaurant, the garlic-tinged air unmistakable. Someone played music too loudly, and a jackhammer pounded out an ear-splitting rhythm.

"Look out!" a chorus of voices cried seconds before something collided with his ankle.

"Sorry, dude. My bad. My board got away from me. You okay?"

A skateboard. His ankle throbbed, but Ian forced a nod of acceptance in regard to the apology and limped along, tapping out his way with the cane.

"Sir? Sir?" a woman called.

Someone touched his arm.

"There's construction ahead of you. That sidewalk is closed. You have to cross back there," she said. "Want me to show you?"

He didn't want to accept help. That negated his challenge and being able to say he'd done it all on his own. But the woman took his arm and walked with him back the way he'd come.

"Straight ahead. The sidewalk leads to the Baker Building. Would you like me to walk you to your destination?"

Like she would walk a dog? "No. No, thank you." He found the button on the light and waited for the tone, making the change in route to the mental map he'd formed in his head. The change added two more crossings to his challenge. Maybe that made up for the woman helping him?

He walked for a bit, the clicking of his cane drowned out by the construction noise. This part of campus had to be on the edge of town because it was a lot busier. Shouldn't he have reached the corner by now?

Ian kept walking, the knot in his gut growing tighter with every step. The sidewalk seemed to be curving, not straight, which meant he'd missed the crossway back to Emma's building.

He stopped, turned his head, and searched the darkness futilely. The university's clock tower began to chime, and he focused on that. The tower was... north, Emma's building east. But like a sick and twisted joke, church bells began to ring, and all the sounds jumbled together. He couldn't sort them out.

A low rumble of thunder rippled through the air, adding to the chaos in his head. A dog barked, traffic roared, even a small plane flew overhead.

Ian turned again, the slick, insidious slide of panic rising inside him. Sweat trickled down his cheek, and the handle of the white cane became slick in his hand.

A loud roll of thunder echoed over the mountains, the ground shaking from the force. The thick, humid air began to move as the wind picked up.

Low, gloating laughter filled his head, and he began to walk too fast. But the sidewalk kept curving, and he didn't know where he was. Didn't know which way to go.

Didn't know how to escape the flood of claustrophobia dragging him under…

I see him." Quinn said, muttering something under his breath.

"What?" Emma demanded in response to Quinn's curse. Quinn never swore, at least not in front of her. None of the men did, except for Ian when he became extremely frustrated. "What's wrong?"

"He's holding on to a pole. He looks bad. Hurry."

Emma picked up her pace, her heart breaking into a million pieces because she knew what had happened. "Oh, Ian."

It was too soon for him to tackle street traffic alone. Why had he done this without her?

Quinn led the way to Ian's side.

"Ian? Ian," Emma murmured again. "We're here." She slid her hand along his arm, down the blazing, rock-hard length to the hand that gripped the street sign. Ian's entire body trembled. "Quinn, go get the car," Emma ordered. "I'll stay with him."

"Those lightning strikes are getting close," Quinn said. "Let me take you inside one of the buildings."

She tried to pry one of Ian's hands loose but couldn't. "No," she said to Quinn. "Just hurry." To Ian she said, "Ian? Focus on me. The sound of my voice. Don't shut me out." He didn't answer her, and she edged closer. "It's okay," she said, trying to soothe him. "It's overwhelming at first, but it gets better. I promise it gets easier. Ian, do you hear me? You're okay."

"No."

The approaching storm nearly drowned out the word, but nothing could hide the pain in his voice. Stark, cold. The sound alone caused a shiver of fear.

He shook the pole, as if he wanted to rip it out of the sidewalk.

"You don't understand. You can't."

"I *do*. Finding your way down the street isn't the same as finding your way through a house. It's easy to lose your way. Everyone panics the first time or so, but I'll help you learn how."

A rough huff of a growl left him, an animal in pain.

"It's not the street! It's-it's the *darkness*. It's swallowing me, Emma. I can't breathe. It never lifts. I can't— I can't do this. I can't be this way."

A panic attack. Oh, she'd had them, too. She'd thought she was dying because that was exactly what it felt like. No air, too hot. Pounding heart. Dizzy and sick and scared beyond all comprehension. Lost. So very, very lost. "You're okay. Listen to my voice. Ian? You're not alone. I'm right here. We're fine. Quinn will be back with the car, and we'll be home soon."

She stroked her hands over his arms, over his back, aware of the strength and the muscle beneath. So strong, and yet so very, very vulnerable. "Oh, Ian, why did you do this? Why didn't you ask me or Quinn to come with you?"

"I have to do it myself. I have to—"

"Why? To prove *what?*" She asked the question, but she knew that answer, too. He'd done this for the same reason she'd ridden her bike after she was blinded, the same reason she swam full-speed.

He did it so the blindness wouldn't win.

"That I could." Another broken, bitter sound emerged from deep within him. "But I can't. I can't escape, and it's *killing* me."

"No. No, Ian, I know it feels that way, but you'll be okay."

"No, I'm in hell. This is hell, *my* hell. I'm trapped."

Like the crack of lightning overhead, awareness struck her in an instant. This was more than a panic attack. This was... "You're claustrophobic? Is that it?"

All those nights at the cellar door, all those times he'd sought oblivion but couldn't go down the steps...

"I thought I could get a handle on it. I thought I could wait it out, but it's not getting better."

Soldiers were taught to never show weakness, never give anyone else an advantage. So Ian hadn't shared his secret and had struggled on his own.

Her heart hurt for him. Frightening enough to be blind. But to be claustrophobic and then lose his sight? "You're going to be okay. You're not in quicksand. Ian? You're not trapped. You're with me. I'm right here, and we will find a way to help you. Listen to the thunder. Can you smell the rain? Hear it coming? Focus on that. It hasn't rained in months. We're both about to get drenched, but it will feel *soooo* good. It will be cool and sweet and wash all the bad away. Focus, Ian. On my voice. P-pray for help to conquer this. Find strength, Ian. It's in you. You can do this."

In the distance, she heard doors to the buildings open up as classes let out, every squeak of the metal latches being shoved in echoing off the brick and concrete. "I'm sorry I didn't figure this out sooner. That you thought you had to deal with this all alone."

"You should go," he said when people began to crowd around them to cross the street.

"I won't leave you." A sharp crack of lightning drew shrieks from the females caught off guard, the resulting boom of thunder rattling the windows and ground, rolling and rolling over their heads. "I'm not leaving you, Ian. I'm staying right here because I love you. Do you hear me? Ian, I love you," she said, unable to hold the words back, her heart bursting with love, shattering with empathy for his pain.

More people crowded around them on their way to parking lots, dorms, and other classes across campus. The skies opened up and the deluge began. Not a sprinkle, not a few drops, but a hard, driving rain that soaked her clothes in seconds.

Emma heard splashes as students began to run, some laughing, some swearing, bumping into her and Ian as they rushed by, attempting to cut across the busy campus exit.

Suddenly Ian bumped her, knocking her backward, off balance. Her foot slipped off the edge of the curb, her grip on Ian's rain-soaked biceps doing nothing to help her as she stumbled into the street.

A car skidded, brakes loud as it tried to slow. Pain streaked through Emma. She bounced off metal, sliding down and tumbling onto the asphalt.

Emma fought off the pain and dizziness as long as she could, trying to move, to get back to Ian, but his hoarse shouts faded away.

Chapter 18

It felt like someone used her brain as a drum. That, or Frank had the TVs and jukebox in The Shak turned up to a throbbing level.

When the noise and pain kept dragging Emma out of sleep, she groaned. "Turn it down."

The complaint worked. The silence was instant—until it resumed all at once and even increased in volume.

Shoot me, shoot me, shoot me. Why so loud?

"Emma?" Laney said. "Emma, wake up. Em? Open your eyes."

"I am awake. Too noisy to sleep."

The comment earned a few chuckles, but the pounding on her brain didn't cease.

"Yeah, well, you've been sleeping most of the day. How do you feel?"

Sleeping most of the day? She took stock of her body and realized she had quite a few aches and pains and something... something was off. "Sore. Where's Ian?"

Ian's big, rough hand fumbled, gently touching her arm and tracking downward until he pulled her hand to his lips and kissed her knuckles. She smiled at the show of affection given the other voices in the room, and blinked her eyes open, wincing from the pain in her head.

She racked her brain but couldn't remember.

"Emma, what's wrong?" Laney demanded.

"It hurts. Everything hurts. It's too bright." The bright white light pierced her skull like ice picks.

Gasps abounded, and the blinds clanked against the window as they were lowered with a zip of the cord. A dull thud—a hand hitting the wall above her head?—plunged the room into blessed shadows. Oh, thank goodness.

"Duncan went to get a doctor," Laney said, her tone anxious. "Hang on, Em. He'll be right back. Don't move, okay?"

Emma was in so much pain she almost snapped at Laney. It hurt to breathe. Why move when every pulse of her heart made her headache worse? "Ian?" She hated how weak she sounded. How shaken. What was wrong with her?

Ian squeezed her hand.

"I'm here. Emma, I'm sorry."

She braced herself against the pain and hesitantly slid her lashes up a notch. The piercing agony was there but not as bad as before and— She inhaled sharply.

The image was fuzzy and wobbly, but when she blinked a few times, the edges began to take shape. Dark. Light. Varying shades of color. "*Oh*," she breathed. "Oh, God, *please*."

"You're scaring us, Em. Talk," Tasha ordered from somewhere in the room. "What's going on?"

She blinked but nothing changed. A sob escaped her. Surprise. Joy. Disbelief. Raw pleasure the likes of which she had never experienced. Until now.

The rush of awareness regarding her new state flooded her so fast she couldn't keep up. Couldn't comprehend. Couldn't *believe* but— "I can see. Ian... I can *see* you."

Sometime later, Emma opened her eyes and froze until she was able to focus on the light fixture above her head. Once she made out the image, the air left her lungs in a rush of relief.

"I take it that's because you can still see?" Laney asked softly.

Her eyes burned with the threat of tears, but they were happy tears. "Yeah." She blinked several more times, waiting for her eyes to adjust to make out the shadows of doors and windows and monitors by the bed. The chair squeak came from her left. Laney. With her long, dark hair hanging over her shoulder. "Where's Ian? What time is it?"

"Outside in the waiting room, and almost midnight. I left the light on in the bathroom, so you wouldn't wake up in the dark. Did it help?"

"Yes. Thank you." Emma turned her head on the scratchy pillowcase and saw that Laney had a blanket draped over her, her feet propped on the railing of the hospital bed. "I thought...I thought I'd dreamt it all. I still can't believe I can see again."

"From what the doc said, you'd better get used to it. Still blurry?"

"Yeah. But I can see you."

"And that's in low light," Laney said, her tone pleased. "Just think of what you could see if I turned on all the lights."

The ache was there but not as painful as before. "Do it. My head is still pounding, but do it anyway."

"Nice try but no. You heard what the doc said. It's coming back naturally, and you need to let it. If you have a headache, you shouldn't overdo it."

"Laney, please?"

Her sister tossed the blanket aside and walked over to the

bathroom door, opening it a little wider so that more light spilled into the room. "Too much?"

"No." Laney stood in the beam of light like an angel, her expression anxious and worried. "You're so pretty."

Laney laughed, the sound watery and choked. She rushed toward the bed and leaned over Emma, hugging her tightly.

"Oh, Em. I'm so happy for you. It's a miracle!"

"I know." Emma inhaled and closed her eyes at the peace flooding her. She and Laney hadn't talked much since the fire, and she had wondered if her sister stayed away because Laney was angry at her. "I'm glad you're here."

"Your friends will never forgive me for kicking them out. They wanted to take turns, but I couldn't leave you," Laney laughed. "Frank said you went out of your way to avoid the wedding ceremony tomorrow. They've postponed it."

"They shouldn't do that."

"He wants you there. And I think Helen's getting a little stressed with details, so it gives them both some breathing room. You did good, kid," Laney teased.

"I'm sorry I scared you. Were you the EMT?" Laney nodded but didn't speak, and Emma felt her sister trembling. "Oh, Laney. You must have been terrified."

"I was. And now I can't even be mad at Ian for knocking you into the street, because if he hadn't... Oh, Emma. Don't ever scare me like that again."

Laney sat on the edge of the bed, wiping at her eyes.

"How is he?" Emma asked, unable to keep quiet about Ian a moment longer.

"You can tell he blames himself for you being here."

"It was an accident. I felt someone slam into him. He certainly didn't mean to knock me off balance."

"I know that. We all know that, but even knowing the end result, it still ticks me off that he put you in danger. You avoid that intersection because it's so dangerous and confusing."

"Laney, he didn't know."

"I get that. And the fact that you can now see means this was probably part of some bigger plan we aren't meant to understand, but that doesn't keep me from wanting to throw up every time I get a squad call and show up to find my sister."

Emma reached out and grabbed hold of Laney's hand. "I love you, too."

"Okay, so no more drama."

"You got it."

"Good. And if you're not gonna sleep, let's plan. What's first? What do you want to do first?"

The change of subject brought a laugh. "I don't know. It's all so overwhelming I'm going to have to think about that. How's Dad doing now? Was he as upset as he was after the fire?"

"At first, but he's okay now. Helen took him home."

Emma snuggled deeper into the uncomfortable hospital bed. Were they always so lumpy? "Are you two still fighting? What are you fighting about anyway?"

"We've called a temporary truce in your honor," Laney said dryly. "But as to what... I guess it's no secret now. I've been scarce because I've been working, and I've started seeing someone."

"Oh? Who? Jim?" Emma asked, referring to Laney's EMT partner. "I can tell he likes you."

Laney shook her head. "No, it's not Jim. It's Rand."

"*Mitchell*? Really?"

Laney's low laugh filled the room. "That's a much tamer response than Dad's, that's for sure."

She could imagine. But only because Rand was nearly her father's age. "How did I not know this?"

"It didn't happen until after the fire. And you and I haven't exactly talked much since then. I feel so bad now."

"It's okay. We've both been busy."

"No, that's not what I meant. The fire— I was angry at you even though I know I shouldn't have been. The stuff that burned was just stuff, and I *know* this but—"

"But it was Mom's stuff. You have every right to be angry."

"No, I don't. It ticks me off that I was so petty to think that way. It's weird, isn't it? If you hadn't taken the job, if you and Ian hadn't been on that corner..." Laney brushed the hair off Emma's face and tucked it behind her ear. "Do you love him?"

"Yes." She wished Ian were there now. She needed to see him, talk to him. Touch him. When she'd opened her eyes earlier and discovered her vision had returned, she'd been in so much pain she hadn't even thought about the time preceding the accident. But now it all came rushing back. Ian's panic, his admission of claustrophobia. Now he had this new change to deal with? How much could he handle? "More than I ever thought possible, considering how I felt about him when we first met. Where is he?"

"In the waiting room with Duncan and the guy who brought Ian in. Quinn? Man, that guy gives me the creeps."

"Quinn's harmless."

"You're not blind anymore, babe. That guy? Not harmless. Anyway, Morgan and Tasha stayed for a while, but they went home. Jolie was still here last I checked, but given the testosterone out there, I'm sure she's probably long gone or else found another place to sit."

Emma couldn't wait to see her friends and family now that her head wasn't threatening to explode, but right now her focus was on Ian. "Has Ian said anything? About what's happened?"

"You mean about you getting your sight back? Not that I've heard. He was here when the doctor finished his exam and gave his report about the pressure being released, though. Why didn't you tell me you've been having headaches for the last couple months?"

"I thought it was just stress. You know, from working so much and then the fire and Roxy and all the changes." The doctor had said her headaches were probably a warning sign of pressure changes taking place that were further aided by her fall into the street. But they would never know for sure. His advice was simply to be thankful for the miracle.

Emma fingered the woven pattern of the hospital blanket, her thumbnail following the ridges and hollows of thread. Those were still too small and blurry for her to see, but if her vision continued to clear, it wouldn't be long.

But as happy as she was, as thankful and thrilled and blessed as she felt at having been given such a gift, Ian's reaction worried her. She remembered him sitting beside her earlier, gripping her hand. The way he'd brushed a kiss over her knuckles and whispered *I'm sorry* over and over before the pain medication had kicked in and she'd fallen asleep.

She could only imagine how he felt. To blame for her falling into the street. Happy for her but sad for himself.

Angry that it hadn't happened to him?

It was too much to process for a man who hadn't been able to cope with his blindness. Maybe he would see that she could help him even more now. Really help him? Or would it make him feel worse?

Emma shifted, feeling every sore muscle in her body. She had spent the day and most of the night sleeping, and now she was awake and in need of a topic to take her mind off Ian and what the future might hold. She wanted to see him but didn't want to rush him. Wanted to be with him but not until he was ready. "So. You and Rand."

"Yes, me and Rand."

"I never knew you were interested in him."

Laney shrugged and took her seat beside the bed, drawing her knees up to her chest and looping her arms around them. "He's nice."

"I know he's nice, but he's quite a bit older, too."

"Isn't age relative? Besides, any guy would be lucky to be as gorgeous as Rand is at his age."

Emma laughed and then winced at the pain it caused. Thank goodness the thumping in her head was down to a mild *womp-womp-womp* that matched her heartbeat. "So is that what it's all about? His looks?"

Rand's age truly didn't matter to Emma, but Laney did matter, and she didn't want her sister getting involved with someone who wasn't right for her.

"No. I really care for him. I'm not sure what it's about, but with him I feel like I could do anything, *be* anything—which is kind of the point, isn't it?"

"I suppose." But did she feel that way with Ian?

"I know you just woke up, and everything is out of whack, but what's going to happen with you and Ian? You just admitted you love him."

Emma rubbed her forehead and temple, trying to ease the ache behind skin and bone. "But?"

"But he couldn't wait to get out of here," Laney said, confirming Emma's worst fears. "With all the people in the room who wanted to stay with you? He couldn't wait to leave. I'm sure it hurts to hear that, but it's really telling, in my opinion."

That it was. But Laney wasn't privy to Ian's fears, either. None of them were except for her. "The news surprised him, too, Laney. He needs time to process things. Wouldn't you need some space if you were him? He's happy for me. I know he is. But put yourself in his shoes."

She refused to allow herself to overthink Ian's absence in light of learning he was claustrophobic. She couldn't imagine that battle, every second of every minute, every hour of every day.

And then to sit by and listen while she received a miracle...

Oh, her heart ached for Ian, and she said a quick prayer. Life wasn't at all fair, was it?

"Okay, fine, I see your point. It would take some getting used to since you met blind and now the dynamic has changed. Just be careful, okay?"

"I will."

"I mean it. The doc said you could've hit your head a hundred times and it not have relieved the rest of the pressure, but it *did*," Laney said.

"What are you saying?"

"That you've been given a second chance. Maybe you should at least consider your alternatives?"

A knot formed in her stomach. "Meaning I shouldn't be with Ian?"

"I'm not saying that. I'm just saying you need to think long and hard before you commit yourself to a man who may or may not be able to accept that he's probably never going to get the miracle you did."

IAN."

Ian awoke to the sound of his name on Emma's lips, the feel of her fingertips sliding over his arm as she crawled onto his lap where he sat in one of the hospital chairs in her room.

"Ian," she whispered again, her voice choked.

He wrapped his arms around her, mindful of the IV and the

soreness Laney had related to those sitting in the waiting room. While Laney had gone for coffee, Quinn had helped Ian return to Emma's bedside in the wee hours of the morning, listening to the soft, even sound of her breathing as she slept.

Her fingertips roamed, every touch followed by a kiss. He felt the slick coolness of her tears on his skin, the way she trembled. "Don't cry. Come on, you should be in bed."

Her hands clutched at him, and her body stiffened.

"No. No, please. I need you to hold me. Just hold me."

He couldn't deny her. It was his fault she had been hurt. He'd stood there on the street like an idiot, frozen by fear, smell of dog shampoo filling his head along with Emma's natural scent and every other smell and sound surrounding him. She could have been killed, and he was to blame.

It was his fault. His fault Emma had been on that side of the campus. His fault she'd fallen into the street. The man he used to be, the soldier, would've been able to keep her safe. Protected her. Instead, he'd stood there and clung to a pole like a child.

"Ian," she whispered against his lips.

He knew what she wanted. To be kissed, comforted.

But with every tentative brush of her lips against his, with every tug of her fingers in his hair, he distanced himself more.

Hour after hour, he'd sat outside her hospital room wondering what kind of man became jealous over such a life-altering event. What kind of man would continue on in a relationship with her knowing he would hold her back?

He gentled her too-harsh kiss and shifted so that her face was in his neck. Her tears branded him, and he sensed he'd hurt her by refusing, but he had to stop her.

Emma was young when she'd lost her eyesight whereas he was a hardened soldier who'd seen and done more than most would in three lifetimes. Emma had the entire world to explore.

The only thing he could do—the best thing he could do for them both—was let her go.

How is she?" Duncan asked the following morning when he spotted Ian in the waiting area down the hall from Emma's hospital room.

"Sleeping. Laney's in the room with her. The doctor said he might release her tomorrow."

"That's good news. She'll be more comfortable at home." Duncan ran his hand through his hair and studied his brother's face. "You should go home. Get some sleep yourself."

"No."

Duncan frowned at Ian's response, at the distant expression on his brother's face. "What's going on?"

Ian's grip on his white cane tightened until his fingers turned red. "Something is off."

"What do you mean?"

"Emma, the accident."

"He doesn't think it was an accident," Quinn said as he joined them, carrying two cups of coffee, a plate of chicken fingers, some fruit, and granola bars.

"Something is off," Ian said again. "I just can't put my finger on what."

Duncan realized his brother was replaying the scene of Emma's accident in his head.

He grabbed a seat, his elbows digging into his knees. "What makes you think it was more?"

Ian explained about Emma's wallet. How it had contained her passkey for the university, and the way things had been moved and changed in her classroom. "Frank found the wallet in Zack's locker at The Shake Shak. Her university ID was missing."

"Okay. The kid's record is for petty theft, but even if he took the wallet and used her ID to walk out with some university property, what does that have to do with the accident? Why would Zack want to hurt Emma? She's the only person standing between him and jail."

"I know," Ian said, "but he hasn't shown up for work or the last couple of classes, and I can't stop thinking it's connected. There have been too many little things happening lately. Things that don't add up."

"Ian, you're worried about not being able to protect her. Are you sure that isn't the reason you think it's more?"

"Ian's instincts never fail," Quinn said. "If he says something's off, it is."

Duncan mulled that over, unable to argue with the logic. Facing down bad guys took some doing, and they had all learned to rely on their instincts. "Okay. I'll do some digging and see what I can find out."

Duncan glanced at Quinn before nodding his head toward Ian.

Quinn lifted his head in silent agreement to stick around and keep watch so Ian wouldn't be alone.

Duncan clapped his brother on the back and stood. "Tell Emma I stopped by."

Half an hour later, Duncan retraced Ian's path from the PAWS classroom to the first corner where Ian had had to change directions. Once the path in front of him was clear, he closed his eyes for a few seconds and kept walking, trying to put himself in his brother's shoes.

The noises, the smells, not knowing what was in front of him.

He rounded the corner on the curving street where Emma had fallen and spotted Zack on the sidewalk by the pole where Ian had stood. "Well, well, well. What have we here?"

Duncan watched as Zack stepped into the street, bent, and picked something up from near the mouth of a storm drain. The guy stared at it a brief second before shoving it into his pocket.

Zack hopped on the back of a motorcycle parked at the curb and took off.

And all Duncan could do was watch as the guy disappeared.

Ian, Quinn's on his way up to you with Emma and Laney. You need to help him get Emma out of there."

Ian frowned at Duncan's order and pressed the cell phone closer to his ear. "Explain."

"I saw Zack at the scene nosing around. He found something on the ground where Emma fell, but took off before I could get to him. I thought he might go home, so I drove to his apartment."

"And?" Ian demanded, not bothering to ask how Duncan knew where the guy lived.

"Cleaned out. Manager said he hasn't seen Zack in well over a week, and he skipped out on rent. But from there, I went to The Shak to check out his locker."

"Anything?"

"Zack had stashed a camera there for safekeeping. Quite an expensive one, too. Not something a guy like him can afford. Anyway, he had pictures of Emma. A lot of them."

Ian focused on one word. "What kind of pictures?"

"Most of them were taken when she was with the dogs or at

the diner, but there are three or four hundred of them on the memory card."

"Three or four hundred? He's stalking her?"

"Looks that way to me. I've got someone trying to run down info on a new address. In the meantime, you and Quinn get Emma out of there. Emma will be safer at the house now that the security is finished."

The elevator dinged, and Ian heard the sound of Laney arguing with Quinn as they walked toward him.

"Fine, if she has to leave the hospital early, she can come stay with me," Laney said.

"No," Quinn countered. "She goes home with Ian. No exceptions."

"They're here," Ian said. He hated feeling so helpless. Helping Quinn get Emma out of the hospital was a joke. He'd be more hindrance than help.

The blind guy slowing everyone down.

"I'll see you at the house."

The phone clicked in his ear, and Ian's hand fisted over the device.

"Ian? Ian, what is going on?" Emma asked. "Do you know what this is about?"

"We're leaving," he said. "Laney, go pack her things."

"Don't give me orders," Laney said. "Answer her questions."

He fought his impatience, remembering a time when his orders were obeyed with no questions asked. "Emma might be in danger."

"Might be? Or is?" Laney asked, her voice rising.

"I'll explain in her room. Quinn? Go find her doctor," Ian ordered. "Make it clear we're leaving, and get instructions on what kind of care she's going to need."

"Stay put until I get back," Quinn said.

Ian nodded, knowing the advice was sound but hating it all

the same. He wanted to pick Emma up and carry her out of there like some white knight, but all he could do was wait for Laney to lead the way toward Emma's hospital room and for Quinn to return to escort them out.

He could love her all he wanted—but he couldn't protect her.

Emma stared up at Ian, her mind memorizing every detail she could make out despite the persistent blurriness.

Ian had several days' worth of stubble on his face, his eyes hidden behind dark glasses. Even so, he looked exhausted and sleep-deprived, his clothes wrinkled, his voice tired. She knew she was the cause. That and her newfound eyesight.

This was the first time she had stood toe to toe with him post-accident, and a shiver raced through her. He was... beautiful. Big and broad and gorgeous, the one person who could relate to all she'd been through.

"Emma?" he urged.

She laid her hand over his on her shoulder and lowered her cheek atop as well. "Come on," she said, her voice husky with emotion.

She turned and noticed Laney watching them, her eyebrows knitted and mouth drawn down in a frown. "He'll explain in the room," she said, knowing it would spur Laney on and prevent further argument.

Once inside her hospital room, Ian kept hold of Emma's hand. "Laney, stay with Emma while I check the bathroom."

"I've got it," Quinn said, entering behind them. "The doc was around the corner. We're good."

"You guys are taking this awfully seriously," Laney said.

"What is going on?" Emma demanded.

"Emma, has Zack ever come on to you?" Ian demanded. "Flirted? Taken your picture?"

"Come on to— No. I mean, he's flirted, yeah, but that's all. It was harmless."

"And the photos?" Ian pressed.

"Bathroom's clear."

Quinn entered the tiny room and stared at Emma, waiting for her answer. She now knew what Laney meant about Quinn. With his size, tats, and scarred body, harmless was not an appropriate descriptive. "A-a few of the dogs at the house and in class. Maybe one or two of me at work. Why? Oh, Ian, don't tell me my father got to you, too? Is this because of the wallet? Everyone knows Zack has a record. Who better to blame than him? Frank hasn't liked him from the beginning. The wallet could've been on the floor *near* Zack's locker, and Frank would have blamed Zack."

Ian slid his hand to her neck, his thumb stroking over her cheek.

"Zack had more than a few photos of you, Emma. He had hundreds."

Emma wasn't sure who gasped the loudest, her or Laney. "Hundreds?"

"Think," he ordered softly. "Are you sure he hasn't done anything else? Made you feel uneasy?"

"No. I mean, he hasn't even shown up the last few times he was supposed to but..." That made Zack look guiltier than ever. "I know I should've reported him to the judge for violating the terms of his parole, but everyone slips up. He could've had car problems or gotten sick. I thought..."

"You'd give him a second chance," Ian finished for her.

"And then a third," Laney said wryly. "Oh, Em. When are you going to stop taking in strays and start living for yourself?"

"Get ready," Ian said grimly, looking as though Laney's words bothered him. "Leave the flowers and gifts. They can be retrieved later."

"Ian?" she asked, gripping his arm when he turned as though to step back outside the door. "Are you okay?"

What she really wanted to ask was, *Are we okay?* But she couldn't. Not yet.

"I will be once I know you're safe."

Chapter 19

You should be resting," Ian said the moment Emma entered the den.

She had been home almost twenty-four hours, and while she had gone to bed upon arrival with a massive headache the doctor said would eventually wane, today she was awake, mobile, and feeling better despite the dull thump that remained. Regardless, she wasn't going to spend her first full day out of the hospital lying in a semi-dark room. "I've rested plenty."

A low *woof* and panting slide of a tongue over her hand alerted her to Tucker's presence in the den. She knelt on the floor and petted the dog, holding him close enough that she could see his sweet face.

Big brown eyes, brown muzzle. Huge paws. Tucker was going to be massive when he was full-grown. Maybe a dog better suited to wheelchair-assist? "You're a good boy, aren't you? But what are you doing in here?"

Owen had insisted on keeping the pups with him last night so she could rest.

"Tucker and I have been hanging out."

"So I see." Realizing too late what she'd said, Emma winced and hoped Ian didn't take the comment badly. "Come on, you. Out. Ian and I have to talk, and you will just distract us," she said, leading Tuck to the door. Once outside, Tucker sat on the hallway floor as though he refused to go far.

Emma closed the door and took a deep breath before she walked over to where Ian sat behind the desk. His features took shape with every step, and she realized that one day very soon, she would be able to see him clearly, either on her own or with the help of glasses.

Today Ian wore jeans and another dark-colored T-shirt. Black or dark blue. She made her way around the desk slowly, straining to focus on his face to get a gauge on his mood.

He swung sideways in the chair as she approached. And even though she thought he stiffened when she got near, she ignored the niggle of unease that slid through her and lowered herself onto his lap, unable to go another moment without feeling his arms around her. Maybe it was forward, but she needed contact with him.

His arms closed around her and held, locking her against him in a tight hug that was over all too soon.

"Ian," she whispered, brushing her fingertips along his neck and the strong jut of his jaw.

He turned his head away from her, his body hard and tense beneath her.

"Ian?"

He lifted a hand and scrubbed it over his face.

"I can't get the sound out of my head."

"What sound?"

"Your gasp when I ran into you."

"Oh, Ian. It was an accident."

"I hit you hard. Hard enough that I knocked you into the street."

"Because someone slammed into *you*. Ian, that's not your fault."

"You could have been killed."

"But I wasn't," she argued softly, praying for the words that would get through to him.

She used her hand to turn his face toward her, nuzzling his lips with hers before pressing him for more, kissing him with all the desperation she felt inside her because she could feel him pulling away from her, and she was helpless to stop it.

Ian didn't move, didn't return the kiss, but she kept her mouth on his, tears burning her eyes because of his lack of response.

Finally, Ian groaned against her mouth, his hands in her hair. Then he pushed her away.

"No."

"Ian—"

"We're not doing this, Emma. As soon as Zack is found, you're leaving."

"You don't mean that."

"Thinking we could be together was a mistake."

"You don't *mean* that," she said again, wishing she felt as brave as she sounded. Her body felt brittle and old, as if the slightest move would make her shatter. She watched him, waited, praying he would change his mind. "You're upset and scared because I got my sight back, because it changes things. You're pushing me away."

"That's right, I am. You need to go."

"Ian—"

"I said get out!"

Face flushed from her anger and embarrassment that everyone in the house and nearby on the grounds had to have heard him shout at her, Emma got to her feet.

This was one of those moments in life where she had to make

a decision, and it had to be quick. Stay, fight for what she wanted —or go.

Laney's words reappeared in Emma's head. This was her chance to create the future she wanted for herself, and in the face of Ian's anger and at the look of naked pain on his face... she hesitated. Because right then, she wasn't sure what she wanted.

She loved Ian, but she couldn't love him enough to heal him. He had to do that on his own. More importantly, he had to be able to accept her, sight and all. And right now he couldn't do that.

She crossed the floor to the door, hesitated, hoping Ian would call her back, apologize. But she waited in vain. Tucker shoved his thick body through the opening and into the room, immediately going to Ian, his tail wagging in greeting.

Ian dropped back into the desk chair and began to pet the dog, his expression so bleak and sad and bitter that she blinked back tears.

Emma left the room but paused outside in the hall when she heard Ian speak to Tucker.

"She needs to go, Tuck. How am I supposed to be with her now?"

The next day, Duncan found Emma sitting on the floor of the hallway facing the terrace and pool. The French doors were open, the force of the heavy rain a loud drone echoing off the walls around them.

He slowed when he saw her, taking in the silent tears trickling down her cheeks and the lost, absorbed expression she wore. "Emma?"

Duncan moved closer when she didn't respond, squatted

down beside her with slow, careful precision that wouldn't cause alarm. "Emma?" he whispered. "You okay?"

"It's beautiful," she whispered, never taking her eyes off the view. "Look at it. The way the rain hits the pool water so hard it plops and makes a splash. The way it makes everything so green and clean and new again."

Duncan shifted so he could sit beside her on the floor, the emotion-packed description hitting a part of his heart he'd thought hardened long ago. His anger with his brother was never far from the surface, and since yesterday's incident had left Emma running from the den in tears, Ian had shut down like he had right after the surgery.

He knew his brother was happy for Emma, but right now Ian couldn't cope with his feelings about the return of her sight, and he was taking that frustrated anger out on her. Ian weighed in on the accident and wanted updates on their efforts of locating Zack, but he avoided all of them otherwise. Emma especially.

And it was taking a toll.

The tears rolling down Emma's cheeks were of sadness and hurt. Appreciation and gratitude. Loss. All because what had happened between her and Ian was so messed up and unfair. Good for Emma, but bad for her and Ian as a couple.

Emma didn't deserve to be punished or tossed away, but that was exactly what Ian was doing. Fool that he was.

Emma wiped her fingers over her cheeks and got to her feet.

"Where are you going?" He didn't want her to be alone. Not when she was upset.

Emma moved as though drawn by a power she couldn't control, toward the open doors. "Out there."

"Emma, it's pouring."

"I'm not going to sit here and be sad. Have you ever danced in the rain?"

Duncan got to his feet. "No, I can't say that I have. You do remember your accident in the rain a few days ago, right?"

"My mom loved the rain. She would take me and Laney out into the yard, and we'd run and play and dance. Dance with me?"

She held out her hand, palm up. Eyes sad but bright with a light that burned from deep within. One so powerful he couldn't refuse her.

Duncan took her hand in his and led the way out of the house into the warm summer rain. What else could he do? He didn't want her to slip and fall. She couldn't afford another bang to her skull.

Leading her off the slippery concrete of the terrace and into the grass, Duncan ignored the sting of the rain in his eyes and twirled her around, smiling at the delight that stole over her face, the sheer joy she expressed at being alive and able to see the rain falling onto her face.

It reminded him to be thankful for the blessings he'd received, Emma being one of them.

Emma's laughter carried across the pool and concrete. Drawn to the sound, Ian moved closer to the window, fumbled for the locks, and pushed the enclosure open wide. She was out there, near the pool with all its memories of hope and companionship.

She laughed, breathless and happy. But when her laughter was joined by Duncan's deep voice singing a lousy version of a popular hit, a knife plunged into Ian's heart.

"That could be you."

Ian didn't acknowledge Quinn's words, but the wood frame

cracked beneath his fingers, giving him away. "Duncan's a better choice. I won't hold her back or get in her way."

Time passed with agonizing slowness for Emma, and the next afternoon, she knew she'd been caught in the act a few seconds before the garage door actually opened.

"What are you doing?" Duncan asked.

She felt silly sitting on Duncan's Harley, but she was so bored in the house with everyone telling her to rest and with Ian avoiding her that she'd begun to explore the many rooms, including the oversized garage. Duncan stored his bikes there and several vehicles as well. She'd sat in the cars pretending to drive and excited at the thought of getting her license, when the motorcycles had caught her attention. "What's it like, riding these?"

"Depends."

He moved toward her, looking handsome in his jeans and dark green T-shirt. Duncan and Ian looked alike, but Ian had a harder edge, one she found appealing because they had shared the same kind of pain. "On what?"

"The reason for the ride, the weather. Some days it's nice to hit the open road and cruise along nice and slow. Some days it's all about the speed and the way the wind clears your head and blocks out everything."

"Oh. That sounds nice." It sounded wonderful, actually. Zack was still missing, and she couldn't bring herself to call Aunt Rose and fill her in on the details—what little there were. Until they found Zack's current location, all they had were a lot of unanswered questions and speculation.

"Emma, Ian will come around."

"So everyone says." Living in the house together, she couldn't kid herself. Everyone knew her relationship with Ian had grown serious—but was now at a complete standstill. They knew Ian didn't talk to her and avoided her any time she managed to catch him in the hall between his room and the den. The only things Ian seemed to tolerate were his friends when they brought him updates on the search for Zack—and Tucker. "I'm trying to be patient. I know I need time to adjust myself," she said, repeating the litany of things she'd told herself since leaving the hospital.

"But?"

"But I got my sight back. My *vision*—and I can't even be happy about it."

"Of course you can be happy about it. We're all happy for you."

"Not Ian."

"No, you're wrong there," Duncan said with a shake of his head. "Ian is happy for you. He's just sad for himself."

She'd told herself that, too.

Emma fingered the smooth leather and fine stitching weaving the seat pieces together. "Is it bad of me to not want him to be sad? To resent him being upset—just a little bit?"

"I think it's understandable."

She exhaled, wishing "understandable" meant "acceptable," because it didn't feel acceptable to her. "I want to celebrate. I want to see all the things I've missed, and I don't want to feel sad or guilty about doing it. I've prayed and prayed for him to come to terms because staying here with him acting like that... It's hard."

"I know. Being stuck here right now is rough, but we have to make sure you're not in danger. Until we can track Zack down, it's for the best."

"Duncan, it was an *accident*. Someone ran into Ian; he bumped into me. That's all."

"Maybe so. But the photos of you on Zack's camera weren't taken by accident. Zack at the scene of your fall *the next day* wasn't an accident. Same with him having your wallet and the incidents in your classroom. The day of the accident, did you or Ian say anything that might have upset Zack seeing as how he has a certain fascination with you? Something that might have angered him enough to shove into you two?"

"I don't—" She broke off, realizing exactly what she'd said to Ian that day. Could it be true? Could Zack have been standing there? Listening?

"Emma?"

She nibbled her lower lip, dazed. "I said I loved him. Ian. I-I was trying to get through to Ian and get him to let go of the post, and I said—I told him I loved him."

Duncan's face twisted in a grimace. Blind, she would never have known he made the expression. It made her realize how much she'd missed despite being able to pick up verbal clues. But why the grimace? Or was it a look of pity?

"That could have been the trigger. All of the things that happened up until then were minor, but if he was around to hear you say you love another man, that could've been what sent him over the edge."

"But why? Zack *never* made a pass at me."

"Sometimes there is no explanation, Emma. Some people are broken inside."

"He's not broken. Zack is nice. He's never been anything but respectful toward me. I'm having a hard time accepting that there isn't a logical explanation for the photos and my wallet being found in his locker."

"Then where is he?" Duncan demanded gently. "Why the disappearing act? Yeah, he seemed like a nice kid. But some criminals are reportedly nice, too. There's no rhyme or reason, Emma. And unless Zack can offer up an alibi and a good reason for why he's fallen off the grid, I think it's safe to consider him a stalker."

Feeling the need to hide, Emma picked up a helmet and fitted it over her head, remembering a childhood game where she'd actually believed if she couldn't see out of where she was, no one else could see her.

"What are you doing?"

"Take me for a ride," she said, not really asking so much as telling and hoping Duncan would overlook her rudeness and just do it.

"Emma, you just got out of the hospital."

"That was days ago, and I haven't left the house since I got here. I'm going stir crazy. Please?"

"I'll take you for a drive in the Hummer."

Big and safe wasn't what she wanted right now. "I want to ride this," she said, fixing the strap under her chin. "You said it helps you think and block out all the stuff in your head."

"You want another concussion?"

"Have you ever wrecked?" He didn't respond—a sure sign he hadn't. "You'll be extra careful with me on board. I know you will."

"No."

"If I spend one more moment here with Ian shoving me away and avoiding me, I'll go insane. Wouldn't that be sad? I get my eyesight back only to lose my mind? Come on, you danced with me in the rain. I could've slipped and cracked my head on the concrete."

"Why do you think I took you into the grass?"

He crossed his arms over his chest and glared at her, but she smiled back at him, waiting him out as she tapped the helmet's surface with her finger. "I'll have this on. One ride?"

Emma knew the moment she got her way. Duncan held

himself so still, but once he'd made a decision, his body loosened and he dropped his arms.

"You're not as sweet as you look, you know that?"

She grinned, unrepentant.

"Ten minutes."

"What? No, forty-five at least," she countered.

"I'll take you down the mountain and back up again, but I won't take you out on the highway."

She thought that over. There was always the second ride for that. "Deal. But you have to drive it like you do when you're clearing your head."

At that he chuckled. Donning his helmet, he swung his leg over the seat in front of her. "Just hold on and whatever you do, don't fall off."

Later that evening, the notes of the piano rose and fell in waves, the song dramatic and sad. Ian listened to Emma play, drawn to the music like the proverbial moth to a flame.

Still, the moment the hair on the back of his neck prickled, he knew he was no longer alone.

"She plays well," Quinn murmured.

The notes of Emma's song lifted higher, drifting to them with haunting clarity.

"Go inside. Sit with her," Quinn urged.

He wanted to. Ached to. But after what had happened the last time they were alone, he couldn't. He didn't know if he had the strength to deny her a second time.

Quinn moved closer. Ian couldn't hear the movement, but he knew Quinn stood directly behind him now, right outside the door where Emma played.

"You like her. You care for her."

"What does it matter?"

Quinn made a sound of frustration. "Because she is hurting, and she's walking around the house like a shadow because her heart is breaking. She loves you. Anyone with—"

Quinn broke off, but it wasn't hard for Ian to finish the sentence. Anyone with eyes?

Ian turned and grabbed hold of Quinn's shirt, fisted his hand until the buttons bit into his palm. "That's exactly why I can't go in there. I can touch her, kiss her, *smell* her, but I can't see her, and I *can't* protect her. She needs someone who can. She *deserves* someone who can."

"Then be that man. Find a way."

Chapter 20

Emma woke up early Monday, her body sluggish and tired from too little sleep. Still, the moment she opened her eyes, she froze then slowly released her breath. She tossed the sheet aside and stumbled to the shower.

The task of shaving her legs now took a fourth of the time, but once done, she remained under the spray, letting it rain down on her head. When her skin wrinkled and the water no longer appealed, she set to work on her hair and makeup. The fine texture of the eye shadow fascinated her, and she found herself staring into the mirror a long time, taking in the changes fourteen years had brought about.

Gone was the girl with the freckles and braces, the acne, and here was a reflection she had to get to know again.

Fifteen minutes later, she was dressed and sipping on coffee as she left the kitchen and meandered along the terrace garden between the house and stable. The pool water sparkled, and her gaze locked on the steps where she and Ian had shared such a special moment.

But Ian's rejection of her had her taking another sip and

turning away from the pain, bracing herself for another day separated by Ian's choosing.

A low-pitched growl sounded. Emma immediately turned to locate the source but didn't see anything.

The sound came again but ended on a whimper of pain.

From the kennel?

Emma rushed toward the structure and tugged impatiently on the big, heavy door. She ran down the aisle and skidded to a stop outside Goliath's pen. The large Dane was lying on her side, panting, two puppies at her feet and another on the way, from the look of things.

Shaking with a mixture of excitement and fear, Emma ran to the old-fashioned rotary phone on the wall and dialed Tasha at home.

"Something wrong?" a male voice said when the ringing stopped. Emma blinked, shocked by the man's presence in Tasha's home at such an early hour. "Uhhh…"

"Emma?"

"Y-yes."

"Sorry," Owen said. "I thought it was Duncan calling."

"No, it's— Can I talk to Tasha?" she asked, her mind whirling with questions.

A split second of silence was followed by Tasha murmuring frantically in the background before she said, "Hello?"

"Did he spend the night?" Emma couldn't help but ask.

"I… Later," Tasha said, the words running together in her sleep-husky voice. "What's wrong?"

"Goli's in labor. You have to hurry. She's already had two."

"She'll be fine, but I'll be there as soon as I can."

"Good. And, Tash?"

"What?"

Knowing just how much Tasha must care for Owen to risk

the talk and rumors, to take such a bold step, she said, "He must really be something special."

"Good-*bye*, Emma."

Smiling, Emma hung up after the phone clicked in her ear.

She wasn't sure what to do to help Goli, but seeing the dog in pain brought tears to her eyes.

Gingerly, in case Goli didn't want company, Emma let herself inside the enclosure and slowly approached. She dropped to her knees at Goli's head and began to stroke the dog gently, one glance showing the pups to be wriggling and squeaking and in good shape. "Look at you, pretty mama. Your babies are beautiful."

The pups more or less resembled rats, but they were beautiful rats, dark gray in color.

Emma was still sitting in the kennel with Goli when Tasha and Owen arrived, followed soon after by Quinn and Duncan.

Goliath was up to a count of five. "How many more? Surely she's almost done?"

Tasha palpitated Goli's stomach. "Definitely one, probably two. Maybe three?"

"Seriously? Eight puppies?"

"First timers average six to eight. But there could be more. We don't know if it's her first litter," Tasha said.

"But so many..."

"She could have a dozen, Em," Tasha said. "Better prepare yourself."

Owen laughed when he heard the news. "A dozen Great Danes. That's something I want to see."

How would she find homes for them all? "Can you tell the paternity?"

Another puppy slipped out of Goli with a low growl.

Tasha took a long, hard look at the puppies. Emma watched her and waited. "Well?" she asked when she couldn't stand it anymore. Tasha blinked several times, a grin curling her lips as she shook her head slowly back and forth in disbelief.

"I'm not sure, of course, but if I had to guess, I'd say... beagle?"

Gruff laughter came from the men watching from outside the gate.

"Beagle?" Emma asked. "*Seriously?*"

"That would be my guess for the time being, yes."

"Where there's a will..." Duncan drawled.

Emma tried to comprehend the logistics. Beagle... Beagle... "Oh, noooo."

"Hey, I could be wrong. When they're a little older, I'll be able to better tell," Tasha said.

"No, that's not what I meant. Tash—Mrs. Marcum. *Davidoff.*"

"Ahhh," Tasha agreed with a nod. "You kenneled Davidoff for her while she went on vacation, didn't you? Well, at least Goli has good taste. That beagle has won prizes all over the eastern United States."

"The dog's name is Davidoff?" Owen asked. "Isn't that a little pretentious for a beagle?"

"Pretentious it may be," Tasha said, "but it appears David triumphed over Goliath again."

Tasha? What's going on?" Emma asked that evening, watching as Tasha approached carrying a gift bag. She'd had a follow-up appointment with her doctor late that afternoon, and on the way home, Duncan had brought her by The Shake Shak for dinner to celebrate Goli's delivery of nine healthy pups.

"Surprise!"

"That's for me?"

All of a sudden, Laney, Morgan, and Jolie appeared carrying balloons, gift bags, and even a cake. The Shak's waitstaff joined them, smiling from ear to ear. "A party for me? You guys! You didn't have to do this."

"We wanted to," Jolie said.

"You know we'll use any excuse to eat cake," Tasha added. Emma's stomach growled at the thought of Morgan's delicious cakes. Having eaten them for so many years, it was about time she saw how pretty everyone said they were and—"Oh, Morgan, it's *gorgeous*!"

The cake was an open book with edible pictures, candy buttons, and fondant ribbons. A beautiful scrapbook ready to cut and serve. Five photos covered the two pages. One of Emma as a child in pigtails sitting on her mother's lap, one of her parents and Laney and Emma together, the third of Emma and Roxy, and two of the *Besties* taken at different times over their many years of friendship.

Emma looked up to find Duncan watching her from across the table. Behind Duncan stood Quinn and Owen. But no Ian.

"He said he wasn't feeling well," Duncan said, answering her unspoken question.

"You knew about this?" Emma asked.

"Are you kidding?" Tasha said. "I asked Owen to get the okay from Duncan since you're basically under house arrest. We were going to have a Girls' Night In at Jolie's, but given the circumstances, the guys insisted on bodyguard duty."

Duncan frowned at Tasha's description but gave Emma a wink. "Well, there was mention of cake, and Quinn isn't much of a baker."

The pieces fell together in her mind. Ian was feeling just fine. He'd simply refused to come.

"Em?" Tasha said.

"What are we waiting for?" she said, managing to hold her smile in place by sheer will.

"Gifts first!" Tasha ordered.

"Open mine," Jolie said, handing her a good-size box tied with a bright red bow.

Emma removed the bow without too much damage and dug inside. "Oh. Oh, Jolie." The cream-colored blanket was delicate and soft. Beautiful.

She ran her hands over the surface, lingering on the feel of it. Was it…?

It was. How many times had she run her fingers over this pattern as she lay on her father's couch listening to the television? Every time she'd gotten sick, she'd wrapped the afghan around her shoulders to ward off a chill.

"Rose let me borrow the one your mom made for her so I could copy the pattern," Jolie said in her soft, sweet voice. "I started on it after the fire. I was going to give it to you for Christmas, but I couldn't wait."

Emma clutched the afghan to her chest and blinked hard. "I love it. Thank you." The words were more breath than sound.

"Oh, great, you made her cry first thing," Tasha chided.

"Well, my gift isn't as emotional," Morgan said, wiping her fingers over her cheek and giving Em a smile. "You've always talked about how you thought it was cool to decorate cakes, so in that box are mini cakes for you to decorate. All ready to go with icing, decorations, the works."

Emma laughed. "Really? Oh, how fun!"

"Mine next!" Laney said. "After I heard what Morgan was making for your cake, I kind of stole her idea and ran with it. I didn't do it myself since you know I'm not crafty, but Rand's sister makes these and sells them. I hope you like it."

Laney's present was an actual scrapbook, the opening pages already designed and ready for Emma to insert pictures. The other half of the book was already filled in with pictures from the past. Most were taken inside The Shake Shak, but some were personal photos from years ago.

"Aunt Rose dug up the old pictures," Laney said. "And she wanted to be here but didn't want to leave Uncle Bruce."

"It's beautiful." Emma stared into her mother's face, ran her fingertip around the bright blue border. "Her favorite color was blue."

Jolie moved to Laney's side and whispered to her sister, and Emma wouldn't doubt Jolie was promising to work on another afghan for Laney next. These were her friends, sweet and funny and wonderful.

"Okay, time to lighten things up some. This is a party, and we're getting way too serious," Tasha declared. "My present has nothing to do with sentiment and everything to do with art." She presented her gift bag to Emma with a grin. "Get ready to have some fun."

"Oh, Tash. What did you do?" Emma asked, wary but smiling. She definitely wasn't an artist in any form.

Beyond the tissue paper, Emma found a Bible with wide side margins for taking notes or journaling. There were all kinds of markers, colored pencils, stamps, ink pads, and pages of designs in bright colors to bring the verses to life.

"You liked the idea of faith journaling when it was mentioned at church, and now you can see to do it so…"

Tears stung her eyes. She couldn't wait to try her hand at this! "I love it. Oh, you guys…"

"Don't get too distracted," Morgan said, "because there's more."

The waitstaff had gone together to buy her a gift card to the local department store so she could go shopping, and some of the regulars from The Shake Shak had taken up a collection to add to the total as well.

"Oh, and for the record, I called Genie and left a message with her," Morgan said. "I can't believe she's not here."

It was surprising, but Emma shrugged off the lapse. "Something must have come up. Thanks for trying. I'm sure she appreciated it."

"This is from all the guys," Duncan said, presenting her with a long, slender box.

From the guys? Duncan, Owen, and Quinn stared at her with varying expressions of warmth and amusement at her surprise that they would participate in the gift giving, but they'd already helped her so much.

Emma glanced up at her friends to find them waiting anxiously to see what was inside before she flipped the top and gasped at the long, slender bracelet.

"Oh, a Pandora! And look at the charms. That's gorgeous!" Morgan cried.

It was. The bracelet was half full of silver charms and bright, sparkling color. She ran a finger over each one, learning the shape of the colorful beads and silver swirls, a cross, dog, flowers...even a fish. The items she'd told Duncan were painted on her childhood walls. Such a thoughtful present. "It's beautiful. Thank you. All of you. I can't thank you enough for all you've done."

"One last one," Frank said, lowering a small box onto the table. "This one is from your old man. And Helen," he quickly added.

Emma unwrapped the last box, thinking nothing else could surprise her, but seeing the key ring and key certainly did.

"When Laney turned sixteen, I got her a car. Since you can see to drive, you should get one, too."

Emma's eyes filled with tears. She gripped the key ring tightly, not caring one bit about what kind of car or color it was but only what it represented. *"Dad."*

She shot out of her chair and into her father's arms, heard him sniffle as he hugged her.

"You deserve it, baby girl. I'm so proud of you, sweetheart. No matter what gets thrown at you, you rise above it. Just promise me you'll drive safe."

"I will."

From there on out, Emma found herself passed around from person to person for hugs and congratulations. They cut the cake and fawned over Morgan's talent, and then she opened her box of mini-cakes and declared she wouldn't decorate them alone. At some point in time, a toast was made, the jukebox turned on, and Emma dragged onto the dance floor.

Then it was late, and Laney had to leave to begin her shift. Morgan needed to get home to her kids, Tash and Jolie to bed for their early workday tomorrow.

Emma said good-bye, hugging each of them and wondering what her life would have been like without them.

"Good party?" Duncan asked when they were in her new car —a gently used SUV with lots of air bags and bulk to keep her safe. She'd handed Duncan the key to drive them up the mountain, but tomorrow, driving practice began.

Emma nodded, rubbing her hands against the soft leather seats. "The best party ever."

At least it would have been—if only Ian had been there.

Chapter 21

Despite Duncan's insistence that she stay holed up in the MacGregor house, Emma attended church on Sunday and her first PAWS class as a sighted person on Tuesday.

For the last four years, she'd matched voices with people and the types of pups they raised. Now seeing them with their animals... It was amazing.

Zack didn't show up for class. Not that she expected him to. She struggled to understand Zack's strange behavior, tried to give him the benefit of the doubt. But disappearing as he'd done and remaining out of touch and in violation of his parole, it was hard to believe anything but the worst. Still, she prayed for him and hoped to be wrong.

She'd demanded to see the pictures Zack had taken, and Duncan had reluctantly shown her. To be honest, seeing the proof that Zack had been photographing her without her knowledge freaked her out more than she cared to admit.

Emma had to inform Aunt Rose, but it wasn't news she wanted to deliver over the phone. Seeing as how she was long overdue for a visit, she had asked Laney to accompany her to Aunt Rose's house after class.

But that was a matter to be dealt with later, she decided, laughing along with her students as they surrounded her, hugged her, and welcomed her back to the fold.

Joey with his dark hair and sloppy clothes, his German Shepherd, Oz, who had the softest brown eyes and a gentle spirit.

Tori couldn't hide her happiness and practically danced right there in front of them all. Her dog, Rosey, a young golden retriever, seemingly grinned with her tongue flopping out of her mouth.

One after one, she went through her class and spent quality time with them, memorizing every feature.

And Genie... "Where's Genie?" she asked the class.

"I saw her at the store last night," Elaine said. "She looked kinda sick."

So that's why she hadn't attended the party. Poor Genie. Emma made a mental note to give the girl a call later to check on her, doubting anyone else would.

Laney was there to pick her up when class ended.

"Are you sure you don't mind?" Emma asked as she and Laney walked Tink to Laney's car. Duncan had texted repeatedly to check in, stating he and Owen would be watching out for them, hanging back in case Zack put in an appearance. "You don't have plans?"

"With Rand? No. Besides, I need to go visit Uncle Bruce, too. Aunt Rose said he's having more bad days than good, and that it won't be long."

"I didn't know that," Emma said, saddened by the news. "Aunt Rose always tries to sound upbeat when I call."

The drive to their aunt and uncle's house was a quiet one with only Tink's panting to mark the passing blocks. Emma was amazed at how much the town had grown since she'd seen it last.

Aunt Rose met them at the door with hugs and held on to Emma for a long, long time.

"I still can't believe it," Rose whispered.

"I know. Me, either." Emma laughed through the moisture choking her. "You look so pretty."

Aunt Rose was pretty. Petite, she wore narrow-rimmed glasses and bright-colored clothes, a little makeup to accentuate her cheeks and eyes.

"Oh, now, none of that. You girls are the pretty ones. Bruce is so excited to see you. Come on, you know the way."

Emma wasn't sure what to expect when she entered her uncle's room. The thought of Uncle Bruce dying left her shaking inside though she knew he was a Christian and heaven-bound.

He'd been such a help after the accident that had killed her mother, stopping by her hospital room and rehab daily to help her cope with the emotional toll.

The bedroom curtains were open, sunlight spilling across the hospital bed where he lay. Emma swallowed the lump in her throat when she saw how skeletal he looked. She moved her hand behind her back, thankful she hadn't come alone. Laney's fingers grasped hers and didn't let go. "Uncle Bruce?"

"Go on, girls," Rose said from behind them, gently ushering them in. "It's fine."

Emma forced her feet to move closer to the imposing bed. Bruce was nothing but skin and bones, his cheeks hollow and tinged a sickly yellow.

"Bruce? The girls are here, dear. Emma and Laney both."

Uncle Bruce opened his eyes, and Emma struggled to contain her emotions. He looked old and so very weak. His beautiful blue eyes—previously always twinkling—dull and sad.

"I hear we need to celebrate."

"Yes," Emma whispered, smiling despite the stinging in her eyes.

"Hi, Uncle Bruce."

Laney greeted their uncle calmly, but her grip on Emma's hand pinched to the point of pain.

"Hello, Laney. My, look at you both. You've grown into beautiful women."

Uncle Bruce lifted his fingers from the sheet. Emma wrapped her free hand around them, forming a human chain.

"You girls are a sight for these tired, old eyes. Tell me how you are," he said. "What have you two been up to?"

Laney talked about her job and the party they had held for Emma at the diner. Emma talked about being in the hospital, how her eyesight had been blurry at first but grew clearer every day since as the muscles became stronger.

"So you like working with Ian?" Bruce asked with a satisfied smile.

Emma tried to put on a happy face and failed.

"What's wrong?" Bruce murmured.

"Nothing," she said. "It's almost dinnertime. What would you like to eat?"

"Don't lie to me, child," Uncle Bruce chided with a hint of a smile. "Tell me, or I'll ask your sister to tattle on you."

She glanced at Laney and exchanged a wry smile. As children, she and Laney had spent plenty of time ratting each other out.

"Ian's having trouble adjusting to Emma regaining her sight," Laney said before she held up her hands and stood. "And now I'm going to go see if Aunt Rose has any lemon cookies." Laney bent and kissed Uncle Bruce's cheek. "I'll be back in a bit, okay?"

"Bring me a cookie," Uncle Bruce ordered.

"You got it."

Once her sister left the room, Uncle Bruce patted the side of the bed.

"Come sit with me and let's talk."

"Uncle Bruce, I'm fine. Ian and I... We'll work things out. You are the one I'm worried about."

"Things have already been worked out for me, Emma. Now, Ian... He is a strong man," Uncle Bruce said. "And I don't doubt he needs time to adjust to the changes your sight has made in your relationship."

"I know."

"But you're still worried. Is that all that is going on?"

Emma held his hand in hers, stroked her fingers over his wrinkled skin. *Oh, Uncle Bruce. What are we going to do without you?* "I guess I can't help but wonder if time is enough. What if Ian doesn't adjust and there's no fixing us? Ian says he doesn't want to hold me back."

"There is that to consider."

She blinked at her uncle.

"Ahhh," Bruce drawled softly.

"What?"

"You're feeling guilty because you're afraid he's right."

"How can you say that? Ian— He's so strong, like you said. He'd never hold me back."

"He'd never *want* to hold you back, you mean. But there would be limitations to your relationship because he's still blind. Ian's not only struggling to accept who he is, but now he must accept the new you as well. The balance of power between you has changed yet again."

"For the better," she countered. "Are you saying he has to hold all the cards or we can't be together?"

"Of course not. I'm simply stating that, as a man, Ian feels even more inadequate because you can see and he can't."

"But I can help him more now."

"No one is arguing that. But a man's pride can be his downfall, Emma, and Ian's has already taken a beating. He is a man who lived to serve and protect. And what about you?"

"What about me?"

"In this case, as much as I love and respect Ian, he is looking at this turn of events with more maturity. You feel guilty for some of the thoughts you've had about your future, but more importantly, you're trying to deny the truth of them."

She ran her thumb over his paper-thin skin, wondering how he'd gotten inside her head so quickly. "Ever since the accident, people have ordered me around. Told me what to wear, when to be ready so they could drive me, where to walk, step. It's gotten better, but I've worked so hard to save money so I could have my own place, do my own thing. Be my own person. And now... I *want* to be with Ian. I *love* him. But I'd be lying if I said there's a part of me, especially in light of his behavior, that just wants to buy a plane ticket for the first flight out to anywhere and *go*."

"Would you feel free if you did that?"

Would she? She tried to imagine it. Tried to picture herself standing on a beach somewhere, toes in the sand, staring at the sunset. But she didn't want to go alone.

Her eyes stung, and she blinked away the pain.

"Why does it make you sad?"

She shook her head, a husky laugh escaping her. "Because I want him there with me, but I'm not sure he'll ever be willing to go."

"Time, Emma. All good things take time."

"Here you go," Laney said, carrying a tray of cookies and tea into the room.

Aunt Rose followed with plates and napkins.

"Emma, I've been meaning to ask you how things are working out with Zack?"

Emma bit her lower lip and exchanged a glance with Laney.

"Not well," Laney stated bluntly. "Zack stole her wallet, and to beat it all, now it looks like he's been stalking Emma."

Rose was in the process of lowering the plates onto a nearby table, but at the news, they fell with a clatter. "What?"

"Yeah. He's conveniently disappeared, too," Laney added, filling them in on the details of the photos.

"*Stalking* her?" Aunt Rose repeated. "Oh, Emma, no. Surely not. Zackary has always liked photography. He wrote in class once that he wanted to be a photographer when he grew up. Maybe that's the reason for the pictures?"

"Might explain the photos, but what about her wallet?" Laney asked.

Aunt Rose gripped her hands in front of her waist. "Do you really think he stole it?"

Emma shrugged. "I'm not sure what to believe. I didn't spend a lot of time with him, but I really thought he wanted to turn his life around."

"Oh, girls. I-I don't know what to say."

Aunt Rose looked at Bruce for a long moment before rushing from the room.

"I didn't mean to upset her. It's not Aunt Rose's fault because she introduced Zack to Emma," Laney said.

"I'm afraid there's more to it than that," Uncle Bruce told them.

Emma shot a questioning glance at Laney before focusing all of her attention on her uncle. "What do you mean?"

Uncle Bruce inhaled, the look on his face one of sorrow. "Girls, you know I don't have much time left."

"Uncle Bruce, don't think like that," Laney ordered. "You have to fight this."

"Yes, He does, and I am hopeful. But some realities must be faced in case I don't receive a miracle. So must some regrets."

Regrets? Emma picked at a cookie to give her hands something to do and licked the crumbs from her thumb. A burst of lemon filled her mouth, sweet and flavorful. But another glance at Uncle Bruce and Emma felt a knot of unease coil in her stomach. This didn't seem to be a "saying good-bye" type of conversation but altogether something different. "What regrets?"

"Girls, I need your help to right a wrong I did to my Rosie."

"Whatever it is, I'm sure it's fine. You and Aunt Rose are the happiest married couple I know," Laney said.

"Happiness is relative. The fact is, a long time ago, I made your aunt do something she didn't want to do, and I've regretted it ever since."

"What did you make her do?" Emma asked.

"I made her give up her baby."

What?

"It's a long story," he said, the words emerging tired and tainted with resignation. "We were having difficulties. Our marriage was going through a rough patch, and we separated. When we got back together, I found out... Well, I found out Rose had strayed outside our marriage vows."

Shock rolled through Emma, obliterated every thought. Aunt Rose had *cheated*?

"There were consequences from her liaison."

Emma struggled to take it all in. She glanced at Laney and found her sister looking equally shell-shocked.

"The baby wasn't yours?" Laney clarified.

Emma remembered asking her mother once why Aunt Rose didn't have any kids. Her mother's response was that it wasn't in God's plan. So how had Rose had a baby no one knew about?

Uncle Bruce closed his eyes and nodded. "The reason we separated was that I couldn't give Rose the children we had always wanted. When she told me... I got angry. When she began to show, Rose went away and stayed until after the delivery because I refused to consider raising the boy as my own. I gave her an ultimatum. To salvage our marriage, she had to give him up."

Laney sucked in a sharp breath, but Emma ignored her to ask, "Why are you telling us this?"

"Because it's *him*," Laney said, obviously making a connection Emma didn't understand.

"Him, who?" She stared at Laney, who was looking in horror at Uncle Bruce.

"It's him, isn't it? Zack? The baby was *Zack*?"

"Yes. Yes, I'm afraid it was."

The news shook Emma to her core. How on earth? How had they kept such a secret for so long? How did no one know? "If she gave the baby up for adoption, how do you know it's him?"

"Rose begged me to make sure the child was adopted by someone in town," he said. "She promised she'd never reveal her identity as his mother, but she needed to be able to see him on occasion and know he was all right. Ian's father was a prominent attorney at one time, before he went on to hold office. He helped me arrange things and kept the adoption quiet."

Emma didn't question Bruce's statement. She had grown up in here. She knew well that such things were possible.

"Who was the father?" Laney demanded.

Lost in thought and remembering Zack's comments about his father's drinking, Emma realized Zack had meant his adopted father, not biological. But Laney's tone drew Emma out of the memories. "Laney, do we need to know that? It's really personal."

"*Who?*" her sister demanded again.

"Frank," Rose whispered from the doorway. "The baby's father was Frank."

Silence filled the room. Emma sat there, stunned, her mind spinning. It was true. She knew the story was true because there was no other reason for Rose and Bruce to look the way they did.

It made her sick to her stomach. Her heart twisted and shriveled in pain. Her father had cheated on her mother—with Aunt Rose?

And then she remembered... "The day of the accident," Emma said softly, her mind whirling. "I overheard Dad talking to someone on the phone. He said 'our son' to the person on the other end when he didn't *have* a son. I was still upset when Mom picked me up from swim practice, and I-I told her what he'd said. That's why she took that curve as fast as she did. She-she was so upset."

Tink whined and rose on her hind legs to brace herself against Emma's knees. Emma petted the dog distractedly, Tink's warm, soft fur comforting.

As bad as Bruce must have felt, Emma could not imagine her mother's heartbreak at finding out so callously about an affair. To have a spouse betray his vows was painful enough, but thank goodness Emma hadn't known the answer to her mother's question as to who was on the other end of that phone call. Her mother had died without knowing Rose was the other woman.

Aunt Rose sobbed, her head hanging low.

"If I've learned anything all these years, Emma, it is that the matter isn't for us to judge." Bruce's hand trembled as he wiped a tear from his cheek. "Had I been able to find forgiveness sooner, raised the boy as my own, maybe he wouldn't have turned out the way that he has. Rosie, I'm sorry. I'm so sorry for taking him from you."

Aunt Rose staggered across the room and sobbed against Uncle Bruce's chest.

"I would have taken this secret to my grave except for the fact I do not want Rose to be alone. Mistakes were made by all of us, none worse than another. We've all sinned. We have all suffered from this, but Rosie needs you now, more than ever."

"What about Mama?" Laney whispered. "What about *her* feelings?"

Aunt Rose's shoulders shook with the force of her cries, but seeing it didn't make Emma feel any better. In a way, she wished she couldn't see it because tears didn't change the wrongdoing. How could Aunt Rose have betrayed her own family that way? Aunt Rose was cookies and book club parties, school projects and sewing. Women like that… they didn't cheat.

Emma opened her mouth to speak, but no words formed. All she could do was sit and breathe and think and mourn. A fly buzzed across the room, trying to find freedom at the window with fruitless, tapping hits against the glass.

For long seconds, Emma was that fly. Able to see freedom, the future, only to be stuck behind the glass, confused about what to do next.

She had a half brother. Her father had denied his own son all these years by hiding the truth.

Where did they go from here? Did Zack know?

Despite the warmth of the sun shining through the windows, Emma shivered. Why had Uncle Bruce told them now? What did he expect them to do?

"Girls, you have to honor a dying man's request. You have to forgive her and help Rosie with the boy once I'm gone."

"Bruce, don't. It's too much to ask of them."

Uncle Bruce wiped away Rose's tears, and Emma's confusion grew.

"I must. Emma, Laney, if there is any decency in Zack at all, I want you to help Rose get to know her son. I took him away from her at birth. I think it's fitting that he comes back to her now. When you find him, tell him the truth."

Aunt Rose left the room soon after Uncle Bruce's request. Silence followed, stretching out until Emma couldn't stand it any longer. She left Laney in the bedroom with Uncle Bruce and quietly made her way through the house.

Rose stood before the sink with her shoulders slumped, her arms wrapped tightly around her middle as though she tried to hold herself together. Emma recognized the pose, feeling much the same in light of all they'd learned. "Are you okay?"

Rose's hand lifted and she pressed her fingertips against her mouth, one quick shake of her head Emma's answer.

Emma's mind flashed to memories of her mother, and she saw the resemblance. Two years apart in age, her mother would have been fifty this year, which made Aunt Rose only fifty-two. Right now, she looked twenty years older.

"I can only imagine what you must think of me. I am so *ashamed.*"

Emma walked deeper into the room. A wave of grief washed over her, the longing she felt for her mother's arms to hold her one more time strong and nearly impossible to bear. "It's... surprising. *How* could you betray her? Uncle Bruce?"

"It wasn't like that," Rose whispered, her voice low and choked with tears. "It wasn't an affair. Your father and Lauren were having difficulties. She'd often accused your father of having affairs with waitresses and cooks at the restaurant, but he'd stayed true, Emma."

"Obviously he didn't. I don't understand how you can love someone and hurt them that way."

"Emma, please try to understand. I was sad and angry because I couldn't get pregnant. Bruce accused me of-of wanting someone else, someone who could give me children. Much like your mother, I accused him of things I knew in my heart he hadn't done. We were all just so angry. The stress was too much for us, and we agreed to spend some time apart.

"I started going to the diner because I was lonely, and it was full of people and noise. One night, your father and I started talking and—drinking. The diner was closed, and every hour brought a new story about an argument we'd had with our spouses. We were comfortable sharing our frustrations because we knew each other so well. We drank too much and things... went too far. Frank regretted the lapse as much as I did. Our indiscretion wasn't a love affair, wasn't long or drawn out. It was a single mistake made by two very lonely, very drunk, very hurt people."

Emma had to think about that. Did her sympathy extend to Rose and her father betraying her mother and Bruce so badly?

"There's no excuse for what we did," Rose whispered. "None whatsoever. I realize that. I've begged for forgiveness every day since. Frank and I agreed that it would *never* happen again, and it wouldn't be discussed."

Emma closed her eyes. "Except for the fact you got pregnant."

A harsh laugh left her aunt's chest.

"Yes. So many years of trying to have a baby with Bruce without success, but one horrible mistake and I couldn't hide the truth of my sins. It was a punishment and blessing in one."

Rose sniffled and wiped away her tears, but more fell.

"Bruce was devastated, utterly, horribly broken. And I was responsible because I'd done that to him. But I didn't feel it was the child's fault, so I begged and pleaded and promised... When you play with fire, Emma, the devil burns you. I've learned that lesson well. Bruce and I had reconciled. But I swore if Bruce would stay with me, give me a second chance, I'd never seek the boy out or let the truth be known. All I wanted was to know the baby was safe and fed. Loved."

"My father agreed to this?"

"Oh, Emma. Frank was as desperate as I was to hold on to our marriages, to make them work. He would have done anything to protect Lauren."

"You didn't think my mother had the right to know?"

Rose looked at Emma and held her gaze for a long time. "If you believe nothing else, believe that we kept the secret to protect her. You can think me horrible if you must, but Lauren was always *fragile*. She would not have been able to handle the truth. It would have destroyed her."

"You don't know that."

"But I do. Once, when we were younger, a boy broke up with her, and Lauren attempted suicide. I couldn't... I couldn't put her through the pain of knowing Frank strayed when it *wasn't* an affair. When it was *nothing*."

"Obviously it was something if it made a baby." Emma walked over to the sink and stared out at the window above it, squinting from the glare. "So you and Dad and Bruce put it behind you and hid the truth. What changed?"

"Zack. His adoptive mother walked out on them. Everything was fine at first. He came to school on time; his clothes were clean. But then things began to slip, and one day Zack came to school limping. I watched him pick at his food during lunch, and at recess he didn't play. When I asked him what was wrong, I touched his shoulder, and he flinched in pain." Rose's voice grew softer, thicker. "His little back was purple with bruises, and there were l-lash marks all down his rear and legs. I couldn't stand it, but I didn't know what to do. If they removed him from the home, where would they send him? I tried to talk to Bruce about it but... he was so angry. I'd promised to keep my distance, and there I was, interfering."

"So you called Dad," Emma said, filling in the blank. What would she have done? She'd gotten physically ill when helping Tasha care for animals who'd been abused, but a child? Or more to the point, for Rose to know Zack was her son, and she'd placed him into the home by giving him up? "That's the call I overheard." She squeezed her eyes closed. "The one I told Mom about before the accident."

"It had to be. But the accident wasn't your fault. *I* caused the upset and the accident and everything that resulted from it. I blinded you; I killed my sister. And after it all happened, I left Zack in the home of an abuser because of my selfishness and greed." She stared at Emma, her gaze haunted. "I just left him there," she whispered, her gaze dazed. "Whatever sins Zack has committed are *my* fault, Emma. Zack is the product of his upbringing, and if anyone should be in there, in pain and dying, it should be me."

Several hours later, Ian stood outside the exercise room and listened to Emma pound on the heavy weight bag, every hit accompanied by a gasp for air. "Are you pretending that's me?"

Two hard hits slammed into the bag. "I probably should be the way you've avoided me."

The end of his white stick came into contact with Emma. "I'm sorry."

"No. If you're going to be sorry for something, at least make it something big. I know you need time to get used to the idea of me seeing again. I don't like it, but I understand. I'm feeling very forgiving about your behavior now. I mean, having an affair qualifies as needing an apology. Or, say, having a kid from the affair and keeping it secret? That definitely qualifies. When I think about it, you avoiding me because you need time to adjust isn't such a big deal in the scheme of things."

Ian couldn't follow her conversation. "What are you talking about?" He tracked the sound of the swinging bag and grabbed hold of it, held it for her next punch. Which wound up being a series of punches landing one after another in rapid succession as she told him of her visit with Bruce and Rose. It was a lot to take in. No wonder she pounded on the bag.

"Does Zack know he's adopted?" he asked, listening to the sound of Emma's breathing. She was getting winded, tired, but she was too upset and fired up to stop.

"I don't *know*," she said, punctuating the word with a slug to the bag. "Laney and I were so shocked at the news, neither of us asked."

"Have you talked to your father?"

"*No*." Another punch. "I don't know *what* to say to him. After Mom died and I was injured, he kind of fell apart, and I *thought* it was because of general stuff. You know, Mom *dying*, me getting *hurt*. I thought he was mourning Mom and the way things used to be. But now there's this whole other level of hurt and I *don't. Know. What.* To do with it!"

"He's still your father. No matter what is ever said or done."

"He's Zack's father, too. Oooh," she said, the word drawn out several seconds, her breathing harsh.

"What?"

"The night of Jolie's party. Dad was upset because I'd hired Zack. He said it was because he always saw Zack's name in the paper as being trouble but now... Dad was looking at his biggest mistake, nineteen years later, right under his nose, and he was probably terrified someone might notice a resemblance or something. No wonder he freaked."

Ian heard the Velcro fastening of the boxing gloves being loosened.

"You can let go now. My arms are ready to fall off."

He released the bag and realized he could smell her. The scent of her hair, her body, and the raspberry soap she favored. It called to him, made him want to hold her.

Was it eight steps to the door or six?

"Uncle Bruce is getting weaker by the day. I think he'd like to see you, Ian."

Considering the man had been a family friend for as long as Ian could remember, he nodded, unable to shirk the request. "I'll have Quinn take me tomorrow. Think you can rest now? It's getting late."

"I'm not tired. We could start on your lessons again," she suggested. "I've been out of the hospital a week, and we haven't done anything."

"No. I'll make sure Duncan pays you the money but— "

"You seriously think this is about being paid?"

He regretted stepping inside the gym to check on her. "I don't want to fight with you."

"So that's it? We're *over* because I can see and you're still blind?"

"It's—"

"You freaking jerk! Spare me. You're not doing this because of me, you're doing it because you're scared! What, are you afraid I'll see you screw up? Is that it?"

"I won't be something else you take care of like your dogs," he countered, the words spilling from his lips. "You think now that you can see, it makes things between us better than it was, but that's not the case. I won't be that guy holding you back."

"Then don't be! Ian, what happened last week when you left the building?"

He scowled, unwilling to go there. "That has nothing to do with my decision. Forget it happened."

"I can't."

"Why not?"

"Because I said I love you, you stupid man!"

The words flowed over him, through him, but they didn't change his attitude toward her. "I'm sorry."

"Sorry?"

He wished he could get her to see what he was trying to do. Egotistical or not, he felt the way he felt. "I can't be that man, Emma. The one everyone pities, the one who makes people wonder why you're with me. I'm trying to look out for you, do what's *best* for you."

"Let me decide what's best for me. Be the man I know you *can* be. Ian, your phobia has a hold on you, and until you learn to control it, you won't *ever* be able to accept who you are. What kind of life is that?"

A limited one—which was the point he was trying to make. "The claustrophobia isn't going away. I've accepted it, Emma. Somehow I'll live with it. But I refuse to drag you down with me. Once Zack is found and arrested, it will be safe for you to leave."

"That's going to be hard to do since I refuse to press charges against him."

"What?" He shook his head, fury rolling through him. "Emma, you have to."

"No, I don't. Zack is—like it or not—my half brother *and* cousin, as weird as that is," she said dryly. "He's family and didn't deserve the life he was given. Uncle Bruce was right about that."

"Emma, Zack Dupré is *stalking* you."

"Maybe. Maybe not. Aunt Rose thinks there is a logical explanation for the photographs."

"And if the explanation is that he's a stalker?" Ian demanded, losing patience. "You're going to let him get away with *hurting* you? I knocked you into the street, but someone *shoved* me into you."

She was silent a long moment.

"I know. But if Zack is to blame, the only thing I can be now is thankful. I will not press charges, Ian. And if you want rid of me? You're going to have to come up with another way to do it."

Chapter 22

The next day in Rose's kitchen, Ian seated himself in the chair Duncan guided him to. Quinn was at home with Emma, acting as bodyguard, while Owen continued the search for Zack.

"I hope you don't mind waiting just a bit," Rose said. "Bruce sleeps so little because of the pain, and he was resting peacefully. He'll be awake soon when the medicine begins to wear off."

"It's not a problem." Ian shifted on the seat to get comfortable.

"I have a call I need to return," Duncan said. "I'll be outside."

Ian nodded and waited until the door shut behind his brother before he asked, "Rose, is there anything Duncan and I can do? Anything at all?"

"No." She patted his hand. "But I thank you for offering. It means a lot to both of us. I'm glad you came, Ian. I've been meaning to check on you, but with Bruce's doctor visits and appointments, time got away from me."

He could only imagine what the older woman was dealing with, and now to have to face her past on top of it? "I know what you mean. I've been intending to check on both of you," he said. "But I haven't handled my blindness very well."

"You are obviously on the road to recovery now. I feel very honored you came."

Ian listened to the older woman bustle about the kitchen. He was able to discern the sounds of a cabinet opening and closing, the refrigerator door. A plastic container lid being pulled off. The scent of lemon filled the air, and like Pavlov's dog, his mouth watered.

She set something in front of him.

"Two lemon cookies," she said with a pat to his shoulder. "And a glass of cold water at two o'clock," she added.

"Thank you."

"Emma was so self-conscious when she was first blinded. She hated eating in front of anyone because she was constantly knocking things over or spilling."

"It's hard to do everything in the dark."

"Yes, it is. I know it's no comparison, but I blindfolded myself for several hours one day. I laid an outfit out on the bed and tried to dress myself, tie my shoes, fix my hair. The phone rang while I was doing it, and when I went to answer it, I stubbed my toes and almost fell down the stairs," she said with a low laugh. "After that, I had a new appreciation for the patience required of the blind."

"I'm afraid I haven't mastered that level of patience yet."

"It'll come. Much like forgiveness, it takes time. I... sense Emma told you about Zackary?"

"Yes."

"Emma and Laney were both very upset when they left, not that I can blame them. Maybe you could listen to Emma? Be a friend if she needs to talk about it."

He nodded, unsure of the proper response given the current status of his and Emma's relationship.

"He's a good boy, Ian. I refuse to believe Zack ever considered hurting Emma. He's made mistakes, I'll admit that, but... he wouldn't shove you or her into the street."

What mother wanted to believe her child capable of such a thing? "Do you have any idea where he'd go?"

"Other than his apartment, the only place I know would be his adoptive father's home. Zack and his younger sister are close."

"That's where Owen was headed today. Maybe he'll find him." Unable to withstand the temptation, he lightly scooted his hand along the edge of the table as Emma had taught him to do.

"Those are Bruce's favorites."

Ian chewed and swallowed and finished off the cookies and water while Rose chatted about the end of the drought.

The sound of a chime echoed through the house.

"Oh, he's awake. Come, I'll take you to him."

Ian stood and allowed Rose to place his hand on her shoulder. She felt bony and fragile, too thin, and he had to take short, careful steps to keep from running into her.

"Look who's come to see you, Bruce. Here, Ian, sit right here on the bed beside Bruce. There's plenty of room."

He'd have preferred a chair but didn't have the heart to protest. Seated, Ian awkwardly arranged the white cane so that it rested against his ankle.

"You look good, Ian," Bruce said.

"So do you."

Bruce chuckled at the joke.

"I see my reflection in your glasses. Good is not a term I'd use."

"I think you're the most handsome man I've ever known," Rose said. "I'll leave you two alone for a bit while I warm up some soup. Press the button if you need anything."

"She worries about me so," Bruce said once Rose left the room. "I'm not sure she's come to terms with what's coming."

"I'm not sure there is a way to come to terms with some things," Ian said, meaning every word.

"Emma says you're having trouble dealing with the return of her sight."

"It's complicated."

"I have some time."

Ian smiled at Bruce's statement. "Emma recently reminded me that she'd said she loved me—but she followed it up by calling me stupid."

Bruce began to laugh, chuckling until he wheezed.

"That's my girl," he said finally. "And your response was?"

"You don't need to be a shrink now, Bruce."

"I'll always be a shrink," the man countered. "Tell me, what was your response?"

"I didn't say anything."

"Hmmmm... I can see why you think the way you do. You're a born protector."

A protector who couldn't protect. Who couldn't get out of his own way? The angled planes of the white stick bit into Ian's hand, reminding him of the wood molding lining the cellar door. How many nights had he stood there, stuck in the darkness of his mind but still unable to go down? No matter what he said or thought or how many times he lifted his foot to take that first step only to stop?

"Relationships are not easy to navigate," Bruce continued when Ian didn't speak. "The balance is precarious and often one-sided, depending on the personalities involved. If you're pushing Emma away because you don't want to be with her, that's one thing, but if you're doing it because you're afraid, Ian, you need to reconsider."

"It's not that easy."

"It never is. I nearly lost Rose because of my treatment of her, and even then I asked things of her I shouldn't have. Now

I'm trying to make amends before it's too late. Don't wait until it's too late, son. We're both prime examples of never knowing what's in store for us. But I can tell you from experience that if you love her, you must fight for her, even if it means fighting yourself."

Ian returned home from his visit with Uncle Bruce that afternoon but immediately locked himself in the den while Duncan and Quinn left to inspect one of the new gates.

Emma paced the floor, unable to sit still or focus. When Genie called about a problem with her dog, Emma realized she had forgotten to call the woman to check on her. Emma invited Genie to bring the animal up the mountain, desperately needing a distraction and feeling bad about neglecting her friendship with the younger woman.

Half an hour later, Genie waited at the door.

"Genie, hi," Emma greeted, squinting at Genie due to the bright sunlight behind the woman. "I missed you at class and my party. Were you sick?"

"I wasn't sick."

Genie ducked her head, and Emma couldn't make out Genie's features because of the mass of hair covering the woman's face. "Oh. Just busy, huh?" When Genie didn't answer, Emma forced an awkward smile. "So, where's Bear?"

"He's, um... I really just wanted to talk to you."

"Oh, sure. Come in." Emma led the way into the living room. "Can I get you anything to drink?"

"Sure. Maybe some water?"

"I'll be right back. Have a seat." Emma turned and carefully made her way back into the hallway and kitchen.

She poured them both cold water from a filtered pitcher, found some fresh blackberries as well as some of the leftover cake from the party, and arranged them on a tray, smiling at the fuss she was making simply because she could see the pretty results.

Done, she carefully made her way back to the living room. "Hope you like chocolate," she said as she carried the treat to the coffee table. It wasn't until she neared the table that Emma looked up and realized Genie stood pointing a gun at her. Emma jerked back in surprise. The tray tilted and sent the dishes crashing to the floor. "*Genie?*"

"How could you? I did everything for you," Genie whispered. "*Every*thing. But it was never enough."

Emma swallowed, her focus on the gun. Cold, hard fear made her dizzy. She couldn't believe what she was seeing, hearing. "P-put that down. Genie, please..."

"*Genie, please,*" the woman mocked. "You're just like the others now. You don't see me."

Emma managed to drag her gaze off the gun to focus on Genie's face. Maybe if the woman appeared wild-eyed and anxious, Emma could think of a way to calm her, but Genie's dull, cold stare scared Emma to no end. "Genie, I see you. I *do*. What I don't understand is why you're doing this."

"Because you were the only one," Genie whispered. "The only one who cared, the only one who listened to me. The only one who wanted me around. *I* was your friend. But now I have no one."

"That's not true."

"It is!"

Emma scrambled to find the words, to say something that would make a difference. "Genie, please. Put that down. Sit down s-so we can work this out."

"No. No, there's nothing more to talk about. I know what I have to do."

"Shoot me?"

"You and the *Besties*... Do you think I didn't hear what they said about me? See how they excluded me? But you— You weren't like that. You were my *friend*. Until you came here."

"Morgan said she invited you to my party. You didn't come."

"I felt bad for what I did—but then I realized I shouldn't feel bad at all."

"What— what did you do? Genie, this is— Put the gun down," Emma ordered.

"No. You caused this. You chose them. You acted all nice but when I tried to help you, you wouldn't let me. You wouldn't move in with me. You replaced me with Zack. You chose them—*all* of them—over me even though, time and again, *I'm* the one who dropped everything to help you because they were too busy to care. They were *mean* to you. You told me they were."

"Genie, friends have spats. I'm sorry. I am so sorry you've been hurt by our actions. *My* actions," Emma said, raising her hands in a pleading gesture. "I had no idea you felt this way."

"I just wanted to be your friend."

Air was hard to come by. After the accident, Ian had said he remembered nothing but the rain and the smell of dog shampoo. Now it made sense because Genie used the same brand. Zack hadn't shown up that day, hadn't bathed the dogs, and she had been so busy, she hadn't had a chance to. "Did you—were you the one who shoved Ian?" She hoped she was wrong. Hoped this was all a bad dream.

"You said you *loved* him."

"Genie—"

"How could you love someone who threw you in front of that car the way he did?"

A shadow filled the doorway.

"Emma? Are you all right?" Ian asked, Tucker at his side.

No. No, no, no. This could not be happening. "Ian, *stop*. Genie's… She's got a gun."

The hot prickle of awareness flowing through Ian's veins warned him something was off long before Emma's statement.

"I think he should come in," Genie countered. "He needs to hear what happens next and know there's nothing he can do."

"Genie," Ian said, hoping to draw the woman's attention, her anger. He had to get closer, between the two women. Had to protect Emma with his body if nothing else.

Images of Kara's rescue flashed through his mind. The gunman's approach and how he'd moved in front of Kara to protect her. That moment in the operating room when the mask was placed over his mouth and nose and everything went black. He shook off the fear, refusing to fail Emma in this moment. *Please, guide my steps. Help me protect her.* "Emma? Where are you?" He needed to place her in the room.

Emma apparently caught on to his thinking, however, because she didn't respond.

"See? Even now you're choosing to protect him."

"Genie," Emma whispered, "*please*. Don't do this."

Ian focused on Emma's voice and frowned. Had she moved toward Genie? "Emma, stay back. Go get Quinn."

"She's not going anywhere," Genie said softly, sweetly.

"Genie, *why*?" Emma asked. "Can't we talk about this?"

"No. You are going to try to change my mind, but you can't. It's too late for that. You had the chance to fix things. All you had to do was live with *me* after the fire."

The air left Ian's lungs in a rush. He had to come up with a way to get Emma out of this. "You set fire to Emma's house?"

"You'd like it if I had, wouldn't you? No, I didn't set the fire. I saw her do it, though," Genie said, sounding smug. "Emma tossed the towel aside and I saw it catch. I could've stopped it, but she had to see I was the only one she could count on."

Emma made a noise. A sob?

"Roxy was inside! You know what she meant to me. How could you *do* that to her?"

"Roxy was another thing that took your attention away," Ian murmured, catching on to the fact that Genie was obsessed with Emma. Somewhere along the way the girl's desperation to have a friend and belong had turned to something more dangerous. "Something you loved."

"Duncan wasn't supposed to hire you, not after that," Genie said.

"Where is Zack?" Ian demanded. "Where does he fit into all of this?"

"Oh, Genie. Did you hurt him?" Emma asked.

"If he's smart, he left town."

Ian inched closer to the sound of their voices and fought off the doubts caused by the conversation he'd had with Genie in the kitchen about his limitations, how he couldn't protect Emma.

"Stay back!" the woman ordered.

"Genie? Genie, listen to me," Emma said. "You don't want to hurt anyone. You're not that type of person."

Tucker whined and then growled, nudging Ian's leg and the hand at his side as he continued toward them, between them?

The dog was just as on edge as Ian.

"Ian, stop," Emma whispered. "She wants to hurt me, not you. *Move.*"

Emma's comment let him know he'd succeeded. "Genie, you don't want to hurt Emma. Put the gun down, or I'm going to take it from you."

Genie's laugh was high-pitched and hysterical. "Go ahead. Try," she dared.

"Ian, no. Don't—"

"*Ahaluna!*"

It happened in slow motion. Ian commanded Tucker to ambush and attack, and Tucker released a spine-chilling growl before the dog lunged at Genie, and the woman screamed.

Simultaneously Ian turned, arms outstretched to enfold Emma. He shoved her down, following her to the floor and protecting her as best he could as the gun went off, deafening in the close confines of the room. "Emma? Emma!"

"I'm okay!"

Ian scrambled up and rushed toward the sound of Tucker's ferocious growls, fighting the darkness and fear and praying he could gain control of Genie before she got a second chance at the gun and shot them all.

"I've got her," Owen said. "Ian, gun's on the floor by the desk. Zack, call the police, and go find Duncan. Zack! Go!"

"You got it," the kid said, his voice high-pitched with fear.

Genie screamed to be freed, demanding Emma's help. Adrenaline pumped through his veins as Ian ordered Tucker to heel and reached out in the darkness, searching once more for Emma. When he found her, he crushed her against him, breathing in the scent of her hair. A sob burst out of her chest, and he held her tighter. "Shhh. It's over."

Ian doubted she heard him. His ears rang from the blast, but he wasn't going to shout the words at her.

"What's going on?" Duncan asked, bursting into the room followed by Quinn.

In short order, the truth was revealed in Genie's rambling bits and snatches of rage and tears and pleas for Emma's understanding.

Genie was the one who'd left the note about Morgan's

husband having an affair, the one who had called in an anony-mous tip that Tasha's vet clinic was illegally dispensing drugs. The one who had taken Emma's wallet and set Zack up to look guilty. No doubt she was also the person who had thrown the brick through Jolie's window. All in a bid to draw them away from Emma so she relied on Genie more and more. Duncan hiring Emma despite her causing the fire had sent Genie into a tailspin that went beyond jealousy and possessiveness into some-thing more.

Owen had found Zack hiding outside the kennel hoping Emma would appear. Zack had heard about Emma's missing wallet and his supposed guilt and had decided to cut his losses and lay low. But when he'd learned of Emma's fall into the street, the guy had felt responsible because he hadn't been there to do his job. At the scene, the kid had found Emma's *Besties* necklace near the drainage ditch and come to return it and proclaim his innocence.

Given all that had happened and been revealed, Ian was glad Emma had refused to press charges against the guy. Especially in light of Emma's newfound relationship with him. As to the pictures, Zack swore he was practicing for a photography contest he wanted to enter, and Ian believed him.

Half an hour later, the police escorted Genie to the hospital for a psych evaluation, and Ian answered a detective's questions.

Genie's off-balance obsession and need for Emma's attention had taken a sadistic turn for the worse, but it was over. Emma was safe.

And now... Now she was free to leave.

Emma rolled over in the bed that night and stared up at the

moonlight shining through her window. She couldn't bring herself to shut the curtains, not when the sky was clear and a full moon glowed.

It was late by the time the police had left, and Duncan had insisted she not go anywhere tonight.

Duncan. Not Ian.

What was she going to do?

Emma closed her eyes and rolled onto her side, staring into the dark and the shadows on the wall.

Are you really going to draw this out? You said you loved him, and he didn't say it back.

Emma pushed herself up in the bed and then scooted to the edge. Tink immediately came to the side and licked Emma's palm in welcome, the gesture so reminiscent of Roxy that Emma smiled. "What do you think, Tink? What should we do?"

The plastic garbage bags Aunt Rose had sent the donated clothes in were stuffed in the bottom of the dresser. Emma crossed the room and pulled them out, packed her clothes and shoes, tossing everything in. It didn't take long.

After a few sniffs, Tink finished exploring. She returned to her corner and curled up, a very human-sounding sigh snuffling out of her.

She'd spend the night, but in the morning she'd be gone before the sun rose over the mountain.

Bags set aside, Emma left her room and wandered through the house, leaving Tink behind to snooze.

She'd been there long enough now that she knew every turn of the hallway, every table and chair and antique desk.

The piano room drew her. She fingered the keys lightly, the *pings* of sound soft and haunting.

She should have left with Zack. He would have driven her to Aunt Rose's house or Laney's new rental or... anywhere. So why had she stayed? Why was she putting herself through this?

A few more hours.

Feeling the walls closing in on her, Emma retraced her steps back toward her room, stopping the moment she realized someone stood at the end of the hall. At the cellar door.

Oh, Ian.

She shook her head at him and at herself, walked toward him on bare feet. Whatever noise she made was drowned out by Tucker's low whines from the other side of Ian's closed bedroom door.

Ian straightened when she was within arm's reach of him.

Inhaling, Emma lifted her hands and placed her palms on his back. Like all the times before, he was hot to the touch, his muscles hard. The cellar door was open, Ian on the threshold but unable to cross it. "This is your test, isn't it?" she whispered. "It's not the blindness per se but the phobia."

"Yeah," he said gruffly. "I don't need the wine. Not anymore. I just need to—I need to go down there but…"

He needs a reason to go down there, she mused.

Ian had come so far. Just stating that he no longer needed the wine to get through a day—or a night—was progress. Because she'd noticed he hadn't argued about his habit for quite some time. But the phobia?

Holding on to him, she ducked under his arm until she teetered on the edge of the top step.

"Emma? What are you—?"

He grabbed her, stepped back into the hall, and tugged her with him. She let him have his way—for now. "Do you love me?"

"Emma…"

He was probably thinking now wasn't the time for such a conversation when he was trying so hard to conquer his fear, but when was a better time? "Do you love me?" she repeated.

His hands tightened on her arms.

"That's a yes," she whispered with more confidence than she

really felt. She rose onto her tiptoes, brushed her lips against his. "Ian... I *love* you. I *need* you and want you in my life. You, no one else. I know you think you're being punished or something, but what if all of this happened so we could find each other? Uncle Bruce's inability to help you, Genie's plan… Why not *believe* it all led us here, to this very moment? If you let me… if you trust me, I will help you, Ian."

She pulled away so she could lower herself onto the first step.

"What are you doing?" His chest rose and fell in rapid, ragged sounds.

She held on to the handrail and took another step down, compelled by a force stronger than anything she'd ever felt. Her other hand skimmed over the light switch, but she didn't turn it on. The dark didn't scare her—being without Ian did. What good was freedom, independence, if he wasn't there to share it with her?

Two more steps.

"Emma, stop. Don't—"

Another step. The wooden stairs were old and creaky but solid beneath her feet. "Let go. Take a step. I'm here for you."

"Stop," he said raggedly.

"Why? What's to fear? It's just a place. I know you don't like the dark, but sometimes even the dark can be good. *Comforting*."

"No."

"Oh, but it can," she said, lowering her voice. "The dark is soft, cool." She took another step down and inhaled the scent of the cellar. It was musky, sweet with remnants of wine, rich from the earth surrounding the house. "You're thinking of it as bad, but if you trust me, I'll show you how to think of the dark in a different way."

Ian stepped to the edge, broad and strong and imposing with the dim lights of the house behind him. Her words were getting to him, intriguing him.

But seconds passed, and he just stood there. Disappointment filled her. She'd made it to the bottom. The poured concrete floor shocked her feet with cold, the temperature bringing goose bumps to her skin. She stared up at him, prayed for him, but he couldn't take that first step—until she shifted her feet in an attempt to warm them and stumbled into some empty wine bottles that tumbled over with a loud crash.

"Emma? Emma, are you *hurt*? Answer me! *Emma!*"

She grabbed her aching toes and hopped, landing propped against the wall, her foot cradled on her thigh. It wasn't until the throbbing stopped that she realized Ian was halfway down the stairs, every measured step awkward and requiring a ragged lungful of air.

But he was coming after her.

For her.

Emma plastered her back to the wall, the light at the top of the stairs blurring briefly from her tears until Ian's shadowed form blocked her view entirely.

"*Emma?*"

"Here," she whispered, gasping when he swung, arms straight, until he found her and yanked her against his chest. She wrapped her arms around his neck and kissed him, relishing the love of her hero.

The lights turned on and Emma blinked. Over Ian's shoulder, she saw Duncan watching them from above, a grin relaxing his worried features.

She waved her hand behind Ian's head, and a second later, the cellar went dark again.

"You scared me," Ian said, releasing her mouth but pressing his forehead hard to hers. "Don't you *ever* do that to me again," he ordered, tempering the order with another kiss. "First Genie and now this— You're going to make me old before my time. Are you hurt?"

"Yes. My heart hurts," she whispered. "It misses you. It needs you, Ian." She kissed him again, used his shoulders for leverage and balance, letting the kiss deepen. "See how good the dark can be?" she whispered.

"Emma..."

"Shhh. Just close your eyes and think of what could be. Ian, you love me, I know you do. Why are you fighting so hard?"

"Because this doesn't mean my phobia has disappeared—or that being with me will be easy."

"Nothing worthwhile is ever easy, Ian. That's what makes us appreciate them even more."

"Does that mean you're sticking around?"

"Does that mean you want me to?"

"I heard you in your room, the drawers opening and closing. You packed."

His hair was cool beneath her fingers. "I can't stay here and not have a future with you. It hurts too much. I love you too much."

"Ahhh, sweetheart. I love you, too," he whispered, the words low and raspy. "Marry me."

It wasn't a question but an order. The best thing she'd heard in a long, long time. "Marry me, and you get my dogs."

A low laugh rumbled from his chest.

"After Tucker responded to my command earlier, I'm counting on it."

Epilogue

Two weeks later, Ian waited impatiently for Quinn to arrive. On any other day, Quinn would have hovered with annoying persistence, but today everyone was busy with wedding preparations.

The service was small, with only Emma's immediate family, Zack included, and friends due to arrive for the celebration. Bruce and Rose had just pulled up to the house, and Ian knew Emma would be teary-eyed, surprised by her uncle's determination to attend after a wait-and-see response to the invitation. Frank was going to walk his little girl down the aisle, then take himself off to the Smokies for a honeymoon with Helen. They had married at the courthouse last week.

"Duncan said you needed me?"

Ian scowled in the general direction of the door. In the beginning, Quinn, Duncan, and all of the others had made a point of scuffing their feet along the floor, jiggling the knob or something so that Ian was aware of their approach. Not anymore. And while he was happy they'd finally reverted back to normal, he hated being caught by surprise. "Yeah. You busy?"

"Emma had me on flower patrol. Turns out Goli and her pups like the taste of the bouquets."

"Who's guarding them now?"

Quinn chuckled. "Zack."

He laughed on behalf of the young man's indignity. "He needs to earn his stripes."

"Exactly. What did you need?"

"Pick up the bear." Ian waited, barely able to make out the sound of Quinn's approach.

Tucker growled and then began to bark frantically.

"Down! Down, dog!"

Ian ordered Tucker to heel.

The barking stopped, but Tucker continued to growl. "You put the bear down?"

"You trained Stupid Dog? In *Cherokee*?"

"Turns out he isn't stupid." Ian called Tucker to his side and scratched Tuck's sweet spot. The dog dropped down and rolled over against his legs so Ian could pet his belly.

"Obviously. But what does this little experiment have to do with your wedding day?"

Pride filled him. "You said you wouldn't mind sticking around for a while. That still true?"

"Why do you ask?"

"I want to start a new business."

"What kind of business?"

"Protection services by the name of Mad Dog Security. Dogs trained to protect but able to slip under the radar because they're seen more as pet than guard dog. Tucker's a perfect example. Emma's busy with her kennel and the PAWS program, but if you're willing to stay on, I thought you might want to be partners."

"I'm listening."

Ian hated that he couldn't see Quinn's expression. "I lucked out when Tucker took Genie on. I wasn't sure he would. But I propose we train him and others to protect our loved ones, celebs,"—he paused, knowing his next statement was stretching it, considering Tucker had a long way to go and was only the first dog but— "and eventually the president or his children."

Quinn whistled. "You think it's possible?"

"Tucker's proof." Ian held out his hand and prayed Quinn would take it. "I need eyes, Quinn. Someone I can trust who doesn't get her feelings hurt when I get irritable."

Quinn chuckled at that. His time with Emma had been an emotional roller coaster, and they had both had some adjustments to make. But it was worth it. He couldn't imagine not having Emma by his side the rest of his life. He'd loved her enough to set her free. At least that was his thinking immediately after the accident that had restored her vision. But after almost losing her again due to Genie's psychotic behavior, Ian had realized he loved Emma enough to take on his demons and fight for her—just like Bruce had recommended.

"Mad Dog Security," the man murmured. "I like it."

Quinn grabbed Ian's hand, and they shook, sealing the deal.

"It's almost time. You ready to head to the altar?"

Ian found his white stick propped where he'd left it and stood. "I'll lead the way."

Ian and Emma were pronounced husband and wife. Their guests applauded. They kissed. The recessional music began, and Quinn breathed a sigh of relief that his imprisonment in the monkey-suit was halfway over.

After the receiving line finally emptied, the photographer quickly ordered them back to the decorated arch for more pictures.

"Don't forget. Emma said you had to smile," Jolie reminded him as she slipped her small hand into the crook of his arm as ordered.

"There's only one way you're going to get smiles out of me, sweetheart."

"Stop it."

"Stop what? I meant a smile for a dance. What naughty thing did you have in mind?" he said just loud enough for her to hear.

She turned toward him as though surprised, head tilted back to stare up at him.

"I love it!" the photographer called out. "All of you—strike a pose."

Quinn smiled as expected and used the moment to his advantage. He wrapped his arm around her slim waist and tugged her flush against him, stared into her eyes and dipped her.

"Great! Hold it! Smile!"

Jolie remained stiff as a board in his arms, her expressions ranging from surprise to anger and a hint of fear. Still, she pinned on a smile for the wedding photographer, and Quinn ignored the way her nails dug into him.

When the shutter stopped whirling and the photographer released them from the pose, Quinn took his time shifting her upright. He'd drawn attention to them from the others, earned more than a few knowing looks, but he didn't care.

"Quinn…"

He released her and took a step back, holding her gaze. "A smile a dance… By the time this guy is finished, every dance will be mine."

Love the Besties? Jolie and Quinn's story is available

now! Get MORE THAN LOVE (FORMERLY THROUGH THE VALLEY) **or read an excerpt below:**

Excerpt MORE THAN LOVE (FORMERLY THROUGH THE VALLEY)**:**

The rich smell of coffee and decadently sweet baked goodies filled the air inside of Cuppa Jo's, and despite her early morning breakfast, Jolie Carter found herself fighting the tempting aroma of the pumpkin spice bread drizzled abundantly in shiny vanilla icing.

Such a weak will, Jo-Jo.

As it always did, the overly critical sound of her mother's voice filled Jolie's head, souring her mood but ending her desire to snag one of the pumpkin slices from the display case.

Jolie grabbed her water bottle from the counter and took a long sip as she walked into the rear storage section to get a new supply of coffee cups. She shoved the plastic-wrapped cups under her arm and took another long sip, wishing someone would create a calorie-free substitute for all the pound-adding goodies that went so well with her gourmet coffee business.

She reentered the area behind the counter and stooped to stow the cups in their proper place only to find herself face-to-glass with a sealed container of replacement pumpkin bread, waiting for its turn to go on display. Shaking her head, she took another large swig of water as she stood.

"Smells good."

Startled by the sudden appearance of Nathan Quinn—how had he entered without her hearing the chime on the door?—she choked and coughed and struggled to catch her breath.

Quinn leaned over the counter separating them and pounded gently on her back with one hand while grabbing a napkin with the other, handing it to her so she could wipe her watery eyes. "Th-thanks," she gasped, still coughing.

"Didn't mean to startle you."

But he does it so well, she thought.

She wiped her eyes and her now-running nose and fought for composure. A mere month ago, one of her best friends had married Quinn's best friend and business partner, officially making her and Quinn acquaintances. But no matter how many times she found herself in the same room as the tall, imposing man with his raspy, damaged voice and intimidating physique, she couldn't get used to it—to him. He was too… much. "It's fine," she said, clearing her throat as she moved away from the counter and out of reach. "What can I get you?"

She tried, as she always did, not to look at the half-circle scar on his throat, but her gaze fell to the thin, jagged line crossing the front of his otherwise tanned skin. Obviously the cut hadn't been fatal, though she imagined he'd spent quite a long time fighting for his life as a result. How had it happened? Why? She wanted to ask but wouldn't let herself.

"Large coffee, black." Quinn's expression darkened to an even more imposing frown, and she wondered if he'd caught her staring.

Coffee, she reminded herself.

His order didn't surprise her. By all accounts, Quinn appeared to be a basic kind of man. He wore jeans and T-shirts, well-worn shoes that looked surprisingly expensive but aged with use.

No, a surprise would have been Quinn asking for one of her chocolate-whipped-and-dairy-laden drinks that rivaled the big-name coffeehouse chains. But then, given his physique, he would burn the calories off in no time. No man obtained those kinds of muscles from sitting in a chair.

But if Quinn wasn't prone to a sweet tooth, what were his vices?

Yet another question you aren't going to ask.

She filled his request, aware of Quinn's gaze following her the entire time. "What brings you to, um, town?"

Making idle chitchat with customers was one of her strengths. Something she'd forced her painfully shy self to learn to do.

But with Quinn… chitchat didn't come easy.

She peeked at him over her shoulder, taking in his six-foot-plus height, broad shoulders and chest, arms barely contained by the sleeves of the black T-shirt he wore. A baseball cap covered short hair the color of her most decadent mocha grind, and he had several days' worth of shadow lining his jaw and cheeks.

She let her gaze drift, noting the scrolling tattoo trailing down his left arm from beneath the shirt sleeve and over his thick bicep.

"Careful."

"Huh?" Hot coffee poured over her fingers and scorched. "Ow!"

She set the cup down with a bang, spilling even more of the expensive brew, and waved her fingers in the air in a poor effort to cool them.

She turned and startled again, coming nose-to-chest with Quinn, who had apparently jumped the counter to get to her so quickly.

"Give me your hand."

He didn't give her a chance to respond. He simply took hold of her wrist and tugged her to the sink, flipping the tap to full blast before shoving her hand beneath the cool water. If it hadn't felt so good, she would've taken him to task for moving behind the counter, but she found herself lacking when it came to words.

Get a grip, Jo. He's just a man.

A big, unsettling, disturbing man who always watched her, seemingly as aware of her as she was of him whenever he was near.

"Better?"

Did Quinn ever use more than five words in a sentence? Better yet, could *she* ever use more than a handful of words in talking to him? "Yes."

She pulled her hand from his and grabbed a nearby towel, ignoring the painful sting in her fingers. "Thanks for the, um, save."

"No problem."

"Let me get your order," she said. "And the— the ten dollars in change you left last time."

"Just trying to help a new business."

No one in this economy had ten dollars to waste. And if he did, she couldn't accept it when there were other businesses in Stone River and the college community around Zailer University struggling a lot more than she was. The coffee business was brisk. It was amazing how hard people would dig for spare change to fund their habit. Not that she was complaining.

Ignoring him as best she could, she grabbed the cup she'd poured for him and dumped a bit of it down the sink before wiping the cup thoroughly to remove the mess. Finally she added a lid, grateful the simple task was complete. "Here. On the house. For the rescue."

Quinn accepted the cup but didn't move.

"You seem distracted. Everything okay?"

Other than seemingly hallucinating on her way into work and making a fool of herself just now, she was peachy.

Jolie ignored his query and slid along the edge of the counter to avoid further contact. She made her way to the moveable section, waiting for him to follow her and go back to the proper side. "I'm fine."

"Sure about that?"

Would he drop it already? Surely she wasn't the only woman who got... *tongue tied* when he was around. "Positive."

If the *Besties* could see her now, she'd never hear the end of it.

They'd tease her about her clumsiness and encourage her to flirt with Quinn. To *smile,* at the very least. But Quinn wasn't her type, not that she really had one.

All she knew was that Quinn was former military turned private contractor/mercenary before he left that life to stay stateside.

Based on the few things Emma had said, Quinn's past was secretive and dangerous and something he never discussed. "Have a good day," she said, quickly lowering the divider. "If you talk to the honeymooners, tell Em I hope she's having fun."

Emma had tutored Ian MacGregor, a blinded former soldier, in ways to come to terms with his blindness before falling head over heels for the man.

Emma and Ian had tied the knot the first week of September but had waited another month to take their honeymoon, just so Emma, who had recently regained her sight after fourteen years of blindness, could see the glorious colors of fall on the drive to board a plane to St. Lucia. Quinn had driven them to the coast since Emma hadn't mastered driving just yet, put them on a plane, and a military buddy of Ian's on R&R had met them on the island to do double duty as tour guide and guard.

Due to his inability to see, Ian had issues with making sure Emma stayed safe, especially after what had happened to her recently when one of Emma's students had stalked her.

"Will do."

Quinn turned away just as the chime on the door sounded, announcing a customer's arrival. Jolie exhaled in relief and focused her attention on the patron walking in, but her smile of welcome froze on her face. She choked again, unable to catch her breath or move. "*Quinn,*" she said before he could walk out the door. "Y-you forgot something."

Quinn froze with his hand on the push-bar of the door, his

gaze zeroing in on her before sliding to the man who'd just entered.

"Give me a minute," she said to Quinn, trying to keep the unease out of her voice. "Have a seat?"

Her heart pounded in her chest, and for a brief few seconds, she actually felt the room whirling a bit. *Please don't leave me.*

"Yeah, no problem," Quinn said, idly moving toward the tables and chairs and displays she had featuring coffees, teas, books by local authors, and other odds and ends the university town seemed to favor.

She stared at the man now standing across from her, gazing at her with a quizzical expression, as if he knew her but couldn't place her.

Was it possible? Could he *not* know her? Recognize her?

"I'd like a large coffee, three creams, two sugars. And one of those," he said, pointing to one of the brownies in the glass case. "But you can finish with him first."

"No hurry," Quinn quickly said, countering the offer.

Her hands trembled when she grabbed the brownie and shoved it into a bag. The coffee was next, and as she placed the items on the counter, she realized it was the fastest she'd ever completed an order.

"What do I owe you?" the man asked.

Money. He needed to pay. She kept her head low so that her hair slid forward and hid her face from view. "Four fifty-three."

"Keep it," he said, handing her a five. "Have a good day."

She stared at the five-dollar bill, vaguely hearing the chime on the door sound as Blake Parker left her business and went on with his life even though his sudden appearance had just shattered hers.

Hot yet numb, she placed the bill in the cash drawer and counted out the difference, adding it to the empty tip jar by the side of the register.

Each drop of the coins pierced her ears and mocked her. Forty-seven cents. Was that really all she was worth?

"What was that about?" Quinn asked.

Quinn's raspy, injured voice pulled her out of her dazed state, and now that Blake was gone, she realized because of her haste to not be alone with him, she owed Quinn an explanation. Her mind scrambled and finally hit on her earlier comment about returning Quinn's too-generous tip. She had forgotten about it after getting burned, but it was the perfect excuse now.

She hit the button on the cash register once more and retrieved a ten-dollar bill, holding it out to him.

"I don't want it, Jolie."

"Please," she said, only then noticing how badly the bill trembled in her grasp. She lowered it to the counter and shoved it toward him. "Take it."

A long moment passed with Quinn staring at her face. Her cheeks were flushed, and sweat beaded on her forehead and at her temples. She felt it gathering and hoped Quinn didn't notice.

"Did you know that guy?"

She wet her dry lips and tried to shrug casually. "Don't laugh, but I-I thought for a second there he was one of the fugitives from the news this morning." She forced a laugh that emerged shrill and off-key, and winced. "Silly, huh? I-I mean, why would a fugitive stop for coffee, right? Sorry to keep you." Jolie wrapped her arms around her waist and squeezed, her nails digging into her skin through her loose blouse. Harder, until pain cleared the fog from her mind. *Please, God.* "Guess I'm jumpier than normal. You know, after what happened with Emma."

Quinn's dark green eyes narrowed on hers. He didn't believe her. And why would he when she was a horrible liar? But it wasn't like she could tell him the truth.

"You're sure?" he asked, his gaze shifting over her face.

She squared her shoulders and managed a nod. She'd been

taken by surprise and shocked by Blake's sudden appearance but — She was smarter and stronger now, not a stupid, naive little girl. "Yes. I'm fine. Take the money. Use it to buy more coffee later," she said.

"I'll do that— If you promise to call if you need me."

"IT HAS BEEN **a while since I have found an author I like this much." - Review of MORE THAN LOVE** (FORMERLY THROUGH THE VALLEY).

Also by Kay Lyons

MONTANA SECRETS SERIES:

- HEALING HER COWBOY
- IT HAD TO BE YOU
- HERS TO KEEP
- MILLION DOLLAR STANDOFF
- HIS CHRISTMAS WISH
- THEIR SECRET SON

THE SEASIDE SISTERS SERIES:

- THE LAST GOODBYE
- LATTES AND LULLABYES
- MAP OF DREAMS
- WORTH THE RISK
- LOST LOVE FOUND

TAMING THE TULANES SERIES:

- SMALL TOWN SCANDAL
- THEIR SECRET BARGAIN
- CROSSING THE LINE
- THE NANNY'S SECRET
- SOMEONE TO TRUST

THE STONE RIVER SERIES:

- WORTH THE WAIT
- NOT BY SIGHT
- MORE THAN LOVE

- LEAD ME NOT
- CHRISTMAS AT HOLLY WOOD
- THEIR CHRISTMAS MIRACLE
- SECOND CHANCES

SMALL TOWN SCANDALS SERIES:

- BRODY'S REDEMPTION
- FALLING FOR HER BOSS
- WITH THIS MAN

SECRET SANTA SERIES:

- SECRET SANTA
- SECRET SANTA II: A CHRISTMAS TO REMEMBER

MAKE ME A MATCH SERIES:

- ROMANCE RESET
- RULES OF ENGAGEMENT
- THE MATCHMAKER'S SECRET
- PERFECTLY MISMATCHED
- BY THE BOOK

CAROLINA COVE SERIES:

- SEASCAPES AND VEGAS MISTAKES
- SEASHELLS AND WEDDING BELLS
- SEA GLASS AND SECOND CHANCES
- SEA BLUE AND LOVING YOU
- SEA VIEW AND SOMETHING NEW

COMING SOON: (LINKS WILL BE UPDATED ASAP)

THE BLACKWELL BROTHERS SERIES:

- BABY BE MINE
- SECOND CHANCE WEDDING
- THE GETAWAY GUY
- OFF-LIMITS LOVE
- FLIRTING WITH FOREVER

Author Bio

Kay Lyons always wanted to be a writer, ever since the age of seven or eight when she copied the pictures out of a Charlie Brown book and rewrote the story because she didn't like the plot. Through the years her stories have changed but one characteristic stayed true— they were all romances. Each and every one of her manuscripts included a love story.

Published in 2005 with Harlequin Enterprises, Kay's first release was a national bestseller. Kay has also been a HOLT Medallion, Book Buyers Best and RITA Award nominee. Look for her most recent novels with Kindred Spirits Publishing.

For more information regarding her work, please visit Kay at the following:

www.kaylyonsauthor.com

@KayLyonsAuthor (Twitter)

Kay Lyons Author (Facebook)

Author_Kay_Lyons (Instagram)

Kay Lyons, Author (Pinterest)

Love Kay's work but want a slightly sexier read? Check out Kay's alter ego Ivy James. The Stone River series was originally

published as The Stone Gap Mountain series. For more information, go to www.kaylyonsauthor.com.

SIGN UP FOR KAY'S NEWSLETTER AND RECEIVE
UPDATES ON NEW RELEASES, CONTESTS, PRE-
RELEASE BOOK INFORMATION, EXCLUSIVES AND
MORE!

**Word of mouth and reviews are the two best ways an
author has to gain attention for their books. While
you're browsing the titles, please consider taking a
moment to leave a short review of this book.**

Thank you,

Kay

9 781953 375711